The Garrison D...
unfo...

The Garrisons:
Parker, Brittany
& Stephen

Three passionate novels from favourite authors
Roxanne St Claire, Sara Orwig and
Anna DePalo

The Garrisons: Parker, Brittany & Stephen

ROXANNE ST CLAIRE

SARA ORWIG

ANNA DePALO

MILLS & BOON

First published in Great Britain 2012
by Mills & Boon, an imprint of Harlequin (UK) Limited,
Eton House, 18-24 Paradise Road, Richmond, Surrey TW9 1SR

THE GARRISONS: PARKER, BRITTANY & STEPHEN
© by Harlequin Enterprises II B.V./S.à.r.l 2012

The CEO's Scandalous Affair, Seduced by the Wealthy Playboy and *Millionaire's Wedding Revenge* were first published in Great Britain by Harlequin (UK) Limited.

The CEO's Scandalous Affair © Harlequin Books S.A. 2007
Seduced by the Wealthy Playboy © Harlequin Books S.A. 2007
Millionaire's Wedding Revenge © Harlequin Books S.A. 2007

Special thanks and acknowledgement are given to Roxanne St Claire, Sara Orwig and Anna DePalo for their contribution to THE GARRISONS series.

ISBN: 978 0 263 89705 0
ebook ISBN: 978 1 408 97072 0

05-1012

Printed and bound in Spain
by Blackprint CPI, Barcelona

THE CEO'S SCANDALOUS AFFAIR

BY
ROXANNE ST CLAIRE

Dear Reader,

There is nothing quite like the culture, colour and romance of south Florida. The sidewalks of South Beach sizzle with the beautiful people, the nightclubs rock with excitement and the sun soaks everything in a golden glow. I know because I've lived in Florida for almost fifteen years, and for much of that time, I worked in Miami and played on the narrow strip of land known simply as SoBe. Because of that, I am thrilled to launch a new dynasty series that is as hot as the tropics and as cool as the neon lights on Ocean Avenue.

In many ways, the Garrison family is typical of the über-wealthy, ultrachic, super-hip residents of South Beach, but they are also men and women with dreams and disappointments, fears and frustrations. And because their stories were part of the Desire™ line, the characters are as rich with conflict as they are with cash. And, best of all, they have secrets that threaten to tumble their empire, or break their hearts.

I fell in love with all the Garrisons, as I hope you will. In this series, you can root for the alpha men, like Parker Garrison, who sometimes lose the control they cherish, and cheer for the lucky ladies, like Anna Cross, who threaten to wreck the order of the men's lives. So grab a pastel-coloured drink, dig your feet into some imaginary sand and discover the world of power, privilege and passion that is the Garrison family of Miami Beach!

Roxanne St Claire

Roxanne St Claire is an award-winning, national bestselling author of more than a dozen romance and suspense novels. Her first book for Desire™ was nominated for a prestigious RITA® Award from the Romance Writers of America, and she is also a recipient of the 2005 Maggie Award as well as multiple Awards of Excellence. In addition, her work has received numerous nominations for a variety of awards, including a SIBA Award for Best Fiction of 2005, a National Reader's Choice Award and a Booksellers Best Award. Roxanne's first book was published in 2003, after she spent nearly two decades as a public relations and marketing executive. Today she writes full-time, while raising two pre-teen children and enjoying life with a real-life alpha hero. She lives on the east coast of Florida and loves to hear from readers through e-mail at roxannestc@aol.com and snail mail, c/o of the Space Coast Authors of Romance, PO Box 410787, Melbourne, Florida 32941, USA. Visit her website at www.roxannestclaire.com to read excerpts, win prizes and learn more!

One

When Parker Garrison strode into the conference room of Garrison, Inc., he noticed three things, despite the blinding sunshine that bounced off the water of Biscayne Bay and silhouetted the figures of his siblings, their mother and a few highly paid lawyers. One, there was no conversation. None. Not that he'd expected a party atmosphere at the reading of his father's will, but it was unusual for a gathering of Garrisons to be quiet. They were, at the very least, an opinionated clan.

Two, his mother appeared relatively sober. All right, it was eight-thirty in the morning and even Bonita Garrison rarely hit the juice before noon, unless he counted the Bloody Marys she consumed in preparation for the Sunday family dinners. But since his father's death two weeks ago, she'd leaned on her liquid crutch early and often.

Three—and most significant—John Garrison's chair at

the head of the mile-long cherrywood table remained empty. A situation Parker intended to rectify.

His sister Brittany practically choked when he eased himself onto the buttery leather and set his BlackBerry on the table in front of him.

"You're sitting in Dad's chair?" Brittany demanded, tapping the digital device that was never far from his right hand.

"It's empty." Parker ignored the implication that he was muscling in on his father's turf. Because he *was*. He was the oldest. He'd run the family's umbrella corporation for the past five years, since his father had given him the CEO position as a thirty-first birthday present.

The rest of them had their hands deep in the Garrison affairs—they each owned one of the properties, whether it was the Grand hotel, a club, restaurant or condo complex. But he'd earned this chair, and not just by birth order. With work, sweat, insight, guts and a few masterful decisions.

"It's disrespectful," Brittany hissed, tapering her brown eyes in disgust and leaning her narrow shoulders closer to make her point. "To the dead."

Brooke reached over and touched her sister's hand. "Relax, Britt. He has to sit somewhere."

Parker threw a grateful glance at his other sister, marveling at how the sisters were twins in appearance only. Brooke responded with a smile that softened her lovely features and accentuated the difference between the sweet sister and the scowling one even more.

Across from Brooke and Brittany, Stephen locked his hands behind his head and rocked his chair easily with a long, muscular body that practically matched Parker's gene for gene, right down to the signature cleft that every Garrison sported on their chin. Stephen's dark eyes danced with wry amusement, his flawless smile white against a face tanned from a recent escape on his sixty-foot cabin cruiser.

"Sit wherever you like, big brother," Stephen drawled. "He may not be using the chair, but I think we're about to feel the hand of our dearly departed father in every corner of this room."

Parker frowned at the comment, and followed his closest sibling's meaningful gaze to the imposing figure cut by Brandon Washington, the young and brilliant attorney who handled the family affairs. Brandon's strong jaw was set as he moved papers purposefully in front of him, his large hands steady and determined. At that moment, he met Parker's gaze, and just beneath the burnish of his espresso-colored complexion, Parker could see…anger? Surprise? Dread?

Whatever Brandon had read in John Garrison's will, the warning look the lawyer gave Parker held a clear message: *You're not going to like this.*

Parker shifted in his seat, tamping down concern. What could the will say that Parker wouldn't like? Nothing mattered to him except control of Garrison, Inc. The money, the properties, the estate—all were secondary to him, all one notch less important than the umbrella firm that invested the profits.

Let the others have their slices of responsibility. He held the biggest piece of the pie dish in his hand. Surely Dad wouldn't have changed his mind about a decision he'd made five years ago, long before he'd known he'd die at sixty-two from a heart attack.

Still, he really didn't like the vibe Brandon emitted. And neither, he could tell, did his mother.

Evidently, Bonita Garrison had picked up the same message, her fragile features drawn from mourning and worry. She pushed at an imaginary strand of jet-black hair, a silver thread catching the light, the gesture one of pure nervousness as she studied Brandon for clues. Were there surprises in store for her today? Hadn't she discussed every aspect of John's last will and testament with the man she'd married more than thirty-seven years earlier?

Maybe not, judging by the quiver of her delicate hands. Maybe she *should* have had a slug of Stoli before they'd gathered. Hell, maybe this event called for a round for the table. If only to numb the still-raw pain caused by losing a man deeply loved by each of his five children. A love, Parker thought bitterly, that didn't exactly extend to their cool and distant mother.

Adam arrived last, the only missing sibling of the five, slipping into the conference room in his usual quiet, detached way, shaking back some of his long, dark hair. He'd have to see a barber if he wanted to be taken more seriously than just the owner of a nightclub—even if Estate was one of Miami Beach's hottest spots. As birth order would have it, Adam was the youngest of the three Garrison men, but sat dead center in the family once the twins came along to claim the joint spot as "babies."

When the lawyer cleared his throat and stood, Parker ended his musings about his family. They'd all work out their various issues and problems, he felt certain. And he'd work out his problems—like the current decline in the Garrison brand that translated into unhappy investors, business partners and patrons.

He'd solve that, as long as he had the lion's share of control. He turned his attention to Brandon with the confidence of a man who rarely lost his focus. That legendary focus had gotten Parker where he was today, and it would keep him there far into the future.

Hadn't Dad assured him of that?

Brandon droned legalese. Next to him, Stephen shot a look of impatience to Parker, who curled his lip in a half smile of response. Brittany doodled on a pad, tempting Parker to kick her under the table and tell his flighty little sister to pay attention. Brooke watched the lawyer, rapt, as did Adam. His mother shifted in her seat, and sighed under her breath as assets were divided and doled exactly as they had all expected.

Suddenly, Brandon stopped talking. He inhaled slowly. He looked at Bonita with no small amount of pity and then leveled his gaze directly at Parker.

"The next section is in regard to the controlling shares of the parent company, Garrison, Inc. Mr. Garrison stated that they are to be divided among his six children."

Parker flinched. Brittany blinked. Stephen leaned forward, uttering a quiet, "What?"

Did he say *six?*

The lawyer must be putting in too many billable hours.

"Uh, there are five of us, Brandon," Parker corrected, a little smile tugging at his lips. "See?" He crooked his head toward the table. "Five."

Brandon responded with a long, silent stare, underscored by a nervous laugh from one of his young associates.

"Five in this room," Brandon said deliberately. "Six in all."

For a split second, no one said anything as shock rolled off the room's residents, bounced all over the table and left a palpable change in the air. Parker scowled at the lawyer, trying to process what he'd said.

Then chaos erupted when Stephen bellowed, "That's preposterous!" and Brittany let out a surprised shriek and Brooke half stood to demand an explanation. Through it all, their mother breathed so hard she damn near growled. Only Adam was quiet, but even he wore an expression of complete disbelief.

Brandon held up a hand, but they ignored him. The noise level rose, the undercurrent of incredulity and fury elevated with each question and demand.

"Stop!" Parker said with a solid *thwack* on the cherry-wood. "Let him finish."

As it had for most of his thirty-six years, a single command brought his younger siblings in line. When the room was finally silent, he said, "Obviously, this begs for an explanation."

Brandon nodded and read from the document. "The controlling shares of Garrison, Inc. will be divided among my six…" he paused and raised an eyebrow for emphasis "…children. The division is as follows—fifteen percent, in equal shares, to Stephen, Adam, Brooke and Brittany."

Parker's chest tightened as he waited for Brandon to continue.

"The remaining forty percent will be split evenly between my son Parker and my daughter Cassie Sinclair, who will also be given full ownership of the Garrison Grand-Bahamas property."

Blood sang in Parker's head nearly as loudly as the eruption that filled the room again.

"Cassie Sinclair is his daughter?"

"The manager of the Bahamas property now owns it?"

"And twenty percent of the parent company?"

"She's not his…"

Bonita Garrison stood slowly, her face ghost-white, her hands quaking. Her children quieted, as all eyes turned toward her.

"The son of a bitch," she said to no one in particular. "The cheating son of a bitch. I'm glad he's dead."

She pivoted and walked out of the room, her shoulders quivering as she tried to hold them square. A barrage of questions, accusations and outraged calls for the truth exploded in her wake.

Now, Parker thought bitterly, it sounds like a typical Garrison family gathering.

But his pulse drowned it all out, and he had to physically work to control a temper he'd long ago conquered.

No damn wonder Brandon had given him that silent warning. And no damn wonder his father had stayed so deeply involved in the day-to-day operations of the Bahamas property.

"Who'd have guessed that?" Stephen said to him, softly enough so only Parker could hear. "The old man had someone on the side."

Parker closed his eyes in disgust. Not because his father had had an affair. And not because that sin had created a sixth Garrison child. But because, for some reason he'd never know or understand, John Garrison had decided to slice Parker's world in half, and give the other portion to some hotel manager living in Nassau.

Some hotel manager—now *owner*—who was his half sister.

He pushed his chair away from the table, determined not to let the bubble of anger brew into a full boil. Instead, he cut his gaze to Brandon's, ignoring the chaos around them.

"We'll talk, Brandon," Parker said. "But I've got a company to run."

Brittany let out a tiny snort. "You have *part* of a company to run."

He refused to dignify the comment, but scooped his PDA off the table, nodded to Stephen in particular and the table in general. "Knock yourselves out, kids."

Without waiting for a response, he left the room, grateful that unlike the rest of them, who would have to travel to various Garrison properties, his office was just down the hall on the twenty-second floor of the Brickell Avenue high-rise that housed the corporate offices of Garrison, Inc.

There, he would find sanctuary and maybe the privacy to sucker punch a wall with no witnesses.

He'd tell Anna to hold every call and appointment. What he needed to do was assess the situation and figure out a solution. That was what he did. Cold, calculating and calm, Parker Garrison manipulated every move of a multimillion-dollar empire, so he could certainly control his insanely bad mood and maybe his father's ridiculously poor judgment.

He ignored the provocative smile of Sheila, the heavily made-up receptionist who manned the front desk of the plush executive offices of Garrison, Inc. He continued directly to his corner office, resisting the urge to rip off his tie and howl in fury, his blood temperature rising with each purposeful stride toward privacy.

As he turned the corner, he expected to see his assistant at her desk, efficiently gatekeeping his world as she'd been doing for a few months since he'd promoted her from the human resources department. But Anna's desk was empty, with no sign of light or life.

At nine in the morning?

Wasn't anything the way it was supposed to be today?

Inhaling sharply, he pushed the door to his office open and closed it without giving in to the temptation to slam it, swearing softly on his exhale.

That was when he heard the humming. Not a normal hum of activity or a printer or even the refrigerator from the wet bar in the corner. No, this was more like a screaming buzz. But that wasn't all. The humming barely drowned out…

Singing.

He paused for a minute, then looked toward the source, behind the partially opened bathroom door discreetly tucked around the corner of his spacious office. Singing?

If you could call that *singing*. More like a sinfully off-key soprano belting out something from…*West Side Story.* She felt pretty? Oh, so pretty? It was hard to tell with the whine as loud as a jet engine drowning it out, and the total flatness of the notes.

Propelled by curiosity and still fueled by a losing battle with his temper and control, he continued toward the sound, the soft warmth of shower steam tumbling from the open door, along with something that smelled like flowers and powder.

He paused at the eight-inch gap in the bathroom door, leaned in to be sure he wasn't imagining things, then just stood there and stared at…

Legs.

No. That didn't do them justice. These were works of art. Heaven-sent. Endless, bare, tight-thighed, smooth-skinned, strip-club worthy legs spread about a foot apart, slipped into three-inch heels and topped off by a barely covered-in-silk female rump stuck straight in the air.

He gaped, mesmerized and only slightly deafened by the noise, which was caused by a blow-dryer aimed at a cascade of dark hair that hung upside down and grazed the marble floor of his private bathroom.

She couldn't sing her way out of a paper bag, but if he

stood here listening and looking too much longer, he'd *need* a paper bag for hyperventilation.

Suddenly, she jerked to a stand, whipped her still-damp hair over her shoulder and faced the mirror, giving him a wide-open shot of a pink lace bra that barely covered her sweetly curved cleavage.

"Oh, my God!" She yelped and spun around, slapping her hands over her and hardly covering a thing. His gaze dropped lazily, taking in the narrow waist, the flare of feminine hips, the low bikini cut of delicate pink panties cupping an alluring apex between those lovely thighs.

Good God, his administrative assistant had been hiding all this under navy pantsuits and crisp white blouses?

"Anna?" His voice sounded as tight as his throat suddenly felt.

"What are you doing here?" she demanded.

The question yanked him back to her face, her appealing features tinged with the shade of her matching underwear, bottle-green eyes bright with embarrassment.

"What am *I* doing here?" He didn't mean to smile. Or stare. But, he was human. And she was…unbelievable. "Last time I checked, this was my office."

She managed an indignant breath—no mean feat for a woman clad only in heels and underwear. "I mean, so soon. What are you doing here so soon? Aren't you in a meeting? With your family? About the will?"

The will. The words whacked him over the head as effectively as if he'd stepped into the shower that still dripped behind her. "I left early."

She threw a pleading glance at the towel rack next to him. She wanted coverage. But he wanted answers. And a few more seconds to memorize every delectable inch of her.

"I wasn't expecting you," she said, still struggling for her always-professional voice.

"No kidding." He couldn't help the tease in his. This was, without a doubt, the bright spot in an otherwise dismal morning.

"I went running," she said, with another desperate look at the towel rack. "It's very humid out there. I needed a quick shower. I thought you'd be a while."

His gaze was slipping again, along with his ability to form a coherent thought other than the one screaming in his brain: How the hell had his all-business-all-the-time administrative assistant concealed that body from him?

And why would she? Most women with a figure like hers would wear as little as possible, as often as they could.

"The meeting ended early," he said calmly, lingering just one more minute on the heels. Did she wear them every day?

He tore his attention from her slender ankles to slide over the neat little turn of her calf and meander back to that silky triangle with a silent vow to buy more Victoria's Secret stock. He zeroed in on a luscious inny navel, then paused just long enough for those lace cups to rise and fall with an exasperated breath.

"If you don't mind, I could use a towel." Her demand was sharp as shock morphed into anger.

She was angry? He should give her a lesson in professionalism, a reminder that she shouldn't be making herself at home in his office. He could treat her like the employee she was, and reprimand her for not being at her desk, or even issue a warning that she shouldn't assume anything about his schedule.

But all he did was smile and tug the towel from the rack, holding it out to her. "Great shower, isn't it?"

Her eyes widened in surprise as she took the welcome cover and wrapped it around her narrow frame, hiding every blood-warming curve. "Yes."

"Gotta love those dual massage heads."

A sneaky smile pulled at her mouth as she tucked terry into terry and formed a makeshift knot under her collarbone.

"Yes. They're great. Both of them." She straightened and lifted her chin, doing her very best to appear the altogether competent assistant who'd impressed him from the first interview. She almost pulled it off, except for the tumbling waves of dark hair that she normally wore in a tight twist, and the fact that the towel barely covered her backside.

He cleared his throat and tried really hard to scowl. "Anna," he said sternly.

"Yes?"

His head pounded with the morning's news followed by the surprise attack on his hormones. But that was no reason to take his anger and physical response out on this young woman whose only real crime was bad timing. Or good timing, depending on your perspective.

"Don't quit your day job to be a singer."

Her smile transformed her whole face, taking what had been plain, passably pretty features to something more stunning. "Not to worry, Mr. Garrison."

But he was worried. Not only had he missed her incredible body, he'd never even noticed her milky smooth skin, or the way the tip of her tongue slipped between her teeth when she smiled, or how nicely her eyes tilted up at the sides. He'd never noticed this lovely woman right under his nose.

So of course he worried. Worried that he was going blind. Or maybe he was just so deep into the family business that he'd failed to see the gorgeous woman who sat outside his office all day long.

He turned to leave, closing the door to give her privacy to dress, and congratulating himself on the return of control and focus. And perspective.

So she was pretty. So she had a body that could bring him to his knees. It didn't matter. What had just happened was nothing more than a close encounter that she would regret and he would forget. She was an excellent assistant and he had an empire to run, a will to contest, a brand to build. He needed his legendary control and focus more than ever.

But, damn, it would be hard to forget those legs.

Anna crossed the Oriental rug that welcomed visitors to the CEO's suite and stabbed the digital air conditioner control until it read a chilly sixty-seven degrees.

But even that wouldn't reduce the burn of embarrassment that singed her from the roots of her hair to the tips of her toes. If it even *was* embarrassment. It was a burn, anyway. As hot and uncomfortable as Parker Garrison's eyes when he'd given her a visual lick from those same roots to those same toes.

A familiar wicked, gooey sensation stirred low in her belly. Really low. Really wicked. Really familiar. And really *dumb* to think about her boss that way.

"Stupid," she chided as she turned on her computer and picked up the phone receiver to listen to voice mail messages. How could she have been so careless? Just for five extra minutes under the ultimate hydro-jet massage from heaven?

God, if he knew how many times she'd treated herself to that shower, she'd be updating her résumé. And she'd worked in human resources long enough to know that the last place she wanted to be was on the job market. No one hired anyone without a check of the Internet—and she knew exactly what would pop up when someone typed "Anna Cross" into a search engine.

Accused of corporate spying...

No, Anna shouldn't do anything that would force her to look for another job. So, she'd better hope her boss didn't think borrowing the shower was grounds for dismissal.

She squeezed her eyes shut as she listened to the voice mail system announce that Parker Garrison had seventeen messages.

Seventeen? What the heck was going on?

By the time she jotted down message number five, she knew. At least she knew that something really bad had gone down at the morning meeting. The various Garrison siblings and a couple of lawyers didn't provide details in their voice mails, but their tone, along with a few clues about "what the will said," didn't sound good.

Parker's door had remained firmly shut since she'd done her level best to exit his office with some measure of dignity, knowing he watched her, knowing he'd seen *everything* she'd been careful to hide. Ever since she'd arrived at Garrison, Inc. four years ago, Anna had done whatever was necessary to stay off the radar, and do an outstanding job as an administrative assistant.

In fact, she'd done such an outstanding job in human resources that she'd been handed the promotion of her dreams when the slot for Parker Garrison's administrative assistant had become available three months ago. Maybe, considering her history, she should have turned it down.

But she couldn't resist the upgrade in status, pay and benefits. Plus, she'd been tucked away on a lower floor for almost four years. Surely, after all this time, her past would remain, well, in the past.

Still, it had become habit to keep a low profile.

Until ten minutes ago when her profile had been anything but low. It had been…damn near naked.

She closed her eyes again as another heat wave threatened, trying to ignore it as she noted each caller. No, that definitely wasn't embarrassment. Nor was it a feminine response to the warmth of Parker's very obviously high opinion of how she looked sans suit. The heat wave that warred with the air conditioner was raw terror.

The only thing she'd ever wanted out of this job, this city and this life was anonymity and peace. No attention—from men or media. No connection—with her boss or his associates. No trouble—ever. And what had just happened in that bathroom spelled *attention, connection* and *trouble* in capital red letters.

She recorded the rest of the messages on a call sheet that she delivered to him hourly, only slightly reassured by the fact that whatever was going wrong in Parker's world, it would divert his attention from her.

Her intercom buzzed.

"Yes, Mr. Garrison?"

"I need you."

Her gut clenched. "I'll be right there, Mr. Garrison."

"I think, Anna—" his voice in the receiver was just soft enough to make her tighten her grasp and push the phone closer to her ear "—you could probably call me Parker now."

Now that I've seen you in your underwear. Her heart wobbled. "Absolutely, Mr.…Parker."

He was still chuckling when she hung up.

"Come on, Anna," she whispered to herself, gathering her planner and pen. Parker didn't strike her as the kind of man to torture and tease a woman, or one who would

assume that just because he'd seen her in the almost altogether that he could have his way with her.

She stood, surprised at how shaky that thought made her
legs. *Have his way with her.*

A stupid, archaic phrase that sent even stupider, more
archaic pulses down her body. So they'd had an awkward
moment.

She rolled her eyes at the understatement. A *really*
awkward moment. And so what if she'd seen a lusty side
of a man she found attractive? Okay, gorgeous. All right,
hot as sin.

She was still a top-notch administrative assistant who
knew beyond a shadow of a doubt that office affairs were
for fools who liked to job hop. And he was a very important, busy man who had an electronic black book with
the name and private cell phone number of every available model, debutante and businesswoman in Miami-
Dade County.

She was still an employee, and he was still the boss.
Period. End of fantasy.

She tapped on his door, opening it as she did. She'd
always done that, but this morning, the intrusion felt more
intimate. He stood at the window, the cordless phone held
to his ear, his attention on the postcard view of Biscayne
Bay. Through a floor-to-ceiling window, sunlight glinted
off blue-violet waves, polka-dotted with pleasure craft and
cruise ships, fringed by emerald palm trees and the pastel
high-rises of Miami Beach on the horizon.

But the real view was inside and, as always, Anna
stole an eyeful.

Parker had removed his jacket, revealing the tailored cut
of a snow-white zillion-thread-count designer shirt pulled just
taut enough to hint at the toned, developed muscles under-

ROXANNE ST. CLAIRE   23

neath. The shirt was tucked neatly into dark trousers, custom-
made to fit like a dream over one drool-inducing backside.

The man was a *god*.

He turned from the window and she averted her eyes
before getting caught worshipping at the altar of his backside.

"Can the legal crap, Brandon," he said into the phone,
sliding one of his hands through closely cropped, thick
black hair. "I don't care what the DNA test results will say.
Can we or can we not contest this will?"

DNA? Contest the will? Anna frowned, but Parker just
nodded to one of the guest chairs in front of his desk,
issuing an unspoken invitation for her to sit. As always, he
seemed utterly calm, the aura of authority that shimmered
around him neatly in place. But there was something different in that clipped voice, and in the tense way he held
his broad shoulders. His control was tied on with a tenuous
thread today.

"Fine, you do that," he said, leaning his head to one side
to work out a crick. "In the meantime, it's business as usual.
My business." He glanced at Anna, who made a show of
flipping her planner to the next clean page so she didn't stare.
Even though she'd become quite adept at avoiding detection.

"Oh, damn it all, I completely forgot." His tone changed
with the admission, and she instantly sat up, prepared to help
him remember what he forgot. That was, after all, her job. Not
ogling his perfectly shaped butt, impossibly wide shoulders
or Adonis-like chest. Parker-gazing was just a side benefit.

"I can't go," he said to Brandon, sliding into the high-
backed desk chair and reaching for his little black digital
device and pressing a few buttons. "But, with the bomb
you just dropped at this morning's reading, I think I need
to be there more than ever."

He paused and Anna tried to psych out what he was talking about.

"But I'm way too swamped to consider going that far away," he added, "unless I charter a jet."

Of course. London.

"I have a ton of work to do this weekend," he continued, "and it's impossible to get anything done on a commercial flight."

Anna slipped a creamy-white card embossed with silver letters from the "pending" section of his calendar. Her fingers glided over the imprint of the International Hotel and Restaurant Association seal, over the gilded script inviting him to the annual ball at Guildhall in London. She'd been meaning to get a response from him so she could RSVP.

He chuckled softly, fiddling with the buttons on the PDA as he tucked the phone into one of those impressive shoulders.

"Yes. A date," he said casually to Brandon, and shot a lazy wink at Anna, which sent an involuntary stutter to her heart. "I suppose I'd need to get one of those, too."

Which of the lucky ladies would win that lottery?

Maxine, whose daddy owned half of Palm Beach? Or the nine-foot glamazon who'd been on the cover of *Vogue* twice? He'd been seeing a lot of her in the past few weeks. Maybe he'd go for that spunky redhead who owned the PR agency that had done some work for Garrison, Inc. last month. Sparks were certainly crackling in the conference room when that one came in for a meeting.

"As a matter of fact, I might have the perfect person." His gaze landed right on her, intense, relentless and unwavering. Exactly the way it had been when he'd devoured her with it in the bathroom.

A low, slow flame curled up her belly and started a familiar bonfire. One she'd become very good at dousing with four simple words that have saved legions of love-struck secretaries: *He's your boss, dummy.*

Suddenly, he stood, turned to the window and copped the voice he used to end a conversation instantly. "Keep me posted, Brandon. And I'll let you know what I decide."

For a moment, he didn't move, but stared at the cloud-less blue sky, his back rising and falling with steady, slow breaths.

Then he turned and trained his midnight gaze on her. "As you can tell, Anna, I didn't get good news this morn-ing."

She set the call sheet on his desk. "That must explain the seventeen voice-mail messages."

He scanned the list, and swore so softly she almost didn't hear it. "Brandon's right."

"About?"

"I have to be at the IH & RA ball in London. It's more important than ever that I maintain…" He paused, assess-ing her as though he was wondering just how much to tell her. "Leadership."

"Your leadership is never in doubt."

He tilted his head, acknowledging the compliment with shuttered lids that said he believed the opposite. At least, at the moment. Then he yanked out his chair and sat, leaning forward the way he always did when he made a decision that he would not second-guess. Not that he'd ever second-guessed anything, ever, in his life.

"Please arrange for the charter jet company to have a Gulfstream V ready to leave tomorrow, very early, from Kendall-Tamiami Executive Airport. That will put me in London Friday evening, with plenty of time to make the function on Saturday and return on Sunday morning. I'll be back in the office on Monday. I'll need the Berkeley Suite at the Ritz-Carlton London. Don't let them tell you it's not available—"

"I'll use your name."

"Yes, and I'll need a limo to and from the event, which is—"

"At Guildhall."

"Right. And I have a driver in London I prefer—"

"Mr. Sanderson with the London Car Company."

He laughed softly. "Yes."

She scribbled the onslaught of instructions. "You'll want some files for the plane," she said.

"Of course."

"The financials on the Grand are up for review next week," she reminded him, still writing. "And you'll need the latest investment results, and the agenda for the exec committee meeting next—"

"Get me everything we have on the Garrison Grand-Bahamas."

She did look up at that, it threw her so completely. "The hotel in Nassau?"

"Everything," he repeated.

"Of course." She scratched another note, swallowing the question of *why?* A good admin didn't ask. "And you'll probably need to review your speech for the business council so I'll include the notes, and you have an appointment with a marketing firm regarding new collateral materials late next week, so no doubt you'll want a complete…" A strange tingling sensation suddenly froze her pen in hand. Slowly, she looked up from her pad to find him staring at her. "You do still want to meet with that firm on Thursday afternoon, right?"

Staring? No. Bottomless brown bedroom eyes practically swallowed her whole.

"What's the matter?" she asked, striking a neutral chord in her voice despite the way her limbs turned heavy.

"Make it easy on me, Anna, and come to London."

Oh. *Oh.* "Make what easy?"

"The *work.* You know so much about my work and you're so incredible...incredibly organized. I can only rationalize this much time away from the office if I'm productive. And with you, I'm productive."

The work. Of course. Why else would he want her to go to London? And why else would she even consider it?

"You can have comp vacation days to make up for the lost weekend," he added, as though she were actually worried about that. He had no way of knowing that her hesitation had nothing to do with losing a weekend, and everything to do with losing her mind. Proximity to the object of her steamiest nightly fantasies could drive her crazy.

"That's no problem," she said slowly. "I don't mind working the weekend."

"Then you'll go." He smiled, a genuine grin that he saved for when he won a small victory in business. Something he did about a million times a day. "Perfect. You'll need something very formal. That ball at Guildhall is over the top."

"The *ball?*" He couldn't be serious. "You want *me* to go to the ball?"

He laughed lightly. "That's the idea, Cinderella. Why would I dig up a date when you'll already be there?"

Like he'd have to dig far. "Because..." She couldn't think of a reason. Except that one.

He's your boss, dummy.

Unless what he'd seen in the bathroom made him think of her differently.

"Mr. Garrison, uh, Parker," she said, standing just so she could gain the minor advantage of height for once. "I'm sorry about this morning. I—"

He pointed toward the bathroom door. "That?" He waved away her concern as if it were no more than a flea. "Totally forgotten, I assure you." Tapping the call sheet, he added, "Better get that charter booked and get all the files in order, and I'll get to these seventeen calls."

Done. Decision made. No arguing or second-guessing or trying to explain that she couldn't, wouldn't, shouldn't go to London with him. Because she could, and she would.

Leaving his office, Anna found Sheila McKay in the act of depositing more handwritten messages.

"These came to the front desk while you were in with Mr. Garrison," the receptionist said. "The phones absolutely haven't stopped since that meeting ended."

"I just gave him seventeen others," Anna said with a sigh. "Looks like it's going to be a busy day."

Sheila wrinkled a picture-perfect nose, which fit her picture-perfect face and body. Anna hadn't been surprised to learn the stunning woman was a former Playmate who'd probably filled her bunny suit very nicely. She'd always been very friendly with Anna, especially since Anna had received the promotion to work for the CEO. But Anna remained distant with all her coworkers.

Friends wanted to know your past.

"So," Sheila said, sliding a well-toned hip on the corner of Anna's desk. "What went down in Garrison land? Did the old man drop a bomb from the grave or something?"

The words *DNA test* and *contest the will* rang in Anna's ears.

"I wouldn't know," she said coolly. Even if she did, she wouldn't tell the receptionist.

He hoped for a clever quip, an easy smile, but got only a shake of her head.

"Just coffee, thank you." When the attendant nodded and moved toward the galley, Anna lifted a paper and held it toward him. "I've compiled a list of pending open items for your attention, Mr. Garrison."

He didn't remind her to call him Parker. Anna Cross was back to business in a big way. It was as though she'd been wearing a sign that said This Is Work, Not Fun ever since she'd arrived at the executive airport and climbed out of her little Saturn wearing her most staid suit selected from a wardrobe that couldn't be called anything but *ultraconservative*. Navy jacket, shapeless trousers, flat shoes.

Where was the girl who felt pretty in pink underwear?

Parker took the list, and reminded himself that he was the one who'd suggested she accompany him to *work*. He'd made that clear. At least, that was how he rationalized what was, at the moment, an impulsive idea brought on by the not-so-semi state of arousal the bathroom encounter had left him in.

He knew why he'd suggested Anna accompany him to London.

But did she? Sure, she was a terrific, grade-A, indispensable administrative assistant. Sure, she was attractive, classy and intelligent enough to make small talk with the high rollers at the hotel gala. And best of all, he trusted her. She had no gold digger's interest in his money, ready to translate one weekend in Europe into a lifetime of luxury like so many of the women he knew.

But, to be honest, not one of those was the real reason he'd made the unorthodox suggestion. The real reason was simple: he liked what he'd seen in that bathroom. And he wanted to see more. And seeing, he knew as sure as he breathed, wouldn't be enough.

Under any other circumstances, he'd make his move and he'd make it in about five minutes, launching a romantic, sex-charged weekend with champagne and hot kisses at thirty thousand feet. Seducing a woman was an art and a pleasure he took seriously. And often.

But something indefinable held him back. Something oddly unfamiliar had him waiting for a clear invitation, a straightforward cue from her.

Maybe she'd take off her jacket, playfully taste his spicy tomato juice, unclip her barrette and give her hair a sensual shake. That was what other women would do. They'd throw in a head-tilting giggle; slide their bare, pedicured feet on his lap and let the games begin.

But not Anna.

She pulled a pair of butt-ugly reading glasses out of her purse and slipped them up her pert nose. She tightened the clip that held her hair severely off a face devoid of anything but lip gloss and maybe mascara. Then she took her copy of his agenda, pointed to item number one, cleared her throat and said, "You mentioned the Nassau property. I have the files."

Not only did she refuse to send a single cue of feminine interest, she doused his low simmer by mentioning the biggest headache in his life.

He took the file and flipped it open.

"Is there something in particular you're looking for?" she asked.

There sure was. Dirt. Problems. Issues. Anything that could get rid of the half sister who'd just been named his equal partner at Garrison, Inc. "Just want to see how the business is doing."

"Last quarter's financials are on the left side, including occupancy rates and banquet revenue," she told him. "On the right, you'll see information about new resort programs and key employee files. The manager of the resort, Cassie Sinclair, seems to be running things quite smoothly."

At the mention of her name, Parker sucked in a slow and disgusted breath. He flipped through the pages, immaculately ordered and filed, frowning at the excellent revenue stream and the strong outlook for the next season based on advance reservations.

"Is something wrong?"

Yes, something was very, very wrong. He wanted the property to be a disaster. Wanted something he could hang on Cassie Sinclair to prove she couldn't be a Garrison.

"No," he assured her.

"Oh, I thought I might have misfiled something."

"Have you ever misfiled anything, Anna?" he asked with a teasing smile.

A soft blush rose in her cheeks. "If you're asking if I ever make mistakes, I think you, of all people, know that I do."

Mistakes like lingering in his shower a little too long? He held her gaze, still hoping for a spark of connection, but she looked away—as she always did—just as Christine returned with the drinks, some fruit and freshly baked muffins.

Parker returned his attention to the file. "The place is turning a nice profit," he said, half to himself.

"You make it sound like that's a problem."

Should he confide in his assistant? Maybe a little shared confidence would loosen her up. At least get her to slide out of that straitjacket she wore. Plus, he needed someone to talk to. Someone he trusted.

He lifted his tomato juice and took a long drink before he dove in. "Cassie Sinclair, it seems, is more than just the manager of the Garrison Grand-Bahamas."

"She is?"

"She's my half sister."

Anna's jaw dropped an inch. "No way."

He gave her a bittersweet smile. "Evidently there is a way. It's called an affair and my father had one for a long time, resulting in the birth of a woman who is now, according to his will, my equal partner in Garrison, Inc. and—" he held the file up "—the owner of this hotel."

"I don't believe it," she said, dropping back into her seat.

"Neither do I. But that's why God invented lawyers," he said with a shrug. "And why I have to make an appearance in London this weekend."

"Will she be there?"

"Oh, I doubt it. But it's only a matter of time until this gets out to the very small and incestuous hospitality industry. It can't help my business. I'm attending this event for visibility and positioning. More of a PR move than one that will impact the bottom line."

"So that's why you were talking about DNA testing and contesting the will," she said. "Oh, and why…your mother…" Her voice drifted off.

So the rumor mill had already started churning.

"My mother has her way of coping." He picked up the drink again. "And I'm afraid it's not Tabasco in her tomato juice."

She gave him a sympathetic look. "Your family is strong. You'll weather this storm."

"I hope you're right."

"You just have to stay focused and keep running everything the way you have. You can't let this distract you."

The unsolicited—and amazingly accurate—advice took him by surprise. "You're right, Anna. Very astute." He smiled and leaned forward, inexplicably drawn to her. "Thank you for being so understanding."

She held his gaze just long enough to give him hope that the cue he wanted was right around the corner. But she just handed him another file.

"When you're ready to go over the agenda for the marketing-firm meeting, it's all in here. And I'm able to take any e-mail dictation now," she added, tapping the open laptop. "I'll download it and send it when we arrive in London."

Oh, yeah. Anna Cross was all business today, and being a smart CEO, he ignored the urge to reach across the space that separated them and unclip her hair just to see what she'd do. She was way too valuable an asset to him to let hormones screw it up.

So he took the cue—even if it wasn't the one he wanted— along with the file, and worked for a solid nine hours, through breakfast, lunch and almost no small talk, until they landed.

Through it all, she never tired, never complained and never even took the damn jacket off. Maybe that was the real reason he didn't make the move to seduce her: they were kindred spirits. Workaholics, both of them, with a bone-deep love for control over their respective worlds.

Sex, in fact, could really screw that up.

By the time they landed and took a late-night cab ride through the still-vibrating streets of London, Parker was entirely comfortable with keeping the weekend on the level of strictly business. He abandoned the idea of taking her sightseeing the next day; they—or at least, he—would work, grilling Brandon Washington on the situation in the Bahamas and tracking the progress of several high-power land deals he had in the works.

Tomorrow night, he would introduce Anna as his assistant and she would no doubt wear her hair in a bun, don a conservative dress and stay stone-cold sober.

"Wow!" Anna froze midstep as they followed the cheerful old doorman into the smothering luxury that was the Ritz-Carlton London.

"Yeah, it's not exactly the Miami Beach hip of the Garrison Grand," Parker agreed. "This is pure old-world sophistication. You either like it or you feel suffocated. I, personally, love it."

"It's fantastic," she said, her voice a little hushed as she took in the three-story rotunda that capped the lobby, trimmed by ornate gilded woodwork.

Smiling at her enthusiasm, he stepped away to check in. But after a few keystrokes and frowns, the formally dressed clerk informed Parker that there'd been an error in the system and Ms. Cross's room was not available.

"Not ready or not available?" Parker asked.

"We are so very, deeply sorry, Mr. Garrison," the solicitous clerk, who obviously had not been in the hotel business long enough to recognize Parker's last name, crooned softly. "We are booked, overbooked and double booked with several very large events this weekend."

Parker knew, without the slightest doubt, that a single word with a manager would get a room. He'd been raised in this business and "no rooms" meant there were a half dozen on reserve.

"Your suite has three bedrooms, Mr. Garrison, and it's quite lovely and spacious," the clerk added. "And perhaps something will become available tomorrow."

Parker squeezed the bridge of his nose, fighting the exhaustion that came with trans-Atlantic travel. He turned to see Anna, who still scanned the lobby with a little bit of wonder in her eyes. There really was plenty of room in that suite. She'd love the decor.

And if it got a little cozy...

He nodded to the clerk. "We'll make due with that, then."

After a moment, a bellman whisked their luggage ahead and Parker joined Anna with a regretful smile. "Slight change in plans," he said.

"Oh?"

"There's no room for you."

She drew back, frowning. "I know I booked it. And, surely, if you tell them who—"

He held up a hand in agreement. "I can fight it, absolutely. But the suite has three bedrooms, all with their own baths, and enough room for a party of fifty people." He grinned. "I believe I had one there once."

She shrugged, a little weariness—or was it wariness?—giving a delicate set to her jaw. "All right. I'm beat, anyway. I just need a shower and sleep."

He tilted his head and put a casual hand on her shoulder to guide her through the lobby. "I only have one rule."

She slowed her step. "Which is?"

"No singing in the shower."

Late the next afternoon, Anna broke the rule.

Secretly, quietly and probably way off-key, she warbled a pathetic version of "Can't Help Loving That Man" from *Showboat* as she let blistering hot water pulse over her skin.

She *couldn't* help it. Showers were made for singing.

Anyway, Parker hadn't emerged from the wood-paneled library long enough to even enjoy the ridiculous opulence of a suite that was about three times the size of Anna's little house in Coral Gables, let alone hear her in the shower. And, oh, what he'd missed while he mumbled and barked orders to his lawyer, his accountant, his minions.

Anna could have spent the day just roaming the endless array of museum-quality rooms, admiring the Louis-the-something furniture, taking in the view of the avenues and stores from every arched window. As it was, she'd lost half an hour that morning just brushing her fingers over silk, damask and velvet pillows of celery and sage on delicate settees and graceful dining-room chairs.

But like always, the best view in the place was the one of her boss, wearing casual khaki pants and a simple but achingly expensive pullover and, God help her, no shoes.

That had been what finally sent her into the streets of London. Not his suggestion that she use the car and driver to explore. Not his implication that he needed complete privacy to conduct his business. No, what sent her out to the shops of Piccadilly, past Buckingham Palace and into the pristine paths of Hyde Park were Parker Garrison's bare feet.

She closed her eyes and paused midsong, water sluicing over her bare skin, as hot as the fire that tightened her stomach into a knot of arousal. She thought she'd seen everything attractive on the man...but she'd never seen such beautiful feet.

Long and narrow, strong boned with the faintest dusting of black hairs on his toes and a high arch where his khaki pants broke.

Oh, Anna Cross, girl, you have it bad. Swooning over feet.

But she'd nearly dumped her china coffee cup when he'd emerged from his room that morning, the shoulders of his red shirt spotted from droplets of just-showered hair, the natural scent of his soap still clinging to him. Averting her gaze from his freshly shaven face, she'd looked down.

Big mistake.

When she'd returned to the suite only an hour ago, he'd still been in the damn library, with the door closed. So she'd decided to start getting ready for the gala, planning to take a lot of time and care with her hair and makeup. After all, he'd said this was a PR move. It would be a PR disaster to arrive with a sad-looking date.

Getting ready might take some time because it had been many years since she'd arrived at a formal affair on the arm of a rich and powerful man. With a hard jerk, she twisted the knobs of the shower, wishing she could shut off the flow of her thoughts as easily. She didn't want to think about the man who'd changed everything. Not her boss, in that case, but her boss's rival.

But ever since she'd taken the job for Parker, thoughts of Michael Montgomery, another powerful, influential man, were close to the surface. The fact that once before she'd given in to a weakness for a handsome power broker with class, humor and style was nothing to be ashamed of, she reminded herself as she applied some makeup and twirled her hair into a French twist.

But her weakness had made her a pawn caught in the cross fire, forced to run and give up her home…all because she'd given in to an attraction to a man who was, ironically, very much like Parker Garrison.

Her father, a very wise man, had once told her that the definition of *fool* was someone who didn't learn from a mistake. She wasn't a fool. Was she?

When she'd been with Michael Montgomery, she'd been twenty-four, young and naive. Now she was nearly twenty-nine, and had successfully escaped her past. Sure, she had a crush on Parker the size of the Garrison Grand, but she was human and female. And she'd managed her attraction for three months.

But now, she was in London, sharing a suite with him, no less. And about to slip into a slinky gown she hadn't worn for four years. And no doubt she'd have to dance with him.

Oh, how much could a girl take before she did something…foolish?

Makeup and hair done, she covered her skin with a lightly scented cream, stepped into tiny bikini panties and opened the closet door to inch the drab navy suit to the side.

He hadn't given her time to shop for something new, she thought as she touched the red silk. And she'd only worn this dress once, so it didn't make any sense to spend money on something else. Plus…oh, forget rationalizing. She loved the dress.

Fingering the plunging neckline, she remembered how beautiful she'd felt the last time she'd worn it—right before her boyfriend had betrayed her, and she'd been run out of Indiana by bad press and false accusations.

She buried the thought. Tonight, she'd just revel in the dress, in the thigh-revealing cut and the backless dip that nearly touched her tailbone and the flared skirt that shimmered like liquid fire when she walked.

Anna reached for the hanger, a little sad she'd cover the revealing bodice and back with a simple black pashmina wrap and take small steps so as not to show too much leg. Because, all rationalization aside, she didn't need to attract any attention.

And she had to remember that powerful, sexy, controlling men with smoldering smiles and mouthwatering bodies were dangerous. Especially, oh, God, especially if one of the things they controlled was your paycheck.

She slipped on the dress, fastened the halter top and added some simple silver earrings and strappy black sandals. She dropped a tube of lipstick and a compact into her evening bag. Now where had she put the wrap?

"Anna?" From the sound of Parker's voice, he was outside her door. "The limo's here."

"I'll be right out," she promised, flipping through the closet for the pashmina. Then two drawers. Then her empty suitcase.

Was it possible the woman who never forgot anything had left the cover-up at home? She closed her eyes and pictured it hanging over the chair in her bedroom where she'd placed it with a mental note to pack it last.

"Damn." She'd forgotten to pack it at all.

"Anna? Do you need help with a zipper or something?"

Or something. She fingered the plunging neckline and swiped her hand over the curve of her hip. Evidently she wasn't going to be able to hide a thing from anyone tonight.

She put her hand on the doorknob and took a deep breath. "I seem to have forgotten my wrap," she said. "I hope that's not a problem."

When she opened the door, she inhaled sharply at the sight of Parker in a tuxedo. Really, there ought to be a law against looking like that.

He merely stepped back, and made absolutely no effort to hide the slow sweep of his gaze over her face and body. "Uh, no." His voice was tight, the way it had been in the bathroom the other morning, and his eyes turned just as dark and hungry. "That is definitely not a problem."

But the way he reached for her hand, and the way that designer tux rested on his broad shoulders, and the way he smelled like cinnamon and spice…oh, that was a problem.

He leaned a little too close and took a deep breath, a soft moan in his chest. "You certainly are good at hiding…things."

She managed a tight smile. "Not really."

Oh, yes. The problems were just starting to mount.

Three

"I thought I should wear a wrap."

Parker gave in to the urge to check her out top to bottom one more time. Anna was stunning. Extraordinary. Perfect.

"*Why* would you cover that up?" he asked.

"I just… I'm cold." She rubbed her bare arms self-consciously, the gesture drawing her breasts together in the most provocative way.

He'd reached to touch her shoulder, but his hand continued over her back, drawing her closer, warming her. "You don't need a wrap. You've got a date."

Goose bumps rose on her skin, and beneath the thin red material that hugged her breasts, her nipples hardened, sending a few gallons of his blood below the belt.

What was that stupid decision he'd made on the plane? Something about kindred spirits and messing things up with sex and…

Never mind. Some decisions just screamed to be second-guessed.

"You look incredible," he said, letting genuine admiration warm his voice as he leaned closer and took a whiff of her musky perfume. "And you smell like heaven."

"Thanks," she said softly, stepping away from him in one easy move. "You clean up nice, too, Mr.—"

He pointed a playful finger at her. "Don't you dare."

"Parker." She smiled and moved another step away. "I'm sorry, it's a hard habit to break."

"I'll help you." Reaching for her hand, he lifted her knuckles to his mouth and placed a soft kiss on her silky skin. "Every time you use the word *mister,* I'm going to kiss you."

Her eyelashes shuttered and the goose bumps returned, but she laughed softly. "Kind of like Pavlov's dog?"

"Nothing like Pavlov's dog." He guided her toward the door. "But consider yourself warned. And every time you force me to kiss you, it's going to get…" He tempered his smoky look with a half smile. "More serious."

Maybe that would nudge her toward that "cue" he'd been waiting for.

"Then I'll have to be very careful of what I say," she promised, her pretty mouth turned up in a teasing smile.

As they walked toward the elevator, he drank in her staggering combination of sexuality and elegance. The gown narrowed at her waist, then flared and then…

Oh, man. The thigh-high slit made his mouth go bone dry. How was a guy supposed to keep his hands out of that treasure trove?

He hit the elevator call button and leaned closer to her. "I have to tell you," he said, glancing down at the open pleat. "You have great legs, Anna."

Color darkened her cheeks. "Thank you, Mist—"

Parker grinned as he dipped down and kissed her cheek. "What were you going to say?"

She chuckled softly. "Thank you, Parker."

"My pleasure," he said, his voice rich with double meaning. Sliding his arm around her waist, he placed his mouth close to her ear as the elevator bell dinged and the doors opened. "Next time it'll be on the lips."

"Well, if it isn't the Grand Garrison himself."

Parker froze at the ice in the familiar voice, the frisson of sexual play extinguished by the sound of an archenemy. He led Anna into the car, sparing Jordan Jefferies no more than a passing glance as he nodded hello. Just long enough to see the tall, muscular man looked tan and fit, and wore a tuxedo.

Parker swore mentally. Jefferies was headed to the same gala, no doubt.

"I'm afraid your escort is too rude to introduce us," Jordan said to Anna. "I'm Jordan Jefferies."

She gave the man a blank look as if she'd never even heard of him before. But how could she not? She must have heard the name around the office. She had to know the Jefferies brothers, both this one and the adopted Emilio, were the bane of Parker's existence. What the hell was he doing here, anyway? He hadn't been on the guest list Parker had requested to see before he'd left.

"Anna Cross," she said politely, shaking his hand.

Jefferies turned her fingers, gave a little fake Euro-bow and kissed her knuckles. Parker seethed silently.

"A pleasure, Anna," Jefferies said.

"Couldn't find a date, Jefferies?" Parker said, only half teasing.

"I decided to fly over at the last minute," he replied, his blue eyes riveted on Anna. "And certainly I couldn't find anyone to rival this beautiful woman."

Anna sneaked a sideways glance of disbelief at Parker, and he wanted to kiss her again for not succumbing to the wiles of this snake. Instead, he slid a possessive arm around her and eased her into his side. Where she'd be spending the evening.

And, if all went well, the night.

The car stopped at a lower floor and when the doors opened, Parker's stomach dropped at the sight of yet another archenemy.

Emilio Jefferies nodded to his brother, but his sage-green eyes swept over Parker, his olive complexion darkening just a little. "Parker. Pleasant surprise to see you here."

Parker doubted that it was pleasant *or* a surprise, but he did the right thing and introduced the other Jefferies brother to Anna.

"I assume you are both headed to the gala," Anna said.

"We are," Emilio acknowledged.

"I'm sure you'll have a wonderful time," she said.

He nodded and looked at Parker. "How is your family?"

"Fine." Parker studied the numbers above the door, calculating just how many more seconds he'd have to exchange oxygen with Jordan and Emilio Jefferies.

"Your sisters?" Jordan asked.

Parker speared him with a look. He'd kill either of his sisters if they even talked to these two snakes. "Fine," he repeated.

"Miss Cross." Jordan directed his attention back to Anna, ignoring Parker. "Are you in the hospitality industry as well?"

"Anna is my assistant," Parker said before she could answer, infusing the pride he felt into his voice.

Jefferies notched a knowing eyebrow. "Well, that must be convenient."

Parker's fingers twitched with the desire to land something *convenient* in Jordan Jefferies's smug face but Anna just relaxed into him, her smile all grace and class. "It certainly is, as Mr. Garrison is so gifted when it comes to mixing business and pleasure."

Jordan drew back as the door opened, surprise and admiration on his sculpted features. He stepped aside and let Anna out of the elevator first.

"You know I love nothing more than taking what you want, Garrison," Jordan murmured to Parker under his breath.

"And I love nothing more than making sure you don't."

"Then you'd better hold on to your assistant."

"I plan to."

"And everything else," Emilio added with a smile that looked more like a sneer.

Parker gave them both venomous looks, then muscled past to walk Anna through the Ritz lobby. They didn't speak until they'd been whisked through the doors and cocooned into a waiting limousine.

"That was the perfect way to handle them," Parker said as he handed her a bubbling glass of champagne the driver had just poured.

Anna accepted it, and tilted her head. "Why, thank you, Mr. Garrison."

She'd used the name on purpose, he had no doubt. Flashing her a victorious grin, he leaned closer and brushed her lips with his.

"Next time," he whispered against her lips, "it's a French kiss."

"Thanks for the warning." The crystal clinked. "Parker."

He sipped the champagne, admired his beautiful date and imagined just how many times he could get her to call him Mr. Garrison in the next few hours.

* * *

In no time at all, Anna surrendered.

How could she not? No woman could resist the magic of a magnificent, historic banquet hall shimmering with a million candles and a thousand elegantly dressed guests. She just gave in to the music, the moment and, of course, the man. The sounds of a full orchestra reverberated off the carved stone walls of Guildhall and echoed from the grandiose stained glass windows. Laughter, tinkling glasses and chatter vibrated around the well-dressed guests gliding across the glasslike marble floor.

From the moment they'd arrived, Parker teased, flirted, danced and introduced Anna as if she were his most prized treasure, keeping one possessive hand on the small of her back.

As they danced to a ballad, he whispered tidbits about the guests, making her laugh with his insights, impressing her with how well he knew so many of the people in his industry.

"That's Davis Brookheiser, the owner of that new line of spa resorts out in California," he said, tilting his head toward an older man who slowly—very slowly—waltzed with an attractive young woman.

"And that's Davis's daughter?" Anna asked, letting just a little sarcasm tinge her voice.

He laughed. "That would be the third Mrs. Brookheiser." Then he frowned a little at the couple. "Maybe the fourth. I've lost track of Davis's trophies."

As the couple danced by, Anna caught Mrs. Brookheiser staring at Parker over her much shorter husband's shoulder. But he ignored the obvious attention, keeping his focus on Anna.

"She hasn't lost track of you," Anna teased.

He applied a gentle amount of pressure to her back,

easing her closer so she could feel the steel muscles of his body and the unmistakable message of desire in his touch.

"No thanks. I've got my hands nicely full at the moment."

Blood rushed through her veins, firing up her nerve endings, making her boneless and light-headed. If he had any idea how many nights she'd put herself to sleep with this very scenario in her imagination. Parker, holding her and making promises with his eyes. Parker, inches from her mouth for a kiss.

Parker.

She took a slow, steadying breath and forced herself to admire the pageantry around her. She had to remember why she was dead set against acting on her attraction. She had to remember why he was all wrong for her.

He's your boss, dummy.

Yeah. Right. She was having a very difficult time remembering that. At the moment, she could barely remember her own name.

"Just imagine how many royals and prime ministers have danced on this very floor," she said, leaning away, striving for casual conversation even though the music and the movement were anything but casual.

But her gesture just gave him an opportunity to lower his gaze to her throat, study the V in her neckline and eventually return for a good, long examination of her mouth. Only then did he politely follow her glance around.

"Many, since Guildhall has been hosting high-end affairs since the fourteen hundreds."

"I guess the association can't hold this event at a hotel," she mused. "That would be like playing favorites."

"Exactly," he agreed. "This has to remain neutral ground for all the members. See that gray-haired matriarch under the arch? Genevieve Dufresne."

"The Swiss resort Dufresne?"

He gave her a satisfied smile. "You do pay attention to the business, don't you? Yes, she is the head of the mighty Dufresne family. So, believe me, there might be a spirit of shared camaraderie since we're all in similar businesses, but there's competition in the air."

"Like in the elevator."

He made a distasteful face.

"Why do you hate them so much?"

The music ended and he guided her toward the table, where she picked up her handbag.

"Let's walk outside," he suggested, pausing to snag two crystal champagne flutes when a white-tailed waiter walked by.

She took hers, but didn't sip. The atmosphere and company were intoxicating enough. They wandered through one of the dozens of soaring archways that led to various halls, a museum and crypts housing centuries of folklore, legends and art.

On a wide stone veranda, where a number of partygoers dallied at tables and benches to enjoy the evening air, they found a cozy bench, blocked by a large planter and secluded from the other people.

"Perfect," he said, taking her hand and tugging her next to him.

"You didn't answer my question," Anna said after a moment. "Why do you hate the Jefferies brothers?"

He gave her a wry smile. "You could ruin a perfectly awesome night with that line of questioning. Truthfully, I don't hate anyone, but if I were going to, Jordan and Emilio would head the list."

"Why?"

"They're ruthless, cutthroat empire builders."

She stifled a smile. "And you're not."

He opened his mouth to argue, but then let out a soft, self-deprecating laugh. "Not ruthless."

"Yes, ruthless."

"Not cutthroat."

"Yes, cutthroat."

"Not... All right." He grinned. "But not underhanded. And I think they are and I don't want that womanizer Jordan around my sisters." He inched closer and draped a possessive arm around her. "Or you."

"Me?" The champagne tickled her nose, mixed with the soft, masculine scent of man. Unable to resist, she nestled into the expensive fabric of his tuxedo jacket.

"Yes, you," he said, his face perilously close to hers.

"He would want nothing to do with me," she insisted.

"Not when you're doing your level best to hide your assets behind your shapeless suits. But the secret's out now." He brought his face closer to hers, and lowered his voice to barely above a whisper. "You are a beautiful, sexy woman, Anna."

She closed her eyes as the compliment washed over her, more potent than if she'd thrown back her champagne and his.

"Thank you," she said, searching for some way to divert the conversation to a less personal area. "So how do you know the Jefferies brothers are cutthroat and ruthless? I don't recall any dealings with them since I've worked for you."

"You sure know how to wreck a moment," he said, a smile on his lips. "Those brothers have made it no secret that they want to give Garrison, Inc. a run for its money. And they are doing a good job," he conceded, taking a swallow of champagne. "They've made some major inroads into the luxury hospitality and entertainment fields."

"You don't strike me as a man who worries about competition."

"Of course I do. I worry about squashing it. And I worry about the fate and status of the Garrison brand, which, as you know, I'm responsible for." A shadow crossed his expression. "At least I was until my father's will was read."

"What's happening to the brand?" Anna relaxed a little, encouraged that the conversation had been steered away from the undercurrent of sexual tension that had been ricocheting off the Guildhall walls for the last few hours.

"We're just taking hits in the media, and some investors I'd counted on have backed out from deals for no apparent reason. Properties I want have suddenly been sold to someone else." He snorted softly. "Usually to someone named Jefferies." After a moment, he added, "I seriously think there's a leak in my company."

A shiver danced down her spine. "A leak?"

"A spy. A mole. A...*someone* feeding inside information to competitors. To the Jefferieses." He turned to her, his expression fierce. "I'm going to find out who it is and ruin them."

White lights burst behind her eyes and it wasn't stars or romance blinding her. It was the hard, cold smack of her past hitting her in the face.

"A spy?" She heard the shakiness in her voice.

"Don't sound incredulous. It happens, you know."

Oh, she knew. She knew firsthand. She knew so well it hurt. "I've read about things like that." The only problem was that when she read about them, her name was in the articles.

Her name—not the man who'd committed the crime. Not Michael Montgomery, a man she'd thought she loved and trusted. A man who'd used her to get into the computer system of her boss, another CEO.

The night air suddenly seemed stifling and the back of her neck burned with perspiration. If Parker ever learned of her past, of the accusation—however wrong—that she'd let her lover access files from her boss's computer, then she would be fired. Of that, there was no doubt.

Who would ever give her a chance to explain? Her old boss hadn't. The media hadn't. She'd just had to run.

"All it would take is one person who has knowledge of my deals to slip the information to one of the Jefferieses," he continued, his voice suddenly sounding distant as blood thundered through her ears.

"Do you think…someone has?"

"I'm certain of it. Jordan and Emilio Jefferies weren't going to come to this gala. They weren't on the list. But then, wham. They show up and no one knew I was coming but a handful of Garrison employees."

Including *her*. At his words, her stomach tightened, her fingertips tingled, her head spun. Only this time, her reaction had nothing to do with attraction, but everything to do with the fear of detection.

Of course, she was innocent. Totally and completely and wholly innocent, and the charges against her had been dropped. But the stain was still there.

Could a man who'd just admitted he was ruthless, cut-throat and competitive even see past that stain? Could he ever see beyond the fact that she had let one other corporate rival into the inner workings of another CEO's desk…albeit unknowingly?

"It really bothers me," he said, still staring into the night.

She had to get the subject changed, fast.

"In fact," he continued, "I'm more determined than ever to find the leak."

She had to get him off course.

"And with the change in my father's—"

She reached up and pressed her lips to his cheek. He froze, then slowly turned toward her. "What are you doing, Miss Cross?"

"What do you think I'm doing, Mr. Garrison?"

He broke into a slow, sexy smile. "What did you call me?"

She lifted her face in invitation, forming the words she knew would derail his train of thought. "Mr. Garrison."

He closed his mouth over hers instantly, kissing her exactly the way he did everything…thoroughly, expertly, with masterful control and brilliant timing.

Parting her lips, she allowed his tongue to explore her mouth. Chills and heat warred over her skin as he glided his hands over her bare back, burrowing his fingers into the hair at the nape of her neck.

She tilted her head, and he deepened the kiss, a tender moan vibrating his chest. He pulled her closer and murmured her name against her mouth.

"Let's go back to the hotel," he whispered in the kiss. "Now."

Okay, she had definitely changed the direction of the conversation.

He stood, pulling her into him. "I want you," he told her, confirming that with a full-body press that left no doubt he was aroused.

She melted into the kiss, torn by a secret delight that she'd caused that hard ridge against her stomach, and the secret horror that he'd find out why.

She inched back, catching her breath. "Parker…I…"

"Unless you'd rather talk business some more," he said with a playful kiss on her nose.

"Not on your life," she said. And, God knows, she meant it.

Four

When Anna sent a signal, she made it crystal clear.

Somehow, Parker knew that would happen. He knew if he bided his time, easing her slowly into a comfortable, sensual, intimate place, she would give him the go-ahead to take that kiss he'd been thinking about all night.

He'd been fighting arousal since she'd opened the door—hell, since he'd found her in the bathroom the other day. Every dance made him want to touch more; every time she laughed or asked a question, leaned gently against him or just sent him a subtle look of pure lust, his jaw slackened for some mouth-to-mouth contact with hers.

He thought he'd imagined the occasional admiring glance in the past, but tonight, Anna's defenses were down. And her interest was up. Way up.

"The limo's right over there," he said, nudging her in that direction. "We don't need to stay a minute more."

A glimmer of uncertainty lit her eyes.

"Unless you want to," he said, placing one finger on her chin to turn her face to him. He trailed that finger down her throat, into the dip between her collarbones, and then lower, barely touching, barely skimming her flesh.

Her eyelids fluttered and her lips parted.

"It's entirely up to you," he added, dropping close to her ear to whisper the words and nibble her lobe.

She arched slightly with a quick breath. Then she closed her eyes and nodded so slightly, he almost missed it. With a firm hand on her back, he walked toward the waiting limo, and addressed the driver.

"We'll go directly to the Ritz, John," he said as he climbed in the car behind Anna. Although it might be fun to play in the limo while they tooled around London for an hour, he didn't want her in a car. He wanted to get her back to the suite and directly in his bed.

He would, however, have to keep her warm on the way back.

Settling in next to her, he offered champagne, but she declined. He touched a button and filled the car with the soft strains of Andrea Bocelli's new-millennium version of classical music and her eyes sparkled.

"I love this music."

"You love music, I noticed."

She smiled. "Broadway tunes are my favorite, actually."

"West Side Story?"

Even in the dim light of the car, he could see her flush. "I'm sorry about that, again."

"I'm not. Use the shower in there whenever you like. Leave the door open." He curled an arm around her and feathered her hair with a kiss. "I liked the view."

"But not the song."

He laughed and moved his mouth to lightly kiss her cheek. "Your heart was into it, that's all that matters to me."

She turned to him, her face suddenly very serious, the laughter gone from her eyes. "My heart's into everything that I do," she assured him. "Even my work."

"Good," he murmured, inching closer to her mouth, not thinking too hard about the sincerity in her eyes. His mind was not on work at the moment. "I like that in a woman."

He kissed her again, working to keep it light and easy, but hot and hard was winning the battle. He tunneled his fingers into her hair and found the comb that held it in place. In one twist of his wrist, her hair tumbled.

He finger-combed it, inhaling the sweet fragrance, gliding his tongue over her teeth. She leaned her head back against the seat so he could kiss the tender skin of her throat and nibble his way into the V of her dress.

She tasted sweet and hot and smooth.

Unable to stop himself, he slid one hand from her nape, down the halter strap to the tender, precious curve of her breast, covering her easily. Instantly, her nipple pebbled against his palm, firing a blast of lava-hot blood through him, pulling groans of pleasure from both their throats.

"Parker." She sighed, lifting herself just enough to let him know she enjoyed the touch.

"Glad we're back on a first-name basis," he teased, dragging his hand along the tight fit of her waist, over her hip and finding the slit that had called to him all night.

His hand hit flesh and her whole body shivered. He chuckled softly into another kiss. "Look what I found," he whispered, tracing the tight thigh with one fingertip, inching higher to torture both of them.

Another moan of delight shuddered through her. He quieted that with a long, wet, hungry kiss, opening his hand to caress the taut muscle of her thigh. His fingers moved higher, over velvety skin, anxious just to touch her once. Just to feel how creamy she was. Expertly, he ran his thumb once over the silky nub of her panties, eliciting a soft gasp in their kiss.

"Maybe we should take the long way back," he suggested, taking one more featherlight stroke over the damp silk between her legs.

Slowly, easily, she closed her fingers over his wrist and slid his hand away.

"Too fast?" he asked. "Too much? Too soon?"

The fire in her eyes said no to all of the above, but she nodded.

He took a deep breath and gave her a reassuring smile, placing his hand on a far less controversial spot on her waist. "I'll wait." He could. His body hummed with need, hard and relentless, but he would wait. "At least until we walk in the door."

She smiled, then caught her lower lip under her two front teeth with a heartbreakingly unsure expression.

"What's the matter?" he asked, cupping her jaw and lifting her face to meet his. "You're not sure? Are you...I mean, you've done this before, right?"

"I had a serious boyfriend when I lived in Indiana." Her whole expression changed with the admission.

He wasn't at all sure he wanted to hear about this boyfriend, at least not at this particular moment. But she obviously wanted to tell him something.

"What happened?" he asked.

She lowered her head, gnawed on that lip again, thinking. "He hurt me. He..."

A natural male fury whipped through him. "He forced you?"

"No, no," she said. "Nothing like that. He just...lied to me. He used me and I..." She sighed and turned to the window. "It cost me my job."

Oh. Suddenly her hesitation was totally understandable. She must have worked for the guy, and this would feel like history repeating itself. And what could he say?

"And you're worried that could happen again," he said.

"Can you, in good conscience, promise me that if I sleep with you, it would never affect my job?"

He breathed slowly, studying her. "I can't promise that, Anna." As much as his hardened, aroused body wanted him to make all sorts of promises, he couldn't actually make that one. Because it might change things in the office. That was life.

The limo slowed in front of the Ritz, and he gave her a moment to smooth her hair. When John opened the back door on her side, Parker watched her climb gracefully out of the car, the sexy red dress clinging to every curve he wanted to explore with his hands and mouth.

Nothing was going to happen to *his* career if they had sex and things didn't work out. He was smart enough to know that. And so was she.

He cleared his throat and willed his arousal to subside as they made their way to the elevator. When the doors closed he turned to her.

"Anna," he said, wrapping the hand that still held hers around her back. "You know what I want. But, it's your call." He resisted the urge to kiss her, but continued. "If that means we end up in bed together, well—" he smiled and touched her jaw with his other hand "—great. But..."

If it meant kissing her chastely good-night and keeping the best administrative assistant he ever had, that was great, too. Not *as* great, but Parker knew when to compromise and when to push.

The doors opened and he took her hand, leading her into the hushed hallway. He pulled out the room key and opened the massive double doors to the darkened suite, the only sound the steady thump of his heart while he waited for her decision.

He'd forgotten to leave a light on, and they stood in the shadows, inches apart. She hadn't spoken since they'd left the limo and he knew the next word she said would seal their fate.

She turned to him and slid her arms around his shoulders, locking at his neck. He resisted a grin of victory, but lowered his head for the kiss he expected.

"Thank you for the most amazing party I've ever been to." She rose on her toes, kissed his cheek and backed away. "Good night, Parker."

He could barely see her disappear into her room, but in the silence, he heard the lock turn. He stood in the dark for a few minutes, tapping the card key against his palm. The card key that she obviously didn't realize was a master and could open her bedroom door.

Smothering a soft sigh, he shook his head, the disappointment finally making it down to the lower half of his body to deliver the bad news.

The lady said no.

He shimmied out of the tuxedo jacket, threw it over a delicate French provincial chair and strode to the bar, flipping over a brandy snifter and filling it with a solid slug of the good stuff. With one hand, he loosened his bow tie and unbuttoned the first two buttons of the tux shirt.

He took the drink to the balcony that ran the length of the salon, folding into a comfortable chair and inhaling the sounds and scents of an active avenue two stories below.

Didn't this beat all? He was in London, in his favorite suite, with a smoldering hot woman undressing in the next room…and he would be going to bed alone.

Why hadn't he thought this through when he'd issued the impulsive invitation? Because he'd been seeing legs in heels and hearing off-key songs in his head, that was why.

Drinking a little deeper than the heavy brandy called for, his throat burned. Hell, everything burned. He wanted her. He really wanted her.

But she wanted…

Now there was an unanswered question. What did Anna want? A promotion? A boyfriend? A husband? A good time?

She really didn't talk about herself so much. She asked a lot of questions about his business; made herself basically indispensable; got him hot, bothered and distracted…but what was her deal? For a minute, he was a little annoyed at himself for not asking.

Then he narrowed his eyes until the city-lit sky blurred and he let the most unsettling thought settle right down on him.

What if Anna wanted…*information?*

The leak at Garrison had started about three or four months ago, right when she'd moved into the desk outside his office. She'd been promoted from HR, where, according to his department manager, she'd been an exemplary, if low-profile, employee.

But, still.

Ice hardened in the very veins that had been molten just minutes earlier.

Was Anna the spy?

Evidence, however circumstantial, started flashing like frozen images of proof in his head. She knew about every deal that had fallen through in the last two months. Of course she did; she had total access to his office. She'd even showered in there! How often had she been in there alone?

The only people who knew he was coming to London were the charter-jet people, maybe someone in his travel department…and Anna. And, in the elevator, she'd acted as if she'd never even heard of Jordan Jefferies, which seemed impossible in their business.

The impact of the revelation catapulted him to his feet, and he bounded back into the salon as the facts popped into his head and fell into place.

She knew the names of competitors. She constantly steered the conversation toward work. She always seemed so interested in the business, and even a little bit nervous around him.

Even on the plane yesterday, she'd dragged him back to open files, forcing him to go over every minor element of every major deal, and then, what had she done when they'd gotten to London? E-mailed it all. She'd said she was sending his e-mail for him, but was someone getting copied on that correspondence? Someone named *Jefferies?*

Oh, man. He almost cracked the crystal in his hand as he reviewed the events of the last hour. As soon as he'd talked about the spy, the minute he'd focused in on the mole in his operation, what had she done?

Classic, by-the-book, take-no-prisoners sexual distraction. Right up to the hotel room, she'd had him panting, pawing and as far away from thoughts of spies as he could be.

What did she take him for? He slammed the snifter so hard on the bar that brandy sloshed over the side and, in one move, he scooped up the master card key he'd left there.

What do you think I'm doing, Mr. Garrison?

He could still hear her seductive voice, feel the pressure of her kiss, the soft breath of a…traitor.

Jamming the card key into the lock on her bedroom door, his heart kicked against his ribs. And he froze. What if he was wrong?

Without making a noise, he turned the knob and opened the door. In the shadows, he saw her shape in the bed, the sheet almost covering her, but for one achingly long, sexy leg draped over it. He heard her sigh and shudder.

Already asleep…or faking it?

"Anna." His voice was sharp, demanding.

She jerked up, pulling the sheet over whatever she wore. "What do you want?"

He heard the tremor in her voice. Was that because she knew he'd figured out her game?

"Please, Parker, I'm sorry if I took things too far."

Disgust roiled through him. Did she really think he'd come in here and force her into having sex?

The sheet fell from her trembling hands, the moonlight revealing that she wore something tiny and strappy, like a tank T-shirt. Something easily lifted and removed.

Against everything he called *control,* his body responded. He was, after all, a man.

But not a stupid man. There was nothing to be gained by accusing her like this. He may have just leaped to one wild conclusion.

Swallowing hard, he gripped the doorknob. "I just wanted to make sure you're okay."

In the dim light, he could see that she very much doubted that was the truth. "I'm fine." She brushed a hair off her face. "Are you?"

The fact that she asked hit him somewhere deep, somewhere he'd rather not be hit by a woman he no longer trusted.

"Yeah. Good night." He closed the door and stared at it for a long minute.

He was probably right, and she was the spy. And if she was, then two could play this game. Now that he knew who his spy was, it was just a matter of feeding her misinformation. And if she really wanted to do her job for the Jefferies brothers well, she would probably have to get close to the CEO of Garrison, Inc.

Very close.

Parker Garrison may have been played for a fool by her this evening. But it wouldn't happen again. Next time, he'd get everything he wanted. *Every*thing.

And he wanted Anna. If he could crush Jordan and Emilio Jefferies in the process, all the better. But he could never let her know that he'd figured her out. In fact, the first thing he needed to do was let her wonder where she stood.

Anna Cross would find out the hard way not to play chess with a master.

Somehow, Anna made it through to Monday morning, but the magic of Saturday night seemed as far away as London when she tucked her handbag into her desk drawer and turned on the computer for the day.

"I didn't expect to see you here today." The receptionist appeared from the tiny galley kitchen that the Garrison executives shared, an empty coffeepot in hand.

"Of course I'm here," Anna said.

"Thought you might make a week of it across the pond." Sheila added a British accent to the last three words, and tempered the tease with a wink. "There were a few early calls this morning. The editor from *Luxury Travel* magazine called about the layout he's doing."

"Okay," Anna said, jotting a note. "Anything else?"

"The secretary at the charter-jet company called this morning to make sure Mr. Garrison *and* Ms. Cross had a pleasurable trip." Her voice was rich with implication and accusation. "So. Did you?"

"You can let them know that it was fine, thank you."

"You're holding out on me." Sheila laughed lightly. "Come on, spill the beans. Is he as demanding in bed as he is in the office?"

Anna managed a very disgusted glare, even though the memory of the moment he'd walked into her bedroom was still vivid. He could have demanded, and she might not have fought him. But he hadn't. And she'd barely slept once he'd backed out of the door, leaving her absolutely aching for more.

"Sorry to disappoint, Sheila. It was all business." Unfortunately. Fortunately. Oh, God, she was so confused.

"Oh, so it's like that, huh?" She beckoned Anna with the coffeepot and a very sympathetic smile. "Come here while I brew the mud. You look like you could use a friend."

Was it that obvious? Parker's distant coolness on the flight home had been a double-edged sword. It cut her because he was so icy, but it relieved her to know she could go back to work and a few steamy kisses had caused no real harm.

Obviously, he'd had a chance to think over the recriminations of an office affair and had decided she was too good an assistant to lose.

Or maybe he didn't want her.

The thought made her stomach squeeze with a sense of disappointment she had no right to feel. But he'd left her so confused. He'd hardly said six words to her on the flight, and three were *See you tomorrow.*

"Ever get involved with your boss before, Anna?" Sheila's question yanked her back to the present.

"No," she answered honestly. The boss's biggest rival, yes. And hadn't that turned out great? "It would be beyond dumb," she added.

Sheila rolled her eyes. "Tell me about it. I used to be a Playmate, did you know that?"

The entire company knew Sheila had worked as a bunny at the now-defunct Miami Beach Playboy Club. "I've heard that."

"Got all tight with one of the managers in the operation."

Anna wasn't entirely sure she wanted this much information, but couldn't help asking, "What happened?"

"What always happens," Sheila said with a world-weary exhale. "He got laid and I got canned."

"Oh."

Sheila nodded knowingly. "But, hey, it was fun while it lasted. That guy could…" She shook her head while she measured the coffee. "Let's just say he taught me some tricks that every girl should know."

"Would answering the phone be one of them?" Parker's voice was thick with sarcasm, eliciting a tiny gasp of surprise from Anna and a snort from Sheila. "Because my line just bounced from the main switchboard to voice mail after ringing about fifteen times."

Anna blinked at his tone. "Sorry, Mr. Garrison." She looked him directly in the eye as she passed through the narrow doorway and managed not to brush one fiber of his thousand-dollar suit. "I'll get your phone." She added some steel in her voice as she hustled toward her desk just as the next line rang.

"Mr. Garrison's office." His name rolled off her tongue,

flipping her stomach as the sight of him had done. This was why people shouldn't get involved at work. Forget what happened to her in the past. She couldn't even say his name without causing a mental meltdown.

"Hello." The voice on the phone was low, rich, female and unfamiliar. "I want Parker Garrison."

Get in line, Anna thought wryly. "May I tell him who is calling?"

"This is Cassie Sinclair Garrison, returning his call."

Anna corralled her scattered thoughts. Cassie Sinclair…*Garrison?* She was using the name now? That would put Parker in a fine…fin*er* mood. She turned just in time to see him heading into his office.

"Mr.—" She blew out a half breath. What did she call him now? Every time she said *Mr. Garrison,* they'd both think of his "warning" kisses. At least, she would.

"Who is it, Anna?" he asked, pausing at his door.

"Cassie Sinclair." No need to have him fume at her because his illegitimate half sibling was using her father's name. Let him find out on his own.

The color drained slightly from his sculpted cheekbones. "I'll take that call." He disappeared into his office, and closed the door with a definitive click, making her feel as shut out as he had on the plane when he'd slept or read the entire flight.

Behind her, Anna got a whiff of Sheila's spicy perfume.

"Not that it's any of my concern," she said, hitching a lazy hip against the arm of the guest chair. "But my experience tells me if you don't clear the air, then whatever is ricocheting off you two is going to do both of you in. And you'll cave first, darlin'."

"Nothing is ricocheting," she insisted. Except her heart. Why was he treating her like this? Would it be different if she *had* slept with him? Was he mad at her for saying no, or at himself for being…a man?

And what a man he was.

"Just clear the air, sweetie," Sheila said, giving Anna's hand a friendly pat. "Tell him you're sorry you did or you didn't, but don't lose your job over it if you can help it. No man's worth a paycheck, trust me."

As if she didn't already know that. "Thanks for the advice."

Sheila winked. "Anytime. And anytime you want to share the gory details…" She pointed toward the closed office door. "I bet that stud knows a few tricks, too."

"I wouldn't know," Anna said, her professional demeanor as secure as the button that held her modest shirt closed tight at the collar.

Sadly, Anna had to admit Shelia knew what she was talking about. As soon as that door opened, she was going to heed the unsolicited advice. She would tell Parker that despite the kisses and the chemistry they felt, they had to remain employer/employee only. But nothing else.

And once she told him that, she could get back to concentrating on her job. Maybe.

"Thank you for calling me back, Ms. Sinclair."

"Actually, I use both my last names. It's Cassie Sinclair Garrison." She ladled extra emphasis on their shared name and Parker just closed his eyes in revulsion.

But he refused to take the bait. "We need to talk about the questionable provisions in my father's will," he said, keeping any hint of emotion out of his voice.

The connection from Nassau was clear enough for him to hear her soft cough. "I'm not aware of any questionable provisions. It was all perfectly clear to me."

She was not going to be easy to manipulate. Well, of course not. Like it or not, she had Garrison blood in her veins and they were a stubborn bunch.

He powered on. "I think you'll agree that there's absolutely no reason for you to be bothered with the responsibility of twenty percent shares of Garrison, Inc. I've been running the company—"

"Not a bother at all," she assured him.

"I make the majority decisions for this company," he said firmly.

"I understand that and I hope you'll continue to do so," she said. "To be honest, I have no desire to exercise my new control, but I'll keep it. I have a hotel to run."

Relief washed over him. "Then I'll have my attorney arrange for you to rescind the shares immediately."

"That won't be necessary," she said coolly, as Parker stood and squinted into the Miami sunshine. "I have no intention of rescinding anything. I just don't want to exercise those shares right now."

He didn't like the sound of that. He didn't like the sound of any of this. "Then why not turn them over to me?"

"Because I don't want to."

She wanted money. Of course. "I will have my attorney draw up an extremely fair offer, Miss…Sinclair."

"It's *Garrison* and I wouldn't trouble your attorney because I will not sell my shares for any price, fair or otherwise."

"Why not?" She had to know he'd offer her well above market value.

"Because they were a gift." She paused for a moment, then added, "From my father."

Parker swallowed the bitter, metallic taste of fury in his mouth. "From your illegitimate father," he ground out.

"Be that as it may, he was and will always be a father to me. You may not know this, Mr. Garrison, but your father spent a lot of time in Nassau and he took very good care of my mother and me."

Forget apathy. Forget leaving family emotions at the door. This woman was doing everything in her power to incense him. And it was working.

"Is that so?" he replied. "Frankly, no one in my family—including *my mother, the one and only Mrs. John Garrison*—was aware of that."

She was quiet long enough to know he hit a mark. "Mr. Garrison, I'm going to make this very easy on you," she finally said.

"How's that?"

"Let's not talk anymore. If you have anything, absolutely anything, to say to me, put it in writing. I don't want to discuss business with you. I don't want to rescind my shares. I don't want to sell my shares. I don't want to hear about your mother. I don't want to meet your brothers and sisters and have a cozy family reunion. Is that clear?"

Oh, she was a Garrison, all right. He didn't even have to see the cleft in her chin to know for sure. "Crystal clear."

"Good. And don't try some underhanded, sneaky way to get rid of me. My father told me you can be ruthless."

He could be ruthless, all right. And would be, if necessary. "I have no idea what you're talking about."

"I know how much this means to you," she snapped back. "I don't put anything past you."

She didn't know anything about him and what meant what to him. "Excuse me, but you're the one who appeared out of nowhere claiming to be a Garrison."

She choked, her own temper obviously torqued. "I haven't appeared out of nowhere. I've been right here, for twenty-seven years, the daughter of John Garrison and Ava Sinclair. There were no 'claims.'"

"You'll have to prove it." The words were out before he could stop himself, erupted by his boiling blood. "We want to run full DNA tests and until conclusive proof is on my desk, my father's will is being contested in court."

He heard her breath escape in frustration. "Fine. Sic your lawyers on me. I don't care. Let me run my property the way I always have. Garrison, Inc. will get the appropriate percentage of my profits. In the meantime, stay away from me and I'll stay away from you."

She clicked off before he could respond. Swearing softly, Parker threw his phone on the desk and strode toward the door, his command that Anna get Brandon Washington on the phone already forming in his mouth.

He whipped the door open and almost knocked her down.

What was she doing there? *Listening?*

He glared at her, and she backed up a step, but lifted up her chin defiantly. "I want to talk to you."

Of course she was listening. The Jefferieses would probably want a full report. He gave her a smile, which wasn't difficult because even behind those little glasses, she was pretty. Very pretty.

"About what?" he asked, keeping his tone friendly.

She took a deep breath and glanced at the clerk who was slowly unloading the morning mail in front of her desk.

"Morning, Mario," Parker said, greeting the man who'd worked for the company since the year his father had opened it.

"Mr. Garrison." He nodded slowly, obviously more interested in the conversation than delivering the mail.

"Please," Anna said to Parker, starting to close his door. "It's personal."

But he put his hand on the wood to keep it open. "How personal?"

She speared him with a look. "Very personal."

He dipped one inch closer and the color immediately rose to her cheeks. For a spy, she sure had a weak spot. Several of them, in fact. One behind her ear, one just at the rise of her breasts and the weakest of all, the soft inside flesh of her thigh.

His body stirred at the thought. Might be time to exploit those weaknesses. "Then why don't we discuss it over dinner, Anna?"

Her eyes widened. "Dinner?"

"Yep. I feel like celebrating."

"You do?"

He cocked his head toward the phone on his desk. "It appears all the problems have been solved," he said smoothly. "Cassie Sinclair is going to rescind her shares. So, let's celebrate."

It wasn't really a lie. He'd win this and Cassie would rescind her shares, or sell them to him. But it wouldn't hurt to see if a little misinformation got dripped into the Jefferies organization.

"Oh, that's wonderful." She brightened, sounding very sincere. How would it sound when she relayed that information to Jordan and Emilio Jefferies? "Would you like me to get Brandon Washington on the phone for you?"

Damn, she was good. Spy or not, she had a skill for anticipating everything he needed. How would that translate in bed? The thought tightened his gut.

"Yes, please. And call Brittany Beach Restaurant and tell my sister to get us the best table in the house tonight."

"All right. Then we'll talk tonight."

They would. And he would plant a few more decoy

targets and then he'd sit back and watch Anna, and Jordan and Emilio, try to hit them. "I'll look forward to it."

The only problem was, he would. All day.

Five

Parker left the office early, met off-site with Brandon and made it to Brittany Beach well in advance of his "date." At seven, the sprawling veranda that overlooked the white sands of Miami Beach was already jammed with the beautiful people ready to blow off summer steam and partake in the edgy atmosphere.

He strode across the whitewashed planks, his sunglasses hiding his observation of a young woman in a bikini top so small a strong wind would loosen it. His sister Brittany had taken a lukewarm restaurant that had little going for it but a primo location and turned it into a fairly sizzling place to dine and be seen. Although Adam's Estate was the late-night destination for the younger club-going set, Brittany Beach had potential.

However, the potential Parker saw was primarily in the fact that the restaurant was located on one of the last waterfront parcels in SoBe still zoned for condos.

Still, Brittany was squeezing what she could out of the restaurant business. Unless it was pouring, the elegant Haitian cotton sofas under cabana tents were populated with self-absorbed Euro models and the men who liked to buy them drinks and dinner. This evening was no different.

"Hey, Parker. Over here." He turned at the sound of Stephen's voice, to see his brother sitting comfortably on one of those sofas, with no model in sight. There would be, eventually.

"'Sup, Stephen." Parker ambled over, offered his knuckles in greeting and took the silent invitation to join him. "You having dinner here?"

"Just stopped by to see how Brittany's doing. Have you seen her?"

"No, but I just walked in. She'll be around."

A pretty blond cocktail waitress in a revealing halter top and low-slung sarong sidled up to their table and flashed a smile. "Hi, guys. What'll it be?"

"I'm having dinner," Parker said, "but not for a few minutes, so just a bottled water for me."

Stephen ordered a light beer and asked if Brittany was around.

"She's in the kitchen," the waitress said. "You're her brothers, right? I'll tell her you're here."

When the waitress left, Parker slipped off his shades to look at his brother.

"How was the water this weekend?" he asked, knowing that Stephen, although he was as much of a workaholic as Parker, spent every free minute on his elegant cruising yacht.

"Gorgeous. A great escape from the mess that has become Garrison."

Parker acknowledged that with a puff of disgust. "You got that right. I talked to our newest sister today."

Stephen yanked his own sunglasses off. "And?"

"And she's added *Garrison* to her last name."

"Oh, man. What did she say?"

"In a nutshell, she won't rescind her shares, won't sell them outright, doesn't want a family reunion and would like to be left alone to run her property." Parker crossed his ankles and peered at the blue-on-blue horizon. "Brandon's filed the legal papers. I'm contesting."

"I don't know if you need it legally, but you have my support."

Parker nodded. "Thanks, bro. God knows if I'll have the others'."

"Adam will back you. And Brooke. I think, anyway."

"What do you mean? What's up with Brooke?" Parker had a well-known soft spot for his sister. "Is she still upset about the will?"

"About the fact that Dad had another family, oh yeah. I tried to talk to her about it, but you know Brooke. She's private."

"I'll give her a call," Parker said.

"You know, I think she's seeing someone, too."

"Really? Did she mention that at the Sunday dinner I missed?"

"No, in fact, she denied it," Stephen said. "But I know I saw her at the Grand last Thursday."

"The day of the will reading?"

"That night, actually. I saw her across the lobby, and some guy had his arm around her. Then he disappeared around the corner with her."

"And you never saw him before?" Parker leaned forward, his brotherly protective streak ignited.

"I only saw him from the back and when I asked her

about it on Sunday, she said I must have confused her with someone else."

"Brittany?"

"Brittany was here that night."

Brooke wouldn't lie, so Stephen must have been mistaken. "I'll have to talk to her, but still, I think she'll support my decision to contest the will. Not sure about her evil twin, though."

Stephen laughed softly. "Brittany's always a wild card." He glanced around as though just mentioning their sister would conjure her up. "I guess it depends what Garrison, Inc. wants to persuade her to do with this restaurant."

Parker shrugged. "I know this is her baby, and I was just thinking she's done a fine job bringing this place into the twenty-first century."

"It's profitable."

"On paper, yes. But do you have any idea how many more millions we'd get if we used this slice of land for condos?"

Stephen conceded that with a nod, saying nothing as the waitress delivered their drinks.

"She'd be devastated if we go that route," Stephen finally said. "You'd have to evict her, technically."

"I know, and I won't unless we're forced to. As long as she's turning a real profit here—and I mean a significant profit—then we can wait. But Garrison, Inc. owns the land, even if she owns the restaurant. If we wait, all that'll happen is that the cost of building will rise, and we'll charge five million for a condo instead of four. But if her business starts to falter, which, knowing the cyclical nature of the restaurant trade, it inevitably will—"

Behind him, a small but firm hand landed on his shoulder.

"Nothing is inevitable." Brittany's voice was as cold as the water he sipped. "Except that yet another poor, unsuspecting fool is up at the hostess stand asking for you. Haven't I seen this one before, Parker?"

She'd heard everything. He knew it. He'd just effectively put his sister on notice. What would that do when it came time for her support in contesting the will? He planted a smile and stood to greet her.

"Of course you've seen her before," he said, reaching to give her a brotherly, if cursory, hug. "She's my administrative assistant."

Brittany ignored his outstretched hands by putting hers on her slender hips. "That's Anna?" She frowned deeper. "She looks different."

"So is this a date or a business meeting?" Stephen asked.

Parker pulled his sunglasses back on. "A little of both, my friends. A little of both."

They both opened their mouths to speak, but he slipped away with a half salute of goodbye before they could bombard him with questions he didn't want to answer.

Anna saw his silhouette before she could make out Parker's face as he walked toward her, backlit by the early evening sun reflecting off the water. He moved like an athlete, so strong and in control of every muscle. He held his head high, his broad shoulders erect, his expensive suit draping perfectly over the body it was cut and sewn to fit.

When, she wondered, would this man stop taking her breath away?

She'd taken the job as his assistant knowing full well that she found him attractive. That hadn't seemed like something that would be crippling. She thought it would add a nice, interesting dimension to her job—the handsome boss.

But she hadn't counted on him being so down-to-the-bone appealing. And she certainly hadn't thought he'd ask her to travel with him and then kiss her senseless.

Of course, to be fair, she had kissed him first.

And there had been nothing *senseless* about it. She'd distracted him. And it had worked. But now they were going back to a strictly business arrangement that would stifle her attraction, and protect her from his digging into secrets that had to remain buried.

As Parker approached, his gaze dropped, quickly but clearly, and his eyebrows twitched in a silent compliment.

"You changed," he said with a smile. "I like that dress."

She'd chosen something black, simple, ladylike. But the way he inspected her, she wondered if he could see right through it. "I had a little time, so I took a run when I got home."

"How long have you been running?" he asked.

From the past? Darn near five years. "I started in high school," she said. "Got hooked on the endorphin rush."

His lips tipped in a smile. "I know the feeling."

"But you get it from work," she replied.

"I get it from a lot of things," he said, his voice so low and rich with implication she actually curled her toes as a hostess approached them.

"Inside or out, Mr. Garrison?" she asked, her sky-blue eyes trained on him flirtatiously.

But he didn't seem to notice. Instead, he put a confident hand on Anna's back and spoke to her. "I suggest we eat indoors because it gets a little raucous on the patio. Unless you'd prefer outdoor air."

"Inside is fine," she said.

"It's more private," he added, stepping a little closer. "Since you wanted to talk."

Yes, she did. And she couldn't let that glint in his dark chocolate eyes or that sexy, musky scent distract her from what she'd come here to tell him.

In a few minutes, they were seated in an alcove more like a bed than a booth, with a sheer privacy drape and a low table that practically begged the occupants to lie down and eat.

"Yeah, this is private, all right," she said, tugging at the skirt that rode up her thighs as she situated herself.

"We can leave the drape open, if you prefer," he said, shaking off his jacket and loosening his tie. She tried to swallow, but her throat had turned bone-dry and her hands itched to undo that tie even farther.

"Need a drink, Anna?" he asked as if he noticed her problem.

"Just water, please. I'm not drinking tonight." She needed every last wit to deal with him.

He ordered them both bottled water, which was delivered with tall, free-form cobalt-blue glasses of ice with curls of lemon and lime. While they sipped, he made small talk, mentioning that he'd seen his brother outside, telling her how the restaurant had changed since his sister had taken over ownership.

"Are you close to Brittany?" she asked, suddenly curious. "She doesn't call you much."

"We have our moments," he told her with a wistful smile. "She's definitely the more opinionated of the twins."

He told her a story from their childhood, something that proved his point about the difference between the twins, and Anna tried to concentrate on the details, but every minute or so her mind would drift to study the full shape of his lips, the marked cleft in his chin so like the ones all his siblings had.

He continued the story and she caught a few snatches, but her gaze slipped to his hair, which was short but thick and a little longer in the front, so that when he lowered his head, a single lock would fall on his forehead.

And his hands. God, she adored those hands. Like the feet, they were all size and strength. She watched his fingers close over the base of the water glass and remembered how they'd felt on her thigh, branding her with heat and desire.

"Can't you just imagine a seven-year-old girl doing that?" he asked.

A little wave of panic dried her throat again. She had no idea what he'd said. "No," she replied, hoping it was the right answer.

His smile was slow and teasing. "No, you can't imagine, or no, you didn't hear a word I said?"

Did he have to be so damn charming? That wasn't making this any easier.

Before she could answer, he leaned on one hand, the one that was perilously close to her hip, and trained that hot, dark gaze on her. "So, what's on your mind, sweetheart?"

Sweetheart. The endearment almost ripped her in half. Pulling up all her inner strength, she opened her mouth to say, "We have to be friends," just as Brittany Garrison arrived at the table, carrying a plate of sushi appetizers.

"I hate to interrupt this obviously important business meeting, but my chef has outdone himself in your honor." She set the plate between them, but looked at her brother. "We wouldn't want to *falter* in the kitchen now, would we?"

Parker plucked a tuna roll and winked at her. "No, we wouldn't, Britt. Do you remember my administrative assistant, Anna Cross?"

Anna reached out to shake Brittany's hand. "Hello, Brittany."

Brittany gave her a thorough assessment. "Of course we've met," she said warmly. "But you only worked for him then. How long have you been dating?"

"We're not—"

"Go away, Britt," Parker said, shooing her with a tuna roll. "It's bad business to annoy the patrons."

She merely shot him a sideways glance. "I need to know what night you want to reserve this place for Mother's sixtieth surprise bash."

He popped the sushi and chewed, wiping his mouth with a linen napkin and nodding in approval. "Nice, fresh fish, Britt. Compliments to the kitchen."

"What night, Parker? I have a business to run so I need to know when I can and cannot accept reservations."

"Accept everything. We're not doing it here. Adam's having it at Estate."

Brittany's elegant, sculpted jaw dropped and she snapped her arms across her chest. "We decided—"

"Adam convinced me."

"Or you made another wholesale decision without discussing it with anyone else."

He shrugged. "It makes way more sense to have it there. The party is a critical PR move for the family." For a moment, he paused and glanced at Anna, as though he wasn't sure he wanted her to hear that. "So, we're having it there."

Brittany's eyes narrowed, Anna obviously forgotten in the midst of a Garrison family squabble. But Parker didn't even notice. Because his decisions were made and abided, Anna thought. And never second-guessed.

By anyone.

Just like, she thought with a sickening wave of clarity, Michael Montgomery. Reminding her of why she'd come to this restaurant with this man: to stop any personal relationship before it started.

"Have a tuna roll, Anna," he said, sliding the plate closer to her. "Let's take this up in private, Britt. This isn't fair to Anna. How 'bout the house special tonight. Would you handle the ordering for us, so we can talk?"

Brittany nodded. "Of course. Enjoy your dinner," she said coolly. "And your date."

Anna sat up a little straighter. "This isn't a date," she said, her words making Parker freeze in the act of reaching for sushi. "But I'm sure we'll enjoy your lovely restaurant."

The corners of Brittany's mouth curled up and she gave Parker a raised eyebrow. "You do that." Without another word, she left the table.

In a move so smooth and fast, Anna almost didn't see it, Parker flipped the drape and shrouded them in gauzy privacy.

"What do you mean this isn't a date?" he asked, his voice only half-playful.

For a moment, she thought he was going to punctuate that question with a kiss, as though that would prove it was most certainly a *date*.

"I guess it's time for us to talk," she said, squaring her shoulders even more. "And please don't interrupt me."

He just lifted a brow, silent.

"I've given this a lot of thought," she started. "Since…Saturday. Since London." Since we kissed. But she didn't need to say that. The thought was reverberating through the small, tight space they occupied. "I think what happened was…" Amazing. Provocative. Tempting. "Not a great idea."

Still, he said nothing, focusing on her so intently, she could feel it singe her skin.

"I like my job," she continued. "I actually love my job. And I'd like to keep it. So, I want to…forget what happened. I'd like to be friends, of course. But you are my boss and I work for you and anything else is out of the question."

She paused, long enough for him to respond. But still, he just looked at her, his gaze wicked and direct. Until it dropped to her mouth and threatened to take her breath away.

"Don't you agree?" she finally asked.

"No." He dipped his head, the word almost lost as he lowered his head, slowly, intently, and kissed her, leaning so far into her that she almost fell back on the bedlike seat. His tongue teased her lips apart as he wrapped both arms around her and pulled her into his chest, the hammering of his heart as shocking to her as the complete ownership his mouth had taken.

Finally, after her ears sang with pounding, pulsing blood, he released her.

"I don't agree," he said, a sneaky smile tipping his lips just before he kissed her again, gently this time, mouth closed, eyes open. "I do not agree at all."

"Don't make this hard for me," she whispered. "You know I like to kiss you. You know I'm attracted to you. But I want to keep my job."

He backed away, just an inch, the playfulness gone from his eyes as he studied her. "Why is that so important to you?"

"Because it's how I make a living."

"Is that the only reason?"

She frowned, confused. "Yes."

"You're not…" He leaned his head in question. "Involved with another man?"

She shook her head, regarding him warily. "I wouldn't have even kissed you in London if I were."

"So there's no other man in your life."

Parker was a possessive man. Was that the reason he was forcing this angle? "No," she assured him. "There hasn't been for a long time."

"And you have no other source of income?"

She blinked at him. "Of course not. I make my living working for you."

"All right, then, I understand what you're saying." He reached for another sushi and gave her a wistful smile. "But I don't have to like it."

She sighed with relief. "I appreciate your respecting my concerns. I know you're a man who gets and takes whatever he wants."

His eyes flashed at that. "If I were, I would have taken what I wanted Saturday night. I wanted…" He closed his eyes in correction. "I *want* you."

"I wanted you, too," she admitted softly, resisting the urge to put it in the present tense. "But I want my job more."

He took a bite of the sushi, still studying her intently. "It's not the only administrative job in Miami, you know," he finally said. "I could help you find another just as good if you really want…to remove that obstacle."

The comment tore her in half. On one hand, the compliment ran deep. He really did want her—enough to try to help her past the hurdle that kept them apart. But on the other hand, she didn't want to risk the search into her background, the hassle and worry of getting another job.

She'd landed this one with the help of a trustworthy friend, but what might get revealed if she hit the job market?

Still, it seemed like a magnanimous gesture on his part. "Would you do that just so we could sleep together?"

"Trust me, there'd be very little sleeping involved." His smile was sinful.

"No." She shook her head in determination. "I want to work for you. I want to stay where I am. I'm learning a lot."

"You're learning a lot," he repeated slowly, the disappointment clear in his expression. "Well, if you change your mind…"

"You'll be the first to know," she assured him. "In the meantime, let's stay focused on business."

His smile was tight and forced, as if he didn't like what he was hearing at all. Another compliment. "Yeah," he said drily. "So you can *learn* more."

He opened the drape with a slow swipe as the waiter approached with their dinner. When it was served, Anna felt the strain of silence.

"You know," she said conversationally, "I was so busy this afternoon I forgot to check your calendar before I left. What's on it tomorrow?"

As he took a sip of water and swallowed, she watched the wheels turning, probably visualizing his PDA screen.

"I have an early-morning meeting with some developers of that North Miami property I've had my eye on."

"Really?" She tried to picture his calendar for herself. "I don't remember arranging that."

"You didn't." He studied his food intently, that stray lock falling on his forehead, tempting her to touch it. "I set it up myself."

"Oh. So you won't be in until, when? Ten?"

He gave her a quick look through his thick lashes. "Yep. Enough time for you to shower in peace."

She laughed softly, grateful for his humor. He may like to be in charge, but Parker had another side to him. A side that was much more human and tender than a man like Michael Montgomery. A very attractive side.

He held a forkful of his roasted duck toward her. "Want to taste?"

It wasn't entirely professional, and it wasn't a move that "friends" made, but she couldn't resist. She ate off his fork and the intimacy of the act pulled at her most feminine core, twisting a pang of arousal exactly the way his demanding kiss had.

As he held her gaze and fed her, she couldn't help feeling that he knew exactly what he was doing to her insides. And he liked it. With Parker Garrison, knowledge was power.

Power she had no doubt he would use—and use creatively.

She knew she'd made the right decision, but she just couldn't escape the sensation that she just might have made her life even more complicated.

Six

"You didn't bring a picture?" Anna threw plenty of exasperation in her voice as she served a cup of coffee to the friend she hadn't seen for far too long. "I don't think I've seen a picture of your daughter since she was two."

Megan Simmons tossed some wavy red curls over her shoulder and tucked her feet under herself as she got comfortable in Anna's kitchen. "Well, Jade's three and a half now and trust me, she's gorgeous. She'll be the first to tell you."

Laughing, Anna bit back the next obvious question. *Who does she look like?* Megan had never revealed the father of her child and Anna respected that. Their friendship dated back to elementary school and one of the reasons it had lasted so long was that they knew when not to pass judgment on each other's actions.

And they knew when to help each other. As Megan had four years ago, when she'd left her consulting job in Miami and returned to Indiana exactly at the time Anna had been up to her earlobes in false accusations. It was Megan's connection with the director of human resources at Garrison, Inc. that had given Anna a much-needed escape, and because of Megan's strong recommendation, she'd been able to get the job without the usual deep background check.

There were times when friends just didn't ask, no matter how much they wanted to know. So, Anna brought the conversation back to the reason they had this unexpected Saturday morning to share some coffee and chat before Anna drove Megan to the airport. "So, how did the meeting go yesterday?"

Megan took a sip, her green eyes widening over the cup. "It was really an interview," she said as she swallowed. "My former boss offered me a partnership in his design firm."

"Wow, congratulations." Anna lifted her coffee cup in a mock toast. "That's wonderful, Megan."

"Thanks. It sure is tempting."

"I'd love it if you moved back here."

Megan's expression grew warm, but wary. "Yeah, it would be great to live near you again, but I don't know."

"You loved Miami when you lived here."

"I know. But Jade has only ever known life in Indianapolis. And she's starting preschool this fall."

"The best time to move," Anna said. "You can start her here. Garrison, Inc. donates to an excellent private preschool. I bet I could get Parker to pull some strings and get Jade in there."

Megan pulled back, a little smile tugging at her lips. "Do you know that since I got here about twenty minutes ago, you've mentioned Parker Garrison about six times?"

Busted. "Have I? I hadn't noticed."

"I did," Megan said drily. "So I guess you're enjoying your promotion from the humble HR department to the lofty executive suites."

"It's different up there," Anna admitted. "It's more exciting. And I'm so busy. It's my whole life."

"It's your *job*," Megan corrected gently, using a voice she probably used on Jade when the child wanted soda instead of milk. "And I didn't say you mentioned Garrison, Inc. I said you mentioned your boss."

"I guess I have. But he's…" How could she possibly explain what it was like to work for someone like Parker?

"He's a Garrison," Megan said, rolling the name on her tongue as if it tasted bad.

"Yes, he is," Anna agreed. "And he's also…" She willed herself not to turn all dreamy and stupid. "Very…"

"Arrogant."

"Well, sometimes. But he's…"

"Demanding."

Anna's eyes widened. "He likes things his own way, but he can be…"

"A snake."

Her jaw dropped. "No. I don't think he's a snake, Megan. He's confident and a leader, he's smart and he's—"

"Flat-out gorgeous. They all are." Megan took a deep drink then thunked the cup back on the table. "Don't get sucked into it, Anna."

"Sucked into what?"

Megan leaned on the table. "I've done enough work for the Garrisons to know what they're made of."

"You consulted, Megan, as the interior designer when they refurbished the Garrison, Inc. offices. You don't really know them. It's not the same as being in their face day after day."

"Oh, I was in their face plenty," she volleyed back, more blood deepening the delicate dusting of freckles across her nose. "Don't forget what happened to you, Anna. You are a living example of what can happen to a woman who is wooed by a man who isn't above using her," Megan said.

"He hasn't used me," she said, defensiveness making her voice tighten as she stood. "And I already gave him the 'we can only be friends' speech this past week at dinner and he's been nothing but business since then."

"It's gone that far? You had to give him that speech?"

"Not that far," Anna mused, turning off the oven and taking a minute to refresh their cups. "We've only kissed. In London. That's all, I swear."

Megan held her cup for a refill. "Why?"

"Why was that all or why did we kiss?"

"Oh, I know why you kissed," Megan said wryly. "You kissed because you were in a ridiculously romantic place and wildly attracted to each other and he whispered in your ear and you melted."

Anna laughed as she put the coffeepot back and sat. "Oh, you think you know everything."

"Not everything. But I know enough."

The need to share the truth was powerful and if anyone would understand, Megan would. "We kissed because he told me he suspects there's a spy in the company and I planted one on him to drag him away from that dangerous train of thought."

"A spy?" Megan's eyes popped. "No wonder you're freaked."

"Can you imagine if he found out that I was stupid enough to let my boyfriend infiltrate my boss's computer system and steal technology secrets at my last job? And then got blamed for it?"

"You'd be okay," Megan said. "I mean, you've been at Garrison for four years or so."

"But now there's the Internet. How long would it take before someone searched my name and found articles in the local Indianapolis papers accusing an administrative assistant of being a corporate spy?"

"You were innocent, Anna. Michael Montgomery finally admitted he did it."

"Yes, I know that and you know that, and even my former boss knows that because the confession happened in the privacy of a conference room in Indianapolis."

"Barry Lynch dropped all charges."

She nodded. "Yes, he did. The boss dropped the charges and the boyfriend fled town and no one bothered to call the papers and inform them except me, and the reporter wasn't interested. Called it an 'old story.' But my name is still media mud."

Megan sighed, obviously unable to deny that. "Barry Lynch is still running FiberTech outside of Indy. Why don't you call him and ask him to vouch for you?"

"I don't want to dredge up old history. He was embarrassed by the lax security in his company, anyway. That's why he didn't tell the newspapers the truth." Anna closed her eyes. "I want it all behind me."

"I know you do." Megan reached across the table and put her hand on Anna's. "And I want you to be careful with Parker Garrison."

Parker again. "Do you even know him, Megan?"

"I met all the Garrisons when I did the consulting job. Cheating runs in their genes."

"Cheating?" Then Anna recalled the latest Garrison scandal. "I guess you're right." She rose and donned an oven mitt to slide the pastry tray out, and as she did, told

Megan the whole story of Cassie Sinclair and her unlikely role at Garrison, Inc.

Megan listened, rapt, then asked, "So this woman over in Nassau is John Garrison's illegitimate daughter?"

"Looks that way. And now she owns twenty percent of Garrison, Inc."

Megan's eyebrow notched. "At least he took care of his child."

At the catch in her friend's voice, Anna turned from the oven, pastry tray extended, but Megan hid her expression behind the coffee cup.

"Would you like a cinnamon roll?" Anna asked.

Megan put her cup down with a little too much force. "But you see what I mean?" she asked, obviously not hearing Anna's question. "See what they're made of? Gorgeous, yes, every last one of them. But can they be trusted? And you, after all you've been through, you have to trust the man you love, Anna."

The tray slipped in Anna's mitted hand, but she caught it. Love. *Whoa.*

"This isn't love," she managed to say. "This is a pathetic crush on my part and lust on his."

Megan's chair scraped the tile as she stood. "You think? How's he treated you since you gave him the speech?"

"Well, he's had a lot of closed-door meetings and placed most of his own calls, so I thought he was trying to avoid me. But…" Her voice trailed off as she tried to think of how to explain what had been happening for the past five days. "But when we're together, well, to be honest, there's been a lot of electricity in the air."

"Oh, really?" Megan meandered over to the counter to help herself to a cinnamon roll. "Like lightning bolts that turn your lower half into liquid and your brain to mush?"

"Yeah." Anna half laughed.

"And every time your hands casually brush when you exchange papers, you sort of shiver and get all tingly?"

"Precisely."

Megan took a bite of gooey pastry, nodding like a knowledgeable expert as she chewed. "And," she added when she swallowed, pointing the roll at Anna, "when he laughs at something you said, the whole room sort of spins and your heart gets all fluttery and your arms get numb from the need to touch him?"

"Every time."

Megan slid her finger along the top of the cinnamon roll, covering it with icing. "You're in love," she pronounced.

"No, I'm not. I'm just in big, fat trouble."

Megan sucked the icing off her finger with a noisy smack and a knowing grin. "Same thing."

The last thing Parker wanted to do on Sunday was trudge up to Bal Harbor for the weekly Garrison dinner. Not that driving Collins Avenue with the top of his BMW M3 down and his floorboard-rumbling stereo at full blast was exactly *trudging,* but he still would rather have spent the evening working on the endless pile of paper that seemed to accumulate on his desk that week.

Because, God knows, he hadn't gotten anything of consequence accomplished at work since Monday. Unless playing games with Anna Cross was "work."

He'd planted three separate false trails regarding business development, and not one of them had resulted in sending the Jefferieses on a wild-goose chase.

He'd tried to draw Anna out from her cloak of professionalism, teasing her with the occasional joke and letting the inevitable contact blister into heat between them. But that hadn't accomplished anything except more than a few restless nights for him and a bad case of unrequited...arousal.

And that, he thought, popping out the classic-rock CD he'd been playing and searching his collection for something that suited his mood, was the problem.

She was getting to him.

Maybe it was her resistance to his obvious interest. Maybe it was the fact that he suspected her of spying and couldn't seem to catch her. Maybe it was the memory of those few kisses, that promise of so much more in London.

He shifted uncomfortably in his seat, the all-too-familiar southbound rush of blood reminding him that whatever the hell it was about Anna Cross, it had an undeniable effect on him.

No matter which way he cut it, rationalized it or ignored it, he still wanted her. A lot.

His fingers grazed the CD cases restlessly, skipping each one. If not rock or jazz or a decent piano concerto, what did he want to hear?

Broadway tunes.

"Oh, man." He tapped the steering wheel and yanked left into the stone gates of the Garrison estate. "That's bad, Garrison. That's rock-bottom bad."

He whipped into an open space behind Adam's smaller model BMW and checked his rearview, raking his hands through his wind-whipped hair in self-disgust. Since when did he have the slightest interest in Rodgers and Hammerstein?

Since that little vixen hummed show tunes while she was filing. Off-key, no less. But when she tapped her toes to some ditty that ran through her head and the tip of her tongue sneaked out between her sweet, soft lips, the next thing he knew he had a sudden need to—

"Don't worry, you're perfect." Brooke leaned over the passenger door of the convertible and offered her brother a friendly grin. "Making all the girls wild, as usual."

He reached over and gave her hand a squeeze. "I'm afraid it's the other way around lately."

That earned him a surprised lift of her shapely eyebrow. "Don't tell me someone's finally gotten under big, bad Parker's skin."

"Not a chance," he assured her, popping out of the car and coming around to give her a hug. "But who are *you* sneaking around with these days?"

All the color drained from Brooke's usually rosy cheeks. "What?" She half laughed and accepted his hug. "You must have me mixed up with my far more social twin."

He released the embrace, but held her shoulders tightly and searched her face, a pang of guilt twisting through him. He'd promised Stephen he'd call her this week and he hadn't even remembered. He'd been so caught up in...Anna.

"Are you okay?" he asked, unwilling to let go of her shoulders. "Stephen told me you've been pretty miserable since the whole Cassie Sinclair thing came out."

Her eyes filled, but she blinked back the tears. "I'm having a hard time, Parker," she replied. "What Dad did was, well, unforgivable. And to let us know like that. During the reading of his will." She inched out of his grip with a shudder of anger.

He slid his arm around her as they crossed the brick driveway and approached the massive glass-and-mahogany entrance to the Spanish-style villa.

"I know how you feel," Parker commiserated. "Mad and hurt and disillusioned. And, hell, we're still in mourning.

I can't believe I'm going to walk into this house and he isn't going to be on the back veranda, drinking in the ocean view, ready to dissect every nuance of the past workweek and plan the attack for the next one."

She raised her delicate jaw so the sunlight caught the dip of the Garrison cleft in her chin. "That's your job now, Parker."

"Don't I know it," he said, the weight of the "patriarch" role weighing heavy on his shoulders. "Those are big shoes to fill."

"No problem," she assured him with a gentle elbow to the ribs. "You've got big feet."

Before they even reached the last of the wide stucco stairs that led to the entrance, the doors opened and Lisette Wilson, the real keeper of the Garrison house, appeared in her standard navy-and-white uniform, looking a bit older than her fifty-five years.

The loss of John Garrison had hit their longtime house-keeper hard, but Parker knew that something more than that was working on Lisette.

"Hello, Lisette," he greeted her with a gentle hand to her shoulder, while she gave a nod to him and a peck on Brooke's cheek. "How are you?" Parker asked.

She answered that with pursed lips feathered with a dozen tiny creases. "I'm fine, Mr. Parker, but I can't say the same for your mother. The bottle has been open since eleven this morning."

He felt his sister sink into him. "Oh," Brooke said. "Thanks for the warning, Lisette."

Behind the housekeeper, Adam strode into the oversize entryway, a frown on his angular face. "I'm leaving," he said gruffly. "Sorry, but I'd rather be anywhere but here listening to her rant about Ava Sinclair."

"Ava who?" Brooke asked. "Is that Cassie's mother?"

"Yes," Parker said. "Brandon Washington has been doing some digging. The woman, Dad's, uh, friend, passed away about a month before he did."

"And I'm supposed to feel bad about that?" Bonita ambled in and leaned shakily on a wide stone column that marked the entrance to a sprawling living room, a glass of something potent in her hand. She shook a strand of hair off her face, revealing some makeup streaked under her eyes. "Maybe your father died of a broken heart when his mistress croaked."

Parker's heart sank. Mother was loud, rough and blasted.

Lisette immediately stepped to her side. "Why don't I take you upstairs to freshen up while the children gather, Mrs. Garrison," she said, as gently as if she were talking to a petulant toddler. "Mr. Stephen should be here soon, and maybe Miss Brittany. I daresay we'll have a full house tonight, and I made braised beef."

"I don't like braised beef," his mother whined, but she allowed herself to be led up a winding staircase, mumbling under her breath as she clutched the wrought iron railing.

Adam blew out a disgusted breath and continued toward the front door. "I'm outta here."

"Wait," Brooke said, going after him. "Come on, Adam. We need to be a family."

"You need to be a family," he shot back. "I need to be somewhere else." He opened the door to leave just as Stephen walked up the stairs. Wordlessly, Adam pushed past his brother with Brooke on his tail.

"Adam, please," she called. "She'll sober up."

"Just enough to insult you, Brooke."

"No, wait, Adam."

Stephen stepped aside to let his siblings barrel by, a bemused smile aimed at Parker. "Another Sunday in paradise, I see."

Parker shook his head. "For this, I gave up work."

Stephen laughed lightly and gave his brother a friendly pat on the shoulder. "Spoken like a true Garrison, bro. But I bet the old man isn't up in heaven saying, 'I should have spent more days at the office.'"

"What do you mean? You're as much of a workaholic as I am," Parker said as the two of them headed toward the back of the house, drawn by the scents of Lisette's cooking and the possibility of a relaxing, private moment together.

Out of habit, they went straight through the bank of French doors to the veranda. A cool breeze blew the dozens of queen palms that lined the limestone patio, exotic scents of tropical flowers wafting from the planters that surrounded an Olympic-size pool that no one actually used.

Stephen ambled to the marble-topped wet bar and poured two fingers of Dad's single malt into cut-crystal tumblers.

"In honor of the old man," he said, giving one glass to Parker and holding the other in a mock toast.

"We're as bad as mom," Parker said drily.

"Nah. This is my first and it's five o'clock."

Parker acknowledged that with a nod. "Yeah, yeah." But he barely sipped the hot, amber liquid, clunking the glass down on the bar. "It's been a helluva week."

Stephen pulled out a leather bar stool and settled next to his brother. "Tell me about it. The bastards are up to no good again."

"Jefferies? What happened?"

"Remember that photo spread in *Luxury Traveler* I negotiated for the hotel?" Stephen said. "Fourteen pages of priceless coverage in one of the top travel magazines in the world?

I worked with the editorial director, schmoozed him, wined him, dined him, let him stay in the penthouse with a young woman who was definitely not his wife. Remember?"

"Of course," Parker said. "That editorial coverage will be equivalent to a hundred thousand worth of ad dollars for the Grand."

Stephen snorted. "Not anymore. He's changed his mind and is waiting for Hotel Victoria to open. He's using *that* as the background for the photo shoot and story about the latest hip and hot hotels in South Beach."

"What?" Parker slammed his hand on the counter. "How did the Jefferieses swing that? No one even knew that story was in the works."

No one, he thought as the whiskey turned bitter in his mouth, but the woman who sat outside his office. Maybe some others, but he distinctly remembered Anna knew about the deal because the editorial director of *Luxury Travel* had called him on more than one occasion.

"I'm royally ticked," Stephen said. "But since it's not paid advertising, my hands are tied. He said it was strictly an 'editorial' decision."

Parker swore softly.

"We got a hole in the dam," Stephen said. "And we can't ignore it any longer."

Parker took a deep drink of the scotch. "I think I know who it is."

"You do? Who?"

He hesitated, but only for a moment. This was Stephen, and they had no secrets. "Anna."

"Anna Cross? Your secretary?" Stephen stabbed his fingers through his hair in disbelief. "Is that why you're dating her?"

"It didn't start out that way, but then she said and did a

few things that made me suspicious. Anyway, I'm not dating her. She wants to keep it all business."

"Sure, so she doesn't get fired and can keep her hands in your files." Stephen sounded disgusted. "What are you doing about it?"

"I've tried a misinformation campaign, but that isn't working. They didn't bite on anything this week."

"Then you'll have to use a James Bond technique," Stephen said, a half smile threatening. "Screw the truth out of her."

A tremor of heat warred with distaste. Not screwing, not with Anna.

"She's keeping me at arm's length," Parker said.

Stephen looked unconvinced. "Come on, ace. You can do this. You're a master."

"I really like her." The admission sounded a little lame, but felt amazingly good. He did like her. Wasn't that at the bottom of all his angst? It certainly explained the sudden desire to listen to the overture from *Camelot*.

"She's using you."

Was that even possible? She was so guileless. "I don't know that for a fact."

"Then find out." Stephen stood to make his point. "Forget misinformation or seduction. Set her up and catch her in the act. Then you can fire her and we can stop this infernal leaking of proprietary information."

Parker lifted his glass and swirled the remaining whiskey. "Seems kind of underhanded, don't you think?"

"And spying on us and feeding information to Jordan and Emilio Jefferies is aboveboard?" Stephen tapped him on his shoulder. "What do you think your father would do?"

John Garrison would have set her up and taken her

down in a heartbeat. Business before personal feelings. Business before *anything*.

"Hey, if she's innocent," Stephen added, "then you find that out, too. Then you can seduce her for real."

"Seduce whom?" Brittany strolled onto the veranda and sidled up to her two brothers. "Who's your next victim?"

"No one," Parker said dismissively.

His brother was right; they had to know the truth. The thing was, if he was wrong, and Anna realized he suspected her, he'd never have a chance with her. Ever.

But if he was right, then he'd be doing the very thing the patriarch of the family should be doing: protecting the Garrison brand.

When it came down to that, he really had no choice.

Seven

By five o'clock on Monday, Anna thought she'd jump out of her skin. Or jump onto her boss's. She'd spent every moment at work next to Parker, at times so close you couldn't slide a hair between them. He seemed to need—or want—her for everything. He had her in his office reorganizing files, requiring her to stay in the room during his telephone conversations so she could take down pertinent information.

He brought in lunch and while they ate, he discussed the possibility of launching an ad campaign for the brand, an idea she'd certainly heard him reject in the past.

Forget the ad campaign. Forget the sudden outpouring of business issues. When he reached over and took her pickle off her paper plate, grinned and asked seductively, "You don't mind sharing, do you?" Anna almost melted into his plush leather sofa. Which she had no right sharing with him, but that was where he'd set up lunch…like some kind of impromptu picnic.

Every overheated cell in her body ached from the torture of being so close without being able to touch, her senses bombarded with the pleasure of seeing him lean over a piece of paper to sign his name, that lock of hair nearly kissing his brow exactly the way she wanted to. Slack-jawed and weak-limbed and awestruck, she watched him shed his jacket at two, loosen his tie at four and unbutton his cuffs to reveal his powerful, broad wrists at five-thirty.

One more minute and she'd start on his belt buckle.

How long could this go on?

"Anna," he chided when his PDA dinged softly. "We forgot the business council meeting tonight."

"We did? I did?" She shuffled through the papers for his calendar. "I don't have a business council meeting on your schedule."

He started lowering the cuffs and buttoning them, sending relief and disappointment colliding through her.

"This meeting was added at the last minute by the board to discuss the next election," he told her.

"That must be why I didn't know about it," she said. That or the fact that she'd gone way past *distracted* and had slid right into *useless* ever since they'd gotten back from London.

Maybe she was trying to sabotage her job; if she didn't work for him, then she could act on all the chemistry she was absolutely certain she wasn't imagining.

If she didn't work for him, she could meet him here late at night and… Her gaze drifted to the leather sofa where they'd eaten lunch, her mind already imagining the stamp of his body on hers; the heat of his hands under her blouse; the wet, warm feel of his lips suckling her breasts—

"But it has to be done by tomorrow morning, so I'm afraid you'll have to finish it tonight."

What in God's name was he talking about? "Which will entail...?" She scanned his desk for a clue to what he'd just told her to do.

"The usual, complete the spreadsheets. It won't take you long. I'm sorry you have to work late. You didn't have plans did you?"

Not unless jogging off nine hours of sexual frustration and then spending the rest of the night fantasizing herself right back into that blissful state constituted *plans*. "No, not tonight."

"Good. To make it easier on you, I've left the data on my computer, so you can just input the spreadsheets right here." He indicated his desk. "You don't mind that, do you?"

Yes, she minded. She had to sit in his chair, his spicy aftershave lingering in the air, his computer under her fingertips. But what she really minded was that she had no idea what he was talking about.

"Um, Parker, which spreadsheet again?"

He laughed softly. "You seem a little distracted today, Anna. You okay?"

"I...I just..." She smoothed her hair and squared her shoulders. "Missing the business council on your calendar kind of threw me."

He waved it off and dragged the charcoal suit coat back on. "I'm referring to the monthly property report for the executive committee. All of the profits from Garrison companies are rolled into that report. My brothers and sisters will be in here tomorrow morning for the exec committee meeting and we'll go over it first thing."

"Oh, of course." Still she frowned, not remembering a document they'd done like that in the past. Didn't all the

Garrisons bring their numbers to the meeting individually, and announce them that morning? Why were they doing it this way?

He slipped some files—she was so distracted, she didn't even know *what*—into his soft-sided leather briefcase and gave her an unreadable look, almost as if he was a little disappointed. He probably was—she hadn't really done her usual bang-up job this week.

Plus, she was getting far less adept at hiding her attraction. Maybe he knew she said one thing to him about their physical relationship, but dreamed of another. Maybe he could tell she was really regretting her decision to keep their relationship strictly professional. Because she was. Deeply. Daily.

"I'll see you tomorrow, then, Anna." What was that expression on his face? Expectation? Hope? Uncertainty? Something was on his mind, but he wasn't saying. Was he hoping she'd change her mind, or had he moved on?

No. She wasn't imagining the sizzle between them.

"I'll be in at eight," she promised him. "And the meeting starts at nine."

He came around his desk and paused in front of her. Inches away, she could feel the heat of him, the sense that he was trying to tell her something nearly buckling her knees.

"Is there anything else, Parker?" Did he hear that note of need in her voice?

"No. There's nothing else." He lifted his hand and brushed a single stray hair from her face, the featherlight touch sparking her skin. Had he noticed she'd been wearing her hair down? "I just... I'm sorry."

"Sorry?" She pulled back. "For what?"

"Sorry you have to work late."

She let out a quick breath, almost a laugh. "I always

work late," she assured him. "And going to a business council meeting isn't exactly a fun time for all."

He smiled, cocking his head exactly the way he would if he were going to kiss her. Her heart walloped so hard, he had to have heard it. Had to have noticed her lips parting, her eyes half closing. He dipped a centimeter.

He was going to kiss her. Her fingers tightened on the papers she held; her gaze dropped to his mouth; her gut clenched in anticipation.

He was going to kiss her, and she was going to kiss him right back.

"Good night," he said gruffly, jerking himself away and marching across the office to the door.

Anna stood stone still for a full minute after the door slammed; the only thing moving was her poor, overworked heart as it tried to redirect blood back into her brain.

Finally, she sank into a chair and took a breath.

She had all night to do his spreadsheets. She needed that run in the worst way. The way she felt right now, she could tear down Biscayne Boulevard, cross the MacArthur Causeway and throw herself into the Atlantic Ocean and it wouldn't erase the fire and need in her body.

But she would try.

"I gave her plenty of rope," Parker said, taking a sip of the draft beer Stephen had just handed him. Instead of hops and wheat, he tasted misery. And regret.

"You gave her all fake numbers, right?" Stephen leaned back on Brittany Beach's comfortable couches as if he didn't have a care in the world.

He didn't, Parker thought drily. Stephen hadn't just arranged an elaborate setup that could ruin a woman he respected. A woman he liked.

A woman he wanted so bad he could howl at the rising moon.

"Yeah," Parker said. "Every single line item a lie." He checked his watch, imagining his dutiful secretary entering made-up profits into a spreadsheet. Would she e-mail that file directly to Jordan Jefferies?

"And you're sure she'll do the work on your PC, not hers?"

Parker nodded. "I set it up that way."

"And you're sure you installed the software?" Stephen prodded. "The one that tracks every keystroke?"

"Yes," Parker answered impatiently.

"Cool stuff, isn't it?"

"Very. I just wish I wasn't using it to bring down Anna."

"To bring down a *spy,*" Stephen reminded him. "I have that on my PC, too. It's just smart protection. Did you know it was invented by a private investigator?"

A P.I. That didn't make Parker feel any better about spying on the woman whose only sin might just be having perfect legs. And a killer smile. And beautiful hair. And that sweet laugh. And a sharp intellect. And—

"You're having second thoughts."

Parker sipped the beer, which still tasted flat and bad. "I'm way past second, bro."

"Hey, if she's the spy, this will be the smartest business move you ever made. You're a hero for trapping her."

He didn't feel like a hero. He felt like a heel. Keeping her close all day long, feeding her BS just to see if she'd spread his lies to the competition. And all the while, every time she moved or breathed or looked at him with all that unmistakable longing in her eyes, his whole being constricted with the fight not to take her in his arms and annihilate her with his mouth.

"What if someone else gets to my computer and it's not

even Anna?" he said as the bizarre thought took hold. "What if she gets blamed for something she didn't do?"

"What are the chances of that?" Stephen asked.

"Slim. None."

"Relax. Here comes Brittany." Stephen gave his sister an inviting wave. "Let's torture her."

But Parker's heart wasn't into teasing his sister, so he let Stephen and Brittany talk while he stared at the horizon.

A beautiful redheaded model glided by and gave him an interested smile, but he just looked past her, his mind seeing a different woman altogether. A little while later, Brittany introduced him to her newest waitress, Tiffany, and he barely noticed her generous cleavage, so she turned her charms on Stephen. Even the arrival of two Miami Heat cheerleaders didn't snag his attention.

Brittany brought him another beer. "Your first one's flat and warm by now." She picked up the barely touched pilsner glass. "If I didn't know you as an arrogant master of the universe, I'd say you were lovesick tonight."

Parker pulled his focus from the darkening Atlantic Ocean to his sister. "I'm not lovesick, Britt."

She laughed. "No argument on arrogant, I see." When he didn't respond, she added, "Then what's your problem?"

He swallowed the smart-ass retort he'd usually give his sister and just shook his head. "Business, of course."

"Of course," she said, perching on the rattan armrest of the sofa. "It's never anything else with you, is it?"

"What's that supposed to mean?" he asked.

She shrugged. "Just wondering if there's a heart in that big old chest of yours, or just a calculator."

Was that how he seemed? To her? To everyone? To Anna? The thought made his chest ache. Not the way a calculator would at all.

A customer called Brittany and she stood, giving Parker a rare squeeze on the shoulder. "Too bad you're such a machine, Parker. If you'd loosen up, I might actually like you."

He looked up, ready to remind his sister that she had the right to be flighty; she was the youngest. He, on the other hand, had the weight of the family name on his first-born shoulders. But Brittany had taken off, and Stephen was flirting with the new girl.

He'd had enough.

"Where are you going?" Stephen asked when Parker stood and set the new beer on the table with a thud.

"I'm leaving," he said vaguely.

Stephen frowned at him. "You changed your mind?"

Parker opened his mouth to argue, but just held up a hand. "I'm going to handle this my way." He hustled away before his brother could argue.

If she was the spy, he'd catch her in the act. Forget tracking her keystrokes and placing blame, he'd walk in and find her there, make her freeze before she had time to close whatever info she was stealing and then they could have it out.

He'd fire her and she'd be gone, no chance for an excuse.

This catching-her-with-software was just not his style.

Propelled by the need to take action, and maybe by the need to see her again, regardless of what he found her doing, Parker was in his car in no time. He zipped back over the causeway and whipped down Brickell toward his office. He parked underground in the high-rise and made it to the elevator in a few steps, his blood already spiked.

Would he tell her he'd set her up? Would she be gone already? The elevator seemed to drag up each of the twenty-two floors as his gut tightened in anticipation.

The soft ding of the elevator echoed in the empty hall. To his left, the wide glass doors of Garrison, Inc. were closed and locked, the reception area bathed in shadows formed by up lighting under the brass Garrison logo on one wall.

He had a key, of course, and turned it quietly, then locked the door behind him. He stood for a moment near Sheila's desk, listening. He heard nothing.

Could Anna be gone? Something like disappointment shifted in his stomach and he walked soundlessly down the hall to his office.

Anna's desk was empty, her computer off. But the file with the spreadsheet information was right on top. Curious, he opened it. It was untouched. She hadn't done it yet? In two hours? Had she spent the entire time raiding his computer?

His door was closed tightly and he paused, wondering if he should just use his key or jiggle the handle. The latter could alert her and she could quickly clear the screen.

But her moves would be tracked with the software.

He jiggled, but it was locked. Quickly, he slid his key in and with a dramatic thrust, pushed the door open.

The room was empty. A Garrison, Inc. logo danced around as a screen saver on his computer. That meant the computer had been untouched for at least half an hour.

He stepped toward his desk, and then he heard it.

High-pitched, heartfelt and as flat as a sick puppy. Singing. She could have danced all night.

Audrey Hepburn might roll over in her grave at Anna's rendition of a signature song, but Parker Garrison simply froze and imagined the woman he wanted...wet, naked and belting out a ballad in the shower.

If she was a spy, he'd fire her. If she wasn't, he'd...

Join her.

In two steps, he was at his keyboard, typing the password to access the results of some investigator's programming.

She hit a high note. It hurt.

He tapped a few more keys and there were the results.

He blinked and leaned closer to make sure he was reading right. And he was. Anna Cross hadn't so much as touched his keyboard, even though she'd had two hours to raid about four dozen "proprietary" files on his hard drive.

Anna Cross wasn't the spy.

A slow, satisfied grin pulled at his mouth. He was so happy that he could kiss her.

He walked to the bathroom door, put his hand on the knob and decided he would do precisely that. And anything else she'd let him do.

Anna held her arms out until her fingertips touched either side of the slick marble walls. The dual shower heads pulsed rivers of warm water down her back and over her chest, giving her the sensation of being suspended in between two waterfalls. She dropped her head back, let her hair slide down her back and nailed the final note with a flourish even she had never obtained before.

The slow, rhythmic snap of one person's applause from the other side of the frosted-glass door hit her as hard as the water.

With a gasp, she twisted the knob that operated both heads.

"Please don't stop on my account."

Oh, God in heaven. *Parker*.

Adrenaline left her whole body quivering. He couldn't see her through the steamy glass, but she still covered her bare breasts automatically.

Taking a deep breath, she dug for a perfectly normal voice. "You said I could use the shower whenever I wanted."

"I did and I meant it. I see you went running."

She remembered her shorts and tank top dropped on the floor outside the shower. "Uh-huh," she managed to say.

Suddenly, a fluffy towel curled over the top of the shower door. "Here you go."

Anna glanced down at her body, her skin rosy from the heat, water still sluicing down her breasts and stomach, into the triangle of curls between her legs.

She shivered, despite the steam.

He was there. Parker. On the other side of that glass. And all she had to do was…open the door. Invite him in. Take what she wanted so much her whole being ached.

"Are you all right in there?"

She didn't answer him, unsure of what she might say, what shocking invitation she might issue if she opened her mouth.

"Anna? Are you okay?"

She reached toward the glass and placed one fingertip on the steam. That was all that separated her bare and willing body from him. One thin sheet of fogged-up glass.

"Why did you come back?" she finally asked.

Behind her, a drop of water hit the marble floor and another dribbled down the drain. Her finger trailed a thin line in the glass, clearing a quarter-inch view.

"I wanted to…check on you." His voice was low and seductive. And so close. He had to be just inches from the glass door.

"I'm fine." She made a second line in the fog. "See?"

His five fingertips touched the glass, leaving ovals where his skin pressed against it. "Yes, you are. Very fine."

She lifted her left hand, and matched his handprint, fingertip for fingertip. "And so are you." He might not have heard her, since she breathed the words.

"Anna." His fingers moved an inch, and she followed them.

"Yes?"

This was the part where he made a light joke about her voice or teased her about his shower. This was the part where he backed away and gave her privacy to change alone. This was the part where he reminded her that she had work to do and he was the boss and she was the—

"I want you to open the door."

Heat and desire rolled through her like the steam clouds in the shower. Her arm trembled, her chest tightened and everything in her that was female curled into a fist of longing low in her belly.

She pressed the door just hard enough to release the latch, but not reveal herself. The barrier was still there, but falling fast.

Through the opaque glass, she saw a dark jacket slide to the ground. The tie, the buttons, the shirt. Gone. She heard the metal click of a belt buckle, the teeth of a zipper, the scuff of a shoe, the soft *whoosh* of falling clothes.

Blood throbbing through her veins, her breathing already labored, she took a step back, and another, until she hit the warm, water-slick marble wall. Behind her, she reached for the faucet, flipped it on with one hand and both showerheads exploded into a pulsing rush of water that streamed over her body.

She closed her eyes, heard the shower door click closed, and felt the heat of Parker as he stood in front of her.

"Look at me," he commanded softly.

She did. His eyes were pure black with arousal, his jaw clenched, his nostrils flared with each ragged breath. Water matted his hair to his head and flattened the thatch of dark curls over the valleys and dips of his broad chest. With her eyes, she followed the water stream as it poured over the taut outline of his stomach and finally flowed over a daunting and mighty erection.

Without a word, he put one hand on either side of her head, caging her in without touching her.

"Anna." He mouthed her name, so softly she felt his breath on her face. "You have no idea how happy I am to know I can trust you."

She blinked into the water that streamed on her face. Why would he say that?

"Of course you can trust me," she said, her fingers curling against the wall as she fought the urge to scrape her hands over every inch of him.

"I just...wasn't sure."

The idea of Parker Garrison, man of certainty and decision, being unsure nearly buckled her knees. All her doubt disappeared with his admission; all her warnings vaporized in the steamy humidity of the shower.

"You can trust me," she repeated, closing her eyes and lifting her face. "And you can touch me."

At the command, he grazed a finger over her wet, parted lips, sliding the tip against her teeth, then following the watery path down her throat. She could hear him inhale with effort and strain as he glided over her breastbone and reached her nipple, making maddeningly slow circles around the peak.

"What else can I do, Anna?"

Her eyes remained closed as she let the silky, delicious touch of his finger send lightning through her. "You can kiss me."

He feathered her lips, so soft she wasn't sure it happened. She opened her mouth and his tongue flicked hers. Slow and steady and with remarkable control, he kissed her, while his other hand cupped her hip, caressing her wet skin, taking teasing strokes of the dips and curves of her backside.

"What else, Anna?" He inched closer so that every wet, hard, sculpted muscle of his body finally pressed against her. His thumb circled her nipple, torturing it to a hard nub as he rocked against her once, fully erect and wickedly hard.

She arched with a soft gasp, marble at her back, man at her front. "You can taste me."

With a groan of pleasure deep in his chest, he took his kisses lower, suckling her throat, licking her collarbone, then nibbling down to her breast. She twisted under his tongue, digging her fingers into his hair to guide his head from one breast to the other.

He gently squeezed both breasts, using his tongue to wipe water and flesh, then sucking each nipple with his eyes closed, as though it were the sweetest treat he'd ever enjoyed. She watched him, shaking, marveling, rolling as her insides twisted into an aching knot of pressure and pleasure.

"Parker," she moaned. "Please."

Straightening, he placed his knees between hers, easing her legs wider, opening her to him.

"What else can I do, Anna?" His voice was rough, with just a hint of tease and humor in the rasp.

He could do anything he wanted. Anything. Everything. And yet, the man who always had control gave her the power.

The thought made her dizzy as she flattened her hands over the soaking-wet hair on his chest, then slowly lowered them, loving every ripped muscle and the smooth flesh that covered them. Finally, she touched him, closing her hands over the velvet skin and sighing at how wonderfully shaped, how completely masculine he was.

She stroked him once and he grew even harder in her palms. She coiled her fingers around the length of him, considering all the things they could do to each other, but wanting only one.

She looked up at him, seeing him through the soft white clouds of steam, his expression intense, his eyes smoky.

"Make love to me, Parker."

The tiniest smile tugged at his mouth. "I thought you might say that," he said, reaching to a shelf above her head.

He tore the condom foil with ease and she took it from him, sliding it over him.

His eyes shuttered as he rose to meet her touch. Then his strong, sure hands gripped under her arms and pushed her up the slippery marble so he could enter her.

Just as he did, he covered her mouth with a ferocious kiss, thrusting his tongue and manhood inside her at exactly the same time, filling her completely.

Their delighted, desperate groans echoed off shower walls, rolled in the mist and gurgled with the water, both of them lost with each single-minded thrust of man against woman.

Shocked by the power of it, she wrapped her legs around his waist, locked her arms around his neck and rode him. Water blinded her now, so she buried her face in his shoulder, inhaling the smell of sex and soap and salt, her body coiling with achy pleasure.

Over and over, he ground out her name, pinning her to the wall, plunging as far into her as he could go, taking them both higher and higher to the unavoidable edge.

And finally she fell, digging her teeth into his skin, spiraling out of control and vaguely realizing that he was falling at the same time, filling her, needing her, loving her.

The steam clouds cleared as they slowly, carefully

slipped down the side of the shower to the floor, staying connected in that most intimate place as Anna remained on his lap, her legs like a vise around his waist.

The position brought them face-to-face, as he kissed her cheek, her neck, her eyes, her mouth, neither of them able to catch their breath.

"Whatever you do," he whispered, "don't even think about singing."

She laughed a little and dropped her forehead against his. "I can't sing."

"No kidding." He kissed her nose. "But you sure can make music."

She narrowed her eyes at him, joking aside. "I have to ask you a question."

"What's that?"

She reached up and twisted the faucet so that the water suddenly stopped. "When you came in here, you said something very strange. Why are you so surprised that you can trust me? That didn't have anything to do with…" She glanced down to where their bodies united. "This. Did it?"

"Actually," he said, his tone deliberate, his fingers winding through her wet hair. "It has everything to do with this. But I was referring to something else."

"What?"

"Let me take you home and hold you in my bed all night, Anna, then I'll tell you everything."

She nestled into him, warmed to the bone by the thought of spending the night with Parker. "Tell me everything about what?" she asked.

"About how I thought you were the spy in our company."

She stopped breathing just long enough to wonder if he noticed the goose bumps that rose despite the heat in the shower.

Eight

<u></u>

Every time Anna tried to form the words to tell him about her past, Parker kissed her.

As the wind whipped her hair in the convertible, he brushed the strands away at every stoplight and kissed her. While driving, he kept his hand on her leg, caressing and sliding up and down her thigh, sinfully intimate and completely possessive. There was no way she could speak coherently, let alone confess her life history.

And what would she say?

Parker, there's something you need to know about me....

No, that sounded as if she were guilty.

Funny thing you would have this corporate-spy problem...

There was nothing funny about it.

Before I spend the night making love to you...

No. No. She just didn't want to give up what she was about to experience. It was stupid, it was shortsighted and it was wrong.

But, she wanted a night with Parker Garrison so much she couldn't risk losing it.

Surely this conversation, this inevitable and uncomfortable conversation, would throw a bucket of cold water on their romance and then she'd never know the joy and pleasure of waking up in the arms of a man she…

Oh, Megan was right. She was in deep, undeniable…trouble.

"So, why'd you do it?" he asked as they reached the intersection at Ocean Drive.

Her throat closed, but she managed an even-toned response. "Why'd I do what?" *Let my manipulative boyfriend have access to my boss's computer and wreck my life?*

"Why'd you change your mind?" His fingers burned through the thin silk of her slacks and he rubbed her leg with his strong, large hand.

"Oh, that."

He laughed, removing his hand to shift gears, maneuvering through traffic, which was heavy, even for a weeknight. Then he slid her a slow, sexy grin and a sideways glance and resumed his private tour of her thigh.

"Yeah, *that.* Back there. In the shower. Big change of mind, don't you think?"

She tucked a still-damp, wind-tossed lock of hair behind her ear as they picked up speed.

She leaned her head back and closed her eyes in resignation. Why lie? "I've always been attracted to you."

"Really?" He actually sounded surprised. "Always?"

"Especially since I started working for you." She gave in to a smile, relieved to be admitting one truth, anyway. "I've fantasized about making love to you about a thousand times."

She felt him tap the brakes, so she opened her eyes to

see him staring at her, his jaw loose, his eyes wide. "Really? You mean, before London?"

She just nodded. "And since."

He shook his head, fighting a smile. "You sure hide it well. Along with everything else, I might add."

"I think getting involved with the CEO is not a wise career move."

He nodded. "I know you do. And you know I could help you get another job."

"I don't want another job," she said softly.

He slowed as they passed the stunning contemporary entrance to the Garrison Grand.

"You could work here," he suggested. "For my brother." Then he narrowed his eyes. "On second thought, you'd be safer working for Brooke or Brittany. Stephen would hit on you."

"I'm not interested in Stephen," she said. "Or working at the Garrison Grand." She glanced at the soaring, dramatic angles of the hotel, lit in pastel spotlights that bathed it in an ever-changing hue of art deco colors. "You'd still be the boss, in essence. You're still in charge of Garrison, Inc."

"Sort of," he said drily, accelerating into a hole in traffic and continuing north.

She should tell him. *Now.* "Parker…"

He turned to her, sneaked in another kiss on her cheek. "Let's make a deal for tonight, Anna. Let's forget you work for me, okay?" He nuzzled her neck for a moment as they stopped at a light. "Just for tonight, be my lover, not my administrative assistant. Let's forget everything keeping us apart and just be together."

The thrill of that danced through her again. His lover. Just for tonight. As for her big confession, couldn't it wait just one night?

Of course, she'd tell him in the professional atmosphere of the office. "But tomorrow—"

He cut her off with a nibble on her ear. "I'll take you home in the morning so you can change for work and we'll be back in the office by eight o'clock, just like always."

She closed her eyes. "But working together…it won't ever be the same."

"No, it won't," he agreed. "It'll be better."

"It'll be awkward."

"It'll be fine."

"It'll be obvious."

"It'll be fun."

She turned her face toward his and kissed him on the mouth. "You always get whatever you want, don't you?"

He grinned and twisted his finger around a tendril of her hair. "Usually, not always. And I want you. A lot. Tonight. Tomorrow." He tugged the hair gently and ignored the guy who honked when the light turned green. "I will make you feel very, very good, Anna. Trust me."

"I already feel very, very good," she assured him. Too good, she decided, to spoil the night with revelations about her past.

When he parked in an underground lot of the sky-high condo called the Tower, he teased her with more kisses. Somehow they made it to the elevator, where he backed her into the mirrored wall as it catapulted to the top floor.

"I live in the penthouse," he told her, toying with the top button of her blouse and pressing his body against hers, clearly ready to make love again. "So we have a minute now."

She laughed lightly, angling her head to give him access. "We need more than a minute."

He moaned softly as he slipped a hand over the lace cup of her bra. "You're right." He settled for a long, lazy kiss as the elevator soared, making Anna feel like the earth had dropped out from under her feet.

The car stopped and opened at the private entrance to the penthouse apartment. He unlocked one of the colossal double doors and led her into his world.

"God, this is amazing." She could barely take in the enormous space, all crisp lines and architectural angles, all shades of sand and coffee and wood, the walls no more than floor-to-ceiling plate glass with mind-bogglingly beautiful vistas of Biscayne Bay, barrier islands and a thousand dancing lights of the city of Miami.

"This is amazing," he repeated from behind her, closing his arms around her waist and pulling her into the granite of his body. "Amazing, beautiful, sexy." He glided his hands over her chest, burying his face in her hair, finding one spot of flesh on her neck to kiss.

She sighed and let him touch her, glorious sensations sliding from head to toe.

"Would you like a tour?" he asked. "A drink? Dinner?"

She turned to smile at him. "You cook?"

"I could scare up some spaghetti. Maybe a salad. Or have the chef at the Garrison Grand send over the special of the night." As though he couldn't possibly keep his hands off her, he pulled her back into him, kissing her forehead and then her nose. "Whatever you like."

She would pay for this procrastination. She would suffer when she had to sit across that desk and tell him that she hadn't been totally honest. She might even lose her job. But suddenly no price was too high for what she craved.

"What I like," she admitted softly, "is you."

His grin was slow and rich with satisfaction. "I like you, too." Then he scooped her up, kissed her on the mouth and carried her farther into the apartment.

* * *

"This wasn't nearly enough," Parker announced as he stole one more kiss outside the one-story Spanish-style bungalow in Coral Gables, the morning sun already burning the leather seats of his car. "While you're changing, why don't you pack a bag for tonight and we'll go out to dinner after work and then…"

Her smile evaporated as she opened the passenger door. "We'll see about tonight. We have to get through today first."

He climbed out, jogging around the front of his car to snag her at the first step of her front porch. "And that isn't going to be easy," he said.

She gave him a quizzical look. "Why not?"

"Because every time I see you, I'm going to want to take another shower." He pulled her in and kissed her. Damn, he couldn't get enough of that mouth.

"See?" She inched away, refusing the kiss. "I told you."

"I can handle a little distraction," he assured her. "Speaking of distraction, can I come in and watch you change?"

She chuckled, then pulled a set of keys from her handbag and stepped up to the patio covered with potted plants and two little wooden chairs.

"Sorry, we don't have time. The executive committee meeting starts in less than an hour." She unlocked the door and gave him a quick smile. "I'll just be five minutes since I already showered."

He grinned at the memory. "I know you're clean," he said as they entered the house. "I washed you myself."

"And so thoroughly," she quipped, sweeping an arm toward the small but cheery living room. "Not exactly the penthouse, but I call it home."

The little room was brightened by sliding glass doors that led to a cozy, plant-filled patio. Comfortable, tropical-print furniture and bright peach walls were bathed in sunshine all on a gleaming tile floor.

"I like your house," he said. It was inviting and unpretentious—just like Anna.

"Stay here, or in the kitchen," she said, a playful warning in her eyes. "You are not invited to my bedroom."

"I'll get there eventually," he said, releasing her hand.

"We'll see." Then she disappeared into the hallway.

She'd already changed this morning, he mused as he rounded the corner and found a sun-washed kitchen full of flowering plants, white cabinets and glossy butcher-block countertops.

She'd already started to pull away, mentally preparing for the workday that they would share. Could they do this? he wondered as he pulled out a ladder-back chair and sat at the table. Could they work together during the day and play together at night?

He'd never had a full-blown relationship with a woman at work. He fingered a fresh hibiscus floating in a bowl, taking a deep breath of the floral fragrance. But he'd never met anyone like Anna. She was smart and competent and wonderful at work…and sexy and giving and satisfying at play.

Could they have both?

What would happen if things didn't work out? Could they keep working together? And what would happen to her when it got out that she was dating—sleeping with—the CEO? Was it fair to her?

The thought of *not* being with her again squeezed his chest. They'd made love at least three times, and still, he wanted more. He woke up with her slender woman's body in his arms and all he wanted was…to do the same thing tomorrow. And the next day.

He felt better than he had in weeks. Better than he had

since his father had died, and certainly better than he had when he'd learned that Cassie Sinclair was his new sister and partner. Anna made the darkness disappear and it wasn't just her body. That was only the package for something truly…beautiful.

He heard the click of heels on tile and looked up to see her enter the kitchen.

"I see my administrative assistant has returned." He couldn't keep the disappointment out of his voice.

She brushed a self-conscious hand over the tan suit she wore over a simple, high-collared sweater loose enough that it didn't reveal what he knew to be luscious curves.

"It's going to be a busy day," she said, as though that explained her plain-Jane wardrobe.

And just like that, the playful, provocative lover disappeared and the professional, pragmatic assistant took her place. Why?

It was almost as if she was hiding something again.

Out of deference to her neatly styled hair, he put the top up as they drove back to downtown Miami. She held her hands on her lap and he filled the awkward silence with some music until they arrived and parked the car.

"I'll be up in a minute," she said.

"Where are you going?"

"I have to get something from my car. It's parked over there."

He understood. She didn't want to walk in with him. Someone in the office might put two and two together and the rumors would fly. Only they wouldn't be rumors. They'd be real. "Okay."

"Oh!" Suddenly a hand flew to her mouth and she gasped. "Parker, I forgot to do the spreadsheets for the meeting this morning. I'm so sor—"

"No problem. We don't need them."

She frowned at him. "What do you mean you don't need them?"

"I can't believe we were so involved last night that I never told you why I came back to the office." He reached to trace his finger along the line of her jaw and under her lower lip to remind her what had them so busy.

She paled slightly. "Why?"

"Not now. I don't want one of my brothers or sisters to beat me to my office. I'll tell you tonight. Over dinner. I promise." He stepped forward and took one more quick kiss. "See you in the office, sweetheart."

Without waiting for her to respond, he hustled to the elevator and didn't realize he was whistling until the doors opened and he found Stephen standing in the hallway outside of Garrison, Inc.

"If I didn't know you better," Stephen said without preamble, "I would accuse you of whistling something sounding suspiciously like…a show tune."

Parker laughed, but didn't deny it as he glanced at the darkened reception area. "No one is here yet?"

"Your front office is usually more efficient," Stephen noted.

Parker pulled out his keys and unlocked the lobby door. "Usually," he said. "But my assistant was busy."

"Busy stealing corporate secrets," Stephen said. "So now we check the computer program to see what your little spy did last night."

"We can," Parker said, hitting light switches as he headed down the hall. "But we won't find anything. I already checked."

"When?"

"I came back last night." He slid another key into his

office door, but it turned before he actually unlocked it. That was funny. It was always locked. Well, he had been pretty distracted after the shower. "Anna is not the spy."

"Are you sure?"

"Yep. She's a lot of things…" None of which he was about to share with his brother. "But she's no spy."

Stephen, however, went straight to the computer and started typing. "So you came back here, but you left the computer on?"

He must have. Damn, that woman had shut down his brain. "Yeah, but I checked it before…" *Before I found her in the shower.* "Before she left."

"Then she must have come back." Stephen's tone was ominous.

"What? No, she didn't. I know that she didn't."

"You're wrong," he said firmly, clicking at the newly installed program. "The bait is gone, bro. Eaten up and swallowed. And e-mailed to…" He clicked a few more keys. "An address of jjefferies@jefferiesbros.com." Stephen stood straight and leveled a hard-eyed gaze at his brother. "We nailed her."

"No." Parker strode toward the screen, trying to make sense of it. "I know that wasn't there last night when I got here. I checked. She was still here."

"Maybe she came back. The office door was unlocked and the computer was on. Would you have left it that way?"

In the state he'd been in? "I might have."

Stephen gave the desk a hard tap. "You have to fire her the minute she gets in."

"No!" Parker insisted. "It wasn't her."

"What's the matter with you?" Stephen growled. "She's the only person who has access to this office, you set up the bait, she ate it and now you fire her."

"I know she didn't come back here last night."

Stephen blew out a disgusted breath. "Unless you were with her all night, bro, you can't be sure of anything."

"I was. All night. Every minute. We left together around eight and we never separated until five minutes ago when I left her in the parking garage."

"Oh." Stephen notched a knowing eyebrow. "I see."

No, he didn't. Parker bit back the urge to correct his brother's impression that this was some kind of illicit office affair. But how? It was an affair; they did work in the same office and what they'd done in that shower definitely qualified as illicit.

"Someone else came in here after we left," he said.

Stephen looked dubious. "Are you positive? Maybe when you checked this last night you missed something. You've never run the program. You might have done something wrong."

"What time did that e-mail get sent?"

Stephen shook his head. "It doesn't say. It only tracks the physical keystrokes, not the time. But I suppose a decent hacker could figure it out. A good P.I., maybe."

"Then I'll hire one."

"And what if he figures out that your new girlfriend is guilty as hell?"

"She's not," he said, not even bothering to correct Stephen's phrasing. Anna *could* be his girlfriend. He'd be lucky to have her.

"But what if you weren't thinking with the right part of your body last night and you thought she hadn't touched your computer, but she had? What then?"

Parker suddenly felt like punching his brother in the smug, superior face. "I'll hire an investigator. She's not the spy, Stephen. I will prove it to you. If there's so much as a traffic ticket in Anna Cross's background, I'll fire her instantly."

Behind him, his office door creaked and Anna cleared her throat. "The executive committee is here, Mr. Garrison."

"She has access to everything," Stephen said in a harsh whisper as she closed the door. "Including the boss. You'd better know what you're doing, Parker."

Had he really checked that computer thoroughly, or had the shower distracted him? He let out a low, slow breath. "I do," he said confidently.

But just in case, he called the company investigator before he went into the exec committee.

Nine

If there's so much as a traffic ticket in Anna Cross's background, I'll fire her instantly.

The words reverberated in Anna's ears all morning long, while the phone rang and packages were delivered and e-mail was sent and received. Life went on…around her. Inside, turmoil raged.

She had no idea what had compelled Parker to make the comment that she'd overheard as she'd opened his door. But it left her with one choice: to tell him the truth before he figured it out.

But that option had a downside that made her whole body ache. She'd lose him. Not that she actually *had* him. But, last night, when they'd made love, she'd felt something so real and powerful. Was that just incredible sex? She didn't know yet, but she wanted to find out. She wanted to find out with every fiber of her being.

But if she told him that her former boyfriend had used

her computer password to access proprietary files—her boss's proprietary files—and that she'd taken a job with Garrison, Inc. without ever revealing that, she'd never get the chance to make love to him again. Parker, she knew, put business before anything personal. Always.

But if she didn't tell him, then their whole relationship was built on a lie. And that was just as bad as losing him.

Wasn't it?

At eleven-thirty, her phone rang and the sound of Megan Simmons's voice rang like real music in Anna's ears. When Megan said she was in Miami for the day for another conversation about the possible partnership, Anna seized the opportunity.

"Please have lunch with me," she begged. "I need to talk to you."

"Are you all right?" Megan asked, concern in her voice.

Anna closed her eyes. *All right* was relative. "I just need to talk to someone who can give me some advice."

"I'm in SoBe," Megan said. "I have a sliver of time until I have to get to an early-afternoon meeting and I was just going to grab a sandwich. Can you meet me at the News Café in about fifteen minutes?"

Anna was already opening her drawer to grab her purse. "Let me turn my calls over to the receptionist and I'll be there as fast as I can."

The trendy outdoor restaurant was teeming with tourists and locals, but Megan had somehow snagged a table right along the sidewalk of Ocean Drive. She was sipping an iced tea by the time Anna arrived.

Before the waiter brought Anna's bottled water, she spilled the whole story of what she'd overheard that morning, keeping out some very important parts...like what she'd done the night before.

"What should I do?" she asked Megan when she'd finished, breathless. "Should I preempt the inevitable or take a chance?"

"You slept with him, didn't you?"

So much for keeping secrets from Megan. "I hadn't planned to tell you that part."

"Why not? It's all over your face, literally and figuratively. Your glowing with satisfaction and…" Megan reached forward and touched Anna's chin lightly. "I believe I see a little beard burn there."

Lying wasn't an option. "I spent the night with him," Anna admitted.

"And that's why this is a dilemma," Megan said thoughtfully. "Because now it's more than a job. Now it's sex."

"It wasn't just sex," she said quietly.

"It never is, to the woman."

Megan sounded like the voice of experience and, as always, Anna had to fight the urge to ask her just what that experience was. Obviously, it had resulted in Jade. But today's impromptu lunch certainly wasn't the time or place.

"The question is," Anna said, "should I tell him about what happened to me in Indiana? If I do, we could both be in trouble. You knew about the accusations against me when you recommended me for the job."

Megan waved her hand. "I'm not scared of Garrisons," she said, "and neither should you be."

"I'm not scared of him," Anna replied. "I'm…crazy about him."

"Oh, Anna," Megan half moaned and shook her head. "Be careful. Men like that, oh, I don't have to tell you. Michael Montgomery was the same way. Controlling. Arrogant. Demanding."

"Parker's not any of those things. And he's not Michael Montgomery, who was a snake and a cheat and a jerk."

Megan snorted softly. "He's a Garrison. So he's all of those things."

"Really, Meg, not deep down inside. When we made love, he was very giving, very gentle. He let me call the shots, gave me every opportunity to say no or at least be sure I knew what I was doing."

Megan dropped her elbows on the table. "Three words, my friend. Run, don't walk." At Anna's look, she added, "You asked for my advice. You don't have to like it, but that's what I'm telling you to do."

"I have another idea," Anna said slowly. "What do you think if I tried to find the real culprit and then told Parker about my background?"

Megan leaned back as the waiter delivered sandwiches. When he was gone, she said, "Okay, let's play with this. That might solve all your problems, and some of Parker's. How could you do it?"

"It would take some sleuthing, but I do have four years' experience in human resources. I know how to interpret a personnel file."

"You could go through phone logs for calls to or from the Jefferies Group," Megan suggested. "Or you could find out who in the company has ever worked for them."

"Although I imagine he's already done all of that," Anna said, picking up a quarter of a sandwich as the idea took hold. "But maybe I could see something he hasn't."

"Anna, shouldn't he just believe you?" Megan insisted. "I mean, if you have any kind of connection or relationship?"

"In a perfect world, yes," Anna agreed. "But we live in an imperfect one. And the fact that my ex-boyfriend stole my password and accessed my boss's files and the fact that my ex-boyfriend also happened to be my boss's biggest rival and the newspapers and company accused me.... Well, it would be very hard for him not to see a pattern."

"*Wrongly* accused you," Megan corrected.

"It still doesn't look good. Even four years later." How long would she be running from that past?

While they ate, Megan told Anna a little bit about her morning interview and how close she was to taking the new job. But by the time the check arrived, the conversation drifted back to Anna's plan.

"Can you get access to some of that information? The phone logs or background checks? From some of your contacts in HR, maybe?"

"Maybe," Anna said. "I'd have to do it quickly. Today."

"Hey." Megan reached across the table and took Anna's hand. "I know you don't want to hear this, but he's just another guy, you know."

"No, he's not," Anna argued. "And I really, really like him. I wouldn't have slept with him if I didn't. I haven't been with anyone else since Michael—"

"Another alpha dog," Megan interjected.

"Parker's not like he appears on the outside, Megan. He's in charge, yes, but he's also, I don't know, vulnerable."

Megan raised her eyebrow in warning. "So are you, Anna." Then she checked her watch and squashed a tiny shriek. "Oh, no. I have to be in my next meeting in twelve minutes."

"Go," Anna said, shooing her with the check in hand. "This is on me. Thanks for listening, Megan."

Megan was already standing and pulling her purse onto her shoulder. "Thanks for lunch. Good luck with your secret investigation. I still think you should run." She blew a kiss. "And I'd better do just that. Bye." She disappeared into the restaurant.

As Anna scanned the restaurant for their waiter, her gaze drifted across the street to a group of pedestrians, where one very tall, dark-haired man stood out.

Stephen Garrison crossed Ocean Drive with determination and confidence, a cell phone pressed to his ear. As he flipped it closed with his chin, he caught her eye.

She nodded in acknowledgment. "I take it the meeting is finally over," she said as he reached her table.

"It is," he said, glancing at the empty seat with a half-eaten sandwich across from her. "Lunching with a Garrison employee, Miss Cross?"

She swallowed at the unmistakable doubt in his voice. The same doubt she'd hear from Parker when she told him about what happened in Indiana. She thought about defending herself, mentioning that she was with Megan, whom he might remember from when she had done work for the Garrisons, but she just shrugged. She'd save her defense for the brother who mattered.

"Just a friend," she said.

He looked around. "Where is he?"

She shifted in her seat. "*She* just left."

"Oh, I see." He gave her a tight smile. "I'd better get back to the hotel. Goodbye."

"Bye." The word stuck in her throat as she watched him walk away, so much like his brother. So much like the man she'd slept with the night before. So much like the man she didn't want to lose.

Should she run? Or try to vindicate herself? She had nothing to lose...but Parker.

Her cell phone vibrated and the caller ID read the main

number for Garrison, Inc., sending little waves of guilt and worry over Anna. "Hello?"

"It's Sheila McKay."

"Is something wrong, Sheila?"

"You tell me," she said with a dry laugh. "Mr. G. just blew out of here when the exec committee meeting ended, said he had an appointment."

She tried to visualize his calendar, which she'd swear had been open that afternoon. "Okay. Does he need me?"

"Not during the day, apparently." Sheila's voice was rich with insinuation. "But he said to tell you he'd meet you at seven tonight at the Opalesce Room in the Garrison Grand."

Her heart rolled around like a tumbleweed. "All right."

Sheila laughed. "Whatever you told him, it must have worked, honey."

"I'm sure he wants to go over business," Anna said, copping her most professional voice.

"Yeah, I'm sure. In the private dining room. I just reserved it for you."

"So he's not coming back for the afternoon?" Anna asked.

"I don't think so."

"All right. Thanks."

She had one chance to make Parker believe and trust her. Could she find out anything in one afternoon?

Parker crossed and uncrossed his ankles impatiently, glancing around the high-end, upscale Miami office. Too bad the slightly stoop-shouldered, thin-haired investigator with the spot-on name of Ace Martin didn't have a chipped Formica desk with a green-shaded lamp. Then he'd be right out of central casting for a B movie called *Ace Martin: P.I.*

But Ace ran an elegant shop, complete with a good-looking receptionist and a few staff members dressed well enough to let Parker know Martin Securities was making a few bucks. Garrison, Inc. had been contributing to Ace's bank account for years.

But this job didn't fall under Garrison, Inc. Parker had asked Ace to investigate Anna Cross on the Q.T. And the urgent call from Ace that had come in at noon left Parker no doubt that something had been uncovered.

"Sorry to keep you waiting, Parker," Ace said as he ambled into the room, his hands full of files and paper. He dropped it all on his desk to give Parker a hearty handshake. "I'm glad you could come over. I didn't want to take all this into your office. Not with our culprit right there."

Parker's stomach dropped. "So you've got bad news on Anna, huh?"

Ace's expression tightened as he went around his desk to sit across from Parker. "I'm afraid so."

He almost swore. He didn't want Anna to be guilty. He wanted her to be… Hell, he just wanted her. And now, he'd never have her. "What have you got? How tight is the connection to Jefferies?"

"I have no idea. I couldn't find one."

Parker gave the other man a sharp look. "Then what's wrong?"

"What's wrong is that your AA has quite a history. Are you aware that you're not the first CEO she's worked for?"

He knew so little about her. Had he even seen her résumé when the director of HR had recommended her for the job as his assistant? Probably not.

"She's been at Garrison, Inc. for four years," he said, unable to deny the little hope and defensiveness in his voice.

"Before that she was the administrative assistant to a gentleman by the name of Barry Lynch, the president and

CEO of a midsize tech firm in Indiana called FiberTech. They make fiber optic cables and such."

A little wisp of jealousy twirled around him. Had Anna showered in Barry Lynch's private bath, too? "And?"

"And she was fired for spying."

This time, he couldn't repress the curse that bubbled up.

Ace agreed with a nod. "Seems she had a very personal and intimate relationship with—"

"Stop." Parker held his hand up, swallowing the sour taste that suddenly filled his mouth. "I don't need the details of how she slept with her boss."

"Not her boss," Ace said, turning a photocopy of a newspaper article around and sliding it across the desk to Parker. "Her boss's biggest rival. A venture capitalist named Michael Montgomery who sat on the board of a competitive company. She dated him for, oh, about a year. Very high-profile guy, wealthy and successful."

At least she was consistent. He glanced at the paper, his gaze darting over a black-and-white picture of Anna with shorter hair. The headline blared Local Secretary Steals Secrets.

"According to that article," Ace continued, "she used her access to spoon-feed highly confidential information to the competitor, which was a company where her boyfriend had about twenty percent of the stock."

Parker flinched as if he'd been punched. History sure did have a way of repeating itself. "What kind of information?"

"The usual. New product launch dates, marketing strategies and new R & D efforts. The implication from this reporter is that she was getting some financial kickbacks."

"Implication? Was anything proven?"

"Actually the charges were dropped by the Fiber-Tech CEO."

Hope curled its sticky fingers around his heart. "Then she wasn't guilty?"

Ace rolled his eyes. "She worked a deal, I'm sure. The boyfriend was kicked off the board of the competing company, and left town. She was fired and moved to Miami about two weeks later. You'll notice that her résumé on file with Garrison makes no mention of the job at FiberTech. And, Parker, if she wasn't guilty, why didn't they run a follow-up story?"

And, worse, why didn't she tell him? She had to know that if this came out, she'd be under suspicion. Why hadn't she told him—in London, the night they'd spent together, all this time they'd been working together?

Because she was doing the same thing again. It was her scam. Maybe being in the bathroom where he could get his first glimpse of her was all part of it, to get closer, to get better information during pillow talk.

His temples throbbed as he reached for the papers. Computer printouts detailed the information she'd given to the competitor. A few pictures of her at social events on the arm of a tall, jet-setting type.

"You can keep all that," Ace said, sliding it into a manila file folder. "Wish I had better news, Parker."

"Hey, we solved a very big problem for Garrison today." Parker took the folder, tapping all the papers together with a sharp rap as he stood. "But send me the bill."

"This one's on the house," Ace said. "Didn't take me but half an hour to get all this off the Internet. I'm surprised she even got the job in the first place at Garrison."

Parker's smile was strained. "She can be pretty charming."

Ace nodded knowingly. "It's obvious she charmed you."

"Is it?" He laughed lightly. "I hate to be transparent."

"Nah, it's my job to read people. If you didn't care about her, you wouldn't be so miserable to hear the truth. You'd just fire her and move on. Which, knowing you, is what you'll do. Business will always trump personal feelings for you, Parker. That's why your dad left you in charge."

Sort of left him in charge. Somehow, in the space of a few weeks, Parker's whole foundation had crumbled. He shook Ace's hand, and barely smiled at the pretty receptionist who called, "Goodbye," and waved pink-tipped fingers at him.

With the top down and music up, Parker cruised through the streets of South Miami and barely noticed the traffic on U.S. 1. In his mind's eye, all he could see was Anna, laughing. Anna, sighing. Anna, wet and wild and wanton in the shower.

Was that all an act to get information?

Something deep inside of him screamed *no*.

He recognized that voice. That was his gut calling, and he usually didn't ignore it. On an impulse, he whipped a left turn and instead of heading home to stew, he barreled the BMW toward Garrison, Inc. He had to know the truth. He *had* to.

If it was bad, he'd fire her and forget her, just as Ace Martin had predicted. But if she could possibly convince him that everything in that file was wrong...

He threw a quick glance at the manila folder on the passenger seat, held in place by his leather briefcase. Damning evidence, all of it. But it all rang untrue to him.

It all rang untrue to a blind man in...lust. Or, worse.

In record time, he parked and jogged to the elevator just as it arrived to take him directly to the twenty-second floor.

Sheila McKay's bright blue eyes widened as he yanked

the glass door open and stepped into Garrison, Inc. "Oh, Mr. Garrison, we didn't expect you back today."

All the more reason to show up. "Is Anna here?" he asked.

Sheila's heavily lined lips curled up. "You two ought to try calling each other. She keeps asking the same about you every time she flits in and out of here to copy files, all breathless like she's in such a big hurry. Guess she wants to get out of here early for your date. I made the reservations, by the way."

Parker's grasp tightened on the manila folder he held. Why was she copying files in a hurry? Why would she ask if he was coming back? The bad taste threatened to return to his mouth. He didn't respond to the receptionist's obvious ploy for gossip fodder, but headed straight through the arched doorway and down the hall toward Anna's desk.

He rounded the corner and froze. Her desk was empty and his door was closed. What was she doing in there?

Showering? God, he could only hope that was the worst of her employee infractions. Slowly, he walked to his office door. He turned the handle silently and opened the heavy cherrywood without making a single noise.

Her head bent over, her back to him, she clicked madly on his computer keys. There was no reason for her to be on his computer. None.

Soundlessly, he walked across the room, leaning a little to the right so he could see what was on the screen. She was so engrossed, she never even moved.

"Damn," she swore softly. "Why can't I find that password?"

All he could see was the Jefferies Group logo. Son of a bitch, that was enough.

"I changed the password."

With an audible gasp, she spun around, surprise and

shock widening her eyes, shame and horror darkening her cheeks.

"The new password is *liar.* That ought to be easy to remember, don't you think?"

"I'm not a liar," she said, forcing her chin up to meet his gaze.

He tossed a folder at her and a dozen papers fluttered around like feathers around her lap and the floor. "Omission counts as a lie, Anna."

She dragged her gaze from his burning brown eyes to the first piece of paper on the floor at her feet. Then she just closed her eyes, placed her hands on the armrest and dug her fingers into the leather. "Will you give me an opportunity to explain?"

"I wanted to," he said, hating that emotion made his voice catch. Steeling himself, he looked over her shoulder at the computer screen. "Until I saw that."

She opened her mouth, then snapped it shut as she stood, visibly shaken. "I knew this would happen. You won't even listen to me. That's why I haven't told you."

He just stared at her, his brain at war with a body that wanted all the papers to disappear and all the lies to dis-integrate.

"Do you believe everything you read?" she demanded.

"I believe you are a very cunning woman."

"Parker, please, I—" She reached her hands up, maybe in a helpless gesture, maybe to touch him, but he backed away before she burned him with so much as a fingertip.

He had no control where she was concerned. For some reason, she got to him. If she touched him or kissed him, the next thing he knew, he'd be listening to her. Believing her.

That couldn't be good for his business. That couldn't be good for him.

"I want you to leave," he said quietly.

Her eyes flashed. "You're firing me?"

"Just leave, Anna. And don't take a single thing with you."

The color that had deepened her cheeks drained, leaving nothing but pale, alabaster shock. "You're firing me." This time it wasn't a question.

"Yes."

"Before you give me a chance to even tell you my side."

"Your side," he said, "is the competition. Why don't you call Jordan or Emilio? Maybe they need an administrative assistant."

She drew back as if she'd been slapped, and guilt sucker punched his stomach, along with the sudden need to hold her and take back the words.

"I won't press charges," he said, stepping back to give her a wide berth. The words and the gesture felt foreign and wrong, but he forced himself to continue. "I'll have Sheila escort you."

She narrowed her eyes at him. "That won't be necessary. I know how to leave a building after I've been terminated."

I bet you do. Something inside him kept him from saying the sarcastic remark out loud.

She walked across the office, and he followed her, keeping the door open so he could see her desk. As she slid open her bottom drawer to get her handbag, he pulled out his cell phone, hit one number and Stephen answered on the first ring.

"Mystery solved," he said.

She pivoted and gave him a sharp, disbelieving look.

"Well done," Stephen said. "Let's celebrate."

He didn't feel very celebratory. "Sure. Meet me at Estate tonight."

Without another word, Anna strode down the hall, head held high, shoulders back, chin in the air. Not at all, Parker thought, the way a guilty woman would slink from the scene of the crime.

"You sure you nailed her?" Stephen said in his ear.

Hell, no. "Yeah."

"I knew you'd do it. I knew you'd make the right choice when it came to the company."

The right choice? This felt anything but *right*.

Ten

The water was as hot as her old Coral Gables plumbing could muster, but it still didn't wash away the sickening sensation of déjà vu.

Anna leaned her head back, lifted her face directly to the stinging spray and flattened her hands on the grouted tile wall.

Oh, yeah. Been here. Done this. Felt this agony.

Water spritzed into her parted lips, over her eyelids, down her cheeks. Not that there were tears to wash away, she thought bitterly. She hadn't even cried once and it was almost ten o'clock.

This time, she was just mad.

All she could see was Parker's torn and pained expression, and all she could feel was the impact of being on the wrong side of that one-of-a-kind focus.

She twisted the knobs and shut off the water, the pipes clanging with the sudden change in pressure. That was usually her final note to a song. But she had no song in her head or her heart. They were too full of regret and disgust.

"Now what?" she said to herself, climbing out of the shower and wrapping herself in a terry robe. "Let's see, Anna, last time you packed up and ran like a scared kitten. Where will you go this time?"

Her voice was bitter and sarcastic as she wiped steam from the mirror with a quick swipe of her sleeve, revealing her own ravaged expression, her lusterless gaze, her sad, sad pallor. She looked like the victim of circumstance she was.

Victim.

"That's a bad word, Anna Cross," she whispered to her reflection. "Very bad."

The thing that stunned her the most was that Parker Garrison had never made her feel that way. He wasn't like Michael Montgomery in that regard. He wasn't like…anybody.

But was he worth fighting for?

The mirror fogged up almost instantly and this time, she used her palm, noisily rubbing against the glass to get a clear shot of herself.

"It doesn't matter if he is or he isn't," she said to herself. "But you are, Anna Cross. *You* are worth fighting for."

The realization was so strong and sudden and clear, it nearly lifted her up on her toes. Why would she just let him win? He was dead wrong. He would figure that out as soon as the next corporate leak occurred.

And then what? He'd come skulking back for more shower sex? No. No. *No.*

But what could she do? Take him on? Deny? Slap him in the face until he listened to her?

Oh, she could waltz up to him at the nightclub where

he was tonight, knocking back drinks with his brother, high-fiving each other on their success in sniffing out the spy.

Yeah, she could march right up to the Great and Powerful Parker Garrison and tell him off. The idea was so absurd, it actually made her smile for the first time all day.

She wandered into her bedroom and headed for the closet, letting the little fantasy take flight. If she would do something like that—just *if*—what would she wear? She stared at the offerings. A gray business suit. A beige shapeless dress. A brown ensemble perfect for…

Hiding.

She'd been running and hiding for so long. Until Parker had seen underneath her gray-and-brown shields. Literally, at first. But then, she'd stopped hiding from him. And it had felt so damn good…until now.

With a soft grunt, she shoved a handful of hangers to the left. Again and again, she pushed her clothes as far to one side as she could squeeze them.

And then she saw the red gown she'd worn in London. She eased it over the rack, and behind that… Oh.

Her fingers closed over the straps of a pure white sheath that fit like a dream and moved as if it were part of her body. She lifted the hanger and smiled at the memory of how much she used to like to wear this sexy, splendid dress.

She held it up and turned to the full-length mirror on the inside of the closet door, taking a little breath when she saw the reflection.

No woman could hide in this dress. In fact, she would jump out and demand attention. Demand that someone listen to her.

A woman could make a point in this dress, she thought.

And when she was done making that point, a woman could make a man suffer just by walking away.

Lovingly, she laid the silky fabric on the bed and, like magic, a song started playing in her head.

Humming softly, she settled into the chair at her vanity, opened up a drawer full of makeup and creams and lined a few up.

She was done hiding and running and worrying and hoping no one knew who she was or what had happened to her. She was done having fantasies fill her brain. She was done letting powerful men make wrong assumptions and wreck her life and break her heart.

By the time she locked her front door and walked to the car, her stilettos were keeping perfect time to her favorite song from *West Side Story*.

Yep, she felt pretty. Pretty strong. Pretty brave. Pretty smart. Much too smart to make the same mistake twice.

The natives were getting restless at Estate and it was only midnight. The DJ had pumped up the beat; the beautiful people were blissed out on strategically situated sofas; the curved, high-tech bars at every corner were three deep with drinkers of pastel-colored martinis and straight shots of dark amber courage. Adam's state-of-the-art mood lighting shifted almost imperceptibly from pink to blue to white and red, washing the Venetian glass mirrors and crystal chandeliers in unearthly colors.

Parker leaned into the cushiony leather of a corner alcove tucked into a towering keystone arch, the Lucite table between him and Stephen empty but for two beers and one PDA/cell phone combination.

The cell phone that didn't ring. Instead, its very presence just teased Parker with the temptation to make just one call. So far, he managed to ignore that temptation.

From where they sat, Parker had a clear shot of most of the lounge and a few of the six different bars, as well as the sweeping staircase that led to this, the lowest and most private level in the forty-thousand-square-foot club.

"You haven't said five words since we got here." Stephen nudged his brother's beer glass with his. "You gotta get over it, man."

Parker swallowed, his gaze moving across the slithering, achingly hip crowd, the heavy mix of perfume and booze and lingering incense as thick as the desperation to look cool.

"I'm over her," he assured his brother, taking a swig of whatever exotic ale Adam had sent to their table. "Trust me, I am so over her."

Stephen laughed. "Actually, I said get over *it*. Not *her*."

"She is it," Parker said softly. "I mean, she is the problem," he added quickly. "Now I have to hire a new AA, I have to figure out what information she leaked, I have to—"

"Lick your wounds."

"I'm not wounded," he insisted. Not much, anyway.

Stephen reached for the PDA. "Come on. Call that model. What was her name?"

"Yvette. Yvonne. I don't remember."

"It'll be in here." Stephen pressed a button and Parker yanked the device from his hands.

"Chill out. I don't want to call her."

"What about that cute little redhead who did the brochure? Weren't you going to ask her out?"

Parker glared at his brother. "Do you actually think I'm going to pick up my phone and hit on another woman right now?"

"Okay, forget the phone." Stephen cocked his head

toward one of the bars. "The brunette in the ass-hugging black skirt has been telegraphing interest since we sat down."

Parker didn't look. "No, thanks."

"Aah, man."

"What? What are you ah-manning about?"

"Come on, Parker. You were with Anna once? Twice? It's not like it mattered. She screwed you, in bed and out of it."

Parker clenched his fist, then relaxed it. He'd be saying the same thing to Stephen if the situation were reversed. "I've known her for three months, Stephen. We built a rapport working together. The sex was just…just…"

"Just sex."

"Not even close." Parker looked out at the sea of people, at the few new ones who ventured down the long red-carpeted staircase. "It was more than that."

"I see," Stephen said.

"No, you don't."

"Actually, I do."

The wry tone in Stephen's voice took Parker by surprise. "What do you mean?"

"I mean…" Stephen lifted his beer, but didn't drink. "The one that got away. It sucks. Big-time."

Parker inched back, looking at his brother in a new light. "Is this the voice of experience?"

Stephen took a drink, his own gaze shifting away, his lack of a response speaking volumes. "Whoa, look at *that*."

"I just told you, Stephen," Parker said, fiddling with his PDA. "I'm not interested."

"You'll be interested in this."

He pressed the button, giving voice to the thought that had been reverberating in his brain for the last two hours. "I think I should call Anna."

"No need," Stephen said.

"Just to see if, you know..." He'd been pretty rough on her. "She's okay."

"Oh, she's fine. Trust me."

"I think I'll call her." He punched in her home number.

"You won't get an answer," Stephen said.

Parker put the phone to his ear. "How do you know that?"

"Because unless I'm mistaken, that vision in white is Anna Cross."

Parker jerked around, his attention drawn like a magnet to the stairs. His jaw unhinged. His eyes widened. His breath caught.

And his heart damn near stopped. "Anna?" he managed to whisper.

Just then, she turned, and the impact of her beautifully made-up face and the intensity of her jade-green gaze slammed his heart back into action. Dark hair cascaded over her bare shoulders, stark against the creamy-white dress. A dress that fit like snakeskin and ended midthigh, showing off those stupefyingly perfect legs.

The PDA hit the Lucite with a clunk and Stephen leaned back and laughed. "This actually might be fun to watch."

"You don't need to be here, Stephen," Parker said with clenched teeth.

"Hey," Stephen said. "She's the enemy. You need backup."

"I don't need anything." Except *that*.

She strode like a white cat, her tilted eyes locked on him, her expression leaving no doubt that her arrival at Estate was no coincidence. The woman was on a mission.

The crowd parted to let her through and Parker's gut grew tighter with each long step she took, fire whipping through his body as he watched her. Along with every single man in the club.

She stopped as she reached the alcove of their table, no smile even threatening. Parker couldn't help it. His gaze dropped and lingered over every curve and cut of her body.

Hitching one hand on her hip, she jutted her chin as though she knew exactly how incredible she looked.

"What are you doing here?" Stephen asked. "Spying?"

"Stephen," Parker said, his attention still on Anna. "I'll handle this."

"No," she said, her voice low. "*I'll* handle this." She placed her fingertips on the table, and leaned just enough to draw his eyes back to the low neckline of her dress and the rise of her breasts.

She wasn't wearing a bra.

His throat went dry and he cleared it, forcing himself to pin her with a glare that would leave no doubt who had more power in this situation. Even if she was towering over him in her high heels, and he was...

Hard as the Lucite table that separated them.

Damn her.

"Mr. Garrison." She almost spat the name. "We haven't finished our conversation."

Stephen started to say something, but Parker held up his hand. "Let her finish or leave us alone."

Stephen didn't move, and Anna drew in a slow, steady breath and stared at Parker. "I am not the corporate spy you are looking for. I don't care whether you believe me or not, because the fact that I am telling the truth will be clear soon enough. Whoever it is—I was trying to find out when you snuck up on me today—"

"I didn't—"

She silenced him with tapered eyes. "Whoever it is," she continued, "will spy again and then you will realize you made a mistake."

"I'm willing to take that chance."

"I'm sure you are. But that's not why I'm here."

His control slipped a little, along with his gaze. "Then why are you here?" To prove she could reduce him to a desperate, sex-starved, lovesick teenager? It was working.

"To tell you that four years ago I was used by a man very much like you. My lover."

The word almost choked him.

"He oozed power and control and authority over everyone."

At that moment, Parker didn't feel very powerful, controlling or authoritative. He was simply mesmerized by the cool, confident woman in front of him.

"I had something he wanted and he took it from me."

"What was that?" he asked.

She smiled. "My password. He stole it, accessed my company's computers and left a trail that led directly and exclusively to me. When I was accused of the crime, he didn't come to my defense. When the newspapers covered the story, he didn't refute it. When I was terminated from my job, he didn't support me. But when the truth came out, as it always does, I was exonerated."

"Why doesn't my private investigator know that?"

"Because the charges were quietly dropped, and the story was no longer interesting and the damage was done, so I ran away without ever forcing the issue or demanding my name be cleared. I was scared and I ran."

"And got a job under false pretenses," he said, trying hard to make his voice sound stern but being totally betrayed by the overload of Anna on his senses.

"Where I spent the next four years as a stellar employee," she snapped back. "But then I made a huge mistake."

"Other than breaking into my computer?"

"I trusted you. I thought that a real heart beat in that steel case of yours. I thought that a real man lived in that chiseled body. I thought that when you were pushed against the wall, you might, you just might, put something and someone before your precious, almighty, profitable company."

He tried to swallow, but couldn't.

"You thought wrong," he said, hating the words the minute they were out. But what choice did he have? In front of his brother and half of Miami, he could hardly stand up, throw his arms around her and tell her she was *right*.

Even though that was exactly what he wanted to do.

She stood ramrod straight and crossed her arms, which made her seem more powerful and in control. And, God help him, sexy. "At my next job, I won't hide who I am, what I've done or where I've been. Because I have nothing to hide. Nothing to be ashamed of. Nothing. But you?" She arched an eyebrow and managed to deliver a boatload of sympathy, pity and disdain with that one muscle move. "That's a different story. Goodbye, Mr. Garrison."

She turned on one ice pick of a heel and walked straight ahead, her body swaying to the rhythm of Parker's thudding heart.

Next to him, Stephen took a long drink. "Think she's lying?"

The PDA buzzed a soft digital tone. Without taking his eyes from the white second skin that moved up the stairs, Parker answered it.

"Yes?"

"Mr. Garrison, my name in Barry Lynch. I'm the CEO of FiberTech in Indianapolis, Indiana."

Parker frowned at Stephen as he processed what he heard. "Go ahead," he said into the phone.

"I was contacted by a private investigator today and if I don't talk to you, I don't think I'm going to sleep tonight."

"What is it?"

He leaned back, closed his eyes and listened as the man talked. When he was finished, Parker clicked off and set the device down.

"No," he said to his brother. "She's not lying. And I just lost the best woman I ever had." He dropped his head into his hands and swore softly.

"Told you it sucks."

Parker lifted his head and looked at his brother. "I don't want to lose her."

Stephen shrugged. "You have to grovel. Apologize. Spend money. Or, embrace celibacy."

"I'm serious. I have to…" *Tell her what she means to me.* "I have to do something."

"I recognize that you are a man of action, Parker," Stephen said. "But I hate to tell you. You can do all that and more and I have a sneaking suspicion that woman is never going to talk to you again."

Parker scooped up the PDA and pushed himself off the cushy leather, already forming a plan, already anxious. "How do you know?"

"Voice of experience."

Eleven

Anna let herself into the dark, silent office without making a noise, her whole body still humming from the confrontation with Parker.

Not that the scene in Estate truly qualified as a *confrontation*. That implied that there were two sides in a discussion. She pretty much owned that round.

Smiling smugly, she turned off the office alarm and kicked off the sky-high heels that had been torturing her toes. They'd done their night's work. He'd all but drooled on his precious electronic gadget.

She glanced at Sheila's perfectly neat desk, half tempted to leave her a note. She hadn't explained this afternoon when she'd left and no doubt Sheila had gossiped about the boss's assistant-turned-girlfriend's sudden departure to everyone from Mario in the mail room on up.

No, it didn't matter. They weren't really friends and gossip couldn't hurt her anymore. She padded down the carpeted hall in bare feet, the silk of her dress cool on her skin. Running her hands through her hair, she practically skipped.

That had felt so good! And the look on his face—the absolute lust and pain and misery in his deep brown eyes— that had felt good, too. Hadn't it?

She paused as she reached her desk, considering that.

She hadn't really intended to hurt him. He was Parker Garrison, after all, and basically invincible. She just wanted the truth out. She hadn't expected that it would twist her heart to see him again, and shoot that fire through her whole body when he'd taken in her drop-dead white dress and had looked as if he might, well, drop dead.

With a soft sigh, she folded into her chair and opened the top drawer. She had personal items, pictures of her family in Indiana, some inexpensive jewelry, a few hair clips.

A suspense novel she'd been reading on her lunch hour and some personal files were in the bottom drawer. She scanned the area for a box or bag that she could put it all in, but didn't see anything. Maybe in the executive kitchen.

In the galley-shaped kitchen, she hit the overhead light and spied a small plastic container Mario used for mail. She picked it up, hit the light switch with her elbow and turned the corner to her desk.

And froze dead in her tracks at the sight of Parker Garrison leaning on her desk, dangling her sandals from one finger.

"You dropped something, Cinderella."

"They hurt."

"Yeah," he agreed. "They killed me."

She refused to react to the compliment. "Shower's in the back, Parker. Left knob's cold. I'm just getting my personal belongings. You're more than welcome to check everything I take out of here or call security to escort me. I'm not doing anything illegal, untoward or improper."

"The way you look in that dress could qualify for all three."

"Stop." She approached the desk, holding her breath that he would move so she could finish her task. "It won't work."

He reached out for her hand, but she jerked out of his touch.

"Anna. I'm sorry."

Her breath rushed out and she cursed herself for it. "It's too late, Parker."

"I mean it," he said. "I'm sorry."

"And I'm sure that pains you to say," she volleyed back. "But if you want forgiveness, you're not going to get it."

"Will you stay?"

She choked a laugh. "No."

"Will you stay at the company?"

"No."

"Will you stay in Miami?"

"No."

This time he sighed, the sad sound echoing in the quiet office.

"Could you move so I could get to my...the desk? I want to finish and get out of here."

"If you stayed, we'd have a chance."

"A chance at what? At what, Parker? Hot sex and...more hot sex?"

His lips curled in a smile. "You make it sound so bad."

She tapped his arm to get him out of the way. Big mistake. In a flash, his large hand covered her arm and held tight. "Anna, please."

She closed her eyes. "Okay, fine. You're forgiven. Now move. I want to get out of here."

"I don't believe you."

"That's a problem we seem to have."

He eased her closer, close enough to smell the warm, spicy scent of aftershave. Close enough to see the individual whiskers of his beard growth and imagine the feel of it on her cheeks. Way, way too close.

"Anna, we can fix it. I made a mistake. I assumed the worst."

"Yes, I know." She nibbled at her lip, studying her desk instead of giving in to the temptation to look into his eyes. If she did, she'd be dead. He'd lean forward. He'd kiss her. She'd open her mouth and her heart and… "That's what really hurt me. You assumed the worst."

He slid his hand up her arm. "Anna, honey, I'm so sorry. I'm going to make it up to you." He dipped his head closer, his lips brushing her hair.

"No," she whispered. "You can't."

He pressed his mouth to her hair, her forehead, and tipped her chin up with one sure finger. "I can."

He could. Of course he could. He could have her in an instant because she was weak for him, weak down to the bone marrow.

As if he knew that, he moved in slow, confident motion, lowering his head, closing his eyes and then covering her mouth with an easy kiss of ownership. Instantly, every nerve ending sang. Her heart kicked against her ribs, a breath jammed in her chest, her arms went numb, her brain went black.

She opened her mouth as he slanted over hers, took his tongue and let him flatten her whole body against him, pinning her between him and the desk, growing harder and bigger against her.

His mouth was warm, tasting of mint and the distant

flavor of some foreign ale. Powerful, capable hands roamed her back and hips, pulling her into him. From deep in her chest, she heard her own voice moan his name softly. Liquid fire licked through her stomach, whipping down her veins, tightening and burning and aching for release.

While one of his hands gripped her backside, the other closed over her breast, her nipple instantly pebbling against the silk and the pressure.

His erection pulsed against her and all she could do was move into it, each arch of her body sending wicked, wild sparks down her spine and into her belly and between her legs.

He's your boss. He's your enemy.

He was Parker and she wanted him more than any man she'd ever met.

His fingers closed over the hem of her skirt, pulling it up over her thighs, higher and higher.

"Let me show you, Anna," he whispered into their kiss. "Let me."

She knew what he wanted and she wanted it, too. Her legs trembled as his fingers inched closer to the apex, closer to where she was already moist and ripe and ready.

She absolutely couldn't say no to him. But she had to. She had to.

He backed away at the first pressure of her hands on his shoulders. Slowly, as if he might hurt her if he moved too fast, he stood, giving her space with his body but holding her firm with his gaze. "Come home with me, Anna. We'll talk."

She almost laughed. "We will not talk. We'll...do this."

"Then we'll talk. Please, sweetheart. Please."

Sanity dripped back into her veins, slowly replacing the bubbling heat of desire. Was this what she wanted? Or was she just acting out another fantasy?

"You can't show someone how sorry you are with sex, Parker."

He closed his eyes. "I'm not just saying I'm sorry. I'm saying I...I...care for you, Anna. I—"

"Stop." God knows what he'd say to continue the sex at that point. "Don't go there, Parker. Don't make a mockery of love."

"I'm not—"

"Because I have practically loved you for three months—more. When I get weak and crazy at your touch it's not because you're so incredibly hot that I can't think— well, you are, but that's beside the point. It's because I've watched you, admired you, respected you for the whole time I worked for you."

"Anna, I—"

She held her hands up. "You didn't even know I existed until you found me undressed in your bathroom. And the minute you did, the next thing I knew it was London, champagne and foreplay. As soon as you suspected I was your spy, everything after that was a game to find out more."

"Actually, it wasn't."

"Actually, it was. And that's fine, Parker. But now that you know you're wrong, you can't just kiss me back into your bed until you get bored with me. No." She shook her head, her heart finally slowing to a normal beat, her brain and body finally composed.

"What could I do to prove you wrong, Anna?"

She thought about that, a pinch of a frown forming. "I can't even imagine. But I'm going home now. Alone." She reached for her package, but he took her arm.

"Anna, don't do this to us."

She stabbed two fingers into the straps of the sandals

he'd dropped on her desk and held them aloft. "There is no us, Parker."

And for the second time in one day, she squared her shoulders, raised her chin and walked away from the man she loved.

Only this time, she broke down and cried the minute she got in the elevator.

Parker stood next to Anna's desk for a long time, willing himself back to a state where he could think. His body didn't want to cooperate. It wanted to tear after that woman; promise the sun, moon and stars and then deliver. It wanted to throw her on the nearest flat surface and make love to her until she couldn't think about all the things he wished he could take back. He wanted to...

It didn't matter what his body wanted. Or his head.

For once, he had to think with his heart. Because if he couldn't do that for Anna Cross, the only woman he'd ever met whom he could really love, then he couldn't do it at all.

What could he possibly do to prove how he felt? He'd offered her the job back, he'd groveled apologies, he'd shown her how he felt.

There had been no ambivalence in her goodbye. That was it. He lost. He lost control. He lost focus. He lost...Anna.

With the thought squeezing his heart, he walked toward his office, unlocked it and stepped into the darkness. Moonlight streamed through the opened window, casting a white sheen all over the papers that he'd tossed in Anna's face, along with the bitter—and wrong—accusations. He bent and picked up the copy of the newspaper article, reading it, slowly.

It was all there. Allegations, accusations, implications.

No proof. Why hadn't he seen that? And why hadn't her boss set the record straight?

His gaze moved to the reporter's name, and the name of the newspaper. *The Indianapolis Star.* He pulled out his PDA and clicked on Barry Lynch's number. Parker wasn't going to sleep until he'd cleared Anna Cross's name. She might never give him another chance, but it was the only way he could think of to prove to her that he…

He did. He loved her.

What a time to figure that out.

Brown, beige, gray, tweed and taupe. It all went in one trunk to be shipped back to Indiana. Standing in her room, ankle deep in clothes, books, linens, shoes and a whole bunch of stuff she had somehow managed to squeeze into that tiny closet, Anna surveyed her little world and mentally calculated how long it would take to pack this up.

She had until the end of the month, but each day in the cheery little house in Coral Gables just made her less…cheery.

The doorbell rang and like a fool her hand hit her chest with the thought of Parker.

But she forced it away. He wouldn't show up at her house at nine-thirty in the morning, or the night or ever. She'd walked away and after a few days she'd stopped hoping he'd follow her. He'd abided by her decision. By now, he was probably halfway through his little electronic black book.

Still, she glanced in the mirror at the ponytailed, makeup-free image of a woman packing to move. Whoever it was, they'd see her like this. She wrenched the door open and burst into a squeal.

"Megan!"

"You quit your job?"

Anna drew back to let her friend in. "The decision was mutual. What are you doing here?"

Megan tossed her handbag onto a table. "I'm here to sign the contract and take the job. I called your office and some throaty thing named Sheila said you were no longer with the company, but if I needed Mr. Garrison, she would be happy to put me through." Megan did a dead-on imitation of Sheila and rolled her eyes.

Anna didn't even want to think about Sheila, or anyone, taking her place.

"I'm taking your 'run, don't walk' advice," Anna said, pulling Megan farther into the house. "And you're really taking the job?"

"I am." She glanced around at the boxes and empty shelves. "And where are you going?"

"Indiana."

"Oh, Anna. Why?" Megan dropped onto the sofa.

"I have to, Megan. I want to go up there and clear my name. I'm going to find my old boss, and hound the newspapers and force the truth to be told. I don't feel like I can do that from here."

Megan nodded. "I guess it's about time you did that. But, jeez, we're like ships passing in the night."

"I know," Anna agreed. "I can't believe I've been here four years and you're coming and I'm leaving."

Megan held up a hand. "Can you tell me exactly what happened to bring this on?"

"Remember the plan to find the culprit and win the CEO's undying affection and true love?"

"I didn't know we'd thrown true love into the mix, but, yeah. I remember the plan."

"It backfired."

"Oh." Megan looked truly sympathetic. "Make me coffee and tell me everything."

Anna did, and Megan listened from a seat at the kitchen table, asking a few insightful questions, but mostly letting Anna spew the whole painful story. Most of it, anyway. Some things just couldn't be shared. Shower encounters, for one.

"Wow, that was gutsy. Especially the showdown at the club. Too bad you didn't have any witnesses."

"Oh, I did," Anna said as she poured the coffee at the counter. "Stephen Garrison was right there and heard the whole thing."

When Megan didn't answer, Anna turned to see Megan fussing with the flower arrangement, gnawing her lip. "That must have been awkward," she finally said.

Anna put the mugs on the table and took a seat. "No, actually, it was great. But, later, in the office. That was…"

"Not so great?"

"That was the hardest thing I've ever done," Anna admitted. "I walked away from him and, God, Megan, I didn't want to. But I did what I had to do and I feel like a stronger woman because of it."

"Oh, God, I know that feeling."

Anna held her cup to her mouth, studying her friend over the rim. "You do?"

Megan pushed her chair back and suddenly looked around. "This place has real potential, you know. Have you ever thought of those beautiful white plantation shutters for those windows?"

"No, but I just had a brilliant idea," Anna said. "Why don't you move in here? You could take over the lease for me and I think the owner would consider lease to buy, but I never could afford that. This place would be perfect for you and Jade."

Megan's face lit up as the possibility took hold. "It would be. Especially with that fenced-in yard. She could get that puppy I've been promising her."

"I'll be out of here in a few days. We could just switch the lease over now. How long are you going to be in town?"

"Just today. I promised Jade I'd be back by tonight." Megan peered at the clock on the oven. "I just stopped by because I had a rental car and an hour to kill before I meet with my new partners." She grinned. "I like the sound of that."

"I bet you do," Anna agreed. "You'll be a fantastic partner. I see great things in your future."

They talked for a few more minutes, discussing how to switch the lease into Megan's name.

"Are you absolutely sure, Anna?" Megan asked. "You don't think you might change your mind and stay? You've made your point with Parker. Sometimes running isn't the best thing to do."

"I'm not running," Anna said. "I'm going up to straighten things out. I have to try and clear my name." She stood, hating the little lump in her throat that she got every time she thought about leaving. "But I might come back," she added. "You did."

Megan nodded and stood. "I'd better run to my new office. I'll call you later," she promised.

As they walked out to the driveway, both of them shielded their eyes against the blinding summer sunshine.

"Leave your winter coats at home," Anna said as they rounded the rental car. "In fact, leave them for me. I don't think I have any left."

They shared a warm embrace before Megan climbed in the car. "I wish you'd change your mind. I sure could use some friends down here," she said.

"You'll make friends so fast, Meg," Anna assured her. "Right now, I have to go back and do whatever I can to clear my name. I guess that means going up to Indiana to face my demons."

Megan hesitated before she pulled the door closed. "You know, Anna, if you really want to face your demons, maybe you ought to figure out where they are. I did."

She closed the door before Anna could ask what she meant. There was a clue there, Anna felt certain, but some things friends just didn't ask.

As Megan pulled out of the driveway, Anna waved once, then lifted her face directly toward the sun. She'd gotten so used to the warmth of Florida, the subtle changes that actually heralded seasons, even the constant humidity sort of felt like…home, now. Sure, her parents were still in Indiana, and that would always be her roots.

But she was a Miami girl now. On a sigh, she headed up the driveway and her foot bumped into something, making her stumble.

She looked down, surprised to see the newspaper that Megan must have just driven over. Frowning, she reached for it, certain she'd already brought the *Miami Herald* in a few hours ago.

As she unfolded it, she just stared at the words across the top. *The Indianapolis Star?*

Megan must have dropped it when she'd gotten out of the car. She must have had it with her on the plane. Anna skimmed the headlines, instantly transported back to her hometown.

The last time she'd read this newspaper, she'd been on the front page of the business section. She'd never picked up another copy, out of spite. She flipped the main section, passed Sports, and then stared at the word *Business* across the top, remembering the burn of humiliation and the physical pain the day that her picture had been right there in the left-hand column.

She froze and blinked. Was the sun playing tricks on her eyes? Because there it was…the same grainy picture. Was someone torturing her by giving her a copy of this paper?

Almost afraid, she let her gaze move to the headline, expecting time to stand still. Expecting to see the headline that ruined her life.

Local Businessman Reopens Corporate Espionage Case.

"Oh, my God," she whispered, clutching the newspaper tighter as she scanned the page for the date. Today's date.

Blood rushed in her head and her hands shook as she let herself read the words.

FiberTech CEO issued a statement yesterday…wrong party accused in five-year-old allegations…former venture capitalist charged with fraud and unlawful computer access…industrial espionage case that mistakenly focused on administrative assistant Anna Cross…Barry Lynch includes formal apology to former assistant…

She stood for a long time, letting the words and the realization melt her hardened heart while the south Florida sun warmed her whole body.

Parker. Parker had done this for her.

At the sound of a car door, she lowered the paper and slowly turned around.

Parker leaned against his convertible, his eyes hidden behind dark glasses, no smile on his handsome, chiseled face.

"I e-mailed them an updated picture," he said. "But they opted to go with what they had on file."

She opened her mouth to speak, but nothing came out.

He levered himself from the car and slid his sunglasses off, dropping them into his pocket. He wore a pale blue T-shirt, khaki shorts and light Top-Siders, like a Ralph Lauren model who'd just stepped off the golf course, his hair a little windblown, his face tan.

He was the most gorgeous thing she'd ever seen.

He took a few steps closer, a slow smile deepening, his beautiful clefted chin just a shadow in the sunlight.

"Barry Lynch asked me to deliver this to you." He reached toward her, holding an envelope.

Holding the newspaper with one hand, she took the envelope with the other. He'd talked to Barry Lynch. Her worst nightmare had taken place. And it had turned into a dream come true.

"It's his formal apology and a copy of the civil suit he's filed against Michael Montgomery," Parker told her. "They had a helluva time hunting that guy down."

She honestly didn't know what to say. "Oh. Parker."

He grazed her cheek with his knuckle. "That's Mr. Garrison to you."

"You did this." She held up the newspaper in one hand, the letter in the other. "You did all of this?"

"I had help. I have a good P.I. named Ace, of all things," he said with a smile. "And Lynch found me first. And—"

"But you made this happen."

He tilted his head in a gesture of acknowledgment and self-deprecation. "I did what any man would do for the woman…he…"

Her heart triple timed, then thudded to a near stop. He *what?*

But he didn't finish the sentence.

"Thank you," she said softly.

He reached toward her again, sliding his hand around

her neck and playfully giving her ponytail a tug. "I miss you, Anna."

That was what he meant. The woman he *misses*.

She closed her hand over his forearm. "I'm sure you're...busy at work."

He laughed softly, tunneling his fingers into the hair at her nape. "That's not why I miss you. Can I come in?"

"Of course...not."

"No?"

"If you come in, then..." She'd be in the shower, on the bed or on the floor in six minutes. Five. "I'll never get done packing."

His face fell. "Where are you going?"

"Indiana." She glanced down at the newspaper. Everything she'd wanted to do in Indiana was done. She looked up at him. "At least, I was going to Indiana. Now it doesn't seem I have to."

He practically exhaled with relief. "Of course not. You can stay."

"Parker," she said softly, almost laughing at his bone-deep belief that he could control everything. "You can't make all the decisions for the world or for me."

"No, I can't," he agreed. "But I need you here, Anna. I still have a corporate spy on the loose, a company in flux and a family in turmoil. I can't fix all those problems without you at my side, Anna."

At his side. As his administrative assistant. His lover, for a while, at least. And then what? She gave her head a definitive shake. "You'll find someone to help you. Sheila's already stepped in."

"I don't mean I want you at my side in the office, Anna."

His voice was so low and serious it sent a million chills down her back.

"You mean you want me in your bed," she said defiantly. "Don't you?"

"I mean I want you in my *life*. In my home. In my bed. In my heart. In my family. In my life." He pulled her closer, tilting her face toward his. "I love you, Anna. I don't want you just to work for Garrison, I want you to *be* a Garrison."

A spark of white-hot delight and disbelief popped in her heart. She blinked into the sun, into his deep brown eyes. "What?"

"Anna, you've changed me. You make me understand that not having control is fine. It's good. You make me believe that there is something far more important than business.... It's love. Anna, I love you. You're smart and sexy and kind and spirited and every bit as strong as I am. I want you to share my life and my name and even my whole, colorful family." He held her firmly, bringing her close to his chest and face to melt her with the fierceness of his focus and sincerity. "I want to marry you. I want to spend the rest of my life with you."

"Parker." His name on her lips was barely a whisper; her breath was so tight and her heart was pounding so hard she thought her chest would burst. "I've been in love with you for so long that I...I just don't know what to say."

"Start with *yes*."

"Yes."

"*I love you* is good. Try saying that."

She smiled. "I love you."

"Now tell me you'll marry me."

"I'll marry you."

"See?" He teased her closer with a flutter kiss. "That wasn't so hard."

"Parker," she repeated. "Let me do this on my own."

With a soft exhale, she slid her arms tighter around his neck and looked right into his eyes.

"Yes, I love you," she said. "And, yes, I want to marry you." She kissed him, slowly and softly at first, then he deepened their connection, lifted her off the ground and suddenly twirled her so fast, the newspaper fluttered all over the driveway.

"Don't leave me again, Anna," he crooned softly. "Don't go back to Indiana. You can pack, but I want you to move in with me. And we'll get married right away. A month, no more."

Joy spread through her whole being and she just clung to his powerful shoulders, warmed by the sun and so much love. "Parker, I can't believe this."

"Believe this." He squeezed her. "Believe me."

"I believe you," she assured him. "I just can't believe that I—I'm going to spend my whole life with you. I feel like I could just…oh." She couldn't grab hold of the right words, so she just tightened her grip on his arms. "I love you so much it hurts."

He laughed and kissed her. "It shouldn't ever hurt again, Anna. Now let's go inside, sweetheart. It's really hot out here."

"Okay," she agreed and then gave him a sly smile. "You still haven't seen my bedroom."

"I thought we'd start with the shower."

"Perfect." She beamed up at him. "Because I feel like singing."

"Oh, *nooooo.*"

Laughing, she took him into her house to start making the music they both knew would last a lifetime.

* * * * *

SEDUCED BY THE WEALTHY PLAYBOY

BY
SARA ORWIG

Dear Reader,

In spite of ambition, deception and family loyalties, the power of true love can triumph over everything else. This is a story of such a love that grows between a man and a woman. On an August night in Miami, when Emilio Jefferies walks into Brittany Garrison's life, he changes it forever, as well as his own. A partnership binds the two together. Brittany, one of the youngest Garrisons, falls in love with the handsome playboy whose destiny becomes linked with hers and passion burns hotly between them.

Obstacles to Brittany and Emilio's happiness abound as an agreement is forged based on lies, driven by ruthless ambition and almost destroyed by family feuds. Even the powerful Garrison dynasty becomes a barrier to them. In spite of this, the love, respect and friendship that builds between Emilio and Brittany is strong enough to triumph over the pitfalls and the disasters that threaten to destroy them. This story is a reaffirmation of love's strength to conquer all.

Please enjoy,

Sara Orwig

Sara Orwig lives in Oklahoma. She has a patient husband, who will take her on research trips anywhere from big cities to old forts. She is an avid collector of Western history books. Sara has a master's degree in English, and has written historical romance, mainstream fiction and contemporary romance. Books are beloved treasures that take Sara to magical worlds, and she loves both reading and writing them.

A very special thanks to Jana Amsler,
owner of Salbute, in Hinsdale, Illinois.

Also, many thanks to Melissa Jeglinski, Demetria
Lucas, Roxanne St Claire, Anna DePalo, Brenda
Jackson, Emilie Rose, Catherine Mann—
you've been great to work with!

One

Brittany Garrison's life had catapulted into disaster. As she stared at the books spread in front of her, she broke out in perspiration even though she was chilled to the bone.

"Now I know why my accountant disappeared," she whispered. If only she had known about Paine Elsdon's embezzlement of two million dollars before his mysterious disappearance, it might have been possible to catch him.

"There's no escaping the truth," Boyd Dumont remarked. "The money could have been deposited into an account in the Bahamas or Switzerland. Your former accountant and your money are long gone from South Beach Miami."

She barely heard what her new accountant said. Seated at a table in his quiet office, Brittany couldn't stop thinking about her family. Last month, she'd overheard her oldest brother Parker's clear intentions to take her upscale restaurant away from her when she failed. Her brother Stephen was just as bad.

Stephen's remarks that she wasn't competent in business drummed in her ears with each heartbeat. Brittany Beach was a growing success. The numbers were there in black-and-white.

"Paine must have been embezzling funds from the start," she said, unaware she spoke aloud. "I trusted him because he came with excellent references."

"This could be the first time," Boyd speculated. "Maybe he got into a pinch and took a little, just to borrow it. Once he crossed that line, he kept on." Boyd shrugged his narrow shoulders as the light glinted on his glasses. "I suspect you won't find him."

"How did he get away with this?" she asked, stunned by the deception of someone she trusted. "The books looked fine."

"Your accountant doctored the books. My guess is, he may have had two sets of books. One for you and another one that he kept."

Her fingers drifted lightly over the cleft in her chin that marked every Garrison sibling. "Let me figure out what to do before there's any publicity," she said, thinking it wasn't public awareness she wanted to avoid, but the knowledge of her family. "We'll notify the law, of course."

"Certainly. But you can't wait long before you have to make payroll, buy supplies and meet the endless expenses of a restaurant."

As if she could wipe away her pounding headache, Brittany rubbed her temples. She should be worrying about how to manage so much debt. Instead, all she could think of was family humiliation. They viewed her, the baby of the family, as incompetent. Even Brooke, her twin sister, regarded her as inept. Now, if she didn't do something quickly, she was going to prove them right.

"Temporarily, other than the authorities, I don't want this embezzlement to go beyond this room."

Boyd nodded his bald head. "My work with all my clients is confidential. But I believe you told me that some of your staff discussed your accountant's mysterious disappearance. Even if you don't hear them, there will be rumors and speculation."

Realizing Boyd was right, she drew a deep breath. "Word travels in the restaurant industry like wildfire," she remarked, pondering her dilemma. "There has to be something I can do," she said, wondering how she could get the capital necessary to keep afloat.

"Brittany, if I may say so, your brothers can bail you out. Even with this immense debt you're in, they're quite well fixed."

"That's what I'm worrying about," she admitted, biting her lower lip. "I want to solve this problem myself."

Boyd sat in a vinyl chair at the head of the table. "That's a noble ambition, but you're going to have to be practical. They'll wonder why you didn't come to them. And it would cost you the least."

"No," she said emphatically, shaking her head. If Parker learned about the embezzlement, Brittany Beach would be gone as if taken by hurricane winds. Parker was a control freak who oversaw all the Garrison holdings. He already wanted her restaurant because the family retained the land, which was one of the last prime pieces of oceanfront property zoned for condos. She knew Parker envisioned condos that would bring in more money than her restaurant.

She rubbed her chin. "Go through this again with me. It's impossible to accept." An hour later, she left his office in a daze.

A week later, Brittany stood in the art deco dining room of Brittany Beach while she talked to her director of services, Hector Garland. The disaster that had come into her life nagged her and she couldn't keep her mind on Hector's conversation. Lost in her own thoughts, she looked around.

From the appearance of the restaurant, no one would guess there was the slightest problem. The cobalt ceiling with soft lights was a contrast to dusky pink walls. Candlelight flickered and bouquets of flowers graced the room. Eating areas, where patrons could lounge while they ate, were cushioned in Haitian white cotton. Cocktail waitresses moved around in colorful halter tops and low-slung sarongs. Outside the main dining room was a partially covered veranda, and beyond the white-washed planks were white cabana tents on the beach. Each tent contained sofas for lounging and eating.

How could such an inviting place be a quicksand of catastrophe for her? Brittany couldn't stop wondering about what she was going to do to save the restaurant and herself.

As she tried to concentrate on what Hector was saying, she noticed a tall, dark-haired man standing in the lobby. She recognized Emilio Jefferies and knew he operated El Diablo, a small, exclusive and popular Cuban restaurant in SoBe that also catered to Miami's jet-set crowd. She had seen her competitor's name and his picture in tabloids, seen him at local happenings and they had met briefly at restaurant events. While she watched, her maître d', Luis Munoz, spoke to Emilio Jefferies and turned to lead him to a table.

When Emilio crossed the main dining room, he moved with the ease of a panther, Brittany thought, watching his long legs and his easy, relaxed stride. In a navy suit and white shirt, he stood out in spite of a clientele of jet-setters, models and buff studs. She knew from Emilio's press coverage that he was thirty-three and definitely single.

"What's he doing here?" Brittany asked her services director, who turned to follow her gaze.

"I suppose he's curious about us," the slender black-haired man replied. "He's eaten here before. Every month we're having more business. Let's hope we grow to rival El Diablo."

She tried to smile, but found it impossible. More business. Less money. She rubbed her hands together, yet she couldn't stop watching Emilio.

"Excuse me, Brittany," Hector said and hurried away.

Barely hearing Hector, Brittany didn't take her gaze from Emilio. He was more handsome in person than in his pictures.

Luis seated him on one of the curved chairs that faced a spectacular view of the white beach. Luis talked to him briefly and left. When Emilio was alone, his gaze circled the room. He looked into Brittany's eyes.

Her breath caught and she stared at him while he nodded and smiled in acknowledgment. She was held by his commanding gaze. With an effort, she smiled in return and then strolled to a table to chat briefly with patrons. Her back tingled and she wondered if Emilio's eyes followed her.

In a few minutes, she left the dining room to return to her corner office, stepping into the spacious room with its polished hardwood floor, teak desk and rattan furniture cushioned in the same Haitian white cotton as the restaurant's other furnishings. A glass wall provided a spectacular view of the private part of the veranda and the beach beyond it. At one end of her office was a long teak-and-chrome table where she worked.

When she was seated at her desk, she pulled up her list of possibilities for funds and read it over again, knowing there was nothing promising. If she didn't do something in the next week, the restaurant was going under.

After racking her brain and coming up with no solution, she went to her private bathroom and looked at herself in the full-length mirror. The brightness of her fiery-red skirt and red silk blouse mocked her dying future as owner of Brittany Beach. Her long brown hair was caught in a clip with tendrils hanging loose and curling around her face. The image in the mirror didn't look like a person facing disaster. She smiled at herself, while inwardly, she churned with worry.

Satisfied with her appearance, she squared her shoulders to return to the main area. When she entered the room, her eyes immediately went to Emilio, who still dined alone. She chose to greet her other guests instead of heading straight to his table as she wanted to do.

It was another fifteen minutes before she approached him. He came to his feet and that riveting moment when she had locked gazes with him across the room was nothing compared to looking directly into his thickly-lashed, crystal-green eyes. She couldn't resist a swift glance over him and was immediately aware of his height. She was tall, herself, nine inches over five feet, yet he was at least six inches taller. His olive complexion added to his rugged appeal, yet it was the aura of sensuality that took her breath more than his physical appearance.

"Please, sit," she said.

"If you'll join me," he replied in a gravelly deep voice that heightened his magnetism. "I've finished eating. Have a drink with me."

"Thanks," she replied. As she started to sit, he came around to hold her chair. When they faced each other, she smiled at him. "Welcome to Brittany Beach. You checking us out to see what the competition is doing?"

"Sure, but I also enjoyed a fine dinner," he replied. She glanced down to see he'd had crab legs with melted butter.

"One of my favorite selections. I hope you've enjoyed your crab."

"I did, but my evening just got better."

She smiled. "I'm sure you flirt as easily as you breathe," she countered, noting an electrifying tension snapping between them. Now she could understand how he so easily attracted women.

"How can I resist?" he rejoined, his deep voice lowering slightly.

"You've been here before."

"Yes. The food is always good, so I come back occasionally. My compliments to your chef," Emilio said, smiling at her with a flash of even white teeth. Creases bracketed his mouth and his handsome appeal increased exponentially.

"Thank you and I'll tell him. Do you always check out your competition?"

"Sure. I'd guess you do, too, and I'd be willing to bet that you've eaten at El Diablo."

"As a matter of fact, I have. The food was also excellent."

"Thanks. I see we draw the same crowd, so we're direct competitors, but you're my most beautiful competitor, no question."

With a jump in her pulse, she smiled at him, yet she suspected he would put Brittany Beach out of business without a qualm if he could. "Thanks, again. I think there's room in SoBe for both of us," she replied tactfully.

"At least until you take my clientele," he answered lightly, smiling in return.

She laughed. "Our restaurants are sufficiently different. You carry dining to a more sensual level than we do here," she replied.

He glanced around and shrugged. "Everything in here is sensual—the ambience, the ability to lounge while you eat, great food, the very attractive waitstaff, music that has a primitive beat. No, I don't think I have the corner on what's sensuous, Brittany."

He said her name in his husky voice that stirred a tingle in her. She enjoyed sparring with him, feeling sparks dance between them, yet she suspected that her reaction was the same as every other female he encountered. The man reeked sex appeal and she was intrigued that he found her enough competition that he would make himself known at Brittany Beach. Or did he have some other reason for his presence?

"I should get you to write our ads," she answered, wondering what was really on his mind. Or was she reading too much into his visit?

"I could do your ads," he said with another flash of his white teeth. "Brittany Beach, fine dining taken to a new level of sensuality by its gorgeous owner."

Smiling, for a fleeting moment she forgot her worries about her finances. "You exaggerate, but I think I'm going to enjoy having you for a Brittany Beach patron," she replied with a toss of her head.

"Next time, join me for dinner," he suggested and she nodded.

"Whenever you want," she answered. "Unless there's a kitchen crisis or some reason I'm needed elsewhere. I see you're through eating. Would you like your own tour? Or have you already seen everything there is to see?"

"Not even remotely," he answered with a twinkle in his eyes. "I suspect there's a lot more to learn about." His tone suggested something more personal than the restaurant. "Let's do it," he said. "I'm already fascinated. I can't wait to see what else you'll show me."

She was amused by him, flattered, even though she was certain every woman he was around received the same flirting and compliments and she knew she shouldn't put stock in anything he said. She suspected he would look around, flirt some more and leave and she wouldn't see him again unless it was at restaurant functions or SoBe events.

He came around to hold her chair and fell into step beside her as she began the tour. She was aware of him close at her side.

"You know we're in the main dining room and you can see the cabana tents beyond the veranda. Off the dining room in this direction are the private rooms and, tonight, all but one are already filled," she said, motioning toward an open door and leading the way inside a small dining area with four long tables. "We can rearrange the tables to accommodate fewer or more than this. Now over this way," she said, leaving the room and switching off the light behind her, "is the lounge. We'll have strobe lights, hip-hop on some nights and, nearly always, hot bodies."

Even as she talked, the music grew louder and they stepped inside the darkened area briefly to watch dancers while the fast music drowned out possibilities for conversation. She touched his arm lightly because she had to raise her voice to be heard over the music. His head swung around and she motioned back toward the hall.

She took him on the rounds of public areas, avoiding any of the private parts of the restaurant and when she had finished, she turned to face him. "There, you've seen Brittany Beach. Would you like to go back to your table or maybe outside? It's cooled somewhat by this time of night."

"Only if you'll join me," he replied, and she shook her head reluctantly because she had enjoyed being with him, but she had already taken a lot of time away from work.

"I'm on duty, actually, and I might join you later, but for the time being, I need to keep checking that everything is running smoothly. Thursdays are busy."

"In that case, I'll call it a night. But I want to talk to you privately. How about an appointment tomorrow?"

Surprised, she wondered what was on his mind that he couldn't have already asked her or talked to her about. She shrugged.

"Sure," she said. "We can set an appointment, or I can take a little longer now and we can go to my office," she replied, curious.

"Right now is fine if you have the time," he replied easily.

"My office is back this way," she said, directing him to a

hallway. Once again, she noticed his height as he walked beside her. They exited the crowded dining room to stroll into a hall where thick blue carpet silenced their steps. In the glass-enclosed reception area for her office, a small light burned.

Crossing the room, she opened the door. When she switched on a dim light, he moved to the middle of the room and pushed open his coat to place his hands on his narrow hips as he looked around. "Nice office," he said. He ran his hand along the edge of her free-form teak desk and she watched his well-shaped fingers slowly, sensuously, rub the smooth surface. "Cool desk," he said.

"Have a seat. Would you like a drink?"

"No thanks," he answered, circling the room to look it over. He dominated the space and she knew the image of him in her office would stay with her.

"We share the same taste in art," he remarked, looking at a Mondrian. "Excellent choices in paintings."

"Yes, I prefer modern art, too. I've seen you at galleries. Take off your coat if you'd like," she said.

He glanced at her and shrugged out of his coat, folding it over the back of a chair. She sat in one of the chairs looking out the window where lights shone on the empty veranda. Green palm fronds waved gently in the breeze. Complementing the tall trees, beds of red, yellow and purple exotic hibiscus circled the base of each tree. The lawn ran to the sandy beach and in the distance, lights twinkled on luxury yachts.

"Attractive grounds, too. This is fantastic real estate," he said quietly. His low voice was velvety when he pulled a chair near hers and faced her. He stretched out his long legs and looked relaxed and her curiosity grew about why he wanted to see her privately.

When she crossed her tanned legs, he glanced down and then his eyes returned to hers.

She tilted her head to study him. "So you did have a reason for coming tonight, besides eating," she said.

"Nope. I came for dinner and thought I'd be back at El Diablo long before now. I got sidetracked. As for talking to you, I intended to call tomorrow and ask for an appointment. I didn't expect to meet you tonight. When I've eaten here before, I haven't seen you."

"Okay. So, here we are. You don't have to wait until tomorrow. What's this about?"

Emilio gazed at her in silence and her curiosity mounted. Whatever he intended to discuss must be serious.

"You know how rumors fly in this business," he said finally.

His words chilled her. She hoped she kept her features impassive while she looked steadily back at him, but all she could think was that there would be only one rumor that would bring a competitor from another restaurant to see her. Was her accountant's embezzlement public knowledge? A suffocating heat enveloped her. If Emilio Jefferies knew about her loss, how long before her family knew?

She reassured herself that Parker didn't know or she would have already heard from him.

"Go ahead," she said stiffly and wished she sounded more relaxed. She was thankful now that they were in dim light.

"Your accountant has disappeared."

"Yes, that's right. And since you know that much, you must know the rest of the story about him. But that isn't why you wanted to talk to me—to confirm something you could verify in other ways."

"No. Do you mind me asking if your brothers know about this?"

"No, they don't and frankly, I'm disappointed that rumors are circulating, because I'd just as soon my brothers don't know about it just yet."

"That's reasonable," Emilio said.

"So what did you want to discuss about it?" she asked, barely able to think about anything except Parker would soon know if he didn't already.

"From the rumors, I gather your accountant is not all that's missing."

"The rumors, unfortunately, are correct. My trusted accountant left with my money. This doesn't have anything to do with El Diablo, though. So what's on your mind?"

"I have a business proposition for you," Emilio answered in his deep voice.

Startled, she again hoped she didn't reveal her surprise. "I'm not selling Brittany Beach," she snapped, clenching her fists in her lap, thinking the vultures were already circling.

"That's not why I'm here," Emilio assured her with a wave of his hand. "You've been doing a bang-up job of running this."

"Then what do you want?" she asked in surprise. "If you expect me to borrow money from you—that's out, as well, because I can always go to my family."

"Ah, I don't think you will go to them," Emilio replied softly. "I'm guessing that if you were going to your ambitious brothers, you would have already gone. I have to admit that I'm surprised your brothers don't already know about your loss."

"They're preoccupied right now with settling our father's estate," she explained, recalling the reading of her father's will last month. She had no intention of telling Emilio what an incredible shock it had been to learn that her father had had a second life and they had another sibling, Cassie Sinclair, who managed the Garrison Grand Bahamas.

She wondered how much that information had circulated, suspecting everyone in the family would be reluctant to talk about it to an outsider. The discovery of the relationship had been stunning and at the time, Parker had been livid. Brittany knew even now, a month later, his attention was on the division of his power.

"Besides, as I'm sure you've heard, Parker's in love, so he's preoccupied," she added. "My other brothers are involved in the same estate issues. I think that's what's given me a reprieve from discovery." She ran her fingers along her skirt, forgetting her family and thinking about Emilio. "If you aren't offering to buy me out or loan me money, what's on your mind?" she asked.

"Quid pro quo—a trade. I cover your loss and, therefore, your brothers don't step in and take over."

Surprised, Brittany stared at him. *Cover her loss.* The words nagged at her and she knew the desperate situation she was in left her few choices. Even so, her first reaction was refusal, because she didn't want a stranger mixing into her business.

"Thank you, but I don't think that's feasible," Brittany answered politely, feeling cold that an outsider even knew about her financial crisis.

"Don't give me a hasty reply," he answered with a wave of his hand, dismissing her rejection. "Let's talk it over."

As she shook her head, he leaned forward and caught her hand, making her pulse jump with the contact. His palm was warm, gently holding hers. In spite of his caring manner, she could feel the clash of wills between them. She pulled her hand away and locked her fingers in her lap to keep from wringing her hands, which was what she wanted to do.

"Your brother Parker, as head of the umbrella corporation for all of the Garrison enterprises, has the funds to cover your loss, but I understand your reluctance to go to your family," Emilio said in a reminder that brought her worries crashing back.

"Right. They're not one of my current options," she said

stiffly, shuddering slightly at just the thought of walking into Parker's office in downtown Miami and announcing that two million had been stolen from her by her accountant. "I intend to work this out myself."

"Ah," Emilio said and satisfaction flared in his green eyes.

She hurt, knowing she was caught in a dreadful dilemma. Everything in her cried out to tell Emilio no and get him out of her office, yet her desperation held her silent. Finally, she couldn't resist asking, "You'd cover my loss. In return, what do you want?"

"A share of Brittany Beach for my investment."

Her immediate reaction was *never*. "I can't do that!"

"Think about it," he said. "You'd wipe out your loss. Your debts would be covered and gone."

Temptation tore at her. An inner voice urged her to accept and the prospects made her heart race. This was the miracle she had searched for, so why were warnings going off steadily in her mind?

"How big a share do you want?" Brittany asked, biting her lip while her mind raced. Everything in her still screamed no, yet if she didn't cover her losses, next week she had to go to Parker.

"That depends on how big my investment is," Emilio replied easily, sitting back in the chair again and watching her. He looked relaxed and sounded as casual and cool as if he were discussing the menu for breakfast. Yet his green eyes were alert and she thought again of a panther, only this time, one ready to pounce on its prey.

She hated to say the amount out loud. It was massive, impossible for her to replace by herself. Emilio waited patiently for her reply. She raised her chin as she wondered how many hundreds of times the total figure had run through her thoughts and kept her awake at night. "It's slightly over two million dollars."

He pursed his lips and sat in silence as if mulling it over.

While she was surprised by his lack of reaction to the horrific amount, she thought about her brothers. If they heard the amount, they would be wild and demanding to know why she hadn't been on top of things and known what her accountant was doing.

While Emilio remained silent, she wondered what he was thinking. She knew the loss was monumental and disappointment shook her while she braced for him to withdraw his offer.

"Two million is a sizable figure. Any hope of catching the accountant?"

"No one knows where he went," she said stiffly, and then they lapsed into silence again. Waiting, she watched as he made a triangle of his fingers and, evidently, mulled over the amount.

"Two million," he repeated. He looked at her sharply. "Do you own the building and land?"

"I own the building, but the land is part of the Garrison holdings."

He nodded. The silence became oppressive and her nerves stretched. Now that she'd had salvation dangled in front of her, she didn't want it yanked away.

"Okay. I'll cover your debts," he declared.

She let out her breath. She didn't know whether she wanted to accept or refuse, but it was a relief to know she had an option.

"So, do you have an idea how big a share of Brittany Beach you want in exchange for your investment?" she asked and then held her breath again while she waited for his answer.

TWO

"If I put that much cash into Brittany Beach, I want a fifty-fifty partnership."

"Fifty-fifty?" Stunned, she hadn't expected that large a percentage, but she really hadn't thought through his offer.

She jumped to her feet and had to move and get away from his steady gaze. Her mind raced over his proposition. She crossed the room to the window to watch breakers hit the shore without really seeing them.

She would have to give up her complete control. Everything in her told her to refuse. With half control, Emilio would be in charge as much as she. She spun around to face him.

"I'd have to share everything with you—running Brittany Beach, all decisions about the restaurant?"

"You sure would," he replied quietly. "It also means that you save Brittany Beach without relying on your family to rescue you. Plus, you'll have my business experience available—the old, 'sometimes two heads are better than one' theory."

"You and I would have to work closely together every day," she said and one corner of his mouth quirked up in a crooked grin.

"Brittany, that would never be a hardship," he drawled.

His words made her pulse jump because he was flirting, yet she couldn't smile in return. She didn't want to take this man as a business partner. She knew his playboy reputation. Sexy and attractive, he disturbed her and she had a reaction to him. Until the past few minutes, she'd enjoyed the evening with him, but that was different from going into business with him.

He had a history as a heartbreaker and she didn't want to become one on the list. She liked being on her own. Another drawback was that she didn't know him. Could she trust him with fifty percent of Brittany Beach? At the same time, while doubts assailed her, his offer hung in the air like a golden salvation.

She couldn't keep from considering what he was proposing. He would cover her monstrous debt—she would not have to borrow money, pay interest and sink deeper into debt. She hoped she kept her features impassive.

"That's a generous offer," she said quietly, walking back to sit facing him. "Why are you extending your help to me? We're competitors and we don't know each other."

He smiled. "Anyone can read the press you've gotten and know you're operating a popular, hip place. You've done well. I consider half interest in Brittany Beach a good investment."

"Thank you," she replied, her mind racing over questions. "We don't know each other. Can I trust you?" she asked, looking into green eyes that were unfathomable. She couldn't guess what he was thinking. How much could she trust a handsome, wealthy playboy who broke women's hearts?

"Cold, hard cash is a good sign of trust, don't you think?" he asked with a smile.

"Yes. Two million is," she said, more to herself than to him. "I don't know if you have a violent temper or if you're a perfectionist and highly demanding," she continued, yet all the time she protested, part of her yearned to accept his offer and toss consequences to the wind. "I don't know whether your employees like working for you."

"You don't have to make this decision now," he replied. "My offer is on the table. Think it over. You can check me out and you can talk to some of my employees."

"I have to decide soon. You know the daily demands of a restaurant. We can't run on credit."

"Garrison credit? That'll sustain you for a time. If you want to know more about me, spend a day at El Diablo and watch me work. You'll get an idea of how I do things and you'll know me better."

He was making her a good offer and being reasonable about letting her check him out, which was reassuring even if she didn't feel she could take him up on his suggestions. She couldn't resist glancing at her desk, too aware of the drawer with a stack of bills that grew bigger daily. "At this point, I don't have the luxury of waiting," she answered truthfully.

"Whatever you need to do. You know my offer. Think about it."

"Frankly, it's salvation," she declared bluntly, wondering if at some point, she might be able to buy back the fifty percent. Or, if they worked well together, it would be a permanent arrangement.

"Do you have any questions?" he asked.

"How involved do you want to be in running Brittany Beach?"

"Until I know your staff and restaurant and everything about this place, I'd like to participate daily in management."

The prospect of constant, involved contact with Emilio sizzled in her. Could she work with this sexy charmer and keep her heart intact? On the business side—his offer was the answer to her prayers. In truth, she had exhausted every possibility for saving Brittany Beach.

Once again, she got up to go to the window while she thought about his offer. In four days, she would need funds that she didn't have. She could borrow enough to get by temporarily, but the moment she got a loan, word might get back to Parker. Friday to Monday.

"Brittany," Emilio said casually, and she turned to face him. "Sleep on it. Or, if it helps, I can advance you a loan while you consider my offer," he said, and that proposal in itself reassured her.

"No. Frankly, I don't have other options. I accept your offer," she replied, feeling as if her future was sealed and it would be a long time—if ever—before she would have full control of her business. She recalled an old song or perhaps a quote—something about dancing with the devil. Was that what she had agreed to? Had she sold her soul to keep her restaurant? Emilio had a reputation that rang bells of alarm the moment he walked into Brittany Beach. Yet she'd enjoyed his company tonight and he'd been reasonable in making his offer and had not pressured her to accept. Besides, the instant she uttered acceptance, an enormous burden had lifted from her shoulders.

"Awesome!" he exclaimed, standing and striding around the desk while he flashed another brilliant, irresistible smile at her that banished her dark thoughts. His contagious enthusiasm made her feel she had made a fabulous choice.

He placed his hands lightly on her shoulders. "Fantastic! This bargain will be great, and you'll keep your restaurant."

"I'll share Brittany Beach with you, is what you mean," she replied, gazing up at him. He was only inches away. His jaw was clean-shaven, his lower lip full and sensual. She could detect his aftershave and was aware of the warmth of his hands through her silk blouse. He was easily the most handsome man she had known and it scared her to think about trying to overlook his appeal and work with him daily.

"My guess is, that we'll have more women customers now," she remarked drily and received another flash of white, even teeth while his eyes sparkled.

"I think I noticed more male customers out there tonight than female."

"It won't be that way for long."

"Don't sound so unhappy about it. If you change your mind tonight, let me know. This deal isn't consummated yet," he said, watching her closely.

Relieved to hear him make such a statement, she nodded. "I guess I'm panicking because I'm giving up part of Brittany Beach."

"Don't look at what you're losing. Remember what you're gaining—Brittany Beach. Plus, an experienced business partner," he added with another engaging grin that again reminded her why females were so drawn to him. She couldn't resist smiling in return.

"How could I question such a deal?" she asked.

"Good! Now you don't look quite like you've agreed for the world to disintegrate."

Her smile broadened. "This has happened so fast. I need to get used to the changes that are coming."

"I predict we'll make more money together than ever," he said in his gravelly, deep voice. "You'll see," he added, squeezing her shoulders and then releasing her to place his hands on his hips. "So how about getting together in the morning to draw up a contract?"

"We're moving fast. Morning is fine."

"We'll go only as fast as you want to go," he said. "I promise. Let me know if you're unhappy."

She nodded again, reassured by each of his statements and hoping he meant what he said.

"At any time until we sign the contract and money is deposited, you can back out of our deal and it's fine. Once we sign a contract, I want to know that I have a lasting agreement. Okay with you?"

"That's fair enough," she replied, unable to smile or display the enthusiasm he obviously felt. Yet she thought he was being more than fair with her.

"As soon as we sign our agreement, I'll deposit the money into your account, and then we'll be in business. From what you said, you have to move swiftly on this."

"Yes, I do," she said, once again thinking about her family and how long before word reached them. Would they have a fit over her taking Emilio as a partner? She was certain any dislike of her new partner would pale in comparison to their reaction if they knew about her loss of money.

"So how about nine in the morning for the two of us to look at a contract tomorrow before we meet with our lawyers?" Emilio asked.

"Let me check my calendar," she said, walking to her desk while he followed and stood close beside her. "Nine o'clock will be fine with me."

"If it's possible, let's get together in the afternoon—you, me and our attorneys."

"I'll try to make an afternoon appointment with my lawyer and you contact yours. I'll use our family attorney," she said as she thought about Brandon Washington, their tall, capable lawyer "He'll be bound by attorney-client confidentiality and I trust Brandon. In the long run, it'll be better to have him because he knows about my business."

"Sure. If I tell mine it's urgent, he'll try to rearrange his schedule."

"Let me give you my attorney's card," she said, opening her desk and reaching for one, which she handed to Emilio. She stepped back slightly, realizing he stood only inches away. Amusement danced in his eyes.

"I don't bite. Might like to, though," he said.

Laughing, she shook her finger at him. She pulled out another card and wrote on the back of it. "There's my card with my cell phone and my home phone."

"If we're exchanging personal numbers, I'll give you mine," he said, pulling out a billfold to get one of his cards. He picked up a pen from her desk and scrawled his numbers and while his head was bent, she looked at his thick, black hair. He glanced up and she drew a deep breath, knowing he had caught her studying him. He handed the card to her and she dropped it on her desk.

"Perhaps it would be wiser to have the meeting at your lawyer's office. I don't care to run into one of my brothers at Brandon's office," she said.

"Good idea," Emilio replied.

She bit her lower lip. "There's something else I'd like to do," she said. "For the time being, can we keep this partnership out of the news?"

He shrugged one broad shoulder. "I suppose."

"It's not you," she said quickly. "It's my family. If we don't make an official announcement, there will be less chance of knowledge of the embezzlement getting back to my family. I've told you, I prefer to work this partnership and Brittany Beach finances out myself."

"I understand about family. They're the best, but sometimes, you want them to let you manage your life without suggestions. If we don't make a public announcement right now, it's okay with me," he said easily, his eyes wide and guileless. "What will you tell your staff, because I'll be here daily?"

While she pondered his question, she focused on a point behind him. "How about simply saying that you're doing some consulting for me, that you're lending your business expertise?"

"That's fine with me," he replied, smiling at her. He tilted up her chin and her pulse accelerated. "See, we can work together."

"At least for five minutes," she remarked, knowing she sounded negative. "I'm still sorting through this and getting accustomed to the idea of a partner."

"I'll remind you again. Get used to the notion of no debt. For your part, that's the big deal and what you want. And remember, tonight, you can still back out."

"You're too good to be true," she replied, wondering about him and if she needed to take the weekend to think over his offer.

"No, I'm not. I'm in the same business and I have money to invest and this looks like a super opportunity. We're going to be great together," he said in a husky voice that instantly removed all thoughts of business from her mind. He smiled. "This partnership will be terrific."

"I'll remind you of that remark when we have the first fight," she replied.

"A fight with you—never!" he exclaimed emphatically as his gaze lowered to her mouth and made her heart miss a beat. "We'll just do things my way," he teased with another charming grin.

"You think I'm going to give in to your every whim?" she asked in a seductive drawl and something flickered in the depths of his eyes as his smile vanished. She knew she shouldn't flirt with him, but it was impossible to resist.

"If I could have one wish—" he began, but she interrupted him.

She shook her head. "If you could have one wish, it would not be that I would yield to your whims! SoBe is filled with really gorgeous, sexy women who will yield to what you want eagerly. I think you flirt out of habit, but I've seen pictures of you too many times and the woman at your side is always drop-dead gorgeous and often a star or famous in another field."

"You don't have to take a backseat to any of them," he said softly as he studied her features.

She laughed. "So compliments come with this deal?"

"Only if deserved," he retorted.

"We've got business to transact, remember?"

"My practical partner," he teased, running his index finger lightly along her cheek and making her pulse flutter.

With an effort, she walked away from him, circling her desk and then turning to face him. "We can make an official announcement about the partnership later, when things are running smoothly. We can have the public celebration and the fanfare."

Emilio placed his hands on his hips again. "I don't need fanfare. I'm satisfied with the bargain we'll make. We'll be an awesome team. This is great, Brittany."

"I hope so," she said.

"Remember, no debt. Hold on to that."

"I'll try," she said,

"I'll go now," he said, turning toward the door and pocketing her card.

"I'll walk with you to the front," she said, hurrying to catch up to him at the door.

He held open the door for her and she left her office feeling as if the past hour had changed her life forever and she would never again be the same.

"Tomorrow morning we can go over what we need in a contract and I'm sure our attorneys will have suggestions. I have a boilerplate contract we can use," he said, but she could barely keep her mind on what he was telling her as she walked beside him and thought about the commitment she had just made. Emilio Jefferies was her new partner.

How long would it take her to get accustomed to that? Probably not long because she was certain he would make his presence felt.

At the front, she stood with him while he waited for a valet to bring his car.

"See you tomorrow," he said. He gave her one last smile before he went striding to his car. She didn't wait to watch him drive away, but hurried back to her office to close the door.

She wished Emilio would turn all management over to her, but she could understand. If she invested in his restaurant, she would want to be involved in running it, too.

Emilio—her partner. The idea of working constantly in close contact with him created a honeyed warmth. In every move and tone and look, Emilio was seductive and it had been exhilarating to flirt with him early in the evening before they got into something serious.

She flung her arms out. "Here's to success, my new partnership and to saving Brittany Beach!" she exclaimed to the empty office. Her relief was enormous. And he had left her an out, which reassured her each time she thought about it.

She hurried around the desk and sat to phone the family lawyer and make an appointment.

Within minutes, Brandon Washington agreed to get in touch with Emilio's attorney and set a time for an appointment. It was an hour before schedules were adjusted and they had an appointment for two in the afternoon the next day.

The sooner the money was deposited in her business account, the sooner she would be safe from discovery about the embezzlement.

She opened her lower desk drawer and surveyed the stack of bills that had accumulated. Now she could pay them!

Brittany glanced at her watch and called Boyd Dumont, the

accountant who had audited the books and found the embezzlement, to tell him her news.

After she had told Boyd goodbye, she made a list of things
to do. The phone rang and her pulse jumped when she heard
Emilio's deep voice. He told her that he wanted to talk so they
could get to know each other a little better and asked her what
time she'd go home.

Smiling, she leaned back in her chair and told him shortly
after one. He said he'd call her then.

Wanting to finish at the office and get home, she replaced
the receiver. Emilio had flirted, charmed her and then made the
fantastic offer. Thinking about talking to him later, she hummed
as she turned back to her list. While she was writing, someone
knocked on her door.

"Come in," Brittany called, and her director of services
thrust his head inside.

"We have an actor and his party and he's agreed to pictures.
I thought you might like to meet him and be in the pictures."

"Of course," she said, knowing this was good publicity for
Brittany Beach. She got up and smoothed her red skirt, and left
with Hector.

It was almost one in the morning when Brittany entered her
two-bedroom condo on the ground floor in an exclusive SoBe
gated area. Always happy to be home, she welcomed the quiet
after the busy restaurant.

Overlooking the ocean, the living room held her books and
favorite Jasper Johns paintings, and after her shower, she
played Otis Redding, turning the music low, enjoying it and realizing that she felt relaxed for the first time since the discovery of the embezzlement.

Wondering what to wear tomorrow, she entered her closet
and looked at possibilities, selecting a white linen suit with a
deep-blue silk blouse.

She held the suit up in front of her as she looked at herself in the mirror, but she was seeing Emilio. She liked him. Tonight it had been exhilarating to flirt with him and enjoyable to talk to him. And she felt a hot physical reaction that she thought he'd experienced, too. She laughed out loud at herself over that one! Emilio probably had the same reaction with every female he encountered. Handsome and sexy, he was one of those men whom women loved. She would have no doubt about that, even if she hadn't seen a multitude of press articles about him buzzing around SoBe escorting socialites or stars. "You better keep your wits with him," she told herself aloud.

Then her phone rang. Eagerly, she plopped on her bed and listened to Emilio's hello.

When she finally told him good night, they had talked over an hour. Afterward, while she tried to go to sleep, she thought about his call. They had talked about favorite things, the newest SoBe restaurant, restaurant menus. Jumping from topic to topic, she'd enjoyed their conversation and she looked forward to seeing him again. Maybe this partnership would be as great as he predicted.

The next hours were restless. She dreamed about Emilio, once waking with thoughts of him still in her mind, drifting asleep again until later, when her eyes flew open and she stared into the darkness as a chill shook her.

Glancing around to see it was almost five in the morning, Brittany sat up while fears and doubts bombarded her. Had she rushed to take a partner too swiftly? Had she once again been too trusting? Emilio had come to her with his offer. Did he have an ulterior motive and, if he did, what was it?

Tossing back the sheet, she paced the floor. With every doubt that assailed her, she reminded herself of her dilemma that had had no solution until Emilio. She repeatedly thought about his promise that she could back out of the deal until they had signed the contract. He had been willing to give her time, to let her investigate him, to let her call the whole thing off. With offers like the ones he'd made, how could he have ulterior motives?

Three

By the time of their appointment the next morning, Brittany had spent an hour going over details for the coming day at Brittany Beach. She was in the main dining room when she looked up to see someone ushering Emilio in her direction. At the sight of him, her pulse jumped. This morning he was dressed in a charcoal business suit and red tie with his snowy shirt.

She had already talked to him twice on the telephone this morning. Over and over she wondered if they could work out an agreement by early afternoon. The speed they were moving astounded her. She finished what she was doing, handed the approved menus to her sous-chef and walked forward to meet Emilio.

"Good morning." She greeted him with a smile as she extended her hand.

"Good morning," he replied, warm appreciation in his eyes as they drifted over her white skirt and blue blouse, down to her peep-toe white pumps with stiletto heels. "You look great."

"Thank you," she said, aware of his hand wrapped around hers. His hand was brown, warm, his fingers well-shaped and his touch stirred a fiery tingle.

"Let's go back to my office. I'll send for coffee," she said.

She motioned him to sit at the table. In minutes, a staff person brought a tray with coffee, tea and orange juice, along with glasses and white china cups and saucers.

When Brittany sat, Emilio moved his chair beside her. "I brought the boilerplate contract," he said, opening his briefcase and removing two copies. When he handed a copy to her, his hand barely brushed hers. Each contact was volatile, and she wondered how long she would continue to have such an intense reaction to him. How was she going to work in close proximity to him if she couldn't control her response to everything he did? When would she view him as ordinary and not get that tingle if he casually brushed against her? She drew a deep breath and turned to focus on the contract.

Emilio pointed to the first paragraph and read aloud. It was an effort to concentrate on business with only inches separating them. She should put a foot of space between them, but she didn't want him to realize his effect on her.

They slowly went through the agreements and stipulations and she stared at the paragraph that gave him fifty percent ownership of Brittany Beach. Once she signed the contract there would be no turning back.

When she signed the papers, though, her debt would be wiped out. Whenever doubts loomed, she reminded herself of what was at stake and what she was getting. Solvency.

She was surprised how swiftly and cooperatively they worked out the details.

By noon, she sat back and confessed, "That went smoother than I expected."

"I agree," Emilio said. "That's another good indicator that we'll work together well."

She had already ordered lunch from the kitchen and they had it delivered to the veranda outside her office.

As she stirred lemon into her chilled glass of iced tea, Brittany's spirits rose another notch. "I have a recent picture of our staff that I'll give you after lunch. Most everyone is in it and their names are printed below. I'll introduce you to as many as I can, but I don't want to have a formal meeting and introduction because it'll make a bigger deal about you being here."

"Sounds okay to me," he said, smiling at her.

She made a notation in a tablet beside her plate. He leaned forward. "You're still working. Let it go through lunch. Tonight, let's have an official celebration at El Diablo. Come join me for dinner," he suggested.

Warnings went off in her thoughts like sirens in a storm. The man was a heartthrob, she reminded herself at the same moment she nodded her head.

"Against good judgment, I accept."

"Against good judgment," he repeated. "Now how do you figure that?" he asked, a dark eyebrow arching.

"I suspect you're a heartbreaker and I definitely think work and fun should be separate."

"Nonsense on both charges. We're sensible enough to mix business and pleasure, and since when isn't that mixed all over SoBe? As for the heartbreaker accusation—I don't think so. I can't recall any teary-eyed ladies languishing in my past," he said with a twinkle in his green eyes.

"Your memory may be poor on the subject."

"Let's celebrate an event that will be mutually profitable. How can you avoid being elated over the future possibilities?"

"I'm happy about it," she said, gazing into his compelling eyes and thinking about her quiet life.

He laughed. "You sound as if you're headed for a disaster. But you said yes, so we're on for tonight. Maybe I can cheer you up."

She smiled. "It's not that bad. I'm trying to get used to what's happening here."

"Get accustomed to me," he said softly. "I'm here to stay."

She laughed and he nodded. "That's better. This is good, Brittany. You'll see."

She felt better and her worries diminished slightly. In spite of his denial, she couldn't imagine that her assessment of him wasn't right on target. Yet she couldn't resist the prospect of the celebration. She shoved away the tablet and placed her pen on the table.

"Very well. I'll put away my list for now. But I do want to say that after we finish eating, let's look around to see about an office for you. We really don't have an extra one that is the size you need."

"Show me what you do have. I don't need anything large."

"Is it going to be a hardship for you to divide your time between your restaurant and this one?"

As he shook his head, wind caught locks of his black hair, lifting them slightly away from his face. His wavy midnight hair was as thick and appealing as his other features. She realized she was staring at him and looked away.

"I have excellent people who can manage El Diablo," he replied. "At first, I want to familiarize myself with your staff and your procedures. I'd like to get to know your regular clientele—which do you have the highest percentage of, regulars or single visits?"

"Both, maybe equally. We're getting celebrities, models, jet-setters—they all generate publicity."

They sat beneath a large blue umbrella, so they were shaded from direct sunlight, but they were outside where the light was strong and Emilio's thickly lashed eyes looked like clear-green glass except, unlike glass, there was a fire in the depths of his gaze that kept her pulse fluttering.

As they talked about trivial matters, Emilio was the one who brought up her family. "I'm sorry you lost your father."

"Thank you. When I was growing up, he seemed powerful and invincible and there's still a part of me that's shocked by his death."

"I think that's natural. Do you see your siblings often?"

"Yes, I do. We try to have a family gathering for Sunday night dinner and we see each other often during the week. What about your family?"

"My brother, Jordan, and I see each other daily. We're the last ones left in our immediate family."

"That's good. There's a lot of sibling rivalry in my family," she said.

"I'll introduce you the first time I have a chance," Emilio replied. Brittany remembered hearing that Emilio's mother came to America from Cuba when he was an infant and she became the Jefferies' nanny. When she was killed, Emilio was adopted by the Jefferies.

"Does Jordan know about your new partnership?"

"Not yet," Emilio replied, "but simply because I haven't had the opportunity to tell him. The first chance I get, I'll let him know. I'll also tell him we're keeping it private for now."

"It'll be more acceptable if it's business as usual when I let my family know. I can't see how they can object to what I want to do with the restaurant as long as it's growing and profitable." She glanced at Emilio's empty glass. "More tea? Would you like anything else to eat or drink?"

"No, thanks."

"Then lunch is over and we can get back to business. Let me show you the offices and after we decide what we'll do about yours, we'll tour the entire restaurant."

Soon the time approached to leave for their appointment with the lawyers. Brittany stopped in her office to comb her hair, once again fastening it up in a clip. She pulled on a cropped, white linen jacket that matched her skirt, pushing up the sleeves and glancing at herself in the mirror before leaving to meet Emilio.

As she walked up to him, she saw the approval in his eyes when he looked at her warmly. "This has to be the best deal I've ever made," he said in a husky voice, taking her arm.

"Don't turn on the charm. We're business partners."

"That doesn't keep me from appreciating a beautiful woman," he replied and smiled at her while he leaned down to open the car door.

It took the entire afternoon to iron out the details they wanted in the contract. Finally, the moment came when she watched Emilio write the check and her heart thudded at the amount, even though she had known exactly what it would be. Relief surged, making her hands clammy. She fought the urge to reach out for the check before he was ready to give it to her.

He held it out. "Here's the money. We need to get it transferred to your account from mine. As soon as we finish here, we'll go to your bank."

With cold fingers, she took the check that meant even more now than when her father had first given her the papers for Brittany Beach. "Thank you," she exclaimed, squeezing his hand.

His eyebrow arched, and she realized he might have misinterpreted her gesture of gratitude for something more. Dismissing the notion, she put the check into her purse.

She realized he must have been certain about her decision to accept his offer because he had everything ready to move instantly, and the notion that he anticipated all this happening raised another flag of warning deep inside her.

She shrugged away the worry. She had no choice, and this partnership would save Brittany Beach.

At half past five they had a brief meeting with her new accountant.

It was almost seven when they finally finished and Emilio pulled up in front of Brittany Beach. "Sure you don't want me to pick you up tonight?"

"Positive. It's not that far and I'll drive myself over."

"See you at half past nine," Emilio said. "I'm looking forward to our dinner. No business whatsoever tonight. This will be pure celebration."

She smiled. "You know the old saying, 'All play and no work makes Jack a lazy bum,'" she said, and his smile widened.

"You made that up."

"I might have," she admitted, grinning at him.

"I think you need to learn how to let go and enjoy yourself."

"I know how to let go," she replied. "You'll see. I can have fun."

"Be ready to have some tonight," he said. "When people come to El Diablo, I want them to have a good time and great food. I definitely want my new partner to."

"See you after nine," she said. She climbed out of the car and walked toward the door, glancing back over her shoulder to find him watching her. She waved and as she went inside, she heard him drive away.

Glancing briefly across the strip of beach at the blue ocean which paralleled the highway, Emilio sped back to El Diablo, sweeping into the drive and circling the exclusive pink stucco restaurant to park near his private entrance. As he turned the back corner, he saw his tall, blond, blue-eyed brother, Jordan, striding to his own car.

When Emilio waved, Jordan turned and approached.

"When I called, they said they expected you, so I stopped by and then found you weren't here," Jordan said. Wind blew locks of his thick blond hair. His open-throat blue cotton s clung to his muscular biceps and broad shoulders. He waved a folder at Emilio. "I need your signature on papers to open another account for Hotel Victoria. I want a separate account for the insurance."

"Sure. I want to talk to you, anyway," Emilio replied.

When they entered Emilio's quiet office, he sat behind his broad granite-and-bronze desk while Jordan sat in one of the blue leather chairs.

"Give me the papers." While Jordan waited quietly, Emilio took the folder from him and scanned the contents. He signed each paper where he was supposed to and then passed the folder back to his brother. "There. You can pay your insurance," he said cheerfully. "How's it coming with the hotel?"

Jordan shrugged. "Fine. We're approaching the opening—and looking to giving the Garrison Grand some real competition with our luxury hotel."

"It's not as big as the Garrison, but it's opulent and should draw the same jet-set crowd. So everything is going all right?"

"A shipment of furniture was delivered to the wrong hotel," Jordan answered, shrugging one broad shoulder. "Other than minor blips, we're sailing along great."

Emilio smiled. "You'll get it all worked out. You're still on schedule, aren't you?"

"Yep. Why did you want to see me?" Jordan asked.

"Remember I told you that I've heard all sorts of gossip from my staff and restaurant friends about Brittany Beach?"

"Yeah, that the accountant disappeared with embezzled millions. The restaurant would be on the auction block soon. The oldest Garrison was taking over. Why? Is any of it true?" Jordan asked.

"I thought there was enough to assume some of the speculation was true, so I ate dinner there and checked it out. The accountant disappeared and money's gone."

"Theft won't slow the Garrisons. They'll replace the money, put the accountant in jail and go on with business as usual."

"Not quite. Remember, Brittany Beach is Brittany Garrison's baby," Emilio said.

Jordan shrugged. "That doesn't matter. Her brothers will step in immediately."

"That's what I figured, but they haven't. They don't know what's happened and Brittany doesn't want them knowing."

Jordan smiled. "Of course, she doesn't because she doesn't want them taking the place away from her."

"I've made her a business proposition," Emilio said. He looked at his brother who was ruthlessly ambitious. "I agreed to pay her debt."

"The hell you did!" Jordan sat up straighter and his eyes narrowed. "What are you getting in exchange?"

"Half of Brittany Beach," Emilio announced triumphantly and was pleased at the sudden flare of approval in Jordan's eyes, but then it was gone as he scowled at Emilio.

"It's the Garrisons' business. They'll never let you get control or take it away from them."

Emilio leaned forward. "The Garrison men don't know it. Brittany and I drew up the contract with our lawyers this afternoon and we signed it. It's a done deal. I now have half of Brittany Beach, and there isn't one thing the Garrisons can do about this transaction."

"I'll be damned!" Jordan exclaimed, staring at Emilio. "Half! Good for you! Congratulations! We own Garrison property! I'm shocked. Doesn't she know we're at war with her brothers?"

"No," Emilio said flatly. "If she had a clue what goes on with her brothers, she wouldn't have responded the way she did. They probably tell her nothing."

Jordan whistled. "How could she not know? Half of SoBe knows what a feud we have with the Garrisons."

"Believe me, she's as naive and trusting as a lamb. She wants to keep this merger quiet, for the time being, until everything is in place and running smoothly. She's telling her employees that I'm a consultant."

Jordan's eyes narrowed. "How much money?"

"Slightly over two million," Emilio answered.

Jordan whistled. "Wow, again. The guy embezzled two million bucks and she didn't know it?"

"She's a baby. I don't know what her twin is like, but they're the babies of that family and Brittany really is one. No doubt a little princess whose daddy tossed this restaurant to her. I walked in there with my proposition, and she accepted it with relief. From the first minute she trusted me."

"Awesome!"

"Jordan, listen," Emilio urged, leaning forward. "Give me time and we'll own all of it. Do you know what a coup that will be? Taking it right out from under the Garrisons. I can see how her accountant waltzed off with her money. She doesn't have business judgment or this embezzlement wouldn't have ever happened. I know I can take Brittany Beach away from her," he repeated. "Give me time."

"Won't that be something! When that happens, Parker and Stephen will go up in flames," Jordan said with a grin. "When the Garrison men learn you own half, they may be ready to yank her out of there and sell you the other half, solely to end a Garrison-Jefferies partnership."

"We'll see how it plays out, but I'm sure I'll get the restaurant."

"That's sweet, Emilio." Jordan stood and tapped the folder against his knee. "I need to be in downtown Miami soon, so I'll take my papers and go. Keep me posted."

As soon as the door shut behind Jordan, Emilio turned to gaze outside while visions of Brittany crowded out other thoughts.

Brittany was an appealing woman, sexy, stirring him easily.

They had a volatile chemistry between them and even though she tried to focus on business, he knew she felt the sparks, too.

He recalled in exact detail the moment he had glanced across her dining room and seen her looking at him. Her fiery-red skirt and red silk blouse had been an invitation. Her long shapely legs were as fabulous as her tiny waist and lush, full breasts.

Thinking about Brittany, Emilio was getting aroused.

She was good-looking and he had enjoyed her company and talking to her. That was a bonus he'd never figured on. He turned to pick up the phone and give her a call.

The minute she answered and he said hello, he leaned back in his chair to prop his feet on his desk. "I wanted to see if you're still happy and if you're looking forward to dinner tonight," he said, nodding over her answer. Twenty minutes passed before she had to go and he replaced his receiver, more eager than ever to see her again tonight. He drummed his fingers restlessly on his desk while he thought about dinner and what he wanted. Anticipation made him eager.

Whistling a tune, he looked around his own office that was a contrast to Brittany's teak and glass and hardwood floor. He had a white marble floor, white walls and a granite desk. There were accents of bright primary colors on his walls in his contemporary art. Deep-blue cushions and blue pots holding palms added more color.

His gaze rested on a particular painting he owned. He looked at the bright colors and abstract shapes by a new artist named Richardson, while he wondered if Brittany would recognize it and remember when he had outbid her for the picture. At the time, they hadn't met and he wondered if she would even recall the incident. If she did, she was going to be less than happy with him about it.

His office was large and luxurious, but he didn't care what kind of office he had at Brittany Beach. He just wanted the fifty percent control that he now had. He'd launched the Jefferies' invasion of the Garrison properties. And he'd acquired a gorgeous partner.

Again, his blood heated when he thought about her and he stood restlessly. He yanked open a top drawer and grabbed up a handful of photos and tossed them on his desk, spreading them with his fingers. The pictures were shots of Brittany Beach, taken last week. A rush of satisfaction surged in him as he picked up one particular picture. Brittany stood in front of the restaurant, talking to a nondescript man who held a rake and Emilio assumed the man was a gardener. Brittany wore a diaphanous skirt and open top with a skimpy blue slash of silk across her breasts. The filmy skirt rode low on her hips and beneath it she wore electric-blue shorts that were as skimpy as her matching top. For a woman who was cautious about love, her wardrobe screamed seduction and sensuality. He smiled and ran his finger over her picture, re-membering the sparks that sizzled between them. He scooped up the pictures to drop them back into his drawer as he decided he would have Brittany and her restaurant, too.

He headed toward his kitchen to make plans for the evening. When he strode through his main dining room, he glanced around at his own restaurant with its ambience of seduction. Tonight, pink and rose lighting would give a heightened sensu-ality to the platforms that contained beds for dining. His pulse jumped at the thought of being with Brittany and he glanced at his watch, counting the minutes until it was time for her arrival.

Shortly after eight in the evening, Brittany returned to her condo to get ready for dinner with Emilio. Anticipation bubbled in her. Ignoring worries, she bathed and selected a black sheath dress that ended above her knees. Black stiletto T-strap pumps added to her height.

As she dressed, she listened to the weather report. A hurri-cane was far out in the Atlantic, but it was on a westward course. In seconds, her thoughts had jumped back to Emilio and she lost all interest in weather, but she'd heard enough to know the storm wouldn't make landfall until Sunday night or Monday. By that time, Brittany knew the storm could change course or dissipate.

With care, she brushed her long hair, pulling it high on one side of her head to catch it up with pins and a clip. Diamond stud earrings were her only jewelry. Finally, she picked up her small, metallic black bag and left.

Beneath a huge red neon sign that proclaimed El Diablo, a drive curved to the front door. As she circled around, she looked at lights splashing over the hot pink restaurant. Beds of exotic red flowers bloomed and lights bathed tall, graceful palms that spilled dark shadows across the green lawn. She stopped in front of the entrance, turning the key over to a valet.

Music played outside and the place was already crowded. When she entered, she crossed to the maître d', to ask for Emilio. While she waited, she looked around. Red flames were painted on hot pink walls in the entrance, highlighted by red-and-orange lighting spilling over the area. Potted palms, banana trees and tropical foliage added touches of green.

"Welcome," came a deep voice behind her and she turned to face Emilio, who smiled as his admiring regard drifted leisurely over her and he reached out to take her arm. "You look beautiful!" he said softly.

The moment she heard his voice her pulse jumped. His handsome looks were heightened by a dark gray shirt that was tucked into gray slacks.

"Thank you," she answered breathlessly, thinking each time they were together her reaction to him intensified.

"Come with me," he said. "We have a private room." He led her through part of the main dining room. "I thought you might want to see all of El Diablo."

"I've eaten here before," she said, glancing around at the beds on raised platforms. Sheer curtains were tied back, or for some, had been loosened to lend a semblance of privacy. Like decadent sultans, people lounged on beds while they partied and ate. One end of the room held a dance floor where couples gyrated to a fast beat. The noise level was high with music and laughter and conversation mingling together. "Food here has always been delicious," she added.

"I hope you were here either because of business, or with a party."

She arched her brows. "You guessed correctly in both cases," she said and his smile broadened. He took her to his kitchen and introduced her to his executive chef, a tall brown-haired man who talked briefly about the night's specialties and his favorite dishes.

As they left the kitchen, Emilio introduced her to his manager. The short blond shook hands with Brittany and welcomed her to El Diablo.

Next, Emilio led her along a hall to a room with a glass door and glass walls. Beyond it was an inner office.

"This is the reception area for my office. I want you to see my office," he said, leading her through another door and switching on a light.

As she looked around, she thought his white office with deep blue accents was as striking as the ocean view through a glass wall. "It's beautiful," she remarked, circling the room as he had done in her office. She paused in front of an abstract oil painting. "The Richardson. This is a new artist and this picture has a story behind it." She glanced over her shoulder at him.

"So you remember," he said, looking chagrined.

"How could I forget you taking this away from me?" she answered noncommittally.

"We hadn't been introduced at that time and when I did meet

you it was much later and, frankly, I hoped you'd forgotten all about the auction."

"Oh, no!" she exclaimed, remembering clearly their contest over the painting as the bidding had climbed and everyone else had dropped out. "You have good taste in art."

"At some point, I wondered if you were bidding it higher out of spite," he said.

She turned and spoke frankly. "I wanted it and I was annoyed that you continued to bid. No, I would have been happy to get it. It's still one of my favorites and I think someday, this artist will be in demand. You made a good investment, although it was crummy of you to keep bidding."

Emilio strolled over to her, standing only inches away and her pulse jumped. "Not one bit worse than your refusal to quit. So you really wanted it?"

"I wouldn't have kept bidding, otherwise, but now I suspect you must have continued because you didn't want to lose. Your suspicions of my motives indicate you took the price higher to keep someone else from besting you."

A smile hovered in his expression as he shrugged one broad shoulder and touched her cheek teasingly. "That might have been part of my reason. It's not often I get to compete with a beautiful woman."

"Thank you for the compliment. I suspect you go into all contests planning to win."

"There's no point in doing something to lose, is there?" he asked softly, and she could feel a challenge running beneath their words. Once again, she wondered how much he would interfere with her running of Brittany Beach.

She raised her chin defiantly and shot him a look that let him know she was a worthy adversary.

She saw a flicker in the depths of his eyes that she'd seen before. It was irresistible to flirt with him.

"You've made my day by joining me tonight," he said in a husky voice that stirred a tingle in her.

"No, I made your day when I signed over half my restaurant this afternoon," she retorted and he laughed.

"Maybe that, too, but tonight equals this afternoon."

"I know better than that," she teased and turned to look at the picture again. "No, I won't ever forget our bidding. I knew who you were. You didn't know me."

"I didn't, but I found out as soon as the bidding was over. After all, I had to know who my gorgeous competitor was. I meant to get over and meet you, but you slipped out of there. Afterward, when we finally did meet, because of the outcome, I didn't think it wise to bring up the auction. Frankly, I figured you'd forgotten."

"Not in this lifetime."

"So, I'm not the only one who doesn't like to lose. I'll remember that."

"Which is sort of a given that we're going to clash," she said, strolling to look at another painting. He stayed where he was and when she glanced back at him, she found him studying her.

"Hopefully, our skirmishes will be as stimulating as that one was."

"You found it invigorating because you won. I found it annoying enough to never forget about it."

"I'll have to make amends some way," he said. "Perhaps I should let you win the next contest."

"Sure, you do that," she said, finishing her tour of his office and turning toward him.

"You sound as if you think it's impossible for me to give up getting my way."

"We'll see. Actions speak louder than words."

He walked up to her and spread his palm in the center of her back. "I don't think we're going to clash in every area," he said in a deep voice and she tingled again and hoped he didn't detect her racing pulse. His mouth was well shaped, his full lower lip was sensual. What would it be like to kiss him? She suspected his kisses would be fiery and as irresistible as everything else about him. Realizing her train of thought, she looked up into a mocking expression in his green eyes. "I'm sure we're not," he added. "We'll find out."

"Eventually," she added, knowing he wasn't referring to auctions or business.

He dropped his hand. "Come along and I'll show you where we'll eat tonight."

"El Diablo looks packed already," she said as they left his office and entered the hall. "People are waiting."

"The weekends always hold capacity crowds. You have to call at least a month in advance to get a reservation," he said, opening another door and stepping back to usher her into a room that was a backdrop for seduction. "Welcome to my private dining room," he said.

Four

"Oh, my!" she exclaimed, laughing. "This is more decadent than in the main dining room," she said.

"Only as decadent as we make it," he retorted with a twinkle in his green eyes.

She shook her head. "Don't get your hopes up," she rejoined firmly.

"That's impossible. You can't imagine how high my hopes are," he said, and she laughed again. Brittany knew she shouldn't be surprised that he was good company.

"In that case, I can tell you that you're in for a letdown tonight."

"Never with you," he drawled. "So far, the evening has started out even better than I expected."

She smiled at him. "I have to agree," she said softly, and he inhaled, his chest expanding. She enjoyed sparring with him too much, even if she was crossing a line. Their light banter left business in the dust and took their relationship in a whole different direction. She felt bubbly with him, challenged and charmed.

"That gives me great hope," he said in a husky voice. "This partnership dazzles me."

"Don't pour it on. This dining room is enough," she added drily, staring at the space.

Soft-red light filled the circular room that was centered with a round bed on a raised platform. Green plants formed a backdrop along one wall. Inviting yellow cushions and pillows were propped against a low wall that surrounded half the bed area. A spread of delectable-looking yellow-and-white cheeses, bright-red strawberries, green kiwi and other tempting snacks were already on a table in the center of the bed.

"Come on, enjoy dining like a sheik," he said, offering her his hand as he kicked off his shoes.

"I thought your dining room was racy. This absolutely screams seduction."

"Ah, then it's doing what it's supposed to," he teased with a gleam in his gaze.

"Not tonight, my dear partner."

"I'll cling to that 'dear.'"

"I suspect you're accustomed to a more intimate endearment. I don't think you'll pay attention long," she said as she removed her shoes and took his hand to crawl onto the bed. His warm fingers wrapped around her hand and she looked into his eyes. The moment became electric and she drew a deep breath.

With an effort, she glanced away and climbed onto the bed, scooting to keep a distance between them. Propping herself against the pillows, she tucked her long legs beneath her and smiled at him. "Soft, red lighting. We're in bed together with champagne on ice. This promises to be an unforgettable evening, but remember, this is a business deal. View me the same as you would if it were one of my brothers who was your new partner."

"That's totally impossible," Emilio answered. "When we're alone and you're only a few feet away, I'm aware that it's you I'm with. And I've looked forward to this time all day. We have a deal to celebrate. Let go, Brittany. Stop being the businesswoman for a few hours," he coaxed.

"I think I stopped being the corporate woman when I got dressed for tonight."

Emilio stood to open the bottle of champagne that was on ice. She watched as he popped the cork, poured the golden liquid and handed her a flute. He sat beside her again and raised his glass. "Here's to a great partnership."

She touched her flute to his and took a sip of the bubbly drink. "I'm looking forward to this. Scared, too, I'll admit."

"Scared? Of me? Never!" he exclaimed. "Why would you be scared?"

"I gave up full control today. That's always scary."

"You'll see, this partnership is going to be awesome. Anytime you're unhappy, promise you'll let me know."

She smiled. "I don't think you need to worry about not knowing if I'm unhappy."

"Does this mean my partner has a temper?"

"I don't call it that," she responded. "What about you?"

"Not ever with you. That would be impossible."

"Don't make rash statements. You said you've had your fights with your brother, so there's a temper."

"Brothers have a way of provoking each other. We're close, but we both know that we're competitive and since we're the same age, we're bound to have clashes."

"Sounds as if I'm describing my life with my twin, Brooke," Brittany remarked.

Her gaze lowered to his full, sensual lips that made her pulse beat faster. It had barely been twenty-four hours since she had met and talked to him in her restaurant and here she was stretched out beside him in a bed and locked into partnership with him.

"Here's to a spectacular future for Brittany Beach," he said, lifting his glass in a toast.

She smiled as she touched her glass to his and sipped again. "So now you have El Diablo, which is successful, and you have part interest in Brittany Beach, which is growing. What are your long-range plans?"

He shrugged. "I think these two places will keep me busy. My brother and I work together on Jefferies' holdings, so I keep up with what he's doing the way he does with me."

"What's he think about your new partnership?"

"He thinks it's a good investment. He's enthusiastic about it, and why wouldn't he be?"

Emilio was propped on the mound of cushions, one long leg stretched out, one leg bent with his arm resting on his knee while he held his glass of champagne. Turned on his side, he was only inches away from her while he waited for her answer.

She shrugged. "I suppose you're right."

"Do you ever take time off?" Emilio asked her.

"Not often. I will in the future. I don't need to now."

"So my partner is a workaholic," he said, picking up a menu. "I need to show you how to enjoy life," he said, handing her a menu.

She leaned back against the pillows to read the suggestive choices, yet the food described beneath the names sounded savory, and she already knew it was first-rate.

"See anything you like?" he asked in a deep voice.

"Of course. It all looks yummy."

"Yummy's right," he repeated, his eyes steadily on her and she suspected he was not referring to the dinner items listed. "Delectable, enticing and I'm starving." With every word his voice dropped and became more of a rasp.

"Concentrate, Emilio, on food," she rejoined, as always her breathlessness betraying her reaction to him.

Smiling, he returned to reading his menu. She looked at his thick eyelashes and his wavy hair that she could too easily imagine combing through her fingers.

"I hope you've found something tasty for dinner," he said.

"I know what I want," she said, closing her menu.

"And so do I," he said, giving her a long look that made her pulse race again.

Emilio pushed a button and within minutes, a waiter knocked and entered to take their orders. Conscious of Emilio's unwavering regard on her, she ordered a fruit and rum drink with her pork tenderloin. When Emilio ordered their appetizers, Cabernet with an entrée of crusted beef tenderloin, and his attention was on the waiter, she took the opportunity to let her focus drift over his length. This tall, appealing man had altered her business already, simply by becoming her partner. What other changes lay ahead? she wondered. She looked up to find him watching her with a faint smile.

"So what are your ambitions, Brittany? What do you want in your future?"

"Right now, I'm totally focused on making Brittany Beach a success," she replied.

"And once it is—then what?"

"I think that'll be sufficient to keep me busy as long as I want to be involved in it. I don't have to try to own half of South Beach the way my brothers seem aimed to."

"You didn't say a word about romance, a partner outside the business, even marriage or a family. Are you burned out on families?"

"Not at all," she denied, aware of Emilio stretched out beside her. "In the future, I want my own family and children someday, but I'm not in a rush. Right now, Brittany Beach takes my time. It won't always."

"With a partner, that should ease slightly."

"So you'll see to it that I have time to get out with men and fall in love," she teased.

One of his dark eyebrows arched. "You're misreading my intentions in this partnership if you think I'm here to free you up to go out with other men. I want to get to know you better, myself."

Her pulse gave another skip as she laughed. "I opened the door for that remark. You know I was kidding."

"I wasn't," he answered.

She sipped her drink and stared at him over her glass. "We'll get to know each other at work."

"Yes, we will," he agreed. "And I'm looking forward to it immensely. So far, my time has never been spent better."

"You're back to exaggeration. You're too accustomed to trying to charm your companion."

Amusement flared in his eyes. "While you are going to give me the unvarnished truth. We'll be a challenge to each other."

"No, no! No challenges here," she said quickly with a wave of her fingers. "I don't want to become a project."

"Brittany Beach is a project. You and I are on the way to becoming friends."

"I'll drink to that one," she said, raising her glass and he touched his to hers with a faint clink, his fingers brushing hers. "To our lasting friendship," she said.

"And wherever it leads us," he added, gazing into her eyes and making her breath catch.

The waiter knocked and served a basket of thick bread slices along with their appetizer of golden tiger shrimp. He poured small saucers of oil and balsamic vinegar for dipping their bread and then they were alone again.

"So what was growing up like?" she asked him and he shrugged.

"I had a good life. I remember moments with my birth mother, but I was only three when she died. The Jefferies were the parents I knew and they gave me opportunities that I would never have had, otherwise."

"They're not still living, are they?" she asked, vaguely remembering hearing that they had both died.

He shook his head. "No. Jordan and I were backpacking across Europe after graduating from college when our folks died in a boating accident."

"I'm sorry, Emilio. That's dreadful! Do you and Jordan get along?"

"Sure. Since Jordan and I are the same age, we're close and, at the same time, we've had our share of brotherly battles, but it was kid stuff, competition. We're both strong-willed."

"So you admit that," she teased.

He shrugged and tugged a lock of her hair. "I suspect someone else in this room is a strong-willed person."

She smiled. "My family sees me as the baby. Even my twin sister does. That's why I'm so determined to make a go of Brittany Beach," she admitted. "I don't tell most people that, Emilio."

"Good. I hope you share things with me. That's what a friend is for," he said. "I understand about families. I was the adopted son, so I always thought I had to keep up with Jordan."

"I imagine you did," she said.

He shrugged. "Well enough," he answered. Studying her, he placed his fork on his plate. "I've known a lot of women, but I haven't had a lot of females who were important friends. You're easy to talk to and you're a good listener and, as partners, we may have a special relationship."

"I hope we're friends. We're going to have to trust each other."

He looked down and touched his fork. She drank some of

her water and when he looked up, his expression was solemn. "Brittany…" He paused and she waited.

"What is it?" she asked.

"I hope we're best friends," he finished finally and she smiled at him, yet she had the feeling he had been about to say something else and she wondered if something bothered him.

The waiter appeared with their entrées and conversation shifted back to food and the restaurant.

After the first bite of her tender pork, she sighed. "This is delicious! No wonder you have such a crowd. People will always come for food like this."

"I'm glad you like it," he said easily.

She took another bite and closed her eyes to savor it as she chewed. "Emilio, this is absolutely scrumptious."

"I hope I can evoke that kind of reaction in you sometime," he said in a husky voice, and she opened her eyes to find him watching her.

Her appetite fled and awareness of Emilio took its place. She took a deep breath as she reached for her wine and sipped, watching him. She felt consumed by his green gaze that conveyed his desire. She set down her glass and waved her fingers at him. "Go back to you dinner," she whispered.

"There are other things I'd rather do," he said in a voice that had lowered another notch.

"Right now, we're sticking to dinner," she said, hoping she sounded matter-of-fact and more calm than she felt. He sat so close and his expression was so intent that she found it difficult to get back to a more impersonal level.

"These beds cause all kinds of trouble."

"Au contraire!" he said in a soft voice. "This is one of the best dinners I've ever had."

"You go back to concentrating on your beef," she said. "And I'll do the same with mine."

"I'm concentrating," he answered and she looked up at him, knowing he wasn't focusing on his dinner. When she pointed to his plate, he smiled.

Her appetite had diminished and she noticed that his was not great, either, in spite of the delicious cuisine. He had already ordered dessert and they ate a few bites of a decadent chocolate concoction they shared before she put down her fork and sat back.

"Thanks for the fabulous meal," she said.

"We can at least dance off dinner," he suggested.

"I agree with you on that," she replied, standing when he did and slipping into her pumps again.

"Which dance floor—our outdoor pavilion and Latin music, or the main dining room with its dance floor."

"I'll take the pavilion," she replied. They strolled through a small lush garden. A bar stretched along one corner of the pavilion and tables formed a semicircle around the dance floor and bar.

After getting a table and ordering drinks, Emilio held her chair. "Excuse me a moment, Brittany. I need to make a quick call."

She nodded and enjoyed watching the dancers while Emilio was gone. When he returned, he took her hand to lead her to the dance floor where he turned her to face him for a tango. His every move was seductive, a reminder of his fit, muscular body.

As they danced, his hot gaze followed every move she made, leaving her warm and flushed. She was aware they had left business in the dust and the evening had changed from a celebration of work.

After half a dozen dances, they returned to their table. "I can see more reasons why this restaurant is so successful," she said, sipping her bottled water.

It was two in the morning before she realized the time and told him she should go.

"Come by the office. I have something to seal our bargain."

Curious, she slanted him a look, but went along with him as he took her arm.

He turned on one soft light and disappeared into his bar, leaning down to pick up something. When he came out of the bar, he carried a large box wrapped in white paper and tied with a huge red ribbon. He carried it to a credenza and set it down. "A present to remember this day and night and the beginning of a fantastic partnership," he said.

Surprised, she looked up at him. "You shouldn't have done this."

"I wanted to," he said quietly. "Go ahead. Open your present."

She started to pick it up and discovered it was heavy. Surprised, she glanced at Emilio, who stood patiently waiting. She carefully unfastened the large red silk bow. "This is too beautiful to open."

"Presents are for opening and enjoying," he said, looking amused. "I didn't know it would be such a production to get into. Christmas and birthdays must take you hours and hours."

She wrinkled her nose at him. "This bow is far too pretty to demolish. I'm excited, but I don't have a present for you."

"That's not the point here. I'm doing what I want to do," he said. "Of course, I didn't expect a production of opening a gift. I do have a knife."

"Heavens, no! We're not cutting this ribbon," she said and bent over to undo the knot. When she had trouble, he joined her and tugged on a piece of the ribbon, leaning near enough that she could detect his enticing aftershave.

"There," he said, and she pulled the bow free and carefully wound up the ribbon and placed it on the table. She tore open the paper to find a large, plain white box.

"I can't imagine," she said, glancing at him while her curiosity grew.

He shrugged. "There's a way to find out," he said, smiling.

She tugged off the lid and gasped as she looked at the Richardson painting. She whirled to look at the empty place on his wall where the painting had been. "Emilio, you can't give me this!"

"I can and I have," he said, smiling at her while he stood with his hands on his hips. He walked up to her and her pulse drummed. She looked at the painting again.

"When did you box this up?"

"Before we started dancing. Andino wrapped it for me and got one of the women to tie the bow. Rather a nice job of wrapping."

"I can't take your painting."

He laughed. "After battling me tooth and nail for it at the auction? Come on—you love it and you know it."

"Yes, but it's yours and it's valuable."

"It's a gift from me to you, Brittany. I want you to have it in celebration of our partnership. Take it and enjoy it."

She drew a deep breath and turned to look at him again. Impulsively, she threw her arms around his neck to hug him. "Thank you! What a marvelous gift!"

Instantly, his arm banded her waist and he held her tightly. She leaned back to look up at him, framing his face with her hands, feeling the faintest growth of stubble beneath her palms.

The minute her lips touched his, his tongue touched her and her mouth opened to him.

His tongue stroked hers, stirring erotic sensations. He wrapped his other arm tightly around her, holding her against his hard length. Her heart slammed against her ribs and she felt as if she were standing in flames.

She returned his kiss passionately as her tongue stroked his. Her pulse roared in her ears and time vanished. She tightened her arms around his neck and wound her fingers in his hair. Desire ignited and she ached for him, holding him tightly, forgetting everything else except his kisses.

How much time passed, she didn't know. Her heart pounded and Emilio's hand slid up her back and he caressed her nape, heightening her need.

Realizing how passionately she kissed him, she pushed gently against his chest.

Immediately, he raised his head and studied her with a smoldering gaze. Her heart still thudded and she hoped she could catch her breath and find her voice. She leaned inches more away from him.

"I didn't mean for that to happen," she whispered, looking into his green eyes that had darkened to the color of a stormy sea.

"I'm glad it did," he said in return, still holding her, studying her features. She shook her head.

"No. We're business partners. I meant to keep things professional between us," she said with her quiet tone covering her stormy emotions, because his kiss had been sensational. She pushed again lightly and he released her.

"Professional went out the window when we began having a long phone conversation and becoming good friends. Tonight, there's dinner, dancing." His eyes twinkled. "And the evening isn't over yet," he said.

"It's near enough over." Smiling, she shrugged. "You're a sexy man. Just don't take my heart."

"I'm a sexy man," he repeated in a husky voice. "Now that really did make my day."

She glanced at the picture, thinking of a way to change the subject. "I want you to know that I love my gift and I'll treasure it."

"Good. That's what I want you to do," he replied, still watching her. "And wipe out a memory of us fighting over it."

Smiling, she shook her head. Overwhelmed by his kiss that had stirred her more than she would have dreamed possible, she tried to gather her wits. She turned to look at the painting again, running her index finger carefully along a corner of the frame. "This really is beautiful."

He came to stand beside her to look at the painting. She was acutely conscious that his arm grazed hers.

"I don't want to carry something this valuable home tonight when I'm alone."

"Wait and I'll bring it to your house when you want me to."

She looked up at him and her pulse jumped again as she saw the desire that still burned in his eyes. "Tomorrow night, eat dinner at my house. I'll come get the painting and, if you want, you can ride back with me."

"I'll be there for dinner and I'll bring the painting." She told him the combination to get through the gate at her condo.

"Emilio, the gift is wonderful! I'm so thrilled. Thank you," she said again, turning to face him.

He placed a hand on her shoulder. "This doesn't mean that I won't outbid you again at another auction," he said, and she smiled.

"Next time, I may not give up so easily."

"I don't think you gave up easily on this one. Now it's yours, and if it hadn't been for you, I could have had it for much less."

"Don't complain, you got it. Only now it's *mine,*" she said, laughing and excited over his gift. She turned to face him again. "What a wonderful evening you've shown me! It's been fabulous."

He crossed the room with her and held open the door. "I'll go out with you."

"Do you have a picture to put in place of the one you gave me?"

"Not now, but I'll get one," he replied casually. "No problem."

When they left the front of the restaurant, he took the stub from her to give to the valet to bring her car. As soon as it arrived, Emilio tipped the valet and went around to open her door himself. As soon as she was seated, he leaned down. "I look forward to tomorrow night and I'll call you in a while," he said.

"Thanks a million. Good night, Emilio."

As he stepped back, she drove away, glancing in the rearview mirror to see him watching her. Her lips still tingled from his kisses.

The evening had been fabulous. She liked his company. His kisses burned her to cinders and dancing with him had ignited desire.

Excitement bubbled in her and she was anxious to get home and talk to him some more. She was shocked to have a partner, to have her debt erased, to have the Richardson oil painting, but, most of all, she was surprised to discover how much she enjoyed Emilio and how much she responded to him. Once again, she reminded herself that was probably the same reaction as most women he knew.

When she entered her empty condo her phone was ringing, and she dropped her purse and made a dash to yank up the receiver and answer.

Smiling when she heard Emilio's voice, she switched on lights and stretched out on her bed to talk. He'd called to say good night and after a quick chat, they broke the connection.

Humming and smiling, she got ready for bed and then was too keyed up to sleep. She kept remembering their fiery kisses that had stirred her more than any others in her life.

Tomorrow night, Emilio would be with her at her place for dinner. She couldn't wait to spend another evening with her new partner. Her fabulous, sexy partner who continued to surprise her.

Five

The next day, Emilio called to say he wouldn't make it by Brittany Beach because he had unexpected situations arise at El Diablo. They arranged to see each other at Brittany's at eight. "You said you like to swim. Bring your suit and we'll swim before dinner," she said.

"Absolutely," he replied. "See you at eight," he added and ended his call.

As the day passed, Brittany wondered how many times she looked at the clock before she finally headed home to get ready for Emilio's visit.

After trying on several outfits, she settled on a blue sundress and sandals. She wore her hair in a thick braid and her anticipation built as she dressed.

Promptly at eight her doorbell chimed.

She opened the door to find Emilio standing with a bottle of wine under his arm, the box in his hands, his swim trunks and towel on top of the box. Dressed in a tan knit shirt and tan slacks, he looked his usual handsome self.

Excited to have him by for dinner, she stepped back and ushered him inside.

His warm gaze slipped over her and she could see the approval in his eyes. "You look great," he said.

"Thanks. Bring the painting in here and, for now, let's put it on the bed in the spare bedroom. Later on, you can help me decide where to hang it."

Emilio followed her into the bedroom to place it on the bed and then he paused to look around at the polished wood floor, wicker furniture and contemporary art on the walls. "Nice room," he said.

"Come on and I'll show you the rest of my place."

She took him through the condo and he looked at everything, stepping into her bedroom to glance at the bed and then at her. "Now I'll be able to picture you in my mind when we talk on the phone and you tell me you're in your bed."

"And that matters?" she asked.

"Sure. I want to know all about you." He crossed the room to place his hands on her shoulders. "I'm discovering I have a fascinating partner."

"I lead an ordinary life," she said.

He grinned. "As if being a Garrison is an 'ordinary life.'"

"Mine isn't so unusual. Hey, it's been a hot, steamy day. Want to swim first?"

"Sure."

"You can change in the other bedroom and meet me at the pool. It's right through the door off my dining room." She left to change into her two-piece dark blue swimsuit and its cover-up. When she approached the pool, he bobbed up, shook his head and swam toward the edge in long, powerful strokes.

Splashing water, he climbed out and her pulse jumped. His

body was lean and muscular. Muscles rippled with every move he made. His taut biceps bulged and he had a mat of dark curls across his chest. He was deeply tanned with his naturally olive skin turned even darker by the hot Florida sunshine. He wore narrow, low-riding trunks and she inhaled deeply. His washboard belly was flat, revealed by the low suit.

She kicked off her flip-flops and dropped her cover-up on a chaise lounge and turned to find him watching her. Desire blazed in his green eyes as they traveled over her.

"You look great! You serve dinner like that and you'll pack 'em into Brittany Beach."

She laughed. "If I serve dinner wearing this, I'll be arrested. Race you across the pool to the far corner," she said, striding past him and jumping in to swim as fast as she could.

She knew when he caught up with her. She had given herself a head start and now she fought to keep up with him, wanting to beat him and wondering why she was so competitive. In seconds, he pulled ahead and when she reached the corner, he was already there with his arms stretched out on the sides of the pool as he lounged and waited for her. "Beat you," he said, teasing her. "You're competitive, Brittany."

"Only sometimes and in certain things. Maybe you bring it out in me," she said and his grin widened.

She splashed water on him and he caught her wrists, playfully trying to dunk her. She grew up with brothers and she twisted to grab his shoulders to take him down with her. They both went under, struggling and then bobbing up and laughing.

He caught her around the waist and yanked her to him. She thought he was going to dunk her again and she reached to hold him, but then she looked into his eyes and her breath caught.

She could tell he wanted her and she knew he was going to kiss her. She became aware of her legs against his, her body pressed against his. He was wet and warm and solid hard muscles. His arm tightened around her waist, drawing her against him.

Her heart pounded as her breasts pressed against his chest. Her lips parted and she looked at his mouth. He lowered his head to brush her lips with his. With a soft moan, she wrapped her arms around his neck and pulled his head down to her. "I said I wasn't going to do this and here I am, doing it again," she whispered.

He covered her mouth with his, his tongue sliding into her mouth to stroke her. She was hot, suddenly burning, even though she was in cold water. She clung to Emilio, kissing him passionately, holding him, aware they were almost naked in each other's arms. She let one hand slide over his smooth, muscled back.

She moved her hips against him as his hand followed the curve of her back, down over her bottom, heightening her desire.

While she kissed Emilio deeply and as passionately as he kissed her, her pulse drowned out all other sounds except the roaring in her ears. She ached for him, wanting more, knowing she was getting more involved with him every time they were together.

She pushed against him and leaned back. "This isn't a private pool," she whispered, barely knowing what she was saying. He looked as if he could devour her. He inhaled deeply and released her, regarding her with a hunger that made her feel as if he wanted her more than anything else on earth. She swam away from him and then turned when she had put yards between them.

"We've had our swim. I'll dress and get us drinks," she said while they both treaded water. She wondered if he knew how badly she wanted to keep on kissing him.

He nodded and disappeared underwater. She swam to the edge and climbed out, retrieving her cover-up and glancing back to find him at the side of the pool watching her.

Warming beneath his steady gaze, she pulled on the blue cover-up, slipped into her flip-flops and headed for the gate. Her back prickled and she knew his eyes followed her every move.

She hurried inside and showered, pulling her hair free and drying it. Thinking about him, she dressed again in her sundress and sandals and tied her hair behind her head with a blue ribbon. His kisses had increased her desire and she knew her awareness of him would be even more intense.

She found him in the kitchen with two glasses of wine.

"I hope you don't mind," he began, but when he turned to look at her, he stopped. "Look at you."

He crossed the room to her and her pulse jumped, as it did constantly when he was near. "Your hair is down," he said, reaching behind her head to tug the blue ribbon free. "I like you this way," he said with a hoarse note in his deep voice.

She shook her head slightly and smiled at him. "It's just plain hair," she said.

"You look great," he said softly.

"Thanks. And you started to say something about me not minding—not minding what?" she asked.

He put her ribbon on a table and turned. "I hope you don't care that I got our drinks. I rummaged around and found glasses. I started the grill on your patio because I saw the steaks you have marinating in the fridge. Unless those are for another night," he said, picking up the glasses of wine and crossing the room to hand her a drink.

"They're for tonight and, my, aren't you efficient to have around."

"You'd be surprised what I can do," he said with a faint smile.

She tilted her head to study him. "Now that does make me wonder. In the meantime, I'll add efficient to your good qualities."

"You say that like there's a list of good qualities and a list of bad. Is there?"

"Do you have a guilty conscience?" she teased.

"No, I don't," he said, smiling at her, but something flickered in his eyes, startling her and she wondered what he was thinking.

"No bad qualities yet that I've discovered," she said. "But I'll qualify it with a 'yet.'"

When he handed her the drink, their fingers brushed and even that slight contact stirred more tingles. "I remember the looks you gave me when we were in the bidding war."

"It's cooler to sit in here," she said, waving her hand toward the room adjoining the kitchen. It was a casual living area with bamboo furniture and had a glass wall that gave a view of the beach and ocean. He followed her down two steps into the room and when she sat on the leather sofa, he sat at the other end, turning to face her.

"Here's to getting to know you better," he said, lifting his glass and extending it to her so she could touch it with hers.

"And to getting to know you, too, Emilio," she replied, thinking about their moment in each other's arms in the pool. "I'd say we're off to a great beginning."

He stretched out a long arm to touch a lock of her hair. She felt a faint tug against her scalp and was aware of his constant scrutiny.

"How many women are in your life? From the media, it looks as if there are too many to count," she asked, her way of reminding him she knew of his magnetism toward women.

"There isn't even one in particular right now. Sounds as if your opinion of me is all wrong where females are concerned."

"I know all the pictures I see."

"Tabloids. You should know better than to put stock in them. So has there ever been a particular man in your life?"

She shrugged. "Not really. The most important was a relationship in college. Long forgotten now."

Emilio smiled. "Good news all around."

"Ready for me to put on the steaks?" she asked, and when he nodded, she stood. Since that first night at Brittany Beach, she had always been conscious of him as a sexy, appealing male, but now, because of their kisses, she was far more aware of the slightest contact with him or even merely when he stood beside her. Occasionally, when he was busy with something, she studied his handsome features and couldn't keep from pausing when she looked at his mouth and remembered his kisses.

Within minutes, he took over the grilling task and she got salads, glasses of water, hot baked potatoes and rolls on the table.

As they ate, she listened to him talk about getting El Diablo started and they compared notes on the beginnings of their two restaurants. After dinner, he helped her clean and put away dishes and the time flew. When they finished, she faced him.

"Now, come with me and help me decide where to hang the painting."

They went to her living room, which had white walls, a polished hardwood floor, bookshelves on one wall. Her furniture was mahogany, more formal, but still with glass tables and contemporary art on the wall. Emilio strolled over to study her Jasper Johns painting.

"Nice, Brittany," Emilio said. He turned to look at the walls.

"I think I want the picture above my sofa," she said, waving her hand toward the plain deep blue sofa. "What do you think?"

"I think what you want is what's best. You're the one who lives here," he said. He walked over to place the Richardson painting carefully on a table and then he returned to lift down the picture that already hung over the sofa. He stood it on the floor and propped it against a wall.

Brittany watched him work, seeing the muscles flex in his back as his knit shirt clung to him. She thought about the moments in the pool when they had been locked in each other's arms and all but naked with only tiny strips of cloth between them. Desire made her hot and her gaze ran over him.

He turned and she looked up to meet his curious gaze. She could feel her cheeks grow warm.

"Can you hold the picture there?" she asked, hating the breathlessness in her voice.

"Sure," he said, pulling the sofa out from the wall slightly. He picked up the picture and held it out, centered behind the sofa.

"I think that looks wonderful. Emilio, I'll tell you again, you shouldn't have given it to me, but I love it!"

"That's what I hoped. After all, you fought tooth and nail for it," he said. "Actually, maybe it'll hang right where the one I took down was. Let's see how it looks."

After he hung it in place, he stepped back and pushed the sofa where it had sat. "What do you think?" he asked her.

"I think the painting looks perfect there. It's where it belongs."

"So do I get another hug and kiss?" he asked.

"Maybe later," she said, smiling at him. "Now I want the painting you removed to go somewhere else." She looked around. "Do you mind holding it over there for me?" She pointed to a space on another wall and he held the picture for a few moments before she shook her head. She asked him to try it elsewhere until she found the spot she liked.

"I'll hang it for you if you have the equipment."

"I can get the carpenter who does work here," she said. "Shall we sit in here to talk where I can look at my painting?" She motioned to a chair. She sat in a wingback chair and he sat in another near her. "This is far more exciting to have the painting now than it would have been if I'd outbid you. I really appreciate owning it."

"So I'm forgiven for outbidding you?"

"I didn't say that," she teased. "No, you're not, and I suspect if we end up at another auction, you'll do exactly the same thing if we both want something again."

"I'm not admitting to that when it might not ever happen," he said, stretching out his long legs and crossing them at his ankles. "So if you ever take time off, what do you like to do besides swim?"

"I like to go to flea markets and art galleries."

"So far, we share the same likes. Do you hike?"

"I never have. Where do you hike around here?"

"You don't around here. Okay, sometime soon, take some time and you show me your favorite galleries and I'll show you mine," he said.

"Deal. I have a couple of new artists I'm watching," she said, studying the picture across the room. She was still surprised he had given it to her and she was so thrilled to have it that she found it difficult to keep from looking at it constantly.

"This erases all the bad thoughts I had about you after the auction," she said, smiling at him.

"I figured you had some dark thoughts about me after you left that day." He grinned. "So now I'm in your good graces. Getting it and then giving it back to you both have definitely been worth my while," he said, his voice dropping a notch.

She knew he was talking about her kiss last night. "I'll enjoy my painting and you tell me about hiking," she said, to get back on a less volatile subject. She listened while Emilio talked about a hiking trip and they went from one topic to another. Later, they went to the kitchen to get pop for her and a cold beer for him before they sat at the kitchen table and talked more.

Finally, with a glance at his watch, Emilio stood. "It's time. Actually, way past time, since it's two in the morning."

She walked to the door with him, where he turned to her. "The steaks were great. The company was even better."

Looking into his green eyes, she saw the desire that she felt. "Thanks again for the picture. What a fabulous gift!"

When his gaze lowered to her mouth, her pulse raced. "This has been a great evening," he said and slipped his arm around her waist, drawing her to him. She placed her hands on his arms, feeling the solid muscles while she looked up at him and wondered if he could hear the pounding of her heart.

"Emilio," she whispered.

Leaning slightly, he covered her mouth with his. When his tongue went into her mouth, he tightened his arm, pulling her up against him as he leaned over her.

With her heart racing, Brittany wound her arm around his neck and clung to him as she kissed him in return. Thrusting her hips against him, she felt his arousal hard against her.

He leaned farther, turning slightly while he slipped his hand along her back and over her bottom. As he pulled her up tightly against him, she moaned. Desire rocked her and she clung to him to keep from reaching for his buttons.

He slipped his hand to her throat and then down to follow the straight neckline of her sundress. His hand drifted feather-light over her dress, down over her breast and a tremor shook her. She tightened her arms around his neck and shifted her hips tighter against him.

While he kissed her passionately, he wrapped both arms around her waist. Finally, she pushed against his shoulders and he released her. She opened her eyes to find him watching her with a smoldering gaze and such desire that she wanted to step right back into his arms. But she knew she shouldn't.

"We have to stop now," she said, trying to get her breath.

"It's been a great night," he said. "Will I see you tomorrow?"

She shook her head. "I doubt it. I take off during the day

and then late in the afternoon I go to Bal Harbour for our family dinner."

"Afterward?"

"I usually go home, unless there's a problem."

"You may have a weather problem tomorrow. The hurricane is heading this way, but it's losing force. They still expect a terrific storm that should hit about midnight tomorrow night or in the early hours of the morning." He hesitated for a moment. "It's been a great evening, Brittany."

"I think so, too," she said while he played with a lock of her hair. After a moment he gave a gentle tug on her hair and let go.

"Take care and thanks again for dinner. I'm glad to see where you live."

"I imagine you'll be back," she said lightly.

"I hope so," he replied and brushed a feathery kiss on her mouth before he turned to go out the door. She stepped outside and watched his long stride as he went to his car, climbed in and drove out of sight.

She shut and locked her door and returned to the living room to look at her new painting, but her thoughts were on their kisses in the pool this afternoon. She still tingled from the kisses they'd just had.

In a short time, she wasn't surprised to hear her phone ring and she rushed to answer it in her bedroom, where she could stretch out in bed and talk.

"What were you doing?" Emilio asked when she said hello. "Let me guess the answer to my own question. You were still looking at your painting."

Smiling, she lay on her pillows and propped one foot on her other knee. "You guessed exactly right. How intuitive of you."

"Do you like it for the painting itself or because you got it after all?"

"How can you ask that! Because of the painting," she insisted, laughing at his question. "It's fabulous and I think you're fantastic for giving it to me."

"Next time we're together, you show me exactly how fantastic you think I am."

"Instead, sometime I'll cook you another steak dinner," she replied.

"That's not the same at all. So what are you doing right now and how are you dressed or undressed?"

She smiled and answered him, going on to other topics until she looked at the clock and saw they had talked over an hour. "Emilio, I have to go or I won't be able to get up in the morning."

"It was a great evening," he told her again and said goodbye and broke the connection.

She got ready for bed and then returned to her living room to sit for another ten minutes to look at the painting, finally crawling into bed to dream about Emilio.

She slept late and as she ate breakfast, Emilio called to talk again, finally telling her goodbye.

She did chores around her place that she needed to do and talked to him once again about three that afternoon until she had to get off the phone to dress for her family dinner.

Brittany wore pale yellow slacks and a yellow silk shirt. She wished she had an excuse to miss this dinner—often the siblings weren't all there—but she thought she'd draw less attention if she attended it.

She tried to calm her nerves, hoping her hawkeyed brothers paid little attention to her, particularly her ambition-driven oldest brother, Parker. Hopefully, by nine o'clock she could escape and the ordeal would be over.

In ritzy Bal Harbour, she swept through the wide stone pillars to the estate and stopped next to Parker's convertible.

Inside, as she hurried across the silent foyer with its sweeping staircase and thick stone pillars, she encountered Lisette Wilson, their longtime housekeeper.

"Ah, Miss Brittany, I'm glad you're here," Lisette said, a faint smile crossing her features as she patted Brittany's wrist.

"How could I miss Sunday dinner?" Brittany responded brightly. "Where's the family?"

"On the veranda wondering when the storm will hit. Dinner will be announced in minutes."

"Then I better join them. I'm late and Mother's going to be unhappy with me."

"These days, she's unhappy with the whole world," Lisette said, her eyes clouding with worry and a frown creasing her wrinkled brow.

"Sorry, Lisette. I know you take good care of her. I don't know what we'd do without you."

"I've been with her a long time—with all of you, for that matter," she said, turning away.

Brittany squared her shoulders, already knowing that her mother's drinking had grown worse since her father's death and suspecting that would be confirmed again in seconds.

She found her family standing on the veranda with its view of the pool and, beyond the pool, the blue ocean. In the far distance, storm clouds were rolling in and Brittany knew bad weather was forecast for later that night.

The moment she stepped onto the veranda, Brooke and Brittany exchanged a look. For a second, Brittany had an instinctive feeling something was bothering Brooke and then the moment was gone as Brooke gave Brittany a vague smile.

Brooke stood talking to Parker, Anna Cross, Parker's fiancée, and Stephen. All greeted Brittany as she approached them. She paused where her mother was seated, smiling at Bonita, who clutched an almost-empty glass in her hand.

"You're really late," Bonita complained, the frown wrinkles in her brow deepening.

"There was a traffic tie-up on Collins that delayed me," Brittany answered truthfully.

"I'd think you'd put the family first when it's only once a week, but without your father, you probably don't want to come home," Bonita said sharply, her words thick and slightly slurred. Dark circles beneath Bonita's eyes had developed since the reading of the will, and Brittany knew her mother did nothing to hide her bitterness over the discovery of another child by their father. Even so, it was difficult to conjure up a lot of sympathy, because Bonita was a cold woman.

"I'm here," Brittany reminded her gently, ignoring Bonita's gibe. When she glanced at Brooke, she saw her twin bite her lip. Bonita's sharp words, even when directed at Brittany, could disturb Brooke.

"Hi, Brooke," Brittany greeted her sister, turning from Bonita, who was finishing her drink. Brittany turned to greet Parker, who had Anna at his side.

"Hi, Brittany," Parker greeted her while Anna smiled.

"Hi, Parker. Anna, it's nice to have you with us," she said. "You're the best thing that has ever happened to my brother."

"I'll agree with that," Parker said, looking fondly at Anna.

"I'm glad," Anna replied. "He's the best thing in my life."

Brittany bit back a sarcastic remark, knowing the two were in love and she didn't want to be unkind to Anna.

"It is getting stormy looking," Brittany said, glancing beyond them at the bank of dark clouds.

"We're in for a tropical storm tonight," Parker said, also looking at the ocean. "They downgraded the hurricane, but we'll still get wind and rain. I hope we're out of here before it hits. It's difficult enough on a sunny day to fight the traffic from here to SoBe."

"I'll leave early," Brittany said, seeing a chance to escape sooner than she had thought. "I want to make sure everything is all right at the restaurant."

"Good idea," Parker agreed. "We should all leave earlier tonight," he added, looking at Anna as if his reason for leaving early had nothing to do with a storm. The warmth in Parker's gaze always surprised Brittany. Her calculating brother was actually in love and it showed. Never would she have guessed that even Parker would be love struck, but since Anna had come into his life, he was in a daze most of the time when Brittany saw him.

"Hi, Brit. I saw the celebrity you had in your club Friday night," Stephen said, joining them. Bonita called to him and he left the group.

"I saw the picture, too," Parker said. "My congratulations. Seems Brittany Beach is drawing an illustrious crowd."

"Thanks, that gives me a warm, fuzzy feeling, Big Brother."

"Do I take that at face value or is there a little bite in it?" Parker asked in a noncommittal voice.

"I meant it. You're all Mr. Bottom Line, even more than Dad was. I'm happy when you're pleased with Brittany Beach. And speaking of Garrison holdings," she said, hoping to get off the topic of her restaurant, "are there any developments about our newly discovered sibling?"

Parker frowned and swirled a drink he had barely touched. "No. She's not interested in us, it seems."

"What a bomb Dad dropped on us," Adam remarked in what was almost a whisper as he joined them and greeted Brittany. "Mother seems to be having a worse time dealing with this, as time goes by, instead of the other way around. Sorry, Anna, but you're part of the family now and all that goes with sharing our lives."

Bonita was across the veranda, chatting with Stephen, both

talking in low voices. Brittany watched them a moment, marveling once again that Stephen was the one sibling who was never the target of their mother's biting criticisms. With the increase in their mother's drinking, Brittany wondered if that would change.

Her mind wandered from the conversation. She relaxed a degree because, so far, no one in the family seemed to have heard about the embezzlement or her new partner. If any of her siblings had, he—or she—would have already said something, Brittany was certain. She fought the temptation to glance at her watch. She knew she had only been there minutes, but she willed the time to pass.

It seemed aeons before dinner was announced, and she noticed that Stephen helped Bonita, who was unsteady on her feet. Brittany could see the grim tightening of Stephen's jaw and knew his disapproval of their mother's drinking was increasing at the same time that Bonita's overindulgence was growing.

The family entered the elegant dining room with its illuminated oil paintings, the ornate ceiling and a low-hanging chandelier. Again, Brittany was amused and surprised to see Parker hovering over Anna as he led her into the dining room.

While talk was lively around the table, Brittany's mind constantly wandered, back to Emilio, to her fear of discovery of her new partner before she was ready.

She glanced around the table, thinking about all their businesses from their father and how each sibling fought for success: Parker, CEO of Garrison, Inc., always kept an eye on everybody's business and usually managed at Sunday dinner to inquire about each sibling's current situation. Stephen owned Garrison Grand, a SoBe premier luxury hotel. Adam, younger than Stephen and Parker, had made a success of Estate, his popular nightclub. Brooke, who was unusually quiet, had The Sands, a luxury condominium building.

Remarks were made about each business, but when Brittany said her week had gone well, Adam mentioned a singer who had been photographed at Brittany Beach and later at Estate and the conversation shifted from Brittany's restaurant to his club.

Finally, to her relief, dinner was over and they adjourned to the veranda once more. With storm clouds approaching, the sky had darkened to indigo. When Parker got the weather report from CNN, they all listened.

"The storm's moving in earlier than predicted and we're going to get high winds and rain within the hour," Parker said, repeating what had been announced. "If any of you need my help, Anna and I can follow you back," he offered to Brittany, who shook her head quickly.

"Thanks, Parker, I'll be fine and I have generators," she said. "But I'll head there now. I'd like to get to the restaurant before the storm hits." She gave Bonita a perfunctory kiss on the cheek and realized her mother was a zombie and totally out of their conversation.

As quickly as possible, Brittany left to fight her way through traffic to SoBe.

She was halfway when the wind whipped up and in minutes, big drops of rain pelted her car. She turned into a parking lot and got out her cell to call the restaurant, telling Hector to get generators if the electricity went off and to put their portable red neon Open sign out near the curb.

"I'll be right there as soon as possible," she promised before she broke the connection and returned her attention to the highway, all worries about family replaced by concern for Brittany Beach.

<u>Six</u>

As she drove, the storm intensified. Wind bent palm trees and set signs flapping. Brittany's anxiety increased when rain began to fall in sheets, making driving slower and more difficult.

Electricity was out in SoBe and when she finally turned onto Brittany Beach's drive, she was thankful to see its neon lights shimmering through the rain and the red neon Open sign blazing brightly at the curb.

Inside, one of the first employees she saw was Hector, who rushed up to her. "Our generators are running," he said. "Business is booming because the rain has driven people off the street and the beach." She thought how they closed Washington Avenue to cars at night and the street filled with people, musicians, vendors, tourists, a mob that would all have to get somewhere inside tonight.

"We've got a huge crowd," Hector continued. "The lobby is packed and customers may have to wait two hours for a table."

"Serve them complimentary mojitos," she instructed. "The drinks should make the wait more tolerable. If they don't want a mojito, offer a soft drink. Pass something to them to nibble on. Get some kind of simple hors d'oeuvres that will be easy to replenish."

"I'll tell the kitchen right away," he said and left.

"Brittany…"

Instantly her pulse jumped because she recognized Emilio's deep voice. She turned to face him. In navy slacks and a navy cotton shirt, he stopped to comb his fingers through his wet hair.

As he walked up to her, his eyes swept over her with warm approval. "I thought I'd see if you need help, but looks as if you're doing fine," he said.

"We have generators," she said.

"Very good," he said, sounding relieved. "There are places that don't have backup power, and they're out of business until the electricity is restored, which may take a while because I've heard there are large residential areas without power."

"What are you doing out in this?"

"I wanted to see if you needed help," he said, glancing past her. "It doesn't look as if you do, and Brittany Beach appears to be busier than ever."

"Apparently, it is," she replied, self-conscious that her hair was windblown and her clothes damp. "Actually, I just got here, myself. Want to come with me to look around and see what's going on?"

"Sure. Maybe there's something I can do to help."

As they entered the main dining room that was packed with people, she glanced through the wide arch and glimpsed the crowd waiting to get a table. "We're serving complimentary mojitos and hors d'oeuvres to people in the lobby while they wait," she told Emilio and received another nod of approval.

"Good. When I came, people were still arriving."

The minute she stepped into the kitchen, she knew something was awry because people were scurrying around and voices were raised and her executive chef's hat was askew, his straight black hair sticking out in all directions. Angier saw her and rushed to her, waving his thin hands.

"We're running out of food. There's a record crowd, and we can't get dinners cooked quickly enough. Orders are backing up."

"Tell me what you need," she said. "We'll get it from somewhere. Let's get some grills out. Put them on the covered part of the veranda and grill outside."

"Two cooks can't get here and, with such a crowd, we're shorthanded," he complained.

"I'll see about the food," Brittany said.

"I'll do what I can to help in here," Emilio offered as she took the list of needed items and left to hurry to her office. She was already on her cell phone, starting her search. For the next half hour she forgot Emilio as she made calls and found places that could rush the supplies they needed.

When she returned to the kitchen an hour later, order had been restored. Rain still drummed steadily and she walked outside onto the covered area of the veranda to see about the grilling. Surprised, she found Emilio in an apron. His dark hair was tangled on his forehead as he turned skewers with shrimp and pork.

She hurried over to him. "You're cooking? I can do that instead of you," she offered.

"You keep up with everything else," Emilio said. "I can grill. If I go out to see about customers, some reporter will pick up on it. We don't want that happening this early."

Nodding, she returned to the dining room. To her amazement, people waiting to be seated still lined the lobby. The complimentary drinks were flowing and as she moved through the crowd and into the dining room, she was relieved to find that everyone she talked to seemed to be having a good time.

The dining room crowd was equally festive. Occasionally, she would find someone who needed to pay their bill or get a drink and she hurried to meet the needs of her customers.

She lost track of time until she realized the lobby was empty and the place had quieted. She left the bar area to go to the veranda, where the grills were off and no one was outside. When she entered the kitchen, Emilio still cooked. He had shed his shirt and wore a white undershirt with an apron over it. His brown body glistened with sweat. In spite of the air-conditioning, exhausts and fans, with all the cooking and the rain and damp, steamy air outside, the kitchen was hot. His muscles rippled as he picked up containers and moved around the kitchen and, for an instant, she forgot everything else, mesmerized by the sight of his muscular back. His shoulders were broad and his biceps bulged and, again, she recalled that moment locked in his arms in the pool. Dark waves of hair fell over his forehead and her mouth went dry while desire sent her temperature soaring.

She realized how she was staring and, with an effort, she tried to get her mind on business. Crossing the kitchen to him, she took a knife from his hand and placed it on the counter. "I think you can be relieved now," she said. "It's getting quieter out there."

"If you're sure I'm not needed here," he said, stepping to a sink to rinse and dry his hands. He removed the apron and picked up his shirt to pull it on while she watched. He caught her looking at him and paused. Realizing how she had been staring at his chest, he sent her a heated look that fueled her longing.

"I'm ready to call it a night. I've talked to Hector and he's staying and Angier is staying. I'm going home. If you want to follow me, you can come in for a drink."

"That's the best offer I've had in a long time," he said.

"Better than acquiring half of Brittany Beach?" she couldn't resist asking.

He smiled. "Let's go before something happens to put you back to work," he suggested. "Ride with me and I'll bring you tomorrow morning. My place is north of yours."

She nodded, happy to turn the driving over to him.

They had his car brought to the door and drove through rain-drenched streets to her condo. Hand in hand and laughing, they dashed inside. "I'm glad to be here," she exclaimed, kicking off her shoes. "What would you like? I'm having pop. I have wine, beer, pop, water—what'll it be?"

"Beer," he replied, moving around and helping her. They sat at the kitchen table and as she sipped her pop, she glanced at her watch.

"Did you know it's almost four in the morning?"

"Time flew past, but we did all right together, you and I."

"I hope you didn't neglect El Diablo to help at our place," she said, while Emilio reached out to pull the end of the yellow scarf tying back her hair.

Smiling, she shook her head and her thick, brown hair swirled across her shoulders.

Emilio picked up his cold beer. "Here's to my coolheaded partner, who handled the crisis well," he said, raising his bottle in tribute to her. "I'm impressed. You did a great job tonight."

His praise warmed her, and she smiled at him as she raised her pop. "Thank you. I'm glad you think so. With generators and your help, we went smoothly through the storm and about half an hour ago, power was restored."

"Serving complimentary mojitos was perfect. The people in the lobby had their own party. So was putting a neon Open sign out on the curb. That's smart. Getting the needed supplies in the storm was a miracle."

Feeling pleased with his compliments, she smiled. "After the mojitos had been flowing awhile I heard the crowd in front singing together."

"SoBe is a party place. The storm excites people and the atmosphere builds. Suddenly, we have a booming night."

"Booming is right! I hope it calms down tomorrow, although the business was unbelievable. Thanks for your help."

"Glad to," he replied. "I have a great partner."

"Thanks. You sound surprised," she said, wondering what he really thought about her. "We're off to an awesome start." She found some of her fears over rushing into accepting his proposal allayed by his cooperation and diligence through the night.

He leaned forward to take her drink from her hand. "This partnership is far better than I imagined it would be, and I had high expectations," he said in a throaty voice. His eyes darkened and held hers while he slipped his hand behind her head to pull her closer. Leaning forward, he brushed her lips with his.

She drew a deep breath. She was on fire with wanting him. His warm lips brushed hers again, taunting and inviting. She shut her eyes, leaning toward him and then his lips covered hers fully, his tongue going into her mouth and setting her ablaze.

Placing her hand against his chest, she trailed her fingers slowly across his hard muscles and up over his broad shoulder. As he kissed her, she moaned.

She barely noticed when he wrapped his arm around her waist. He pulled her to her feet against him, bending over her to kiss her passionately.

While desire raged, she thrust her hips against him. Leaning away abruptly, he sat on a chair and pulled her onto his lap. His green eyes devoured her, making her feel as if she were the most desirable woman on earth.

"You're beautiful," he said. His voice a rasp as he wound

his fingers in her hair and tilted her head back to kiss her throat. His tongue drew a fiery path from her ear, across her slender throat while her heart thudded. Hot and hard, his thick erection pressed against her hip.

"Emilio," she whispered, scalding sensations bombarding her.

Twisting free the buttons of her silk blouse, he pushed the soft yellow material off her shoulders. Cool air washed over her while he unfastened the clasp of her bra and it fell away. When his big hand cupped her breast, she cried out with pleasure that heightened swiftly. His thumb lazily circled her nipple.

"Emilio, we're going too fast!" she gasped.

"Shh. I know what you want," he whispered and leaned down to take her breast in his mouth. His tongue circled where his thumb had been and she moaned. Wanting all of him, she ached with need. Desperate to kiss him, she wound her fingers in his hair and raised his head.

For one brief moment they looked into each other's eyes. The mirrored desire in depths of green fanned the flames tormenting her. Then she kissed him hungrily, as if it were their first kiss and she had waited a lifetime.

No man had ever kissed her or affected her the way Emilio did effortlessly. A look, a touch could set her pulse pounding and snatch her breath away.

How long they kissed, she didn't know. She felt his hand at her waist and then her slacks were pushed down and his fingers drifted across her bare middle and slipped lower.

Closing her fingers around his wrist, she tugged his hand and stopped him from exploring lower. With an effort she opened her eyes. "Emilio," she whispered.

He raised his head and gave her another burning look that clearly conveyed his desire. "I want to set you on fire," he murmured as he cupped her breasts and watched her while his thumbs circled her nipples.

"You already have," she whispered. Closing her eyes, she moaned and held his wrists. Pleasure enveloped her and desire pushed her toward tossing aside all reservations.

"You want me and you want my kisses," he whispered, leaning down to take a nipple in his mouth and slowly circle the pouting bud with his wet tongue.

She cried out and framed his face in her hands to pull him up to kiss him hotly.

"You melt me and make me want you," she gasped finally as she leaned away. The minute she pushed lightly against his chest, he released her. When he did, she stood, trying to get herself composed and desire under control as she pulled on her clothing. "You're going too fast for me," she said breathlessly.

With a smoldering look as he watched her dress, he came to his feet. "I want you, Brittany."

Fighting the urge to walk back into his arms, she inhaled. "We have to go slow. I can't do this," she said and he nodded, placing his hand against her cheek while he looked at her intently.

"I'll go now," he said, heading for the front. She followed, getting her clothes together. At the door he turned to look at her and scalding desire still burned in his expression and made her pulse skip.

"I'll see you tomorrow," she said.

"I'll pick you up in the morning. Is nine too early?"

"Not at all," she replied.

He glanced at his watch. "That's not so far away. Okay, nine it is. See you in the morning," he said and turned to walk to his car.

She watched his long-legged stride and remembered being in his arms.

Thinking about his hot kisses made her pulse race. Was she

going to be another broken heart in his path? If so, would it jeopardize their business relationship?

Unable to answer her own questions, she locked up and switched off the foyer lights. She thought of Emilio's compliments again and felt another warm rush of pleasure. She knew she was starved for such approval because all her life she had been put down by her family. When it came to praise, she knew her vulnerability. Though she was mindful of how susceptible she might be, Emilio's remarks filled her with satisfaction.

And tonight had laid to rest some of her fears. When Emilio had wanted this partnership, she had jumped at the chance without hesitation or checking to see if there was any reason that it wouldn't be in her interests to accept. Yet tonight he had worked diligently, doing a hot, taxing job that he didn't have to do at all.

Twenty minutes later, her phone rang. Smiling, she picked up the receiver and heard his deep voice.

"Is it too late for a short call?"

"No. After such a hectic night, I'm not that sleepy. Maybe I'll relax while we talk."

"You can doze off and I won't mind. Again, you saved the place with your practical management tonight. I'm getting happier all the time about this partnership."

"Good. So am I," she said, although she thought it was for different reasons than what he was saying. She curled up on her bed to talk to him, listening to his deep voice and the rain still drumming on the windows.

After twenty minutes, she told him good-night and in seconds, she was asleep.

Friday morning, Emilio called to say he would leave his place in about ten minutes and come to Brittany Beach. She replaced the receiver, going to look at herself in her bathroom mirror and comb her hair again.

In a lime-green skirt, sandals and a lime cami with lace across the top and spaghetti straps, she knew he would like her outfit. Her hair was one long braid down her back. She started to comb it out and redo it, but then gave a shake of her head and decided to leave it.

Satisfied with her image, she went to her desk to check over the week's receipts. From the time of the deposit, she had looked often at the books. She could never get enough reassurance that the debt was covered. She'd realized she had exchanged one problem for another. She no longer had to worry about embezzlement, losing Brittany Beach or humiliation with her family. Instead, she fretted about falling in love with Emilio, who was a heartbreaker.

Charming, virile and sexy—she was drawn to him more each hour they spent together.

If he sat in her office even silently poring over books, her concentration was ruined.

She glanced at her watch and decided to check on the kitchen and see if the restaurant had received their supplies for the day. As she crossed the dining room and glanced outside, she saw Parker slow in front and a valet hurry to meet him.

She whirled around and dashed back to her office, yanking out her cell phone to call Emilio. The instant he answered, she cut him off.

"Emilio, come later this morning. Let me call you. Parker is here and I'd just as soon you two don't meet today. Let's give it a bit longer."

"Fine. Call and tell me when you want me to come."

"I will," she said, relief surging and then dying swiftly. Parker never came to Brittany Beach early in the morning. Had he learned about her new partner? When she hurried toward the lobby, she bit her lip. Worry tormented her because she could imagine Parker's ire over her acquiring a partner, even if it was an experienced, successful one.

Looking very much the businessman in his conservative white shirt, navy tie and navy slacks, Parker strode into her lobby. She had to admit, Parker wore authority with as much ease as he wore a tie. A stranger seeing them for the first time would guess Parker was the owner of Brittany Beach, not Brittany. Emilio had that same take-charge air and she wondered as time went by if she would have as difficult a time holding her own with him as she sometimes did with Parker.

"Morning, Brittany."

"And to what do I owe the honor of a visit from you at this hour?" she asked, hoping her voice sounded cheerful and hid her anxiety.

He shrugged. "I had an appointment with a contractor in SoBe. I was in the vicinity and I haven't had breakfast, so I thought I'd stop and catch a bite here if your kitchen is open."

"Sure, come in," she said, relieved to discover his harmless purpose. "I'll join you for coffee. We can eat outside on the veranda or in a cabana tent. It's beautiful this morning," she said, wanting to keep Parker away from the kitchen and her staff, where he could hear about Emilio.

They sat in one of the cabana tents and gazed at blue ocean and blue sky with gulls circling high overhead, occasionally swooping to the water and soaring again. Parker ordered and soon had orange juice, steaming coffee and ham and eggs in front of him.

"I should've called," he said as he ate. "How did you manage through the storm?"

Brittany lowered her coffee cup. "We got along fine. We have generators, so we kept right on serving and cooking. There was a huge crowd. We served complimentary mojitos to the customers waiting for a table—and some had to wait until after two in the morning."

"Good thinking, Brittany, with those drinks," Parker said, studying her while he finished his orange juice.

"Don't sound so grudging, brother dear," she replied, unable to keep the sarcasm out of her voice.

"I meant it. Some places had to close in the storm and some were so bogged down trying to wait on people, that customers left in a huff. Probably a lot came here. Complimentary mojitos was a smart move. I'm sincere in what I said."

"Okay, Parker, truce," she said, knowing it wouldn't last. "I like Anna."

"That's good, because she's part of our family now. How're profits besides the night of the storm?" he asked, going back to the subject of Brittany Beach.

"Still increasing. You'll get the monthly report."

"Good. We're all growing steadily and I'm looking at some more property."

"Our father trained you well. You've filled his shoes as he expected you to do."

"Thanks, but I don't think I can ever do what he did."

"Of course, you can," she said. "Heavens, I didn't think I'd ever hear you cast a shred of doubt on anything you do."

He gave her a crooked smile. "I thought we had a truce, my wicked little sis," he said, and she smiled sweetly at him.

"We do. Want anything else? More toast?"

"Nope. I hate to eat and run," he said, glancing at his watch, "but I've got an appointment back at the office and traffic will already be snarling up."

She strolled to the lobby area with him and stepped outside. "Come back, Parker."

"Sure. Thanks for breakfast. The food was great."

She watched him stride to his car and as soon as his vehicle disappeared, she phoned Emilio, who said he would be at Brittany Beach shortly.

Brittany went back to the receipts and concentrated on work, trying to ignore the image of sea-green, thickly lashed bedroom eyes that danced in her thoughts any time she was apart from Emilio.

Half an hour later she heard a light knock at her office door and when she called to come in, she looked into the warm eyes she had fantasized about through the past hours.

"Good morning," Emilio said in his deep voice as he entered her office. Dressed in a navy knit shirt and gray slacks, he looked refreshed, too handsome.

"Hi," she replied, smiling at him while her heart hammered.

"Think I could talk you into taking a break and having a cup of coffee with me?"

"Yes, you can," she said, tossing aside her pen, knowing her work suffered from his presence. She stood and when his gaze traced over her, one of his dark eyebrows arched and a corner of his mouth lifted in a crooked smile.

"My day has improved vastly," he said in a deeper voice, taking another slower, more thorough assessment that started heat rising until she wanted to fan herself. "The SoBe crowd should flock to Brittany Beach today. At least the males."

"SoBe's filled with women in tight, cool clothes. It's too hot here to be bundled to your chin."

"Thank heavens for that one! And SoBe's not overflowing with women who look like you do. You look great, as usual," he said.

"You'll spoil me with your compliments. Except I remind myself you probably do that with everyone—or maybe every female."

"Hardly. And definitely not everyone," he said, smiling at her while she pressed her intercom to the kitchen to ask for coffee, rolls and orange juice. "It's a pretty morning. Want to sit outside?" she asked, and he nodded.

In minutes, they sat on her private part of the veranda and sipped from steaming cups of black coffee.

"Parker stopped by to eat breakfast because he was in the neighborhood. I think next month we can announce this partnership."

"Don't rush it, Brittany," he said. "Let's get our partnership established."

"I think it is," she said and shrugged. "Now, what's on your mind this morning?" She looked up from her coffee to see a somber expression on Emilio's face. It was gone in a flash, but she wondered if something about Parker had disturbed him.

"There's something I want to discuss with you," Emilio said.

In the outside light, his sexy, bedroom eyes looked more green than ever and she had a difficult time concentrating on anything else. He withdrew a paper and handed it to her, his fingers lightly brushing hers, yet the contact was volatile. She knew her desire built daily and she tried to quell it, but failed most of the time.

Trying to focus on what Emilio wanted, she unfolded the paper and scanned the contents, to find a résumé by a chef from Brazil.

"And why are you showing me this?"

"You have an excellent chef, but it might be good to have two. You have a fine staff of cooks and a good sous-chef, but this way, you would have two very special, world-class chefs."

Instantly, she bristled and thought that Emilio was stepping in to run things after little more than a week with Brittany Beach.

Trying to control her annoyance with him, she shook her head. "Thanks, but I don't think so. There has to be one person in charge in the kitchen. My chef isn't going to want to share the task. He's very territorial."

"Wait before you rush to a hasty decision on this," Emilio urged in a mild voice, but she could feel the clash of wills. She suspected he was struggling to stay patient and pleasant with her about doing what he wanted.

He sat back in his rattan chair with his long legs stretched out. He looked as fully in charge as her brother Parker had earlier this morning.

"What will you do if Angier Lougee leaves you, particularly with short notice?" Emilio asked. "It happens."

"I'll face that when it occurs, which it may never."

"If you have two chefs, you won't have to worry about losing one," Emilio persisted, leaning forward and resting his elbows on his knees while he focused an intent, steady stare on her that merely increased her anger. "Brittany Beach will gain a splendid reputation for its fare because you'll have more than one expert and more imagination at work here. This man has a marvelous reputation." He paused to let her think about it.

The idea held no appeal for her, and she shook her head. "Can you imagine two in charge in one kitchen? That's bad enough in a home," she said. "No, I definitely don't want a second chef."

"You're making a hasty decision," Emilio insisted. "Listen to me. Two chefs are not a problem," he said with as much assurance as if she had capitulated. "Here's what we can do."

"You have this all worked out," she said and this time she couldn't keep the sharpness out of her voice.

"Stop being angry with me and listen," he said. "We put Angier in charge. We pay Remigio Tiago, the chef I want to hire, the most money. Everyone is happy."

"Until Angier discovers that Remigio makes the highest wages. Then he'd walk on us."

"How will he ever find out? Remigio isn't throwing it in his face. I won't tell him and neither will you. No one else will know. Angier will never be aware that Remigio gets paid more. We'll hire Remigio with the stipulation that Angier is in charge. Angier remains the executive chef."

"And you think your chef will go for this?"

"I'm sure he will."

"It's crazy, Emilio!" she exclaimed, throwing up her hands. "Angier is touchy about his kitchen. And believe me, it is *his* kitchen. He has it arranged the way he wants."

"I think Remigio can go along with that. I'll make it worth his while and he'll understand about Angier."

She looked around to find Emilio's gaze drifting languidly over her or lingering on her breasts, and she tingled from head to toe. Her heartbeat raced, and she fought the taunting memories of his hot kisses and momentarily forgot chefs. When she realized silence had grown and a faint smile hovered on Emilio's face, she shifted her thoughts to their conversation.

"Make Remigio the second sous-chef and we alternate their schedules so the sous-chefs don't work at the same time," Emilio answered without hesitation. For all she knew, he had already made arrangements with Remigio. She faced the fact that part of her stubborn refusal and her annoyance was because she had dealt with her control-freak brothers all her life and she suspected Emilio was one, too.

Trying to keep an open mind, she drew a deep breath and thought about Emilio's arguments.

"Are you taking over my life, plus fifty percent?" she asked bluntly.

One dark eyebrow arched and he leaned closer. "How I wish I could take over your life. And maybe your fifty percent, too, but no, I'm not in either case. If you don't want it, I'm not pushing this on you. I'm presenting my case because I think this will be better for both of us. Actually, a good deal for Angier, too. If you can't tolerate it, say so," Emilio said disarmingly, smiling at her and waving his hand as if he didn't care in the least what she decided.

"You bluff better than my brothers. They can't blithely deny their interest in something when they really want it."

"I mean what I say," he said and leaned back while he watched her. His green eyes looked guileless, but she didn't think Emilio was nearly as unconcerned as he acted. She thought about what he wanted and what he'd suggested.

"It has possibilities," she admitted. "Maybe. I want to think about it."

"Great. Read Remigio's background and training and experience. You'll see you'll be getting an exceptional chef. We'll have a much stronger position and more to offer customers."

She realized Emilio had a strong argument. At the same time, a stubborn streak in her screamed to stay in complete control and say no. Now was the time to assert herself. If she yielded now, it might be more difficult the next time they disagreed.

He leaned forward. "With both these master chefs we can have a fantastic menu. I've already done this at El Diablo. I don't ever want to be caught without an executive chef."

"You filled in last Sunday rather well, yourself."

"Grilling—that's simple. I don't concoct blue-ribbon recipes and mouth-watering dishes. Remember, if he doesn't work out, we can always get rid of Remigio."

"Let me think about it," she said.

"Fine. I don't want to pressure you, but chefs who are really first-rate, are snapped up quickly. And they aren't available often. This is an excellent chance to get him."

She smiled. "So you are pressuring me to make a decision right now," she said.

He brushed tendrils of hair away from her face. His touch

was feather-light, yet as always, he stirred tingles with every contact. "Do what you want," he said, smiling at her.

"I have some orders to sign," she said, standing to go to her desk. In minutes, she was bent over a stack of papers, trying to concentrate, but unable to stop thinking about Emilio, who worked quietly at the table only feet away from her desk.

She realized instead of growing accustomed to having him around and less susceptible to him, she was doing the opposite.

That afternoon at three o'clock, she found Emilio in the kitchen going over the menu with the executive chef. As soon as he saw her, Emilio left Angier and joined her.

"Were you looking for me?"

"I'm going to my condo."

"I'll go out with you because I was going back to El Diablo," he said, turning to walk with her. They left together, stepping outside into sweltering late afternoon heat that made her think of a quick dip in the pool at her condo.

In the parking lot, he placed his hand on her arm. "Until later," he said and brushed a kiss across her lips.

"If our staff see you do that, you'll start wild rumors."

"I imagine the wild rumors are already flying," Emilio said with amusement sparking in his green eyes. "Until tonight."

He was gone then, striding to his car to climb inside and drive away before she had the door closed as she sat in her black car. She drove out of the lot, remembering his mouth on hers, recalling his hot kisses. Her reactions to him were instant and intense. They talked over an hour nearly every night now after they both went home from work. She'd been to a gallery with him, had him at her place, spent hours with him at work and outside of work.

As she drove home, she continued to think about him. She liked his company and could talk freely to him. She could depend on him in a crunch at Brittany Beach. He was sexy

beyond any man she'd ever known. Was she falling in love with
Emilio?

In her quiet condo, she went for a brief swim, glad to see
the empty pool. As she enjoyed the cool water and exercise,
she thought about a second chef and decided Emilio's arguments were valid. Did she want to let him get his way so
quickly and easily? That was the big question that plagued her
because he was another take-charge male.

She splashed as she floated on her back and wondered if she
really had any choice to make. She suspected he was going to
get his way. Giving up, she resolved to agree to his suggestion
and see how it worked out. Emilio could deal with the change.
She flipped over and swam laps, remembering how Brooke
never did like to swim, wondering if her twin would ever change.

After a few minutes, Brittany went inside to bathe and dress.

After her bath, she studied her clothes. She knew what
Emilio liked and what was sexy to him and turned him on. In-
decision racked her and she picked first one outfit and then
another before tossing aside caution and selecting a hot-pink
shirt and hot-pink skirt and pink high-heeled sandals.

Seven

It was eleven that night before Brittany turned around in the bar to find Emilio lounging against the doorjamb while he watched her.

He walked over to her. "Hi. Think I can have a dance?"

"I don't seem to be needed in any particular place right now so, yes, you can," she replied.

He took her hand and led her to the lounge dance floor and turned her toward him. Dressed in brown slacks and tan shirt, he was as handsome as ever. Black locks of hair fell over his forehead. It was the searing need in his crystal eyes that stirred her own longing.

Wordlessly, they began to dance and the air between them sparked with fire. She knew she was wearing a sexy outfit, dancing a hot, Latin number that meant moving her body in an enticing manner. Tonight, she wanted to be appealing to him. Desire burned a steady, hot flame in her.

Was she ready to throw consequences to the wind? She knew she already had. As she danced around him, she watched him and their surroundings vanished.

Her world narrowed to the flashing lights, a pounding beat and the sexy male moving his hips and long legs and watching her with that devouring look that made her feel as if she were the most desirable woman on earth.

When the dance ended, he took her hand and they left the dance floor and headed toward a table. As they moved through the crowd, she noticed Juan, one of the waitstaff, step into the lounge and look all around and she withdrew her hand from Emilio's. "I think I'm wanted," she said, hurrying to the door and waving at Juan. The minute she walked up to him, he began to talk.

"Someone swung open a door and hit Hector. He's lost consciousness and Luiz called an ambulance."

"Let's go see," Emilio said from behind her. Taking her arm, they hurried after Juan, who led the way to the kitchen where Hector lay on the floor with his eyes open and a compress on his forehead. Waitstaff and chefs were clustered around him and moved back to give Brittany and Emilio room.

"I'm okay," Hector insisted when Brittany knelt beside him. "Cancel the ambulance. I don't need one."

"I know, but you should still get checked out by professionals," Brittany said, concerned about him even though it was reassuring to have him say he was all right. "Lie still until they get here." She glanced up at Emilio, who had called 911, and she heard him tell them to turn the siren off when they entered the Brittany Beach drive and to come around to the back to the kitchen door.

He clicked off and looked at Brittany. "I'll take you to the hospital when Hector goes."

"I got knocked out," Hector grumbled. "I'll be all right."

"Let them look you over to make sure," Brittany said. "I insist and we'll cover any charges the insurance doesn't."

"I'll wait outside for the ambulance," Emilio said and left.

When the paramedics arrived, the time seemed to move slowly as they took Hector's vital signs and checked him over and talked to Brittany. Finally, Hector got to his feet and it was agreed that the ambulance wasn't needed, that Brittany and Emilio would take Hector to the emergency room.

It was almost two in the morning when they left Hector at his home with his wife and Emilio drove Brittany to her condo.

"Come inside and have a drink," she said as he parked in front of her door.

"You won't have to ask twice," he said, getting out and striding around the car to help her out.

In minutes, they had on soft music as they sat in her back room. Emilio had a beer and she had pop and she had kicked off her shoes. "Once again, thanks for your help," she said.

"Sure. I'm glad he wasn't hurt badly."

"I wouldn't have been able to sleep if he hadn't gotten checked by a doctor, even though he didn't think it was necessary at all."

"I'm sure his wife agreed with you," Emilio said. "Now right before that happened, I remember dancing with you," he said, his voice getting deeper. He reached over to take her drink from her hand. "I liked that. How about another dance?"

"There's not much room…."

He stood and set aside his beer, taking her hand to lead her into her kitchen, where only a small light burned. "You can hear the music in here," he said, pulling her into his arms to slow dance.

She moved with him, relaxing and forgetting the problems of the evening. Her awareness of Emilio became more intense. His warm, hard body pressed against her. He held her close.

Desire ignited and she wrapped her arms around his neck to hold him while they swayed slowly.

They danced two dances and then he leaned back to look into her eyes. Her heart slammed against her ribs. She could feel his desire, white-hot, mirroring her own feelings, and then he lowered his head to kiss her.

The minute her lips pressed against his, her insides clenched. His tongue plunged into her mouth and stroked her. Bending over her, he kissed her deeply. His tongue explored her mouth as if he would devour her. And she wanted him to.

Her desire raged and she ached to have no barrier between them, to touch and kiss and caress him. Healthy and strong, he made her burn with longing, and she wanted to discover his powerful, male body.

She had no idea how long they stood kissing. Soft music played in the background, but she was barely aware of it.

Emilio picked her up, holding her in his arms as he turned to carry her to her bedroom, where he set her on her feet and switched on a small table lamp that shed a faint glow.

She wrapped her arms around his neck and stood on tiptoe to kiss him again.

In a few minutes, she leaned back and tugged his shirt out of his slacks. Her fingers fumbled with the buttons at his throat, twisting them free. He brushed away her hands and yanked his shirt over his head, tossing it aside. She looked up into his smoldering gaze that was as sexy as everything else about him. And then her attention lowered to his muscled chest and she ran her hands across him while they kissed.

He slipped off her top, and she had to raise her arms to get free of it. She wore nothing under it and he inhaled, making his chest expand.

Flames of desire filled his eyes while he cupped her breasts in his large, tanned hands. "Beautiful," he whispered. "So beautiful."

Closing her eyes in pleasure, she gasped and clung to his muscled forearms.

He leaned down and his tongue encircled her nipple, hot and wet, making her tremble. Desire pooled low in her, a primitive craving for him. She moaned with relish while exquisite sensations streaked from his kisses. For a few minutes, she simply clung to him and drowned in the kisses and caresses he showered on her.

His thumbs circled her nipples slowly, as lightly as a feather, yet incredibly tantalizing, driving her wild with need.

As torment built, she ran her hands over his chest again, enjoying the bulge of muscles and his strength. She tangled her fingers in his mat of black, curly chest hair and then slid one hand along the column of his neck. Tangling her fingers in his thick hair, she kissed him hungrily, wanting more of him by the minute.

Her hands slid low to unfasten his slacks and let them drop away. She hooked her thumbs in his low-cut briefs. His thick rod bulged out of them, hard and ready for her, a black mat of short curls surrounding his ample endowment. Watching him, she slowly peeled down his briefs and he stepped out of them. His thighs were muscled, covered in a sprinkling of dark curls that were a tantalizing roughness against the smoothness of her legs.

She knelt to caress him and lick him, slowly sliding her tongue along his throbbing shaft. Groaning, he wound his fingers in her hair while he stood with his legs slightly spread.

"Brittany," he whispered.

Slowly, she ran her tongue over him while one hand went between his legs to stroke him, to tease and stir him as he did her. Her other hand slid over his hard bottom. His body was as solid as granite, ready and magnificent.

With another groan, he reached beneath her arms and pulled her up. When they looked into each other's eyes, she could see her own intense craving mirrored there. He drew her into his tight embrace, kissing her hard and leaning over her, his erection thrusting against her while she clung to him.

"I want you more than I've ever dreamed of wanting anyone," she whispered between the kisses she showered on him.

When his arms tightened, his kiss deepened and her heart surged.

His hands unfastened her skirt to let it fall around her ankles. While they kissed, she kicked off her shoes. His hot gaze played thoroughly over her, lingering on her breasts. When his dark hands slipped lower to take the straps of her thong in his fingers and peel it off, she stepped out of it.

Standing again, he placed his hands on her hips and held her away while his eyes traveled slowly over every inch of her. "First, I look," he whispered in a rasp. "Next, I touch and feel and then last, I kiss every inch." She shook, wanting him and wanting to do the same to him.

"You're gorgeous, fantastic!" he exclaimed, his gaze still drifting so slowly over her while his fingers skimmed lightly across her breasts and then lower, over her belly.

She cried out with pleasure as he caressed her.

She started to do the same to him once again, but he yanked the covers back on her bed, picked her up and placed her on it. Moving beside her, he held her close against his hard length while his other hand roamed over her.

Clinging to him, she let one hand drift over his smooth, muscled back. "I want you, Emilio," she whispered. "Now," she urged.

"Soon. Not yet. I want you more passionate."

"I can't be! Love me," she exclaimed.

Ending their conversation, his mouth covered hers. His hand slid along her hip and upper leg and then between her legs. With a cry that was muffled by his kiss, she thrust her hips against him.

He shifted, moving between her legs and his dark head dipped lower, while his tongue went where his fingers had been.

Hot and wet, his tongue circled her feminine spot and she cried out, arching higher for him with need exploding in her. His tongue drove her wild, stroking her, building her torment and pleasure.

"Emilio! Love me!" she cried out, her hands reaching for his thick shaft. "I want you now!" she cried and bit her lip. Her eyes were squeezed shut and sensation rocked her.

Finally, he raised to look at her. "Do you have protection?"

When she shook her head, he pushed her aside, getting up to find his discarded trousers.

As he returned, she drank in the sight of his muscled, lean body and long legs. He was sexy, ready for love. He retrieved a packet from his billfold and climbed back on the bed.

When she shifted and spread her legs, he moved between them. His gaze drifted slowly over her and his fingers played with her.

"You're the most beautiful woman I've known," he said. "And the sexiest."

"I don't believe you, but I like to hear you say it," she whispered. "Come here." She held her arms up to him, longing to kiss him. "I want you inside me."

His eyes darkened as he inhaled deeply and paused. While she drew her fingers along his thighs, he put on the protection and then he lowered himself, the tip of his shaft pressing against her.

When he kissed her, she wrapped her long legs around him and her slender arms around his neck to hold him close. Eagerly, she ran her hands over the curve of his bottom and the back of his hard thighs.

He filled her slowly and she felt as if she would burst from his thickness, yet she wanted him and she moved her hips, meeting his thrusts with her own. She knew he was struggling for control, trying to increase her pleasure and desire, but she was driven with a primitive desperation.

She held him with her legs and stroked him, trying to drive him to the point where he had taken her, where his control was gone and the ultimate release was the only thing that would satisfy him.

With a sound deep in his throat, he kissed her as he filled her slowly again, moving with a restraint that built her need to pure torment.

Finally, his control was gone and he pumped into her, moving hard and fast and she matched him.

She spun into an erotic world of passion and intimacy. They rocked together, building toward the climax.

"Emilio!" she cried, unaware of calling his name, her hips moving frantically with his, while need pounded like her racing heartbeat.

"Brittany!" he gasped. He thrust into her, taking her to a brink and then she cried out and climaxed, feeling spasms rock him as he climaxed with her.

Her pulse roared and rapture blossomed, exploding with her release. She cried out again, clinging to him, feeling his strong back that was covered in sweat. They both gasped for breath.

"Don't stop," she whispered, wanting to prolong the ecstasy, wanting this moment to last when they were one and he was hers and she was his. For now, life was bliss.

As he slowed, he kissed her. She held him tightly, relishing his body, his sexiness, his manhood. "I could kiss you all night," she whispered, running her hand over his smooth back.

He showered kisses on her temple and finally he slowed and let his weight rest on her. He turned on his side, taking her with him and, blissfully, she gazed at him.

"So sexy," he whispered. "I'm lucky to have found you, Brittany." A satisfied look passed between them. She framed his face with her hands and kissed him tenderly. When she raised her head, he rolled onto his back and she slid beside him, placing her head on his shoulder while he held her close and their legs entwined.

"Things changed between us tonight," he replied solemnly, and she smiled.

"At the moment, it's a wonderful change."

He studied her and brushed a kiss on her forehead. "I want to hold you all night. You set me on fire. You're beautiful."

"You're rather appealing, yourself," she said, running her index finger along his jaw, feeling the faint growth of stubble.

"I want to be with you, looking at you, kissing you, making love to you," he said lazily.

"Help yourself," she said and she raised up to run her hand lightly over his chest. "Look all you want."

As she caressed him, his eyes darkened. She traced her fingers across his flat, washboard belly, going lower and moving to his thighs, watching as he stirred.

"Two can do that," he said, his voice getting deep. Releasing her, he stepped off the bed and picked her up. "Ready for a warm shower?"

"I'm ready for anything with you," she said, feeling bubbly, desire reawakening in her.

He set her on her feet in her shower and turned on the water, then wrapped his arms around her and kissed her hungrily.

As warm water spilled over her, she rubbed against him, letting her hands slide along his sides.

Desire was a hot flame, making her move her hips against his. His shaft thrust against her, hard and ready.

They soaped each other and rubbed away the soap and finally he turned off the water while they dried and he pulled the towel slowly and lightly across her taut nipples, the friction a sweet torment. Next, he slipped it between her legs to cause another fiery friction. She gasped and wrapped her arms around him to kiss him.

He picked her up to carry her into the bedroom back to bed, where he held her close. "This is the best night ever," he said in his deep voice that was a rumble against her ear.

Raising up, she leaned forward to let her nipples touch his chest and she rubbed lightly against him.

He toyed with her hair and watched her while she ran her fingers slowly up the inside of his thigh and leaned down to rub her nipples against his belly this time. She was getting aroused, feeling his warm body and fueling her rising need. Sex with him had been great—as she had expected.

Suddenly, he rolled her over on her back and he straddled her, placing his hands on both sides of her face as he gazed into her eyes. Her heart leaped. "Are we going to make love for hours?" she asked.

"I plan to," he said and then leaned the last few inches to cover her mouth with his.

She wound her arm around his neck and held him tightly. His hands were everywhere, sliding over her, caressing her, rubbing her and the spiral started again.

In minutes, she was gasping, wanting him inside her more than before, shocked by her own need that was compelling beyond what she would have believed possible.

And then he retrieved another condom. He stretched on his back and settled her on his thick shaft, plunging into her as she moved on him. While he was inside her, hot and hard, his hand played with her nipple and the other hand rubbed her feminine bud. She moved faster, need building, sensations bombarding her from his hands and his erection and his loving.

She squeezed her eyes closed and rocked on him, the exquisite torment growing until release burst inside her and she climaxed.

He pounded into her, holding her on him while he climaxed.

The roaring of her pulse deafened her. Sex with Emilio was better than she had hoped, lustier and more satisfying, yet each kiss and caress forged a link in a chain that bound her heart to him irrevocably. She knew she could be plunging headlong into heartbreak, but at the moment, she didn't care.

Finally exhausted and covered in perspiration, she sprawled over him. "You're fantastic, Emilio."

"Your gorgeous, sexy body is impossible to resist," he said, playing with her hair. He rolled her beside him and held her close while he smoothed her hair away from her face. "We're good together, Brittany."

Warm pleasure filled her and she held him tightly, feeling their hearts beating together while she rubbed her cheek against him. "I'm happy."

"Great," he said. "I hope you always are," he added and she looked up, hearing a strange note of concern in his voice. She wondered what was bothering him.

"Sounds perfect," she said happily, not wanting to interrupt their moment.

They made love through the early hours of the morning until finally, Emilio climbed out of bed and headed for the shower. "I have to go home, but I'd rather stay here in bed with you."

She rolled on her side to look at him. He was virile, naked and aroused.

"I don't think you're going anywhere right now," she said in a sultry voice, moving sensuously on the bed. He inhaled, as his gaze drifted over her and he came back to pull her into his arms and it was another hour before he got up and found his cell phone to call and tell his general manager that he wouldn't arrive at El Diablo until late in the day.

When he returned to bed, he took her into his arms. She twisted to look at him and wrap her arm around his neck. "I'm glad you're staying."

Eight

They spent the morning making love and finally, by mid-afternoon, Emilio insisted he had to leave. She walked to the door with him, where he turned to kiss her one last time. When he released her, she looked up at him.

"Brittany, last night, today, it was all the very best ever," he said, sounding sincere.

Her heart jumped and she looked into his unfathomable green eyes. He was somber, looking intently at her and she wondered what was going through his thoughts.

"You look worried, Emilio. Is something wrong?"

He gazed at her in silence, while something flickered in the depths of his eyes and she realized she might have been intrusive with her question.

"Am I treading on something private?" Brittany asked, wishing she hadn't quizzed him.

He placed his hand on her shoulder. "You can ask anything

you want. In some ways, I feel closer to you than to anyone else I've ever known," he said, and she drew a deep breath. She rested her palm against his cheek.

"That's the nicest thing you could possibly say," she said softly. "That's even better than the picture you gave me."

He shrugged. "We've gotten to be friends, Brittany. I know I can count on you."

"Yes, you can," she said, "but don't look so unhappy about it."

He smiled at her and slid his hand behind her head to pull her to him to kiss her. She put her arms around his neck to return his kiss, her heart beating fast because his words had made her feel a stronger bond than ever with him. Finally, he released her.

"I'm not unhappy. Just the opposite," he said, flashing one of his spectacular smiles. "Now I better go," he said. "But I hate to. I'll call and we can talk," he said. "I'm going to miss you terribly."

Nodding, she blew him a kiss and he headed to his car.

Emilio drove to his condo and walked out on the terrace and cast his attention into the distance without seeing the beach or ocean. Instead, he saw Brittany's lush body over his, her tongue stroking him, her mouth raised to his, but then he thought about the past hours and how she had given totally to him. Before, she had trusted him with her business. In the past two nights, she'd trusted him with her body. And he had deceived her in business. He knotted his fists in frustration.

For several years, Jordan and he had fought with the Garrison men. If Emilio and Jordan could wipe out the Garrison competition, they would. They intended to cut into it as much as possible. And when he'd gone after Brittany Beach, Emilio had thought it a mere extension of all he'd already dealt with in the Garrison family. Brittany had been ripe for picking and he had pursued her restaurant.

He was caught in a trap of his own making, Emilio realized. He had violated her trust. And she had given him her trust—the most a woman could give a man—complete intimacy.

If he admitted the truth to her, she would hate him. And if he didn't tell her and she discovered it—which she would when she finally broke the news about her partner to her family—she would despise him.

Wind blew locks of his hair as he stared out to the horizon. He knew he was ruined, no matter what happened. He didn't know if confession would be one degree better than letting her discover the Garrison-Jefferies feud from someone else.

Emilio clenched his fist again in frustration. There was no good way out of his problem. He thought about Brittany in his arms, pressed against him, beautiful, sexy, trusting.

What a bastard he'd been! He couldn't blame her for hating him and the thought pained him. It surprised him how badly the deception hurt and how much it worried him. Was he beginning to care for her? Really care in a manner he'd never known before in his life? He had never gotten closely involved with any of the women who had been in his life. It had been lust and excitement. This caring was something new and he didn't like it because he hurt.

Brittany was important to him. He shared interests with her. She was sexy, fun and he could trust her with his secrets. She wasn't interested in his money. She was frank and truthful and dependable.

He was into it now and it was only a matter of time until everything blew up in his face. Then what would he do? Finding no solution, he turned and went inside, preparing to go to work.

By the time he was in the car, his thoughts were on the past hours of lovemaking with Brittany and his spirits had lifted. Forgetting his worries, Emilio drove toward SoBe and El Diablo. He wanted Brittany and couldn't wait until he could see her again.

He'd been infatuated many times, but he didn't remember being consumed by desire for someone before. Brittany was special and different.

Last night and this morning had been the best ever. Whatever that chemistry between them, it was unparalleled and fantastic. He was getting aroused thinking about her and he wanted her right then. He ached to hold her, kiss her and make love with her again. With a groan, he realized he would have to go hours before he saw her and even more time before she would be naked in his arms.

As he turned into the parking lot and drove to the back of El Diablo, he swore because Jordan's car was in the lot. Right now, Emilio didn't care to see his brother.

He climbed out of his car and into his office, where Jordan sat writing in a tablet.

"Well, hello. I thought you'd be here half an hour ago." Jordan tilted his head to study him. "You look like the weight of the world is on your shoulders."

"Actually, no. I'm doing fine," Emilio lied, wanting to avoid discussing his dilemma with Jordan, who looked cool and casual in a blue shirt and chinos and deck shoes.

"So how's business—particularly Brittany Beach?" Jordan asked, still scrutinizing his brother.

"Business at both Brittany Beach and here is booming."

"I heard when we had the storm, that Brittany Beach was one of the places to be in SoBe."

"Right. It was packed until the wee hours of the morning."

"Her brothers still don't know, do they? When they find out, you'll have war. Of course, what could they expect? Send a flighty baby sister out who doesn't know squat and someone will have her skirts over her head before she knows what happened," Jordan said lightly and grinned.

While he tried to curb his temper, Emilio's insides tightened and he gripped the arms of his chair. "She's not flighty, Jordan. I misjudged her, and so have they. Actually, she's a damn good businesswoman."

"Uh-oh. Sounds like a man enveloped in lust. I can't believe Brittany Garrison has any business sense."

"She does. I'm telling you that in the cold light of morning," Emilio said seriously. "I misjudged her because she had the embezzlement and she accepted my help so quickly. She's shrewd about the restaurant business and the night of the storm, she managed quite well," Emilio insisted, wishing Jordan would go and take his annoying opinions with him.

"So it may be more difficult than you expected for you to take the whole thing away from her."

"I'm not doing that," Emilio said flatly, and Jordan frowned.

"Your feelings for Brittany Garrison come before the Jefferies' interests?" Jordan asked with surprise and annoyance in his tone.

"That's my business, Jordan," Emilio snapped.

"If you put her before our interests, you're a traitor to the family."

"Dammit! You take that back."

"You're siding with a Garrison. Deny that one."

"Did you want to see me about something?" Emilio asked, clamping his jaw closed and trying to hang on to his temper. He glared at his brother while Jordan glowered and Emilio tensed, wondering if they were going to come to blows. "What do you want?"

"Really, nothing. Only to see how it was going with El Diablo and with Brittany Beach." He stood. "I'm going because I can see that I'm not wanted, but I'm telling you, bro, you better dump her and work your fifty percent from afar. Don't let her come between us. I don't want to have anything to do with a Garrison."

Emilio wanted to jump over the desk and take a swing at Jordan. Instead, he controlled his temper and glared at his brother as he stood.

"Those Garrison men are going to be madder than hell when they find out what's happened," Jordan persisted. "And when she discovers how much you deceived her, she's going to be angry, herself."

"Go to hell, Jordan."

"Brittany Garrison isn't for you." Jordan turned and strode out of the office, slamming the door behind him.

Emilio swung his fist through the air, wishing he could hit something. Frustrated and angry, he decided to go to the gym for a workout.

Two hours of exercise didn't change his grim outlook. He was steeped in deception with Brittany and he didn't see any way out of it, except to confess the truth to her. This soon in their relationship, he didn't want to do that. At this point, he was certain he would lose her.

And he hated to see Jordan leave his office in a huff. Emilio swore out loud. He didn't want to drive a wedge between Jordan and himself. His thoughts jumped back to Brittany.

Tonight, he would be with her and eagerness made him forget everything else and stop worrying about confessing to her. For now, he wasn't going to worry about it. Tonight, he would take time and savor every moment with her.

The damnable Garrison Sunday dinners were a threat. Every time the Garrisons were together, chances of Brittany discovering his deceit shot higher. Maybe soon she would care enough for him to forgive him when she learned the truth.

Yeah, right, he said to himself, shaking his head. He could imagine her fury that wasn't going to end with forgiveness. He knew he postponed the inevitable, but he wasn't ready to lose her.

He went by his home that night to shower and change. He

dressed in gray slacks and a navy shirt. After combing his hair, he left for Brittany Beach.

By the time he walked into the restaurant, it was ten o'clock. Drums pounded out a slow, sensual rhythm in the lounge and dancers gyrated in the semidarkness. Emilio peered through the flashing lights for a glimpse of Brittany.

Then he spotted her in the dining room and his pulse jumped. Her short skirts and clinging silk tops turned him on— actually, the body they revealed was what turned him on. Tonight, she had another outfit that hugged her slender hips and flat belly and he ached to peel her right out of it.

Her top was a blue halter that ended high above her midriff and revealed a bare middle, shoulders and back. She was hot and he could look at her forever, but he wanted far more to kiss and taste and caress her as he had last night.

He crossed the room to her, walking up behind her. Emilio didn't want to startle her, but she was turned away from him. Her long hair was looped and clipped on the back of her head and he wanted to reach out and take that clip out of her hair and let it fall over her shoulders, which he would do as soon as they were alone. Soon, she would be naked in his arms in his bed. Just as quickly as he could get her out of Brittany Beach and back to his place.

"Brittany," he said softly, reaching to take her arm and turn her to face him. His pulse raced and he felt as if he had waited months for this moment, instead of merely hours.

"Hi!" she exclaimed, flashing him a warm smile that made his heart jump.

"You haven't seen my place. Everything's going smoothly here. Let me show you where I live," he said. "Can you leave with me now?"

"Give me time to tell people," she said, giving him an eager, heated look that sped his heartbeat even more.

In minutes, they were in his car heading for his condo, which was the penthouse of a high-rise oceanfront building. As soon as he closed the door behind them, he pulled her into his embrace. Brittany flung her arms around his neck as if she hadn't seen him in years.

While they kissed, he lifted her up into his strong arms.

Brittany was oblivious to where he carried her, and barely conscious of the bed beneath her when he lowered her and stretched out beside her to kiss her.

She pushed against him and raised up. "Wait a minute. Slow down, here. I've never been in your place before. I want to see where I am."

"I got carried away," he replied in a rough voice, caressing her nape.

"I think I'm the one that got carried away—to bed," she said with amusement and they laughed with each other.

"I'm glad you're here," he said. "I'll show you around and then I'll have my way with you," he teased, standing and offering her his hand, which she took as she stepped off the bed.

"I can't think of anything more delightful than for you to have your way with me, unless I get to have my way with you," she retorted, and he draped his arm across her shoulders.

"All right. Do you want the grand tour now?"

"Of course," she said, looking around his large bedroom that held a king-size brass bed. She walked about, looking at his shelves with books, pictures and trophies for swimming and golf. She turned to face him. "You have swimming trophies. No wonder I couldn't beat you across the pool. You're a pro."

"I'm not a pro. Those are high school and college trophies. Just admit it. I can swim faster than you can."

"You could last week. Maybe not this week," she said with haughty disdain.

He grinned. "We may have to go for a midnight swim and settle this again."

"Don't be so smug. You've won trophies and I'm a mere amateur."

"Darlin', you're the most adorable amateur I've ever seen and if it makes you happy to win, next time, I'll throw the race," he said, walking over to her.

"Don't you dare! I win on my own merits or not at all," she snapped, knowing they were teasing and it was all in jest.

"Oh, well. There are other things we can do where I can come out on top."

"You definitely come out on top in some ways I can think about. Want me to show you?" he asked and she shook her head.

"Not yet. You said that you'd show me your condo."

"You're in my bedroom," he said. She looked around at the polished hardwood floor, the brown leather furniture and the teak dresser, a teak desk, shelves with books, bronze statues and framed pictures, a plasma television. Modern art with vivid colors accented the darker tones.

"This room fits you," she said. "And now I'll know how things look when I talk to you on the phone."

He took her arm. "Over there is the bathroom. I'll give you a special tour of it and my shower later," he said and she smiled. He led her outside on his terrace and she gasped at the view. "You can see the lights along the beach and the street below, but beyond that is the ocean, with yachts and boats and, occasionally, the big cruise ships. The view in the day is spectacular. On the other side of the condo, you can see all of SoBe and Miami and a million lights."

"It's fantastic," she said.

"Yes, it is. I've been waiting all day."

She turned to look up at him, knowing he was not talking

about his view. "Wait a few minutes longer and show me around. I'll try to make it worth your time," she said in a sultry voice, flirting with him.

He draped his arm across her shoulders to show her a formal living room that held traditional oak furniture, elegant sofas and chairs. They walked through his dining room, that was equally formal, with a table that would seat twenty.

"Here's where I live," he said next, and she entered a room with contemporary rattan furniture covered in material with earth tones of warm browns and orange. She could see a media room beyond it and then he took her to his kitchen, a cheery yellow-and-white room that held state-of-the-art equipment.

They looked at another bedroom with a king-size teak bed and contemporary furniture in primary colors. As she looked around, he came up behind her to wrap her in his arms and nuzzle her neck.

"Now, you've had the royal tour. I want to do my own touring," he said quietly in a hoarse voice that made her breath catch. He turned her to face him, reaching out to release the clip that held her hair behind her head.

Over two hours later, he stepped out of bed and picked her up. "We'll shower and then have a late snack," he said, smiling at her.

Joy bubbled in her and desire was reawakening. As he carried her across the room, she glanced outside again at the view of a long string of lights far below and then darkness spreading away to infinity. "You have the best view in the world up here."

"Indeed, I do," he said in a husky voice, looking down at her and she forgot outside. She was warm, naked, held against his bare body in his strong embrace. She tightened her arm around his neck and kissed his shoulder.

Stepping into his bathroom, Emilio switched on a light and she looked at a huge black-and-gold, marble-and-glass bathroom.

"This is enormous. You could get lost in here," she said, gazing at a sunken tub, a huge shower and a dressing area.

He stepped into the shower and set her on her feet and she forgot her surroundings, except for the tall, dark-skinned man holding her waist. He ran his fingers lightly across her breasts and she inhaled.

They started with soap and washcloths, but in seconds, the cloths were tossed aside as they kissed and caressed each other's warm, wet bodies.

Eventually, he put on protection, braced himself and picked her up. She wrapped her long legs around him as he settled her on his thick rod and she moved wildly on him.

When she climaxed, she cried his name and sank against him, pleasured and wrapped in his arms. Ecstasy enveloped her. He thrust into her, as release burst in him and his breathing gradually slowed.

Afterward, she slid down to stand. They showered and dried each other before moving back to the bed where he held her close against him until he fell asleep.

Long after his breathing was deep and steady, she raised up to look at him. His dark lashes were feathered above his prominent cheekbones. He had become her partner and then her friend and now her lover. She'd had fun being with him, looking at art, flirting with him, even working together and their phone conversations were great, but now the friendship had deepened for her into something stronger. She knew she was falling in love with him. She wondered how important she really was to him.

She remembered the moment this morning when he said that he felt closer to her than anyone he had ever known. That had been a stunning admission and she couldn't imagine he had told that to any other female. She had thought about it all through the day.

She touched him on his shoulder. "I love you," she whispered, leaning over to brush a kiss so lightly on his mouth.

His arm tightened around her and he held her close. She started to tell him that she was sorry she had awakened him, but then she saw that he still slept, so she snuggled against him and wrapped her arm around his narrow waist to hold him close.

Glancing at the clock, she saw it was only a few hours until sunrise and it was already Sunday morning. Tonight, she faced another family dinner. Each week was a little less stressful than the one before because she had moved further away from the disastrous embezzlement.

It was three in the afternoon before she kissed Emilio goodbye to leave for her own place. Emilio had called a car service to take her home. "I'll see you later tonight," she said. "I have to get this Sunday dinner over with."

"Skip it once."

"I'm tempted, but I think I should go. It's not the same, though, without our dad. Not at all. Mother is having a tough time and she's trying to deal with it," Brittany said. "At least our dinners don't last late."

"Come straight back here," he said, his green eyes intense as he waited for her answer. "I'll want you in my arms again," he added and she nodded.

"I will," she promised. "I'm going to miss you," she said, not yet ready to tell him that she had fallen in love because she didn't expect to hear those words from him.

"You look gorgeous, as usual," he added. "Although it's best when you wear nothing."

Wrinkling her nose at him, she smiled. "I'll call you when I leave Bal Harbour," she said, blowing him a kiss and leaving.

There would be no storm to cut tonight's dinner short and she dreaded the evening. Their mother's drinking was making dinners more tense.

Her impatience grew as they all sat around the table and she had to resist the urge to continually glance at her watch. She tried to make an effort to join in the conversation. Parker, in his usual white shirt and dark tie, looked the authority figure. Brooke was unusually quiet and Brittany once again sensed something amiss with her sister.

"You're quiet tonight," Stephen remarked to Brittany. Turning to him, she shrugged.

"I guess I'm preoccupied. Mother seems worse," Brittany whispered, glancing toward the end of the table.

"She is worse," he replied quietly, and a muscle worked in his jaw. "Lisette is worried sick about her. Mom stumbled and missed a step this week and almost fell. She's okay, but things are getting out of hand."

"Lower your voice," Brittany said.

"You think she'll pay any attention to any of us?" he snapped. "She's already in a stupor."

Brittany glanced at her mother, but all she could feel was relief that Stephen was focused on their mother and he didn't seem to have any knowledge of Emilio.

"How are things going at the Garrison Grand?"

"Fine, but that reminds me of something I wanted to mention to Parker," he said.

Relieved to shift the conversation from her and glad every time a topic came up that had nothing to do with Brittany Beach, she tried to keep focused on the conversations.

"Parker, we need to update some of the decor at the Garrison Grand. It's getting overdue," Stephen said.

"The hotel has to stay first-class," Parker replied. "Wilkins and Tyler did some work for me that was good."

"I've heard Megan Simmons is back in town as a partner at her former interior design firm," Anna said. "Megan's reputation in that field is growing. I'd think all of you would like her work."

"I'll second that recommendation," Brittany added, happy to stay on the subject of the Garrison Grand. "She did the project at Garrison, Inc. headquarters four years ago, Stephen," Brittany added. "Remember?" she asked, certain he did because he and Megan were a couple when Brittany met her.

Looking shocked, Stephen frowned. "Megan's back in town?" he asked Anna and she nodded.

"I didn't know you knew her," Anna said.

"Why don't you call her?" Brittany asked her brother, surprised by Stephen's reaction to Anna's announcement.

"I'll look into the matter," Stephen answered with a clipped tone to his words. Brittany knew her brother and when something flickered in the depths of his brown eyes, she wondered what disturbed him. If it had been Parker, Brittany would have suspected he didn't want others telling him what to do, but Stephen was more receptive. Still, he had a definite hesitation which surprised her because, for a while after Megan disappeared out of Stephen's life, Brittany suspected he was carrying a torch for her. Perhaps she'd been wrong.

Stephen's gaze swung to her and she smiled and looked away, wanting to avoid any close scrutiny, herself. She didn't know what was going on with Stephen, but if he focused on his properties instead of hers, she would be happy.

Parker could hardly take his gaze from Anna. With a smile at Anna, he looked up. "I'd like everyone's attention," he said and glanced around the table again. "I want to make an announcement."

Conversation died, and all of them turned their attention to Parker, except Bonita, who was studying her drink and swirling her glass slightly. As they waited, Brittany couldn't imagine what Parker had on his mind.

His eyes sparkled and she realized she had never seen him look that enthused over any deal he had made. Anna was radiant as she smiled at Parker and he took her hand. "Anna and I are getting married. We decided to marry Saturday afternoon."

There was one second of stunned surprise and then the siblings started talking and asking questions at once. Parker raised his hand for quiet. "Before you quiz us, let me tell you our plans, and then see if you still have something you want to know. This is short notice, so we're not having attendants because the wedding is within days. We'll marry at the Garrison Grand on the beach and then have a party. We'll have announcements sent out tomorrow, but I'm having my secretary call our closest friends. Can all of you be there?"

There were nods and positive replies and Stephen stood and raised his glass. "Here's a toast to the happy couple. Best wishes from all of us for a long and joyful marriage."

Everyone raised their glasses in a salute to Parker and Anna and later, the minute dinner was over, Brittany and Brooke both went to Anna to welcome her into the family again.

It was nine when Brittany finally got away and as soon as she was in her car, she called Emilio to tell him she was on her way.

The second he opened the door to his condo, she walked into his arms.

Clothes were strewn from the door to the bedroom, but she barely noticed. She ran her hands over him as she kissed him and felt as if she had been away from him forever. "I can't believe how much I missed you," she whispered.

They made love through the night and slept for a couple of

hours after the morning sun spilled into his bedroom. Finally, she sat up and dressed.

"Emilio, it's almost eight in the morning! I have to go home and get to Brittany Beach. You've ruined me."

"Are you complaining?" he asked, pulling her into his arms to smile at her. She wound her arms around his neck.

"I don't think so," she said. "Kiss me and I'll see if I have a complaint."

"Gladly," he said, covering her mouth with his. Her heart thudded and she was amazed how she continually wanted him more. He excited her more all the time. Her pulse raced and his kisses melted her and she didn't care if she ever got out of bed or home or to Brittany Beach.

It was two hours later when she rolled over and sat up, pulling the sheet to her chin. "I do have to go now."

"I'll order breakfast sent up from the restaurant next door. You can eat with me," he said, stretching out his long arm for the phone and placing an order. "Now, we shower."

"No way. I'll shower in your guest bathroom," she said and hurried to gather her things. He crossed the room and caught her before she left, turning her into his arms. She saw that he was aroused and she shook her head.

"I have to get out of bed, Emilio," she insisted.

"One kiss. You walk around like that—"

"I'm covered in a sheet, for heaven's sake!"

"I know there's nothing under that sheet except a beautiful, naked woman," he said and kissed her long and hard. Finally, she pushed away and hurried to the shower, closing the door and knowing she would have to resist him again or never get away today.

They ate on his terrace with a view of the ocean and yachts at anchor.

"What a beautiful day," she exclaimed.

"I can only see a beautiful woman," he said, reaching across the table to touch her cheek lightly.

She smiled at him. "This is good."

"Very good," he repeated. "How was the family dinner last night? I never got to ask you."

"Fine. Parker and Anna announced they're marrying Saturday at the Garrison Grand on the beach. Parker is so in love that he's a different person."

"I doubt that," Emilio remarked drily. "Your brother is all business and practical. Falling in love isn't going to change him much or for long."

"You'd be surprised."

"Damned surprised," Emilio replied with such force that she looked up.

"Have you had a conflict with Parker?"

Shrugging, Emilio toyed with his ice water. "Everyone in Miami knows your brother—I should correct that to say every businessman in Miami. Tourists don't know the Garrisons. Now enough about Parker. When do we get to be together again? I have appointments and business at El Diablo today. How about eating a midnight dinner with me tonight here at my condo?"

Feeling giddy with happiness, she laughed. "Midnight supper? Sounds ridiculous, but how can I refuse you?" she asked and lost her appetite for her breakfast at the look in his eyes. Desire flamed while he stood and came around to pull her to her feet. Wrapping his arms around her, he kissed her.

She didn't know how much time passed before she pushed away. "Now I have to go. I'll be with you tonight."

He walked to the elevator with her where he kissed her again and wanted her to come back inside with him, but she said goodbye and left.

She drove straight to Brittany Beach to find the noon crowd already gathering.

* * *

By eight o'clock that night, she had talked to Emilio a dozen times and the midnight dinner had been moved up an hour. As she stood in the dining room, she saw Parker striding across the room toward her. Her first thought was that something had happened to their mother.

Instantly, that concern was replaced. With a frown wrinkling his brow, Parker was charging toward her without looking at anyone except her. He was furious and she could guess why. Parker had discovered Emilio was her partner.

Nine

"I take it something's wrong," Brittany said as Parker walked up to her.

"Yes, it is. We'll talk in your office," he said, looking over her head, gazing around the dining room. She was certain that he'd heard about Emilio and was looking for him.

With her heart drumming, she led the way and as soon as they had her doors closed, she turned to Parker, whose face was red. "I assume you've learned I have a partner," she said, raising her chin.

"Dammit, yes. Stephen wanted to come, but I told him I'd take care of this. He'll probably call you. How the hell could you do this?"

"Don't swear at me, Parker!" she snapped, her anger soaring over his high-handed ways.

"You deserve more than swearing. We've let you keep this restaurant, but you've betrayed us. I want to boot you off and take the place. Then see how well you and your partner do."

"Don't you dare, Parker!" she yelled at him, her temper boiling. "You know if our father were alive, he would never let you evict me!" she yelled. "You leave me alone. This is my business to run as I see fit."

"When you take in the enemy as your partner, that's it."

"What are you talking about, 'the enemy'?"

"You know damn well what I'm talking about!" Parker retorted. "You know the Garrisons and the Jefferies feud like the Hatfields and the McCoys. We've fought those damned Jefferies over more deals than I can count. They've tried to ruin every Garrison thing they can or compete with us and we've been at war with them for the past few years. Our father fought them like crazy."

Stunned, she stared at him while her mind reeled and all her anger drained away. "What are you talking about, Parker?"

Glaring at her, he took a deep breath. "You didn't know that we have a feud with Emilio and Jordan Jefferies?"

"No, I didn't know that," she answered. "What war with the Jefferies?" she asked, beginning to shake.

"I'll be damned, you don't know!" Parker exclaimed and frowned at her. "They compete with us and want to ruin us if they can. They want to build an empire like we have. They try to beat us to buy property that we want. They've used blind trusts and other people representing them and now this? Emilio Jefferies becomes your partner?"

"I didn't know anything about a Garrison-Jefferies history," Brittany said stiffly. She had been deceived by Emilio. He had been after Garrison business. No wonder he had made the suggestion to her and offered his money and help.

What a dupe she had been! On top of that hurt was the knowledge the family didn't bother to keep her informed about things all the others knew.

"I don't know how you could keep from knowing about

them when they've caused us so damned much trouble," Parker grumbled.

"Why didn't any of you tell me?"

"I suppose it didn't seem important."

"I know why," she said bitterly. "You don't think it matters what I know or don't know. Well, I wouldn't have taken him for a partner if I'd been informed. You should tell me what's going on."

"Most things don't involve you or Brittany Beach and you know it. How much percentage did he get?"

"Fifty percent," she admitted, and Parker grimaced as he mouthed a word, but didn't say it aloud.

"A Jefferies has half!" Parker stormed, his frown deepening.

"Keep me informed if you don't want me to do something I shouldn't. What did you expect?"

"Damn well not for you to go out and take in our worst enemy and hand over fifty percent of the restaurant! Damnation, Brittany, if our dad were alive, he'd take the place back from you. We can't take Jefferies' half now. That's his. He's got a Garrison business. I'll bet those Jefferies had a blast celebrating and if you think they didn't split their sides laughing at the deal they put over on you—think again."

Parker's words stabbed like a knife because she knew they were true. She rubbed her forehead. All the nightmare accusations of her family that she was inept, flighty and didn't have business sense—every charge haunted her because she had proved them right.

Angry and hurt, she glared at Parker. "I didn't know, Parker."

"Well, now you know and he's got half of this! Damn, what a fool he's made of you! He better lie low and stay out of my sight. I swear, I'll punch him out. Is he here now?"

"No, he's not and he won't be tonight," she answered.

"That's good for him. He's got half your business. I'm sure he plans to take it all from you. We're not going to let him do that, Brittany."

"I won't let him take my part away from me," she said, knowing that Parker didn't think she was competent enough to stop Emilio.

"Damn straight he won't, but I'm the one who'll see to that. He got half from you and I'll bet he did it easily. Do you have the contract?"

"Of course," she said. "Brandon has the original." She walked around her desk to unlock and open a bottom drawer.

"Brandon?"

"He has to observe client-attorney confidentiality, so don't go yelling at him. He couldn't tell you no matter how badly he wanted to." She withdrew a folder and carried it to Parker. "Did Brandon know about the feud?"

"Yes, I thought all of SoBe, including you, knew it," Parker huffed. "But Brandon couldn't tell you for the same reason he couldn't tell me about your contract with Emilio—attorney-client confidentiality."

"I guess you're right. He was noncommittal, but I sensed disapproval. I figured it was because he knew you wouldn't like me taking in a partner. He suggested I talk it over with you, and I told him I didn't want to."

"That makes me feel better about Brandon. You should've taken his advice."

"I didn't know the reason for it."

"That doesn't matter, Brittany."

"Parker, you don't think I have a brain in my head!" she accused, glaring at her brother, who scowled in return.

"Thank God you had Brandon do the legal work, though," Parker said, ignoring her comment in which she was certain he concurred. "I trust the contract to be okay if he had a part in it, but I still want to see it. I'll have a copy made and get this back to you. What did you get out of the deal?"

"Emilio has a two-million-dollar investment and he'll lend his restaurant expertise," she said stiffly, hurting badly while anger burned. Emilio had deceived her from the start. She'd trusted him as much as a person could trust another and he had violated that trust completely.

"With two million they acquire a Garrison property. Does he know you don't own the land?"

"Yes, but he doesn't know that you would evict me in a flash. He assumes it's a Garrison deal so I'm here to stay."

"Why didn't you come to us if you wanted two million or advice or any other damn thing?"

"My family doesn't exactly work cooperatively with me," she said with sarcasm lacing her voice. "You know you wouldn't have wanted to give me money to put into this and you would have stepped in and taken over. Admit it, Parker. You're just waiting for an excuse far less than this to take Brittany Beach."

"What got into you, to take anyone into your business? Why did you do it?"

"I thought I was doing something that would be good. This place is turning a profit. It's popular and profits increase every single month. I can invest more in it to make it grow." She knew her reason sounded weak, but she was not about to tell Parker about the embezzlement.

"I'll tell you, Brittany, I don't want the Jefferies in our business," Parker said.

"Don't evict me. I have a successful place. When I start to lose money, then we can talk about eviction. Until then, I'll take you to court."

"You'll lose," Parker said.

"I know that, but I'll tie you up and cost Garrison, Inc. money until you'd wished you'd left me alone."

"That's a hell of an attitude!" Parker complained.

"I'm trying to save my restaurant. The one Dad gave me. What about your outlook when it comes to ousting me because I took in a Jefferies, when you didn't tell me you had a feud with them?" she asked in exasperation. "I'll do something about Emilio because I didn't know there was a feud, but you leave me and Brittany Beach alone."

Parker nodded. "All right, but come to me if you want money. Don't go to outsiders. You should've let us put the money into this."

"You know you would have refused," she repeated. "Don't expect me to believe anything else. If I'd known," she said bitterly, "I wouldn't have taken him in. I'll deal with him, though."

"Keep me posted about what you're going to do and what that partner of yours plans," Parker ordered.

"I will," she promised, wondering exactly how she would deal with Emilio.

Parker nodded and thumped the folder with the contract against his leg. "All right, Brittany. Keep in touch."

Feeling numb, she walked with her brother to the front and watched him go outside and talk on his cell phone while he waited for a valet to bring his car. She was certain he was talking to Stephen about meeting to look over her contract with Emilio and decide what they were going to do next. Moving woodenly and hurting all over, she returned to her office.

The moment she closed her door, her shoulders sagged and she couldn't keep tears from coming. She had been betrayed by a man she had fallen in love with and trusted.

What a little fool he must think she was.

Emilio's money may have been the only way that Brittany Beach could have been saved. But that didn't have anything to do with her heart and the deception and betrayal by Emilio. She hurt because she had given him her trust and her love and her body.

While she had been falling in love, had he and Jordan Jefferies been celebrating her naiveté and gullible acceptance?

Blind with tears, she stumbled toward the sofa to put her face in her hands and cry.

Suffering pain and anger and humiliation, she sobbed. His deception was agonizing. To know she'd been used, crushed her.

Finally, she stood and went to her bathroom to wash her face in cold water. Along with her hurt was fury over being duped, but she knew when she broke off with Emilio, what would be left after the anger had cooled would be agony.

She stared at her reflection, wanting to look composed when she saw him later tonight. Tomorrow she was taking the day off from working at Brittany Beach.

At the moment, she barely knew what she was doing.

Sitting at her desk, she switched off the lights in her office, stared outside, watching whitecaps roll in while she hurt over Emilio. She remembered the day she had asked him if something was wrong and he told her she could ask him anything she wanted. Now she could understand why he looked worried, because of guilt and the deception.

Finally, it was time to go to Emilio's condo. The sooner she broke off with him, the quicker she would begin to recover. Except, she wondered if she would ever really mend. She hoped she could control her emotions. She didn't want to shed tears around him.

She tried to concentrate on her driving, being careful because she knew she was on a rocky edge. From the lobby, she phoned to tell him she had arrived.

His voice was warm and deep. "Come up."

Stiffly, she stood in the elevator as it rose to his floor.

She stepped out in the short hallway in front of his door. He had his door open and he lounged in the doorway. Dressed in navy slacks and shirt, he leaned one broad shoulder against the doorjamb. His smile faded the moment he saw her.

"Brittany? What's wrong?" he asked, approaching her.

He walked up to place his hands on her shoulders. "What's happened?" he repeated, studying her with concern in his green eyes.

"Let's go inside," she said, knowing his hall was probably private, but she didn't want to be interrupted.

He turned to drape his arm across her shoulders as they walked into his condo and he closed the door. He turned her to face him. "What is it?"

"Parker came to see me tonight," she said. Emilio closed his eyes and rocked back on his heels.

"Brittany, let me explain," he urged. He took a deep breath, angry with himself for not confessing to her before she discovered the truth from someone else.

"My brothers have already told me about the Garrison-Jefferies feud." Her voice was cold and she stood stiffly facing him. She had lost all color, and he ached because he knew he'd hurt her.

"There's a feud, and that's why I wanted to buy into Brittany Beach," he declared earnestly. "But then, after I began to work with you, things changed and I didn't know how to tell you."

'Oh, please, Emilio! We've had enough deception between us. You used me and you got what you wanted. You've hurt my family and me. Don't add more lies and try to deceive me further. I don't want to hear any of it," she said in a tight voice as she wound her fingers together until her knuckles were white. He wanted to go wrap her in his arms and convince her that he was sincere, but he knew he couldn't. He felt as if he were sinking into quicksand that would destroy him and he knew the whole terrible situation was his own doing.

"If I'd admitted what I'd done, you would have been angry and hated me for it. If you'd learned about it from your brothers, I knew you'd be hurt and furious with me. Either way, I was doomed. To be honest, I wanted a few more nights with you when we got along well together and could make love before I told you the truth, but I was going to. I swear, I was. I knew I had to."

"Now you don't have to," she replied coldly, and her words cut into him. "For a few days you stay away from Brittany Beach."

It was over between them. There was no forgiveness in her stance and he hurt and wanted to undo what he'd done. "Brittany, listen to me," he said, approaching her to take her into his arms.

She jerked away from him. "Don't touch me! I trusted you, Emilio. You knew I believed you and you took that faith and trampled it."

"Brittany, listen to me. You're not giving me a chance here—"

"What did you give me?" she retorted and his guilt deepened. "I'll never trust you," she vowed. "We're not going to work together from here on, Emilio," she continued. "We'll arrange our schedules so that we're not at Brittany Beach at the same time."

"You're not going to listen to me at all, are you?" he asked, realizing she had shut her mind to everything he was saying.

"Get it through you head—I don't believe a word that you tell me and I don't want to see you. I'll talk to my lawyer and he can contact you and your attorney to work things out. You've taken advantage of me and deceived me and I don't want any part of you."

"I thought we had something good between us," he stated quietly.

"Coming from you, that really cuts it," she said. Her eyes flashed with fire. "You got it all from me," she said with her voice dripping with venom. "You really weren't trying to help and you weren't interested in Brittany Beach, except as a way to erode the Garrison holdings. I was a pawn in a game you were playing and you were exploiting me."

"You're not hearing one thing I'm saying to you."

"I hear you all right. I just no longer believe you," she replied.

"My feelings for you haven't changed, and I want to be with you," he said, gazing at her imploringly.

"Brittany, listen to me," he said, taking her shoulders again.

"Let me go, Emilio. I'm leaving now. I'll get someone to call you with my new schedule. When I'm at Brittany Beach, stay away. I don't want to talk to you. We've said it all right now. It's over. You got your Garrison property and you seduced me. You probably were aimed at taking one-hundred percent of Brittany Beach. That accomplishment I can keep you from doing."

"You're not being fair."

"And when were you fair?" she accused him, her brown eyes darkened with rage. "I'm out of here forever. And I guess it'll take you all of one evening before you have another adoring female draped on your arm and in your bed. By this time tomorrow, you'll forget me, except for the fact that your duplicity has been discovered and, hopefully, you can't do any further damage to the Garrisons."

"It won't be that way, and I don't want to hurt the Garrisons, particularly you," he replied.

"I hope my brothers ruin the Jefferies!"

"I don't give a damn about that," Emilio replied tersely. "It's you that I don't want to lose. I mean it, Brittany."

"We've said all there is to be said." As she headed away from him, he knew she was walking out of his life and it hurt more than he would have guessed.

Catching up with her, he walked in silence beside her and opened the elevator. When she stepped inside, she faced him.

"Don't go like this," he said.

"Goodbye, Emilio. I hope I don't see you again for a long, long time. That's the one thing you can do that will please me."

Knowing it was useless to argue with her, he stared at her, knowing he would never forget this moment. Her brown eyes were wide and still blazed with fury. Her thick brown hair was tied loosely behind her head. Her mouth was as soft and tempting as ever, but she wouldn't let him touch her again. She was beautiful, desirable and no longer part of his life.

The doors closed and she was gone. He felt as if his heart had been ripped out and taken away. As she descended to the ground floor, he watched the brass arrow above the elevator. When the arrow stopped at one, he could imagine her stepping into the lobby and walking out of his building and his life.

In a daze, he returned to his empty condo and went to the terrace to look at the traffic below, knowing she was down there, heading back to her place or Brittany Beach.

"I'm sorry I hurt you and I wish you'd listen," he said to the empty air. "I already miss you," he added, realizing he wanted her to an extent that stunned him. Had he fallen in love with her?

As he stared at the highway and tried to sort out his feelings, he frowned. He'd never been truly in love in his life. And he'd never hurt like this.

He shook his shoulders and told himself that he wasn't accustomed to women breaking off the relationship with him and he'd get over Brittany soon, the same as he had always recovered from other splits. But those other times, he had been the one to end the affair, so from the beginning he had been doing as he pleased.

Staying in his empty, silent condo was no way to get over

Brittany's loss. He picked up his billfold and keys and left to drive to El Diablo, where he could forget Brittany Garrison.

As he drove, he thought about his fifty percent of Brittany Beach. It would be a miserable partnership now for both of them. He no longer wanted to continue the feud with her family. What would he do about Jordan? He knew he couldn't convince his brother that they should call off the feud.

Getting his cell phone, Emilio contacted Jordan and got him to agree to stop by El Diablo in the morning so they could talk. Grimly, he broke the connection and headed toward his restaurant.

At half past ten, looking fresh and fit, dressed in gray slacks and a gray shirt, Jordan came striding into Emilio's office. "Morning. What's up?"

"Thanks, Jordan, for coming by," Emilio said.

"What happened to you? You look like you've been hit by a bus. What's gone wrong?"

"Have a seat."

"Something's happened, so don't keep me in suspense," Jordan said, sprawling in one of the leather chairs and placing one foot on his knee.

"Parker Garrison discovered the partnership."

"Whoo, hoo!" Jordan exclaimed with jubilation. "I hope they're burning with fury and frustration."

"They are, and so is Brittany."

Jordan's smile faded and his eyes narrowed. "So what difference does that make? Dammit, Emilio. Don't tell me you're going soft for a hot body. You can replace Brittany in five minutes."

Emilio ground his jaw closed and tried to hold his temper, knowing if they got in a fight he wouldn't get anywhere with Jordan.

"Jordan, I care about her feelings," Emilio said, walking to

the window to look outside and trying to remain calm enough
to reason with Jordan.

"Don't be ridiculous! She's a Garrison. You went into this
wanting to take advantage of her naiveté, which you did with
great success. You intended to capitalize on it and get all of
Brittany Beach from her. Now, because she's letting you sleep
with her—and I'm sure she is or we wouldn't be having this
conversation—don't go all soft about a Garrison."

Emilio spun around, striding toward Jordan to halt only feet
away. "You don't know her. She's special. She's a good businesswoman. I've got feelings for her. I'll admit that I care
about her. She's different from other women."

"The hell she is!" Jordan argued, coming to his feet to glare
at Emilio. "You've let her come between us. From the beginning, this is what I warned you about. You go soft on the Garrisons and she'll split us apart, Emilio. Is that what you want?"

"Of course not! You know I don't want a rift to occur. Listen
to what I'm saying. We're doing fine without Brittany Beach."

"We're keeping that restaurant," Jordan insisted. "You get
over her! She's not for you. From the beginning, you've lusted
after her and she's probably hot in the sack, but so are other
women. Get rid of her and let's go on with building our empire.
We've got a great start. Don't tear us apart and wreck everything over a little hot number."

"Don't call her a 'hot number,'" Emilio ordered.

"You've let her come between us," Jordan retorted, his frown
deepening while his blue eyes blazed. "You've aligned your
loyalties to the Garrisons. Although I know that the Garrison
men won't welcome you."

"I don't give a damn about them, and I don't want us ripped
apart," Emilio replied.

"Damn straight, but we will be if you let some woman come
between us."

Emilio doubled his fists and swung at Jordan, who ducked and the swing went wild without any contact. "Stop it!" Jordan shouted, stepping back out of Emilio's range and raising his fists. Locks of his blond hair curled over his forehead, while Emilio's black hair was as unruly. Emilio's chest heaved, and he fought to curb his anger.

"You're going to let her come between us, Emilio. Your loyalty should be to *us*."

"You don't have any interest in Brittany Beach, so whatever I do there, you have no control over it."

"Dammit, are you going to let her buy you out of the partnership?"

"I don't know what I'm going to do," Emilio replied bluntly.

"I'm glad our parents didn't live to see you turn traitor to the family."

"That's a hell of a thing to say!" Emilio admonished.

"If you come to your senses, give me a call," Jordan said and strode out of the room, slamming the door behind him.

Emilio's anger soared that Jordan was stubborn and unreasonable. Brittany Beach wasn't that important to them. They'd been doing fine without it, and Jordan was turning a blind eye to what Emilio wanted.

He knew Jordan disliked the Garrison men as much as he did. If Jordan would only listen and give him a chance, Emilio thought.

He swung his fist through the air in frustration and anger. He hurt over Brittany and he hated that Jordan would be unreasonable about his feelings for her. He knew his brother had a stubborn streak. Now, there was a split between them and it might widen until they couldn't bridge it.

Emilio stomped outside, standing on his patio and watching waves roll in and recede. What was he going to do about Brittany Beach?

His thoughts jumped to Brittany. He missed her. He couldn't

go an hour without thinking about her and wanting her. He cared about her and if that drove a wedge between him and his brother, so be it. Brittany was more important.

Startled that he would feel so intensely about her, he drew a deep breath. He acknowledged that she was the most important person in his life. He had known that he felt closer to her in some ways than he did to anyone else, even his brother, but he hadn't stopped to realize how vital she was to him. Why hadn't he seen this before?

Already, he missed her. He ached to go inside and phone her if for nothing else, just to hear her voice. He missed her and images of her, naked in his arms, smiling up at him, of her hands fluttering over him, of her kissing him, tormented him until he groaned and ran his fingers through his hair.

His cell phone rang and he picked up to hear his secretary telling him that Hector Garland, director of services for Brittany Beach, was in the office and wanted to see him.

"Sure, tell him to come in," Emilio said, going inside and crossing his office as the door opened and she ushered Hector inside. When Hector entered, Emilio offered his hand.

"Hi, Hector. Have a seat, please. What can I do for you?" Emilio asked as he pulled a chair around to sit and face Hector, who had a folder in his hand which he held out for Emilio.

"I brought a schedule that Brittany wanted me to give you. If you'll please follow this, the two of you will be at Brittany Beach at different times," Hector said in a brisk, businesslike voice as if he were talking about supplies they needed for the coming week.

Hurting, Emilio hoped he kept his features impassive as he accepted the folder, opened the flap and glanced at a schedule for each day of the week. "Very well. Reassure her that I'll stick to this schedule."

"Thanks," Hector replied, sounding relieved. "She asked

that anything you want, please either go through your attorney or call me or one of the other employees who can relay the message to her. She prefers that the two of you no longer have dealings with each other," he said, avoiding looking Emilio in the eye until he finished. He took a deep breath and faced Emilio. "I'm sorry."

"Thanks. So am I. Maybe with time, it'll work out," he said perfunctorily, not believing it would happen and not caring to discuss the matter with Hector. "I understand and I'll do what she wants," Emilio continued, wondering if he would keep his word on that one. He could feel the chasm between Brittany and himself widening further, getting impossible to span.

"I think that covers everything," Hector said with so much cheer, Emilio wanted to grind his teeth. "Do you have any questions or comments for me to take back to her?"

"Only what I told you a moment ago. I'll follow this schedule."

"Fine," Hector said. When he stood, Emilio came to his feet. Hector extended his hand. "As I said, I'm sorry for the split between the two of you, but this seems a workable arrangement."

"Brittany Beach has experienced, competent staff, so we'll get along," Emilio said, thinking the restaurant should thrive, but he didn't know how well he would fare in the coming weeks. Or what he would do eventually about Brittany Beach. He walked to the door with Hector and told him goodbye. The minute he closed the door behind him, he flung the folder across the office and papers spilled out on the floor.

Pacing the room, Emilio finally yanked open his office door, leaving to head to the gym and try to forget Brittany for an hour, if possible. How long before he would get over her? Like a heady wine, she was in his blood. Unlike the wine, she wasn't going to wear off any time soon.

"Dammit, Jordan!" he swore softly as he climbed into his

car. What a muddle life had become. He was paying a heavy price for deception. Was Brittany's anger enough to make her glad to be rid of him and not hurt over the end of their affair? How much had she really cared? What was she doing this moment, he wondered, wanting to be with her.

"Brittany, Brittany," he whispered while a hundred questions plagued him.

Ten

Saturday afternoon, Brittany dressed in the bedroom of a suite she had at the Garrison Grand. She had the suite so she could stay in the hotel after the rehearsal dinner and party they had last night and where today she could have a private place to change clothes.

Suspecting this wedding would be an emotional ordeal for her to get through, Brittany dressed with care, looping and pinning her hair on top of her head. A few tendrils hung down to curl slightly around her face. She smoothed the skirt of her pale yellow sleeveless silk dress and studied her reflection. While she stared at the mirror, all she could see was black wavy hair and thickly lashed green eyes. She hurt and the pain seemed to steadily increase, instead of lessen.

She resigned herself to misery and figured the time would come when the past would be a memory and the dreadful longing that enveloped her now would stop.

She suspected that she would love Emilio all her life, but she hoped she was wrong. Tears threatened and she fought them back, hating how weepy she had become when, until loving Emilio, she'd rarely shed a tear since becoming an adult.

Breaking into her thoughts, her cell phone rang. She answered to listen to Brandon, who was in the hotel for the wedding reception and wanted to know if he could talk to her privately for a few minutes. He asked her to meet him in the coffee shop, but Brittany gave him her suite number and told him to come up where they would have the most privacy.

Figuring Brandon had something that he wanted to discuss about her contract with Emilio, she walked through the suite to pick up any clothing she had discarded in the sitting area. The white carpet and white furniture looked pristine. A vase of fresh mixed flowers added to the inviting ambience and there were splashes of color in the ornate paintings on the walls and decorative pillows on the white sofa.

She carried clothes to the bedroom to hang them in the large closet. The bedroom held oak furniture and a king-size bed with a cheerful duvet of primary colors, yet neither pretty rooms and furniture or a family event could lift her sense of hurt and loss.

The knock at the door was light and she hurried to open it and smile at Brandon as she offered him her hand. Dressed in a navy suit and white shirt that complimented his tanned brown skin, he stepped inside to shake her hand.

"Stephen told me that you're here in the hotel and that you wouldn't mind if I called and wanted to talk to you."

"Of course not," she said. She motioned toward the chairs. "Please, have a seat."

As tall as Parker, Brandon moved with the energy of a well-trained athlete. He sat in a straight-backed chair and she sat on a matching one that was turned slightly toward him. "What's up, Brandon?"

"I've tried to call before but when you didn't answer, I didn't leave a message. I know Parker and Stephen—and your whole family now—have learned about your partnership with Emilio Jefferies."

"Yes. Parker and Stephen finally calmed down."

"I wanted to talk to you myself. When you first called me about the partnership, you know I couldn't warn you further than I tried to, because of my attorney-client relationship with Parker and Stephen."

"I understand, and Parker and I discussed your position. I know you couldn't reveal their situation with Emilio and his brother. I told Parker that you tried to discourage me from entering into the partnership. I didn't guess the real reason for your remarks."

"That's the most I could say, but I felt terrible, Brittany, because I knew you were going into something that would enrage your entire family. Parker and Stephen were wild about it because they fight Emilio and Jordan constantly."

"I must have been the only person in SoBe who was ignorant of the feud," she said bitterly, and then remembered Brandon and tried to smile at him. "Sorry, Brandon. None of it was your fault at all, and don't worry about it. I understand, and you did your ethical best to keep me from it."

"Thanks for being understanding about this, because I know it's caused you pain. If I can do anything to help you in any way—"

She shook her head. "Forget it, but thanks," she said, interrupting him. "It was one of life's lessons, both for me and my brothers, who in the future may not keep me in the dark about business matters."

"Well, I hate that it happened." Brandon stood. "I'll go now. It'll soon be time for Parker's wedding."

"I really meant what I said. Don't worry about telling me

about the Jefferies, because I know you did all you could," she said, standing when he did. "It was particularly kind of you to come by to talk to me about it."

"It's damn little when you consider what happened," he said. "I'll see you shortly," he added.

Smiling at him, she hoped that she had convinced him that she held him in no blame, whatsoever. When he left, she closed the door and leaned against it. What would she have done if he'd told her about the feud? She'd had nowhere else to turn. Yet she knew she wouldn't have entered into the contract with Emilio. How could he have been so duplicitous with her?

Before going downstairs, she went back to the bedroom to look one more time at herself. Knowing she had to get through this wedding without losing control of her emotions, she reminded herself again that today belonged to Parker and Anna and she didn't want to darken it in the slightest. "No tears for the next five hours," she said aloud to her image in the mirror.

"Damn you, Emilio!" she snapped, wondering if he and Jordan were still celebrating the wreckage they had caused in the Garrison family.

Taking a deep breath, she really looked at herself and decided her appearance was fine. She had lost a slight bit of weight, but nothing noticeable yet.

When Parker returned to work after his wedding, she wanted to talk to him about taking the land where Brittany Beach was located. If they were evicted and had to find another location, she figured Emilio would want out of the partnership. She knew that Parker would help her buy Emilio out in a flash.

On the other hand, if Jordan and Emilio were set on ruining the Garrison empire, they might hang on, just to have part of the Garrison property. If so, she wanted to sell her half and find some other job and, again, her brothers would help do anything, she suspected, to get her out of business with Emilio.

She left her suite to go to her brother's wedding.

They had a private area on the beach where chairs had been set up. The sunny afternoon was perfect, with only a faint breeze, whitecaps washing ashore and receding. The deep-aqua water met a blue sky. A band was to one side of sprays of red and white roses.

Brittany slid into a seat by Brooke, who looked unusually glum. Studying her twin, Brittany knew distance had grown between them, yet there was still a bond that would always be there.

"Are you all right?" she asked Brooke, who turned to look into her eyes. Brittany's suspicion strengthened that something worried Brooke, but Brooke merely nodded and smiled.

"I'm fine. What about you? Adam told me about Emilio Jefferies. Sorry, Brit."

Nodding, Brittany bit her lip. "Thanks. I didn't know anything about our feud with the Jefferies, but I'm sure you did," she whispered, unable to curb a surge of anger over her family's attitude toward her.

"Yes, I did and I figured you did, too," Brooke said. "Otherwise, I would've told you. Here comes Adam to seat Anna's mother," she said and Brittany glanced around at an attractive woman on her youngest brother's arm.

"Look at Stephen," Brooke hissed. "He's going to seat Mom and he looks unhappy."

Brittany glanced around to see Bonita walking beside Stephen. Her mother's step was steady and she had a faint smile. She looked more like her old self, in a beautiful pale blue silk dress. Brittany knew from talking to her that Bonita had been drinking since morning, yet she was hiding it well so far.

The minister appeared, striding to the front, followed by

Parker in a charcoal suit. Parker's gaze went to the back where Brittany guessed Anna waited for her entrance cue. Parker looked happier than ever.

Something twisted deep inside and she clenched her fists and fought thinking about people in love.

Then the wedding march began and everyone stood and turned to watch the bride.

Eleven

On the arm of her father, Anna looked radiant in a short, white silk sleeveless dress with a low-cut *V* neckline. She wore a spray of white flowers in her hair with a veil that was turned back. Her sparkling green eyes were locked on Parker. A pang stabbed Brittany as a different a pair of thickly lashed green eyes taunted her memory, and moments in Emilio's arms swept her thoughts, far from Parker's wedding. How she ached for Emilio.

She tried to concentrate on Parker and Anna repeating their vows, but all she could think about was Emilio. She glanced at her watch several times until Brooke turned to give her a searching look.

When the ceremony was over and the party started, Brittany was relieved. The band's lively music played. Tables had been set up and white-coated waiters formally dressed—except for their sandals—moved through the crowd. A buffet was spread on three long tables with an array of appealing dishes, but

Brittany had no appetite and she simply carried a wineglass so no one would bother her about a drink, but she didn't want that, either.

Brittany was happy for Parker and Anna, but she hurt and she wanted to be away from the crowd and home, where she could be alone with her pain. Knowing that she had a room in the hotel and soon could escape to solitude, she forced herself to move through the crowd and welcome guests. She didn't feel like partying, and it was an effort to try to keep a smile on her face and remain friendly.

She congratulated Anna, giving her a hug. "Welcome to the family. You're officially my sister now."

"Thanks, Brittany," Anna replied with a big smile. "That's kind and I hope we truly are."

"You look gorgeous."

"Thank you," Anna repeated, and then Brittany turned to hug Parker.

"Congratulations, Big Brother. I didn't think this day would ever happen. I wish you and Anna all the best."

"Thanks, Brittany. I appreciate it and I can't quite believe this day is here, myself," Parker said amiably and grinned, turning to look at his bride. Brittany wondered if he was even conscious of the crowd, family or friends. She laughed, patting his shoulder as Adam appeared.

"Congratulations, brother. May you be married a hundred years," Adam said and turned to Anna. "Anna, Brittany, Parker, this is Heidi Summers," Adam said, introducing a tall, stunning blonde whom everyone greeted perfunctorily.

The kind of beautiful woman that Emilio might like, Brittany thought bitterly, recalling pictures of Emilio with models and rising starlets.

She didn't wait to hear Parker's reply, but left with a softly mumbled, "Excuse me, I'll speak to Mother," she said.

She spotted Bonita, who was seated at a table with Brooke beside her. Brittany squared her shoulders and walked over to talk to them. She should sit and relieve Brooke, who would probably like to escape Bonita's sharp criticisms, but Brittany didn't care to compound her glum feelings by sitting with her mother.

In spite of her increased alcohol dependency, Bonita continued to be stylish, which surprised Brittany, yet she suspected they could all thank Lisette, hairdressers and some clerks in exclusive shops who sent clothes out for Bonita's approval. Always thin, she had lost weight and become even more fragile-looking since her husband's death.

Vowing she wouldn't stay more than another ten minutes with her mother, Brittany did her dutiful daughter act and walked over to sit across from Brooke and their mother.

"Hi, Mother. Beautiful wedding, wasn't it?"

"I don't know why she couldn't have the formal church wedding that Parker deserved," Bonita replied sharply. "The beach is dreadful with all this sand everywhere." Bonita's words were clipped as she studied Brittany. "I heard about you taking in an enemy of the family as your partner. How could you do that?"

"I've been over this with Parker. I didn't know Emilio was a Garrison enemy. No one told me about the Garrisons and the Jefferies," she replied stiffly, realizing even their mother had known about the feud. When they kept her in the dark about everything, what did the family expect?

She tuned Bonita out and, in seconds, stood and moved away, feeling chilled and clammy in spite of the warm August afternoon. It was almost September. Time would help, she reminded herself.

Adam approached her, carrying two drinks. Wind tangled locks of his black hair.

"You beat a hasty retreat," he said, looking at her with curiosity.

She shrugged. "I talked to Mom, who's more critical than

ever and probably had too much to drink by ten o'clock this morning."

"I know," Adam answered grimly, his blue eyes clouding with worry. "I haven't introduced Heidi yet, and I don't know that I will, although our mother is hiding her liquor well, so far."

"She's had plenty of practice. And it won't matter whether you introduce your friend or not. Mom won't like her. Adam, when are you going to get rid of the bimbos and settle down?" she asked her tall brother. "You're thirty."

"I love beautiful women," he answered with an infectious grin. "Sis, it ain't gonna happen," he joked. "If I want someone with a brain, I can go talk to Parker and Stephen. That's not why I'm with Heidi," he said and moved on as she shook her head.

"Womanizer," Brittany said softly under her breath, always surprised that Adam had a way with women, because as far as the family was concerned, he was a loner. Often excusing him for it, Brittany knew that he was younger than Parker and Stephen by quite a few years, while she and Brooke had grown up doing things that wouldn't interest a boy. He was a notorious playboy and she wondered how old they would all be when, and if, Adam ever settled.

As she wandered through the crowd, speaking to first one guest and then another, she saw an unmistakable tall, pretty redheaded woman dressed in a sleeveless green sheath. She stood talking to Anna. Brittany knew Megan Simmons and strolled to the two women to say hello.

"Megan," Brittany said, "I heard you were back in town, and I'm glad you're here."

Turning, Megan smiled. "Hi, Brittany. Thanks. I'm a resident again. I was talking to Anna, who's a beautiful bride."

"Yes, she is," Brittany agreed, smiling at Anna. "We're fortunate to have her in our family and she's turned my all-business brother into a human being."

Megan smiled while Anna laughed. "Thanks, you two," Anna said. When she glanced across the crowd, Brittany knew she was looking at Parker. Suspecting Anna was barely listening to any conversation even when she was involved in it, Brittany looked at Megan.

"I heard that you're a partner in your former design firm now. Congratulations!"

"Thanks," she replied. "I'm getting settled in and started. This is a great place to be an interior designer. I love the art deco that makes SoBe unique."

"Come to my restaurant, Brittany Beach, sometime soon. If you'll let me know, I'll buy your dinner."

"Thanks, Brittany," Megan said, smiling at her. "That's a nice offer and I'll take you up on it," she said, but something in her voice made Brittany suspect that Megan was merely being polite in her reply.

"Here comes my brother," Brittany said, seeing Stephen with a somber expression as he strode toward them. He had shed the coat to his navy suit. Wind caught locks of his jet-black hair and he moved with that same athletic ease that Emilio did.

"It was really nice to see you, Brittany," Megan said hastily. "Best wishes to you, Anna, and to Parker. If you both will excuse me, I see someone," Megan added and turned to hurry away, disappearing into the crowd of milling guests.

"What was all that about?" Brittany said, looking at Anna, who shrugged.

"She seemed to be enjoying everything until seconds ago," Anna remarked. "I guess she saw an old friend."

"Here's Stephen," Brittany said, watching her brother stride up to them.

"That was Megan Simmons, wasn't it?" he said as if to himself. "How come she left so quickly?"

"I don't know," Anna answered. "She said something about seeing someone."

"Stephen, did you hire her to do the Garrison Grand?" Brittany asked. "I think she's really good at what she does."

His gaze searched the crowd and, for a moment, Brittany wondered if he had even heard her question.

"I've called her several times to talk to her about the hotel, but she won't return my calls," he said.

"Did you leave a message?" Brittany asked.

"Yes, I did. I'll get in touch with her," he said and Brittany noticed a muscle worked in his jaw. "Excuse me, you two," he said and left them, turning his head to look at the guests.

"Well, what was all that about?" Brittany asked.

"I don't know. I can't imagine why she isn't returning Stephen's calls. Maybe Parker should call her."

Brittany laughed. "Stephen will not get his big brother to call her for him!"

At that moment, she saw Adam and Heidi approaching. "I'm leaving you to Adam and his latest woman, who will probably be replaced tomorrow," Brittany remarked drily and moved on, looking to see who else she'd missed talking to. She saw Brandon in a cluster of men with Parker. He glanced her way, nodded and smiled and she waved her hand in return.

"Brittany," Brooke called and Brittany turned to find Brooke approaching her.

"So you escaped from Mom's side," Brittany said.

"Yes. Some old-time friends are with her and Lisette is hovering in the background, so I left."

"Adam's good about watching her on Sunday evenings, but he won't want to now with a hot blonde hanging on his arm."

"Stephen has his yacht, Adam has his women," Brooke said. "I think Parker has his concerns. Anna is a big influence on him."

"An astounding influence," Brittany agreed and heard a commotion.

"Oh, saints in heaven!" Brittany exclaimed, stiffening, and Brooke reached out to grab her arm.

"Brittany, what's wrong? Are you all right? You look as if you've seen a ghost. What's the racket?" Brooke asked and Brittany broke free to start running.

Twelve

To Brittany's horror, Emilio had crashed Parker's wedding!

For an instant, her heart stopped and she forgot everything except him. He was in a conservative charcoal suit and, in spite of his angry expression, looked incredibly handsome. Then her heart-pounding second of shock was gone.

Emilio shouted at Stephen and Adam, while the brothers, including Parker, yelled at Emilio, whose jaw was set in a stubborn line. Brittany's heart pounded. There could be only one reason for Emilio to crash Parker's wedding.

"No! Get out!" she yelled, knowing her cries were lost in all the shouting.

Adam and Stephen restrained Parker, who was ready to fight Emilio.

Brandon took Emilio's arm, but Emilio pushed him away and charged ahead, searching the crowd and then looking at her.

Before he could get to Brittany, Bonita stepped in front of

him, and he stopped in his tracks. Everyone froze, as Bonita waved her fist at Emilio.

"You bastard!" she snarled. "You're a deceitful outsider who tried to steal what wasn't yours," she continued. "You've never belonged in society, anyway!"

"Oh, my heavens!" Brooke exclaimed. "We've got to get Mom," she said as she rushed forward.

Bonita continued to insult Emilio, who had made it past all the Garrison men, only to be halted by their mother.

Adam and Brooke rushed to Bonita and each took her arm and walked her away from Emilio.

Brittany knew they needed to get Bonita away from the guests. Alcohol had taken its toll on her. Then Brittany forgot about Bonita as she watched Emilio, who rushed toward her while stunned guests stood as if captured in a picture.

"Get out of here," Brittany said in a low voice. "You've caused enough trouble."

"I have to talk to you and I'm not leaving until I do," Emilio informed her. She saw the steely look in his eyes and knew he meant what he said. Her pulse roared in her ears and she wished she could faint and be oblivious to everything.

Instead, she jerked her head and put her hand on his arm. "Come with me. Hurry!" she said, glancing beyond him to see Stephen and Parker starting toward them.

She rushed with Emilio into the hotel, praying they didn't encounter her mother inside.

It seemed an eternity to cross the lobby and get an elevator, but finally doors closed on them and they were alone. She was breathing as hard as if she had run a race as she looked at him.

"I want to talk to you and I want you to listen to me," he said.

"You picked a poor way to do this."

"You won't take my calls. You won't come to the restaurant if I'm there and you leave if I arrive unannounced."

"Indeed, I do," she said, raising her chin in defiance, ignoring her racing pulse or the ache caused by seeing him. "You know I don't want to be with you, or even talk to you and this is a strain right now. Besides that, you've interrupted the wedding reception and created bad moments that Anna and Parker will remember the rest of their lives."

"For that, I'm profoundly sorry, but this is the only way I could get to you. I'll apologize to your entire family and try to make it up in some manner to Parker and his bride. I had to see you. I want to talk to you, and you've put me off long enough."

She rode in silence until they reached her floor. She unlocked the door to her suite and they stepped inside. As soon as they did, Emilio closed and locked the door while she dropped the key onto a table.

When she turned to face him, he withdrew a thick sheaf of folded papers from his inside coat pocket. "This is for you. I want you to read it over and decide what you want to do," he said solemnly.

Surprised and puzzled, she took the paper from him and unfolded it to see that she was holding a contract. "What's this?" she asked, glancing at him.

"It makes you sole owner of Brittany Beach once again. You can buy back my part and, because of the anguish I caused you, I'll sell it to you for a million and a half. Brittany Beach will belong solely to you."

Stunned, she scanned the contract and saw it was exactly what he'd told her. "You'd do this?"

"Yes, to try to make things right for you."

"Does Jordan know about this?"

"Not yet, but he will," Emilio replied calmly, his gaze going slowly over her features as if he were trying to memorize them.

"Doesn't he have to agree to this?" she asked.

"No. I can do what I want. You buy it back and the money will go into our business account."

"He won't like it, will he?" she persisted, amazed at what Emilio was doing.

"No, but returning what I took from you is more important. Your feelings come first with me."

Shocked, she looked again at the contract. She could buy him out and her restaurant could be hers once again, solely a Garrison endeavor. "What happened to this big feud between our two families?" she asked.

He shrugged. "I want no part of it. Jordan hasn't changed, so he's determined to build a Jefferies empire to rival the Garrisons and he'll clash with your brothers."

"He'll be so angry with you," she said, staring at Emilio and thinking about what his offer really meant to her. "He'll be even angrier if you don't get back your full two million. How can you do this if it drives a wedge between you and your brother?"

"It's necessary. I don't want to fight any Garrison, one woman in particular. I hope Jordan will come around. Whether he does or not shouldn't matter to you. I know you and your family would like to buy back my partnership. Is Brandon here? He told me he was coming."

"Yes, he is," she said, barely able to get out the words.

"I've already signed the contract. Turn to the last pages and you'll see my signature. If we add yours in front of a notary, it's a done deal and you will once again be sole owner of Brittany Beach. You'll have your restaurant back and you can go on packing them in and running Brittany Beach and your brothers will leave you alone to do so."

Shaken, she stared at him. "I'm overwhelmed and don't know what to say."

He took the few steps necessary to close the distance between them. Reaching out, he folded her cold fingers in his warm, strong hands. His intense regard made her pulse hum and, in spite of all that had happened, she wanted him and wanted his arms around her.

"I miss you more than I thought possible," he said in a rasping voice that made her tremble. "I love you, Brittany."

Her surprise deepened even more, and she looked at him while her heart accelerated.

"Our families hate each other," she whispered, thinking how angry her brothers had been at Emilio.

"I can't do anything about families, mine or yours. I just know what I want and it's you. I don't want to go through my life without you in it. I love you. I want you to marry me."

Another shock jolted her. While Emilio's words echoed in her thoughts, she felt consumed by the pure green of his eyes that bored into her. Their families might not ever like each other—was she ready to live with that? She couldn't answer her own question, but she did know that she loved Emilio. She took a deep breath and stepped closer to wrap her arms around his neck.

"I love you," she whispered, standing on tiptoe to kiss him.

His strong arms banded her and drew her into his tight embrace as he leaned over her to kiss her passionately. His deep, long kiss conveyed all his feelings for her.

Her heart thudded and she wound her fingers in his hair and knew Emilio's love was what she wanted more than anything else. She tipped back to look at him, framing his face with her hands. "It's been terrible to be away from you," she whispered. "I love you and, yes, I'll marry you."

His eyes blazed with desire and he dipped his head again to kiss her hard. Suddenly, she didn't want the barriers between them. Her hands flew over him as swiftly as his fluttered over her. She twisted free buttons and slid down his zipper and in minutes, clothes were discarded as they kissed. He picked her up into his arms to carry her to the bedroom.

Emilio yanked away the linens on the bed and placed her on it, kneeling to kiss her throat and then trail kisses lower to her breast. She moaned and sat up to wrap her arms around him while he bent over her and his mouth covered hers as he kissed her passionately.

She felt starved for him, and ran her hand over his warm, muscled shoulder as she kissed him.

He shifted, showering kisses lower to her breasts, taking her nipple in his mouth to circle the tip with his tongue. His hand drifted across her belly and between her thighs.

He stopped, walking away to retrieve a condom from the pocket of his pants and then returned and moved between her legs.

Her heart raced with eagerness. She reached for him, wanting to pull him to her, aching for him while she watched him put on the latex shield. She ran her hands along his muscled thighs and then he lowered himself to thrust into her.

Wrapping her legs around him and her arms around his neck, she held him tightly as her hips arched against him and she moved frantically with him. How starved she was for him! "Emilio, I love you!" she cried.

Wanting him more than ever, she rocked with him, the tension building to white heat. Finally, she shook with release while she felt him shudder with his climax.

Ecstasy replaced need as her breathing slowed and she relaxed in his embrace. Taking her with him, he rolled on his side and held her close to kiss her with satisfaction. "I have to hear you say it again," he whispered and leaned back a fraction to look at her as he stroked her hair away from her face. "I love you. Will you marry me?"

"Yes, I'll marry you."

He looked at her solemnly. "We both have families that won't approve. You may face a real battle with them and I know I will with Jordan. Are you ready to live with their anger?" He placed his finger on her lips. "Think about it before you answer me."

She wound her fingers in his damp chest hair and ran her hand over his hip while she imagined how furious each member of her family would be. Bonita would be in a rage. So would Parker and Stephen. Brooke and Adam—they might accept it. Emilio shifted his hand away to toy with long locks of her hair.

"I'm not giving up the man I love to keep my family happy," she replied and saw some of the tenseness go out of his expression, even though he still watched her thoughtfully.

"It won't be easy. I can promise you that."

"Since you'll let me buy back your partnership at a bargain price, none of them will be as angry as they were, except my mother. Right now, she's furious over other things. She's got problems, Emilio."

"Jordan will still compete with them and annoy them, so don't hope for peace," Emilio said. "The feud will continue. Make no mistake about it, Brittany."

"I know you're right," she answered soberly. "But I'm sure about what I want to do." Suddenly, she flashed a broad smile. "Oh, yes, I'll marry you," she repeated with joy, pulling his head down to kiss him a long time.

Wrapping his arms tightly around her, he kissed her in return. Finally, when she leaned away, she studied him. "Are you sure about what you're doing? You're not exactly the marrying type."

"That's because you hadn't come into my life."

She smiled and hugged him.

"I never want to go through days without you—and nights. Especially the nights. I couldn't sleep or eat or work. I love you and I want you with me and I want to marry you," Emilio repeated.

She kissed him again and finally snuggled against him. "I love you," she whispered. "I can't say it enough."

"I can't hear it enough," he answered. "When we marry, perhaps we can run our two businesses together. We were doing a good job the short time we worked together."

She raised up slightly to prop her head on her hand and study him. "You'll let me run El Diablo with you?"

"I'll give you El Diablo if I have to, just to get you to marry me. Of course, I will. You're doing a great job with Brittany Beach and your family, including Parker, acknowledged that until I got involved in it."

"They still don't know about the embezzlement."

"That's history and they don't need to know. What about running our businesses together?"

"I think it sounds like a great idea," she replied, smiling at him and running her index finger along his smooth jaw.

"Brittany, I interrupted Parker and Anna's wedding, which I'll apologize for and send them some kind of gift to make up for the disturbance. I think in the interest of smoothing things over now, you should go back to the reception for a time while I'll slip quietly away."

"You're probably right," she said with a sigh, hating to part.

"When you leave here, I want you to call me and meet me at my condo."

"Family events take time," she replied, winding a short lock of his hair around her finger as she leaned over him. "I think I should wait until tomorrow at Sunday dinner to announce our engagement, because I don't want to do so right now. This is Parker's and Anna's time and all the attention should be on them.

"Later, I'll call Parker and leave a message on his cell phone about our engagement. Parker won't care what happens for a time because he's so in love with Anna that he's in a daze."

"When you go downstairs, take the contract and show it to

Parker and the others. Brittany Beach will revert to the Garrisons."

"Your cooperation will go a long way toward smoothing things over with my family. Maybe you can drop by after dinner tomorrow so you can meet the ones you don't know and get reacquainted with Stephen and Adam on a better basis. Parker and Anna won't be there because they'll be on their honeymoon."

"If they don't want me, don't push it," Emilio said as he sat up. "I don't want to, but I'll shower and get out of here."

She slipped her arms around his neck to pull his head down and kiss him while her heart raced with joy and eagerness. Finally, she released him and watched him cross the room. He was nude, fit, virile and she wanted to call him back to bed, but she knew they had to wait.

It was thirty minutes later when she stepped outside, paused and searched the crowd still enjoying the reception. The moment she spotted Parker, she hurried to him and tugged on his arm.

Standing in a crowd of guests, Parker laughed at something someone said. He glanced at her and his smile faded. Excusing himself, he turned to walk away with her.

"I want to talk to you. Emilio gave me this," she said. She held out the contract. He glanced at it and her and then took it from her and scanned the first page. His head came up and she could see the surprise on his face, which for Parker was unusual.

"He let us buy him out? And for less money? What strings are there?"

"It's signed. No strings. As soon as I sign it and have it notarized, Brittany Beach is mine, plus half a million that he put into the business."

"I'll be damned." Parker's eyes narrowed. "No one does this unless there's a reason."

"There is a reason, Parker," she declared flatly, wondering

how her family would take her relationship with Emilio. "Emilio and I love each other."

"I'll be damned," Parker said again, staring at her intently. "Emilio Jefferies? You're sure, aren't you?"

"Yes, I am."

"He damn well must love you to do this. His brother may never speak to him again," Parker said, looking at the last page and Emilio's signature. "You'll alienate yourself from your family, as well," Parker said sharply.

"That won't be anything new," she said, his words cutting into her. "Go on and enjoy your wedding party. I'll let Stephen and the rest of the family know about this contract and Brittany Beach."

"I'm shocked," Parker admitted. "It isn't often I get surprised by someone, but this is twice Emilio's surprised me."

"Go on, Parker. Enjoy your day," she said, giving him a small push. He smiled and walked away and she suspected he was already thinking about his bride again. She glanced around for Stephen, to show him the contract.

It was nine o'clock that night when she walked into Emilio's condo and into his arms.

She felt even more urgency to kiss and love him than she had earlier in the afternoon and he seemed to share the feeling.

Later, when they calmed and he held her close against his warm, naked body, she ran her hand across his chest. "I couldn't wait to see you," she said.

"I couldn't wait for you to get here." He shifted to look at her. "There's something I've been thinking about. How much did you search for your accountant?"

"I hired a private detective who worked about two weeks and said the man was no longer in Miami. He could have gone anywhere in the world, so I gave up. Why?" she asked, toying with a lock of Emilio's black hair.

"I'd like to hire a P.I. to hunt for him. Let the P.I. take some time and have enough funds to do a thorough job. We might be able to find the guy and get your money."

"I don't think you'll find him."

"Do you have any objections if I give it a try?"

"No, I don't, but I think you're wasting your money."

"I might be, but I want someone to try to track the guy."

She twisted to kiss Emilio lightly and then she smiled at him. "Go ahead and hunt for him."

"I love you," he said, gazing into her eyes. "I want you in my arms every night. Just a minute," he said, extricating himself and slipping off the bed. She watched him in the dim light of the bedroom as he left the room and returned.

He slid back in bed beside her, pulling them both up on pillows and holding her close against him. "I have something for you," he said. "Hold out your hand."

"What on earth?" she said, looking at him. "You can't have it in a pocket and I don't see that you have anything in your hands." Then she noticed one fist was closed and she looked at him questioningly.

He held out his hand. "This is for you." He opened his hand and she gasped. A huge diamond sparkled in the soft light. The seven-carat diamond was on a gold band, surrounded by rows of smaller diamonds.

"Emilio! It's beautiful!" she cried.

"Hold out your hand," he commanded and, when she did, he slipped it on her finger. It was heavy, the thick gold shiny, the diamonds dazzling and she turned her hand first one way and then another.

"It's magnificent!" She looked at him and then threw her arms around his neck to kiss him and push him down in the bed and, within minutes, she forgot about her ring and was lost in making love with him.

Sunday, she stayed at his condo until mid-afternoon, when she suddenly sat up in bed. "I want to get home early to talk to my mother and tell her about our engagement before telling the others."

"That's the right thing to do. I should go see her and see Parker, to tell them that I want to marry you. If your oldest brother hadn't just married, I would have waited to ask you until I told him."

"Thank goodness you didn't! Don't be old-fashioned about this."

"I intended to be quite old-fashioned about it, but I've blown it a little by proposing first."

"I want to call her and tell her I'm coming early," Brittany said and climbed out of bed.

Later, as she finished combing her hair under Emilio's watchful gaze, she glanced in the mirror at him. "How do I look?"

"The only way you could look better," he said, letting his eyes drift slowly over her pink shirt and gray slacks, "would be naked."

"Why did I even ask," she said, and took one more look in the mirror before facing him. "If everyone is receptive to my announcement that we're engaged, I'd like you to come to the house tonight. Can I call you?"

He looked amused. "Want me to drive to Bal Harbour and eat somewhere nearby so I'll be on hand?"

"Would you?" she asked in surprise. She was excited and eager to get their engagement into the open for the world to know.

"I don't mind," he said easily, amusement dancing in his green eyes. "I'll have my cell phone. Give me a call."

"Sweet!" she exclaimed. "You're wonderful!"

He caught her around the waist to kiss her long and hard until she pushed away. "I have to go," she said, twisting free and hurrying to get her purse and car keys and kiss him goodbye once more at the elevator door.

Excitement bubbled in her and even the prospect of her mother still being angry over Emilio's appearance yesterday couldn't dampen her happiness.

Dressed in flawless white silk slacks and a matching blouse, Bonita waited alone on the veranda, the ever-present drink in her hand.

Brittany kissed her mother's cheek and sat beside her. "I wanted to talk to you before the others come. Stephen said he was going to tell you that Emilio offered to sell me back my ownership of Brittany Beach. It'll be half a million dollars less than he paid."

"He should do that. It was awful of him to take advantage of you," Bonita said and sipped her drink.

"He's made up for it. Mother, he's asked me to marry him, and I wanted to tell you first. He said he wanted to come meet you and tell you."

Bonita focused on her daughter and Brittany remembered better times with her mother. Brittany reached over to pat her mother's hand. "I love him."

"Don't let him break your heart. I've seen his pictures in the paper," Bonita said. "He likes women."

"He loves me and I love him very much."

"Don't rush into this, Brittany. His family feuds with our family. You'll go into a marriage that has obstacles before it even starts. That kind of man isn't faithful. Your marriage won't last."

"Yes, it will," she said, disappointed and sitting back in her chair. "We love each other and we plan to marry," she said firmly.

"Have you set a date?"

"No, we haven't."

"Think about it and give it time. Men like that—he's not going to be a good husband."

"I think we'll love each other all our lives. We like to be together. We like some of the same things. We work well together. That's more than a lot of couples have."

"You have no idea what the future will bring. A man like that, wealth and looks and a playboy, he can't be trusted," Bonita said, frowning.

"I think he can and I love him. Sometime tonight, I want to tell the rest of the family. After dinner, I'd like to ask him to come by to meet you and Brooke. He knows the men in the family."

Nodding, Bonita took a long drink. "Men are rotten," she said quietly and Brittany suspected Bonita had already dismissed her and her announcement from her mind.

Brittany heard Stephen talking to Lisette and she stood to greet him. "Here comes Stephen," she said, relieved to have the moment with Bonita over as she turned to see Stephen stride onto the veranda.

Dressed in a tan sport shirt and chinos, he look fit and happy as he greeted her. Soon, the family was all together, seated in a circle. Brittany was surprised how pleasant the atmosphere was. Brooke, who was in blue slacks and a blue-and-white silk shirt, sipped a glass of water.

Stephen gave Brittany a long, searching look. "Here's a toast to Brittany. Here's to sis for having her restaurant and a tidy chunk of money back in her sole ownership," he said, surprising her.

"I'll be happy to toast that," she said, as she raised her glass and the others did at the same time. They lightly touched glasses.

"I'm glad that's made the family so happy," she said, smiling at them, thinking nothing could mar her joy this night.

"So do you plan any changes as soon as you're back as sole owner?" Stephen asked and she shook her head.

"No. Nothing really changed, anyway. It wasn't a long time that Emilio was involved."

"No, it wasn't. By the way, all of you, next week I'm having a casual party on my yacht. Everyone's invited. It's a bunch of friends, but family is always welcome," Stephen announced and conversation shifted from her restaurant.

Brittany could hardly concentrate on the conversation that swirled around her on the veranda or later at dinner. Eagerness simmered in her and she waited, trying to decide if this was the night to break the news of her engagement or if she should wait.

Her siblings seemed in good moods and, for once, there wasn't much tension at the table. Dimly, she wondered if Parker's absence on his honeymoon contributed to a more relaxed atmosphere, but she decided that wasn't the difference. Finally, she couldn't wait any longer.

"I have an announcement," she said and everyone except Bonita looked expectantly at her.

"If it tops the one you had yesterday," Stephen remarked lightly, "let's hear it."

"You might not think so, but I think it does." She fished in her pocket and slipped her ring on her finger beneath the table and then raised her hand. Adam was the first to notice.

"Uh-oh," he said. "I see diamonds," Adam said, grinning. "What a ring!"

"Emilio asked me to marry him and we're engaged," she said, smiling broadly. "I've already told Mother."

"Brittany!" Brooke exclaimed, her eyes widening. "You and Emilio?"

"You're marrying a Jefferies," Stephen said evenly and she wondered if he hated the thought. She looked at him and smiled, but he didn't return her smile.

"I've warned her against marrying a Jefferies," Bonita said glumly.

Everyone started talking at once and Brittany answered their questions and finally waved her hand at them. "I want to call Emilio. He came to Bal Harbour because I asked him to and I want him to come to the house and get acquainted," she said, looking directly at Stephen, who would be the most likely to object.

"I think that's a good idea," Stephen said, stepping into the void left by Parker as a family spokesperson.

As soon as they finished dinner, she rushed from the table to call him. Next, she went to the kitchen, where she found Lisette and told her the news, which was received with all the warmth Brittany had hoped her mother would show.

Half an hour later, the family was on the veranda when Brittany's phone vibrated and she left the family to take the call. Emilio said he was at the front door, so she hurried to greet him. The minute she opened the door, she stood on tiptoe to kiss him.

He was in navy slacks and a navy sport shirt and he looked handsome.

"How'd they take the news of the engagement?" he asked.

"Fine," she said, hoping he didn't ask in particular about her mother. "They'll be friendly. You'll see. And come with me real quickly to the kitchen to meet Lisette."

She took his hand and as soon as he had met and talked a few minutes to Lisette, they walked through the house to the veranda, where the men came to their feet as she introduced Emilio to Bonita and Brooke. He already knew Stephen and Adam, who shook hands with him.

To her relief, everyone greeted him with a friendly smile; even Bonita rose to the occasion and was the gracious hostess for a few minutes before lapsing into silence.

"Welcome to the family," Brooke said, smiling at him as if

there had never been a problem and Brittany had a rush of gratitude for her sister.

"Thank you, I feel very fortunate," Emilio said, draping his
arm lightly across Brittany's shoulders.

"Have a seat," Stephen urged. "You're the man of the hour,
anyway, for your magnanimous gesture, letting her buy out
your ownership in Brittany Beach. How could we not welcome
you after that?" he asked, and she wondered if there was a
ripple of tension between Stephen and Emilio, but they both
smiled and she relaxed.

Her relief increased when Emilio seemed to fit into the
group and was his usual charming self. Once her worries about
the announcement and how he would be received were over,
she simply wanted to be alone with him.

He showed interest in Stephen's yacht and, in a short time,
she was surprised to listen to Stephen inviting Emilio to come
with Brittany to his party.

By ten o'clock, Emilio stood. "I've enjoyed this, but it's time
I should get back to South Beach. Thanks for the fine welcome
you've given me," he said.

Brittany stood and when they had all said goodbyes, she
walked to the front with Emilio and stepped outside with him
to stand on tiptoe and kiss him lightly.

He slipped his arm around her waist and held her close.
"Come to my condo from here, will you?"

"Yes. They liked you. Stephen liked you enough to invite
you onboard his yacht."

"Your oldest brother may be the tough one to win over.
We've had some royal battles over property and deals."

"We're not going to worry about Parker now," she said and
he smiled at her.

"I love you," he said softly and leaned over to kiss her. In
minutes, she pushed against him.

"I'll see you before long," she said and watched him get in his car and drive away.

Humming, she joined her family. "Thank all of you for being yourselves and nice and welcoming him," she said.

"He's acquiring a family," Adam said.

"And he may be losing a brother," Stephen added drily and Brittany wondered if he was right. She sat and talked to her family for the next half hour and then they all told Bonita good night.

As Brittany was getting into her car, Brooke hurried out. "Brittany, wait," she called and joined her sister. "Congratulations again and I'm happy for both of you."

"Thanks and, again, thanks for being so nice tonight. That could have been awkward, but it wasn't."

"I know. I'm glad."

Brittany impulsively hugged Brooke. "Thanks again. You take care of yourself."

"Sure," Brooke replied seriously and stepped back, while Brittany climbed into her car. Brooke turned to go to her own car.

It seemed an eternity until Brittany finally entered Emilio's condo. Smiling at her, he drew her into his embrace. "I couldn't wait to be alone with you!" he whispered, leaning down to kiss her.

Ecstatic to be engaged and to be in his arms and have had her family accept him, Brittany kissed him. Finally, she leaned back and looked up at him. "I love you," she whispered.

"You're my life, my love. I know I have to be the most fortunate man on earth."

Joy welled in each of them and spilled over into huge smiles. They could hardly take their eyes from each other, wanting to memorize this moment. She knew she was fortunate that she was held tightly in the embrace of the man she loved and would love all the rest of her life.

"You're the best thing that ever happened to me, Brittany," he said, becoming serious.

"How I love you!" she whispered. She leaned forward to kiss him—this tall, handsome man she would love forever.

* * * * *

MILLIONAIRE'S WEDDING REVENGE

BY
ANNA DePALO

Dear Reader,

I love writing about intelligent, resourceful, strong women, and Megan Simmons, the heroine of this book, is no exception. Megan's trying to hold her life all together—the child, the job, the family move—until Stephen Garrison walks back into it.

To say these two have been dancing around each other for a long time is the least of it! Stephen owns *the* trendy hotel in South Beach, and now he's out to discover Megan's secrets.

Have you ever had a hotel stay that made you feel as if you're getting away from it all for a while? Now imagine getting involved with a guy who knows how to provide you with that kind of luxurious pampering all the time. I hope you enjoy!

Wishing you the best,

Anna

Anna DePalo discovered she was a writer at heart when she realised most people don't walk around with a full cast of characters in their heads. She has lived in Italy and England; she learned to speak French, graduated from Harvard, earned graduate degrees in political science and law, forgot how to speak French and married her own dashing hero. A former intellectual property lawyer, Anna lives with her husband and son in New York City. Her books have consistently hit bestseller lists and Nielsen BookScan's list of Top 100 bestselling romances. Her books have won an *RT Book Reviews* Reviewers' Choice Award for Best First Series Romance, and have been published in over a dozen countries. Readers are invited to surf to www.desireauthors.com and can also visit Anna at www.annadepalo.com.

For Susan Crosby and Barbara Daly.
Thanks for the mentoring.

One

When Megan Simmons left Miami four years ago, she'd struggled every day to regain her equilibrium and put the past behind her. But her equilibrium had eluded her, and the past had dogged her every step.

Now, at the sound of the knock on her open office door, she glanced up from the documents on her desk and into the eyes of the man she'd once thought she'd never see again.

Her breath left her in a whoosh.

She put down the papers she was holding.

"Your new partner is hard at work already, Conrad."

His voice went through her like fine cognac. It *always* had. Particularly in bed.

This time, though, she immediately sensed the danger. Stephen's words held a note of cynical amusement.

Her eyes traveled to the second man at her door. Conrad Elkind's offer of partnership in the interior design firm she used to work for as an employee was the reason she was back in Miami.

"Good news, Megan," Conrad said heartily. "We've got an assignment to redesign part of the Garrison Grand. Stephen here was so impressed by the job you did on the Garrison, Inc. building four years ago that he requested you work on this new project."

Her eyes shot back to Stephen. From the look on his face, she knew this was no mere coincidence.

Stephen's lips twisted. "I asked Conrad not to let the cat out of the bag until we'd sealed the deal."

She felt the blood drain from her face. If she hadn't already been sitting down in a chair, she'd have collapsed into one.

When she'd moved back to Miami, she'd known she might run into Stephen, but she hadn't expected to be working for him within weeks of being back at her old firm.

Someday, in the not too distant future, she hoped to be a *senior* partner. Her firm would be Elkind, Ross, Gardner & *Simmons*. Now, however, Stephen loomed like an immovable obstacle in that path.

She composed herself and stood, even as her eyes

shot daggers at the man who'd haunted her days and not too few of her nights.

"What an *unexpected* compliment," she announced as she came around her desk.

She was dressed in a sand-colored skirt suit paired with an emerald blouse that echoed the color of her eyes. She was glad now for the professional armor, though—in a nod to the hot, sunny weather—her feet were encased in strappy tan sandals.

The end of summer in Miami was still *hot*. The September sun radiated outside Elkind, Ross & Gardner's cool offices, and its rays filtered through the blinds on her office window, hitting her back.

Still, though her sandals lent another two inches to her five-foot-nine frame, the boost wasn't enough to counteract Stephen's intimidating presence. At six foot three, he loomed over her, radiating a charisma and sex appeal that were palpable.

He was the epitome of tall, dark and handsome, with jet-black hair and coffee eyes, and a body that looked as if it would make military basic training seem no more rigorous than a stroll in the park.

She'd seen evidence of his effect on women four years ago. They'd *swooned* over him. *She'd* been stupid enough to swoon over him, too.

Even now, she felt a tingling that went all over.

She wondered whether it was the cleft chin—a Garrison family trait—that did it for some women.

But unlike screen idol Cary Grant, Stephen was a living, breathing playboy nonpareil.

A quick glance at his left hand was enough for her to confirm he was still single.

Conrad glanced at his watch. "I've got a phone conference starting in five minutes, so I'm going to leave the two of you to talk and get reacquainted."

Getting reacquainted was the last thing she wanted to do with Stephen Garrison, ever, but she forced herself to nod. "Thanks, Conrad."

When the older partner had retreated, her gaze came back to Stephen, and of its own volition, her chin rose a fraction.

Then she caught herself. It was ridiculous for her to feel defensive. *She* had nothing to feel defensive about.

"Hello, Stephen. Won't you have a seat?" She turned to head back to her desk. "I'm sure we can help you with whatever it is you're looking for."

"That's what I'm counting on," he said silkily.

She heard him close the office door, and she couldn't help but think of the sound as the opening bell in a boxing match.

She turned to face him. "I suppose it's too much to hope that your appearance here today is a mere coincidence."

"You guessed right," he drawled. "It's taken a while, but I plan to get the answers I'm looking for."

"Why do I get the impression we're not talking about the Garrison Grand?"

"Four years ago, you left Miami without a backward glance."

"You mean I left *you*."

A muscle jumped in his jaw.

"No one leaves a Garrison, is that it?" she said, hands braced on hips. Hips that now had experienced childbirth.

Motherhood had instilled in her a newfound courage, changing her from the woman she'd been four years ago. She'd do anything to make sure her daughter had the future she deserved, including struggling with the demands of single parenthood.

Including coming back to Miami.

Last month, she'd uprooted herself and Jade from her hometown of Indianapolis, and returned to Miami, though she knew it was the Garrisons' town. She'd been lured by the promise of a lucrative junior partnership in her old design firm.

Now, looking more closely at Stephen, she realized the intervening years had wrought a change in him, too. She knew he was thirty-one now, only a year older than she was, but he had a physical maturity he hadn't possessed the last time she'd seen him.

It wasn't that he looked different. He was still as good-looking as ever.

It was more that he wore his power more easily.

His air of command had lost its harsh shine and achieved a subtle luster.

Subtle, but more dangerous, she reminded herself. With that thought, she blurted, "How did you know I was back in town?"

He shoved his hands in the pockets of his bespoke suit and sauntered closer, completely comfortable in an office that should have been her domain.

She thanked her lucky stars that she hadn't set out any photos or revealing mementos. She also prayed Conrad hadn't mentioned anything too revealing about her private life.

"How did I know you were back in Miami?" he repeated, as if taking his time to consider her words. "Now that's the central question, isn't it?"

For all his smoothness, she couldn't miss the quiet danger in his voice.

His eyes held hers, and she felt as if she were drowning in their dark depths. "It seems you never mentioned to your friend Anna that you and I used to be lovers."

Oh, Anna, Megan wailed silently. Why, oh why, did you have to mention me to Stephen Garrison?

Yet, she could hardly blame her friend. She'd kept Anna in the dark—she'd kept *everyone* in the dark—about the debacle in her life four years ago.

Stephen's lips twisted sardonically. "If you wanted your return to Miami to remain a secret, you should have sewn up that hole with the brand-new Mrs. Parker Garrison."

He was right, of course, but it didn't make the pill any easier to swallow.

"You know, it's funny," Stephen went on, his tone implying it was anything but humorous, "there we were sitting around Sunday dinner at my parents' estate in Bal Harbour a few weeks ago when I happened to mention I was looking for an interior design firm to update the Garrison Grand." He paused. "One guess as to what Anna said."

Megan compressed her lips, but Stephen apparently wasn't looking for a response.

"She mentioned her friend Megan Simmons had just moved back to Miami to be a partner at Elkind, Ross." Stephen rubbed his jaw, then paused as his eyes focused on her again. "I didn't even know you and Anna were friends."

"That's how Anna got her start at Garrison, Inc. four years ago," she said tightly. "I'd gotten to know people in the HR department at Garrison headquarters when I was working on the redesign there, and I recommended her for a job. She was ready to leave Indianapolis."

She braced her fingertips against the top of her desk. Her legs felt rubbery, but since Stephen had yet to mention Jade, she guessed Anna had left out she had a daughter now.

"Right," Stephen said, sauntering even closer. "Four years ago would be right about the time you skipped town."

"I *decided* to leave Miami, yes." She'd *fled,* but these days she'd learned when to run and when to stand her ground.

"Of course," Stephen went on, seeming not to have heard her, "if you hadn't run off like a scared rabbit when I headed your way at Anna and Parker's wedding reception recently, we could have had this conversation elsewhere."

She'd hoped he hadn't spotted her mingling among the guests at Anna and Parker's lavish beach wedding, but clearly it had been a false hope despite her quick departure.

Her fear of coming face-to-face with him had almost kept her from attending, even without Jade, but loyalty to Anna had ultimately won out.

Still, she wasn't about to concede an inch. "I did *not* run away."

He quirked a brow disbelievingly.

"I just refused to sully Anna and Parker's wedding day with an unpleasant conversation."

He laughed humorlessly. "Spare me the drama."

"Is it so hard to believe there are women who don't want to flirt with you?" she retorted, her temper igniting.

"I haven't found any who've turned down an invitation to my bed, sweetheart," he shot back. "Including *you*."

"Yes, but I was the one who ultimately walked away," she countered, then went on the offensive. "Does it bother you, Stephen? Did I ruin your perfect record with women when I dumped you?"

A muscle ticked in his jaw.

She tilted her head. "You know, I promise not to tell...."

His eyes narrowed, his lips becoming a thin line, and for a moment, she worried she'd gone too far.

They'd always been good at pressing each other's buttons. It was what had added an element of exhilarating excitement to their short-lived affair.

She reminded herself, however, that nothing *she* could do now could match *his* betrayal at the end of their affair.

He searched her face. "Did you run because I was getting under your skin?" he mused, his voice lowering. "Were things getting too hot in the bedroom for you? Was your cool facade in danger of melting?"

She sucked in a breath.

"You know it was good," he murmured.

"Don't flatter yourself!"

She hadn't wanted an ugly confrontation four years ago, so she'd walked away without an explanation—without a goodbye. She'd been afraid that if she faced him with her knowledge of his betrayal, he'd convince her to stay.

Because she knew she was weak where he was concerned. Because she was intimately acquainted with just how charmingly persuasive he could be.

He shifted a step back suddenly, laying off some of the pressure. "Why did you leave?" he asked bluntly.

"I told you in the last conversation—"

"A phone message."

"I wanted a clean break," she lied again.

"After dodging my calls for days," he accused.

"You were out of town on business."

"Yeah, and then you were—supposedly."

"I was never good at breaking up," she countered, "and it was clear to me our fling was coming to an end."

As clear as the woman whom she'd seen leaving his yacht, she added silently.

His jaw clenched. Evidently, he didn't like her response, but he also wasn't going to dispute her belief.

She read his silence as confirmation, and her stomach dropped sickeningly. Obviously, if she hadn't called it quits first, Stephen would soon have been giving her his "it was good while it lasted, babe" talk.

"There, that wasn't so bad, was it?" he taunted finally. "A simple explanation for why you ended the affair. You could have given it to me at Anna's wedding without an ugly scene."

Perversely, she felt her temper rise again. "Are

you suggesting that if you'd had a chance to talk to me before now, you wouldn't be here today with a brand-new project for Elkind, Ross?" she demanded. "Because if so, I don't believe it. I know you too well, Stephen."

"You *used to* know me well, sweetheart," he responded silkily. "About as well as any woman who's shared my bed."

She was just one in a crowd, Megan thought bitterly. *As if she could ever forget.*

Yet one more reason Stephen must never, *ever,* know about Jade.

She could bear working for him if she had to. She just couldn't bear having him jeopardize what mattered most.

Stephen stared at the woman who'd walked away from him four years ago without a second glance.

He'd wanted her from the moment he'd seen her, coming out of a conference room at Garrison, Inc., right after her firm had inked a deal with his older brother, Parker, to refurbish the offices at Garrison headquarters.

She'd been laughing at something Parker had said, and the laugh, combined with everything else, had hit him like fine aged whiskey burning a path to an empty stomach.

She'd been intoxicating. A tall redhead with legs

that went on forever, and a body that was all curves. A Jessica Rabbit come to life in all her bombshell glory.

He'd pictured her beneath him in bed, those long legs wrapped around him as he lost himself inside her.

And the reality had lived up to the billing—for the first time in his jaded experience with women.

Their five-month affair had been explosive. They'd spent weekends aboard his yacht, just enjoying each other, then had sneaked away in the middle of the workday for lunchtime sex in a hotel room.

Fortunately, he'd owned—and still did—the most luxurious hotel in Miami's trendy South Beach, and he kept a private suite there for his own use.

On days when he was done meeting and greeting the high-rolling hotel guests who'd come to frolic in the sun and party in nearby nightclubs, and he didn't feel like heading back to his four-bedroom villa and estate near South Beach, he could crash at the hotel.

This particular day, however, was supposed to be about putting a coda on unfinished business. Instead, he was irritated to discover, she still had as much an effect on him as ever.

The urge to touch her was irresistible, despite the fact that *she* had chosen to end their affair four years ago with a curt phone message.

He'd tried to contact her, always getting her voice mail, until he'd discovered from the receptionist at her design firm that Megan had given two weeks' notice and skipped town to go back home to Indianapolis.

To hell with it, he'd decided. His male pride had been stung, and he'd already put it on the line enough by breaking his cardinal rule: don't look back.

He'd never been dumped before. He was used to leaving women, not having women leave him. His breakup with Megan had been the first time he'd experienced being cast aside, and he hadn't liked it.

"Why are you here?" Megan demanded now, her green eyes flashing.

To get some answers, and as it happens, I need to hire an interior designer. He'd figured he'd enjoy having Megan on his payroll, playing it until he got some answers, and in the meantime, keeping the pressure on—letting her see just what she'd walked away from.

Now, he shrugged. "Isn't it obvious? I need an interior designer to update the look of the Garrison Grand. Your firm has done work on various Garrison properties in the past, including the Garrison Grand."

"Why ask for me?" She gestured around her. "Any number of people in this office could help you."

Because I'm going to enjoy seducing you back into my bed. "Because you're one of the best interior designers in town, and you're the one who's most familiar with the Garrison account."

He hadn't shown up with the intention of reigniting their affair, but now he'd seen her again, the idea appealed increasingly.

Her response as to why she'd ended their relationship had been only a little more satisfying than the one she'd given him by phone, and he wasn't sure he bought it: their affair had been so hot, he thought his fingers would be singed.

Now that she was back in town—and back in his orbit, by his own doing—he intended to dig a little deeper.

Conrad had told him he and the other partners had lured Meghan back to the firm. They needed new blood, and she was that good.

Megan opened and closed her mouth. "But we—"

"—slept together?" he finished for her.

At her indrawn breath, he arched a brow. "You have a problem working for former lovers?"

"This is the first time I've had to face the situation!"

"What? Worried about maintaining your professionalism?"

"It's not *my* professionalism I'm worried about," she retorted.

He swept her a look, letting his gaze linger on her chest before coming back to meet her mutinous gaze.

He smiled slowly. "Then you have nothing to worry about."

She raised her chin. "I'll ask that someone else be assigned to work on the Garrison Grand."

"Careful, sweetheart. The Garrison property is one of the most lucrative accounts your firm has going. You wouldn't want to be the one who caused your firm to lose it."

Her eyes widened, and color seeped into her face, masking the dusting of freckles there—freckles that he'd spent one memorable night kissing, one by one.

"You wouldn't dare," she gritted.

He shrugged. "Since you're just back in the office, I'm assuming you've got the most time to devote to a new account. You're going to find it hard to explain to your partners why you can't."

Her shoulders heaved, and her lips compressed.

"Fine," she said finally.

He looked back at her blandly.

"But our relationship this time is strictly business."

He inclined his head. "Whatever you say…Meggikins."

He was going to enjoy coaxing Megan Simmons back into his bed. And this time, she'd leave only when he asked her to.

Two

Megan stepped past the liveried doorman and into the cool lobby of the Garrison Grand.

The change was a welcome respite from the heat outside. She'd dressed for the hot weather in a lime-green sheath dress with a short matching jacket, her feet encased in strappy sandals.

A couple of men sent appreciative looks her way.

She knew that as a tall redhead in heels, she was hard to overlook—even if she wore her hair tied back and constrained, as it was today.

What she *wasn't* used to, she thought, as she looked around at the hotel guests in the lobby, was the cool sophistication of Stephen's world.

She'd almost forgotten what this world was like, having spent the past few years variously wiping baby food off her shirt, reading nursery rhymes and teaching Jade how to use the potty.

Now though, as she surveyed the women with lithe tanned bodies dressed in halter tops or less, and the men projecting a chic style in khakis and designer shirts, she knew she had to gird herself for today's meeting.

Glancing to her left, she noticed Stephen walking toward her from across the lobby.

She watched as he was waylaid by an employee, then as his progress was halted again by someone who appeared to be a familiar hotel guest.

When he finally approached, she said, "I thought I was meeting one of your executives."

"Change of plans," he said, cupping her elbow and gently steering her with a subtle pressure.

He slanted her a look. "That is, unless you *mind* it's me."

"No," she responded automatically. Since she had been the one to call their relationship strictly professional, she had no choice but to stick to the script. "Of course I don't care."

Of course I care. Just being in the same room with him was enough to make her tense and jittery.

As it was, little shock waves coursed through her from the casual contact of his hand at her elbow.

They walked across the majestic soaring lobby

toward the elevators. One end of the lobby led to the street, and the other end, with columns alternating with billowing white curtains, opened onto the Garrison Grand's private beach. The smell of surf and sand wafted in.

She hadn't been able to stop herself over the years from reading the occasional news article about Stephen and the Garrison Grand. The hotel had kept a fantastic reputation while she and Stephen had been dating, but it had surpassed itself since then, becoming the *it* place for the rich and famous who flocked to South Beach.

Walking through the lobby now, she could understand why. Stephen seemed to keep everything new and cutting edge.

"I'm looking to redesign some of the meeting rooms on the second floor," Stephen said. "Then we can talk about other changes—what else needs to be revamped and updated."

His deep voice buffeted her like the warm jets of a hot tub.

This is not going to work, she thought. How could she stand to work with him when she couldn't even think straight?

Yet, she had no choice. After Stephen had left her office yesterday, she'd gone to see Conrad. The meeting had confirmed everything Stephen had said: everyone else in the office was too busy with other projects to be the lead person on the Garrison Grand, and they were looking to her to be a team player.

Now, as Stephen called the elevator and they rode up together, she felt the air between them fairly crackle with tension.

When they stepped out on the second floor, they walked down a hallway with recessed lighting along either side of its carpeted floor.

He gave her a quick tour of the business center and various conference rooms. They ended up at the end of the hall, where Stephen opened a set of double doors and ushered her inside the last empty conference room.

As she walked past him, she was careful not to brush against him. She didn't think she could stand it.

This conference room contained a long, rectangular, glass-topped table that looked as if it could seat twenty. Like the others, the decor was modern, with high-backed office chairs and all the proper business amenities: phones, a flat-screen television with a DVD player, and a projection screen that appeared as if it was normally hidden behind a wooden wall panel.

"I find it hard to believe," she observed after looking around and turning back to Stephen, "that anyone can work in paradise's playground."

It was a thought that had increasingly hit her during their brief tour.

A smile slashed across Stephen's face. "*I* do," he

said, then added drily, "That's why you can't see the beach from this room or the others."

She walked farther into the room, trailing her fingertips along the top of the table before setting her purse down, putting together the thoughts and ideas that had been formulating since the beginning of their tour.

He watched her.

"Very modern," she mused.

"Very," he agreed, "but I'm not looking for merely modern. I want different—unique—and that means changing to stay ahead of our competitors."

She turned to face him. "Are you thinking of the Hotel Victoria?"

"Just back in town, and you've heard of it already," he quipped.

She lifted her shoulders. "I'm an interior designer. Of course I'm interested in news of a hotel opening."

"Well, don't be too impressed," he advised. "Jordan Jefferies is an imitator, not an innovator, and I'm more than ready for a fight."

Stephen's comments reminded her of everything she knew about him from four years ago. He was still strong-willed, powerful and competitive.

Seeking to change the direction of the conversation, she said, "The conference rooms are different from the rest of the hotel. They don't have the same white theme—"

His lips quirked. "We were looking for something a little more professional for the business rooms. White is the ultimate indulgence."

"Decadent luxury," she agreed.

It was what his celebrity guests came for. She could only imagine what his cleaning bill amounted to for the hotel. She knew most of the guest rooms were decorated in white, with splashes of color lent mostly by fresh flowers and marble accents.

But then again, given the room rate at the Garrison Grand, she could well imagine Stephen seeing healthy profits.

She thought about the suite at the hotel that Stephen kept for his personal use. It had also been done in white, she recollected. But unlike the other suites in the hotel, the room rate there had been a night of passion in Stephen's bed.

She felt herself heat at the thought.

"What are you thinking?" he said, and she jumped.

"I was just mulling the possibilities," she said quickly, trying to cover her lapse. "It occurred to me to do a takeoff on the decor in the rest of the hotel. White and dark blue. White leather, midnight-blue velvet. Different textures, different fabrics."

She spoke rapidly, sketching her idea for him, the thoughts spilling from her. "White to echo the calming relaxation of the rest of the hotel, midnight-blue for business. Navy is a business color, but we'll subtly undermine it by casting it in sinful velvet and giving it a unique hue."

His long-ago familiar lopsided smile appeared. "Tell me more."

It was easy to think *sinful* in his presence, she wanted to tell him.

Her heart beat rapidly.

There was a time, four years ago, when they'd been so hot for each other, they'd have abandoned their business meeting to sneak away upstairs and have frantic sex in his hotel suite, kissing and holding hands in the elevator as soon as the doors closed.

Or he'd have locked the door, and taken her right here.

Not anymore.

And she shouldn't be having such lascivious thoughts about a client, she reminded herself. Particularly him. She was mommy material now.

She glanced around. "We'll replace the wood paneling with sound-soak material to help with the acoustics and lighting. It comes in an off-white color, but with a suede finish, so it'll blend with the decor."

He smiled. "Sounds good."

"It'll sound even better when I've had time to draw up plans," she responded as she walked back toward him. "We'll need to move the business center, too. It should be convenient but less obtrusive. Right now, from what I saw, it has too much glass, in my opinion."

"I'm liking it even more," he replied.

"Aren't you lucky, then, that you got me before Jordan Jefferies did?" she joked, then could have bitten off her tongue as Stephen's eyes darkened.

She watched as his gaze traveled over her. "Yeah, I *got* you," he drawled before he met her gaze. "The question is, when will I have you again?"

Her stomach flipped. *"Never."*

"Never is a long time, sweetheart."

"I thought we agreed to keep this relationship strictly professional."

"We did?" he murmured.

"That would put sexual innuendo on the wrong side of the line," she informed him.

"How about dinner?" he asked, his voice flippant even as his look heated her all over. "Would having dinner together be on the wrong side of the line?"

"Mo—" She stopped to clear the catch in her throat. "Most definitely."

"Too bad," he murmured.

Yes, too bad. Then she caught herself.

No, not too bad. He was lying, cheating vermin, and she'd be three kinds of fool to fall under the spell of his seductive charm—again. What was wrong with her?

He looked at her hair. "Why is your hair up?"

"It's hot."

Outside. It's hot outside. But she felt as if she was burning up right in here.

Before she could stop him, he reached up, and with an efficient move, released the barrette holding her hair in place.

A cascade of dark red hair followed.

"Much better," he remarked. "I always liked it better down."

"Stop it." She didn't know whom she was angrier with, him for putting the moves on her, or herself for her breathless reaction.

"It was good four years ago," he stated.

"Yes, and it's over now."

"Easily rectified. Have dinner with me."

Stephen being Stephen, it was more a command than a request.

"I can't. I need to go—"

She clamped her mouth shut. He'd gotten her so discombobulated, she'd almost said she had to go relieve the babysitter. It was an excuse that came effortlessly to her lips. She'd grown accustomed to using it over the past three years.

"You have to go, what?" he asked.

"Nothing," she responded. "When I have something down on paper for this project, I'll call you."

Then she grabbed her purse and brushed past him in her haste to get out of the room.

Stephen stood looking out his office window, his suit jacket hanging open and bunched above the hands shoved in his pockets. He had a rare moment for calm introspection.

He'd come on strong with Megan earlier. Maybe too strong, he admitted to himself now.

She'd reacted like a deer caught in headlights. It was far different from the way she'd reacted to his pursuit four years ago. Then she'd flatly refused to go out with him, but the unaccustomed taste of rejection had simply spiked his interest.

He'd made up reasons to show up at Garrison, Inc. headquarters, even recruiting Parker so he would know when Megan was due to show up there.

He'd engaged her in casual conversation, and eventually discovered they'd both been captains of their high school swim teams and they were both football fans, though she followed her hometown Indianapolis Colts while he was a Miami Dolphins fan.

More importantly, he'd liked the fact she was ambitious without taking herself too seriously. It was something he could relate to.

He'd discovered she'd left her home in Indiana and come down to Florida because of the career opportunities in the interior design field. She dealt with the aesthetics of workplace and hospitality environments, while his aim was to make his hotel the premier accommodation in Miami by focusing on cutting-edge design.

To his chagrin, he'd also discovered his reputation

as a player had preceded him and Megan was understandably wary.

"Why won't you go out with me?" he'd asked her one day, bestowing one of his trademark killer smiles. He'd found from experience that the direct approach often worked best. "It's been rumored I'm actually a reasonable dinner partner, decent arm candy and even a fairly good kisser."

Her lips had twitched. "Yes, and that's not *all* apparently. I know about your reputation."

"Rumors of my prowess have been exaggerated," he parried, not averse to shamelessly self-serving comments.

She laughed. "Can I quote you? It's rare to hear a guy like you argue for once that his image has outstripped the reality. Still, I noticed you didn't say *greatly* exaggerated."

"A guy like me?" he repeated, pretending to look wounded.

"Mmm-hmm. Exactly like you," she said archly, turning back to her work.

Still, he'd eventually caught her at a weak moment one day and coaxed her into having an overdue lunch with him at a corner bistro. She'd relented, and their affair had taken off from there.

Yet, back then she'd never had that apprehensive quality around him that she'd exhibited earlier today.

People changed, of course, but he wondered what could have triggered it in this case.

Still, he didn't intend to let the pressure off Megan. He wanted her—sooner rather than later.

Three

When Stephen showed up at her office two days later, Megan was prepared to act as if their encounter in the Garrison Grand's conference room had never happened.

She gritted her teeth now as she led the way down the hall to Elkind, Ross's storage rooms, where they kept fabrics, carpets and wall coverings.

She was determined to keep this an all-business relationship even if it killed her.

She could feel his presence behind her—authoritative, confident, all male—and wished now she'd worn something more severe than a wrap dress and heels to work today.

They stepped into the secluded and very empty storage room, and Megan couldn't help thinking that there were some requirements of her job that she could easily do without right now.

Stephen looked around at the shelves surrounding them. They were all piled high with materials.

"So this is what things really look like around here," he said, his voice tinged with amusement. "I was beginning to think, judging from your austere office, that this was a place where even a paper clip wouldn't dare to be out of place."

"I haven't had a chance to settle in yet," she responded.

Let him think what he liked, she thought. She didn't want him getting any hints of her life as it was now.

She walked toward the back of the room to search for the samples she was looking for, and he followed, then stopped beside her. In his dark pin-stripe suit, he pulled off the look of restrained power effortlessly.

Retrieving a small chip from a cardboard box, she said, "This is a sample of the type of wall covering I'd like to use in the conference rooms."

As he took the chip from her, their hands brushed, sending awareness shooting through her.

"As you can see," she went on, determined to ignore the sensation, "it's not quite white, but close enough, I think."

"Right," he muttered, but his eyes were focused on her, not the sample in his hand.

She scooted over to another shelf. "And these are examples of the fabrics I'd like to use. This is the white leather—" she tapped a bolt of fabric "—and this is the midnight velvet."

She watched him feel the leather, his tanned hands dark against the lightness of the fabric, and an erotic charge went through her.

Cursing her wayward mind, and seeking to distract both him and herself, she yanked the bolt of velvet fabric forward with more force than necessary.

"As you can see, the color has a depth and a richness to it that make it more than merely navy-blue. It's plush, and at the same time, fairly easy to clean thanks to the wonders of new industrial processes."

He reached out and touched the fabric, his hand slowly stroking over it.

She nearly gulped. It was impossible, she belatedly realized, to have this conversation *without* a sexual subtext.

"You're right," he said, gazing directly at her. "It's...sinful."

She could see amusement lurking in his eyes. Damn him. He knew exactly the effect this conversation was having on her.

The sudden ring of a phone made her jump and broke the spell.

Stephen arched a brow.

"We keep a phone in the supply room," she explained, hurrying over to a nearby cabinet, "in case anyone needs to be reached while they're working."

While they're being seduced by the look in a client's eyes.

Picking up the phone, she said, "Hello?"

"Megan, it's Tiffany."

What a time for her babysitter to call! Maybe it hadn't been such a great idea to tell her secretary to forward any important calls. She cast an involuntary look at Stephen from the corner of her eyes.

"Is anything wrong?" she asked.

"Just checking in."

She groaned inwardly. "Thanks. That's thoughtful."

"Jade wants to go to the park," Tiffany continued, "so we might not be here when you arrive home. I didn't want you to worry, so I thought I'd call now. If we don't beat you back, we'll be on the way."

"That's fine."

"We might stop for some ice cream."

"Just remember what she's allergic to," she responded in a lowered voice.

"Will do."

When she hung up, Stephen asked, "Is everything okay? I heard you mention the word *allergic*."

She thought frantically, even as she struggled to appear composed.

"Ah, it's a client I'm taking to lunch," she fibbed. "I was just reminding my secretary to bear in mind what the client is allergic to when making reservations." She waved her hand around. "You know, ah, ethnic cuisine and all."

"Right."

She cleared her throat. Time to get out of the pressure cooker that the storage room had turned into. "If you follow me back to my office, we can consider the layout of the Garrison Grand redesign in greater detail."

What was Megan hiding? She'd appeared furtive when speaking on the phone in the storage room earlier in the day.

Stephen stared out the window of his office, his fingers steepled, his feet crossed on his desk.

He knew she wasn't married. She didn't wear a ring, and he figured Megan would be one to change her surname when she got married.

Maybe there was a boyfriend in the picture.

His lips thinned at the thought of Megan with another man. Still, her reaction to his asking for a date *hadn't* been to say she was seeing someone. She'd been about to say something, but he was fairly sure it wasn't that. She would have finished her thought otherwise, because a steady boyfriend would have afforded her an easy excuse to turn him down.

Still, he wondered how many lovers she'd had since their breakup. He'd hardly been celibate himself. They're were plenty of beautiful women in South Beach who were only too happy to hook up with the wealthy and good-looking owner of one of the trendiest places in town.

But none of those relationships had gone as deep as the one with Megan. When his mind had slipped its leash and he'd compared those women to her, they'd come up short.

He thought back to Megan's accusation. *No one leaves a Garrison.*

Yeah, it had irked him to be dumped. Particularly since, as far as he was concerned, their relationship had been just fine. The sex had been great, and she'd challenged and fascinated him out of bed, too.

She was the one woman he'd actually given thought to settling down with.

"You look severe."

He looked at his open office door and noticed his new sister-in-law, Anna, holding on to the doorjamb.

He pushed away from his desk and lowered his feet.

Anna walked into the room. "What were you thinking? I could practically see the storm clouds."

"Nothing," he said, standing. "What brings you to the Garrison Grand?"

He kept his personal life private, including the particulars of his short-lived affair with Megan.

Still, now he knew Anna and Megan were friends, he figured his new sister-in-law could be useful to him. He wasn't averse to doing some subtle digging.

"Parker and I are having dinner at the Opalesce Room," Anna responded.

He flashed a smile that more than one woman had characterized as devilish. "Come to invite me along?"

Anna laughed. "Hardly. Parker and I are still honeymooners."

"Yeah, how can any of us forget?"

The change in his brother had been extraordinary. The guy actually seemed to be in love, which—given the train wreck their own parents' marriage had been until their father had died—was some feat. It also spoke volumes about the woman before him.

His parents' marriage had been marred by Bonita Garrison's drinking. Still, after John Garrison's sudden death from a heart attack, everyone had been shocked to learn he'd fathered a love child.

"Actually," Anna went on, "since your brother is going to be late, I thought I'd stop by on the off chance that Megan might be around. I know she's working on the business center renovation."

"She came by yesterday." He didn't add she'd hightailed it out of there after his thwarted pass.

Anna looked momentarily disappointed, then

shrugged. "Oh, well. I suppose I'll catch up with her soon." After a moment, she added impetuously, "I'm glad you hired her."

"Yeah," he said, coming around his desk, "I didn't know until you mentioned it that you were close friends with one of Miami's best up-and-coming designers."

"In fact," Anna admitted, "I have Megan to thank for my start at Garrison, Inc. four years ago. She'd gotten to know people in the HR department while she worked on renovations at Garrison headquarters."

"So she said. What are friends for?" he remarked flippantly as he made his way to a side cabinet that held a small refrigerator and beverages.

Recently he'd suspected Anna of corporate espionage, but he'd been proved wrong. Someone, though, *was* leaking secrets to the damn Jefferies brothers. Last month, editorial coverage and a photo spread in *Luxury Traveler* that he'd been working hard to negotiate for the Garrison Grand had somehow fallen through, and the magazine had instead—by strange coincidence—decided to profile Jordan Jefferies's soon-to-be-opened Hotel Victoria.

Fortunately, Parker had asked the family's private investigator, Ace Martin, to ferret out the traitor. It didn't help matters, though, that one of his younger twin sisters had just decided to get herself engaged to Emilio Jefferies.

"Drink?" he offered.

"No, thanks. Parker should be here any minute."

Stephen poured himself some bottled water. After watching his mother drink herself silly, he was careful with the heavy stuff.

"Anyway, I'm glad you hired Megan after I mentioned her for the project here at the hotel," Anna continued. "I'm glad I was able to return the favor she did for me."

"I'm sure she can't thank you enough," he responded tongue-in-cheek, thinking of Megan's reaction when he'd shown up in her office.

"I also convinced her to take over the cute little house I was leasing in Coral Gables."

He turned back toward Anna, and took a sip of his drink. "You don't say?"

Parker appeared in the doorway behind his wife, and Anna turned.

"Great, you're not as late as I thought you'd be," Anna said.

Parker gave his wife a quick kiss.

"Leave it for dessert," Stephen said to no one in particular.

Parker flashed him a grin, and Anna looked embarrassed.

Stephen raised his glass in salute. "Enjoy your meal."

Thanks to Anna, he had more important matters to attend to, starting with calling over to HR at Garrison headquarters and finding out his sister-in-law's old address.

Four

He scanned the house numbers, and when he found the modest little home in Coral Gables, he pulled up at the curb and parked his Aston Martin convertible.

As Stephen strode up the well-kept front lawn, he scanned the home's facade. It was hard to tell if anyone was home.

The house was painted white, with light blue shutters and trim providing vivid contrast. Flower boxes spilled over from the front windows, and some small bushes dotted the lawn before them.

He pocketed his sunglasses before finding and ringing the doorbell.

It was a late Saturday afternoon, and the temperature hovered modestly in the mideighties. Megan could be anywhere, he thought. She could be out running errands or seeing friends. If she wasn't home, his plan was to try another time.

He rang the doorbell again.

He knew just calling Megan up and asking for a date wouldn't work. She'd already turned down his invitation to dinner.

So, he'd decided to show up on her doorstep unannounced. He figured he could offer his help for what remained to be done moving in, and in the process, he might even persuade her about dinner.

She was bound to be more relaxed outside of work.

On top of it all, he was more than a little curious about what Megan was hiding. At the Garrison Grand the other day, when she'd abruptly cut herself off, the alarmed look that had crossed her face had been telling.

Showing up at her house would give him a good opportunity to discover any secrets.

With that thought, he rang a third time.

After waiting for a few moments, and again receiving no response, he resigned himself to trying again another time.

He turned to leave when a distant laugh suddenly stopped him.

The laugh came again, and this time he thought it was coming from the rear of the house.

Changing direction, he cut across the lawn, then

turned the corner and walked along the concrete path that ran along the side of the house.

As he neared the backyard, he could tell from the sound of movement that there were definitely people outside.

"Mommy, the green."

"Okay, Jade. Just a minute, honey."

He recognized the second voice as Megan's.

Even as his mind roared to life trying to make sense of the conversation—*Megan, a mother*—he turned the corner into the backyard.

His eyes rapidly took in Megan, her back to him, sitting at a plastic picnic table opposite a little girl. They were finger-painting and wearing matching smocks.

The little girl looked up suddenly and stared at him.

He stared back—and felt the breath leave him.

The girl had dark brown hair, pulled back in a ponytail, and her large brown eyes stared at him innocently.

But the characteristic he zeroed in on was her cleft chin.

He was all too familiar with the trait. He viewed it every morning when he shaved, and he saw it in the faces of his siblings.

All the Garrisons had cleft chins.

The girl looked to be around three, which would make her the right age....

His mind froze.

The little girl smiled and pointed. "Mommy, there's a man here."

He watched as Megan looked over her shoulder.

When she saw him, her eyes widened and her lips parted. Color drained from her face.

She owed him some answers big time, Stephen thought grimly.

He could read the truth in Megan's reaction, could see it in his daughter's face. *His daughter.*

"Hello, Megan." Given his fury, he was surprised by how even his voice was.

Not in front of Jade, her eyes seemed to beg him as he stepped forward.

"And who is this pretty girl?" he asked, looking over at Jade.

The little girl giggled. "I'm Jade."

A door opened and slammed. "Sorry, I'm late—"

Stephen turned to see a woman—a cute blonde who looked to be in her early twenties—stopped in front of Megan's back door.

Megan rose. "That's okay, Tiffany. I was just entertaining Jade with some finger-painting."

Stephen noticed Tiffany gazing at him as if she recognized him.

More likely than not, she did. If she and her friends partied at the Garrison Grand or one of the other hot spots among the Garrison properties, chances were good she would have seen him. Or maybe she recognized him from the newspapers.

"My name is Jade, and I like green!"

Despite the charged atmosphere, Stephen couldn't help smiling at the little girl's outburst. The tyke had personality.

Megan looked down at her daughter. "Time to clean up, sweetie."

"But, Mommy, we're not done!"

"Why don't I finish painting with Jade?" Tiffany offered, stepping forward, though her eyes remained on him.

Doubtlessly, Stephen thought, she was wondering what he was doing standing in Megan's yard.

"Yes, Megan," he drawled, "why don't you let Tiffany take over, since you and I *need to talk.*"

His tone said she wasn't getting rid of him. He wanted answers *now*.

Their eyes met and clashed until Megan broke contact.

"All right," she said finally, then raised her arms to untie the smock from behind her neck.

Because Tiffany continued to look at him curiously, he said smoothly, "Aren't you going to introduce us, Megan?" Then without waiting for a response, he held out his hand. "Hi, I'm Stephen Garrison."

Jade's father. Megan's former lover. The guy who just found out he has a child.

"I thought I recognized you!" Tiffany exclaimed. "You're the owner of the Garrison Grand, aren't you?"

"Yes," he acknowledged, then shook Tiffany's hand.

He was used to women stating the obvious when meeting him for the first time.

He knew his effect on the opposite sex. He was tall, well-built and rich. Three qualities women loved. When they weren't slipping him their phone numbers or hotel keys, they were finagling an introduction from friends.

His image blended with that of the Garrison Grand: life in the fast lane.

"Get around, don't you?" Megan remarked drily.

He arched a brow as he stepped toward where she stood, waiting for him. "I'm locally known, if that's what you mean."

He could tell Tiffany was following their exchange avidly, which made it all the more imperative that he and Megan find a place where they could speak privately.

"Listen to what Tiffany says, sweetheart," Megan said to her daughter before turning to walk toward the back door.

He followed, watching Megan's hips swing in tailored shorts and a light blue T-shirt, her feet in flip-flops.

She could have been any suburban mother trying to entertain her kid on a hot weekend afternoon.

Except now he knew she was the mother of *his* kid.

He trailed her through the house to a cozy living room furnished with tropical-print furniture and strewn with toys.

She stopped and turned to face him.

"Why the hell didn't you tell me I had a daughter?" he began without preamble. "And don't bother denying it. She's got the Garrison features, right down to the cleft chin!"

She folded her arms in front of her, almost hugging herself. "I thought it was best."

"You…thought…it…was…best?" Fury made him enunciate every word. "Best for whom? *You?* Because I can already tell you, honey, it sure as hell wasn't best for me." He stabbed his finger in the direction of the yard. "And it's questionable whether it was best for that little girl out there to be raised by you alone and denied all the advantages I could have provided for her."

He'd just given voice to her own niggling doubts over the years, Megan thought.

There were times when she'd thought about contacting Stephen. Times when she'd wondered whether she was doing the right thing by not telling him of Jade's existence.

And then she'd thought about his betrayal and his playboy lifestyle, and realized all over again he wasn't father material. There was no way he'd be happy to learn he'd accidentally fathered a child.

Now, though, he'd found out about Jade in the worst possible way.

Still, she rebelled at his judgment of her.

"Why?" he asked.

"It was clear to me our affair was coming to an end."

"Try again," he snapped. "You've used that line before. It may have sufficed as a reason for breaking up, but it doesn't explain why you kept my daughter from me."

"What would you have done if I'd told you?" she flung back at him. "Would you have accused me of deliberately getting pregnant? Of trying to trap you?"

He stared at her hard. "My reaction is beside the point. I had a right to know."

"You gave up that right when you proved yourself untrustworthy."

"Untrustworthy? What the hell is that supposed to mean?"

"It means you were seeing other women. *Having sex with other women.*"

He didn't move a muscle.

Just let him deny it, she thought angrily.

"You're crazy," he said finally.

"I saw *her,*" she responded, dropping her arms. "I saw her leaving your yacht the night I was coming—"

She cut herself off.

"The night you were coming to tell me you were pregnant?" he finished for her, guessing.

"She said you were the best she'd ever had."

"A nice compliment if it had been *true*," he retorted, "but I wasn't sleeping with anyone else."

She threw up her hands. "What was I supposed to think? She was straightening her dress while she spoke to me! She was leaving your yacht, it was late, and you had a reputation as a player."

A reputation that she'd been well aware of. She'd only gone out with him after he'd pursued her persistently while she'd worked on the renovation of Garrison headquarters. Even then, it had been against her better judgment. Of course, once she'd found out about his cheating, she'd castigated herself for her naiveté.

"I can hardly remember who you're talking about! Women have thrown themselves at me—"

"And that's the problem," she retorted. Definitely not Daddy material. Not then, and not now. "You're the Garrison Grand's owner. You operate in a sophisticated world."

A heartless world.

A muscle worked in his jaw. "Even if I'd slept with someone else, it doesn't justify your hiding Jade."

"Oh, yes, it does," she responded. "It meant as far as you were concerned, we weren't serious. It confirmed you were still a player. I knew you wouldn't be thrilled to discover I was pregnant."

If she couldn't trust him with her heart, how could she trust him with her baby?

At least, that's what she'd told herself whenever she'd had doubts about keeping Jade's existence a secret.

"How can you be so damn sure of my reaction when I'm not even sure what the hell my reaction would have been?" he tossed back, then raked his hand through his hair. "How could you have gotten pregnant? We used protection."

She'd wondered the same thing for a time. Now, she shrugged her shoulders. "I took some antibiotics for a sinus infection. They must have interfered with the pill."

He just continued to look at her fixedly.

She steadied herself. "The question is, where do we go from here?"

She dreaded raising the issue, but it was a question that had to be asked.

"I'll tell you where we're *not* going, and that's back to you excluding me from Jade's life."

His words chilled her. The thought of Jade somehow, someday, being taken away from her was her biggest fear.

"What do you mean?" she breathed.

"I mean," he said, his expression flinty, "you're going to marry me and publicly acknowledge I'm Jade's father."

"*What?* You can't be serious!" Even as her heart thudded, she tried to wrap her mind around the idea and couldn't.

"But I am, *sweetheart,*" he responded implacably.

"And if I say no?"

His face closed, hardening, and she got a glimpse of Stephen, the ruthless businessman. "Then I'll take you to court to establish my parental rights. I'll use every means at my disposal to give you the legal battle of your life and to get access to my daughter."

She knew those means were formidable. Stephen had wealth, power and political influence, not to mention the Garrison empire to back him up.

Still, she managed to find her voice, and say evenly, "I'd probably win a custody battle. The law is on my side as Jade's mother and the one who's raised her."

"You couldn't afford a fight, and even if you could, would you want to risk it?" he shot back.

No, she acknowledged, if only to herself. She knew Stephen had the money to hire the best lawyers in town, which would make for a protracted and messy battle. He could very well win generous visitation rights, at the least.

"Think about it," he said, seeming to read her mind. "One way or another, I'm in your life."

"I *could* fight you." She wasn't without some means herself. But she knew she was out of her league with Stephen.

And that was the heart of the matter. He'd always been out of her league, in every way.

"Yeah," he acknowledged too quietly, "but think about your career. You just got a new start in Miami. You don't have the time for a legal battle, and your professional reputation will take a hit."

She hated that he was right. Her professional reputation *would* suffer. Interior design was such a fickle business. Who would want to hire a woman whose personal life was a disaster? Who might be trailed by reporters to their doorstep?

Stephen had influence in this town. He was a trendsetter and more. She knew there would be people who'd want to keep on his good side—and that would include not doing business with the former lover with whom Stephen was involved in a messy child-custody fight.

"Why are you doing this me?" she whispered, distraught.

"Isn't that my line?" he countered. "Why did you do this to me?"

She opened and closed her mouth.

"No matter what," he said flatly, "we're joined at the hip."

"Oops, sorry to intrude!"

Megan turned and saw Tiffany standing in the doorway from the hallway to the living room. She had no idea how long the sitter had been there.

"I didn't realize you were still here, Megan," Tiffany said, "but I thought I'd check because you usually tell me when you're leaving." Then glancing from Stephen back to her, she added, "Didn't you say your dinner was at seven?"

Megan closed her eyes. She'd almost forgotten about her business dinner!

Opening her eyes again, she looked at her watch. It was nearing six. She'd have to hurry.

Tiffany looked from her to Stephen, and evidently judging that she'd walked in on a heated conversation, she took a step back. "I left Jade in the kitchen. Call me if you need anything."

When the sitter had retreated, Megan looked back at Stephen. "I have a business dinner in a little over an hour to court a potential new client. That's why Tiffany came over."

She'd made an exception to her rule not to let business intrude on her weekends with Jade because Conrad had asked her for a favor. She was supposed to meet Conrad and the potential client at a downtown Miami restaurant—and she wasn't even dressed yet.

Stephen looked at her coldly. "I'm giving you until Monday to make up your mind. And I'm only giving you that amount of time because I know you're scheduled to come by the Garrison Grand and we can talk then without having Jade around." He paused. "You already got *four* years."

Megan watched then as Stephen strode to the front door and slammed out of her house.

But *not* out of her life, she thought with a pang.

Five

The Mediterranean-style Garrison estate in Bal Harbour should have felt like home, but it didn't.

Still, Stephen reflected, even now with John Garrison gone, and his extramarital affair and its illegitimate child exposed, not to mention Bonita's heavy drinking, they all still felt obliged to maintain the illusion of a happy family gathering over Sunday dinner.

Yet, it was rare for all the Garrison siblings to be present, and tonight was no exception.

Stephen looked around the room. Bonita sat at the head of the dining room table, and his younger brother, Adam, and younger sister, Brooke, sat across from him.

Missing were Parker and Anna, and Brooke's twin, Brittany. Stephen figured the newlyweds had better things to do, lucky dogs. And since Brittany had recently decided she was in love with Emilio Jefferies, she preferred avoiding tense family dinners.

Now, as they chewed dinner mostly in silence, Stephen reflected on how an outsider might perceive tonight's gathering.

Valuable artwork hung on one wall, and in front of the opposite wall sat a china closet displaying various crystal pieces. Potted ferns sat in two corners of the room, and Greek columns flanked an arched entry. Overhead, a magnificent chandelier hung from a painted domed ceiling.

The room, like the rest of the estate, was majestic—and cold as ice.

His gaze came back to his family. Better to bite the bullet, he thought grimly.

"I just found out I have an illegitimate child," he announced into the silence.

Brooke gasped, and Adam froze.

Bonita stopped in midmotion, her wineglass halfway to her lips.

Given the shock waves that the discovery of John Garrison's illegitimate child had recently sent through the family, he had no illusions about how his news would be received.

Suddenly Bonita gave a raucous laugh. "Just

like your father, except you don't have a wife to trick."

He ignored the outburst, though it was uncharacteristic. He was the only one of the Garrison offspring that his mother didn't criticize, but he knew his news was a bombshell. "There's a three-year-old little girl named Jade."

"How?" Adam asked, raising the question he knew must be in everyone's mind.

He held his brother's gaze. "I had a relationship with her mother, Megan Simmons, when she did some interior design work at Garrison headquarters."

Bonita shook her head. "Just like your damned father!"

He heard the note of betrayal in his mother's tone, and felt his face tighten. "I'm planning on publicly acknowledging Jade as my daughter as soon as possible."

And marrying Megan, he added silently, if he got his way. He planned to do everything in his power to get his way.

Bonita's hand came down, her glass hitting the table with a thud and sending red wine across the white tablecloth. "You will do no such thing, do you hear me? I will not have the child of another tramp in this family! I will not tolerate another slut getting her hands on the Garrison fortune!"

He faced his mother. "You have no say in the matter," he ground out.

"I'm disappointed in you, Stephen," Bonita said, her voice frigid despite her inebriated state. "First your father betrays this family, then you do. Don't we have enough turmoil to deal with?"

In fact, he'd been thinking the same thing, but he rebelled at putting Megan in the same category as his father's faithlessness.

His fling with Megan may have been careless, but it sure as hell hadn't amounted to marital infidelity.

And it wasn't the fact that he had fathered a child out of wedlock that bothered him. It was having a child and not acknowledging her for years that, for him, created uncomfortable parallels with his father.

The longtime housekeeper, Lisette, appeared in the archway, no doubt having heard raised voices.

Bonita knocked a wine bottle to the floor, sending more wine, as well as glass this time, everywhere. Then she rose unsteadily to her feet.

Stephen stood, and Adam did the same.

Immediately, Lisette moved to Bonita's side. "Let me help you, Mrs. Garrison."

Stephen watched, along with Adam and Brooke, as Lisette helped Bonita from the room.

His hands bunched at his sides. He figured Lisette, as well as the missing Garrison family members, would find out soon enough what caused tonight's ruckus.

"Well, another rockin' Garrison family dinner!" Adam said, then picked up his glass and raised it in a mock salute before taking a swallow.

"Why don't we continue this conversation outside on the patio where the wet bar is?" he said to Adam and Brooke. Outside, they would be away from any prying eyes and open ears among the household staff. "We can let the staff clean up in here."

They'd almost finished with dinner, anyway. He looked down at the spilled wine and broken glass in distaste.

"Sorry," Brooke demurred. "I think I'll pass."

Stephen noticed his sister continued to look pale.

"Is something wrong?" he asked. "Did my news shock you that much?"

"N-no," she stammered.

He searched her face. "You look upset."

"I'm concerned about Mother's drinking." She lowered her voice. "Did you notice she drank almost a full bottle of wine at dinner—before she spilled the rest?"

Yeah, he had, and he hated to think how much his mother had imbibed *before* dinner.

Still, he had to admit that sometimes *he'd* felt the need for a fortifying drink before a Garrison family dinner.

They'd all moved to one end of the dining room, and he gently chucked Brooke under the chin. "Don't worry, kid. Let our mother deal with her own problems. But if it makes you feel better, I'm planning on having a talk with her."

Fat lot of good it would do, but he'd try. For some reason, today's dinner aside, Bonita usually held her tongue with him, and he figured that gave him some leverage. He'd also have to make clear that he wouldn't tolerate his mother taking any more cheap shots at Megan.

After he and Adam had said goodbye to Brooke and had retreated outdoors to the patio, he went to the marble-topped wet bar to pour himself a Scotch on the rocks.

The patio was dominated by an Olympic-size pool and lined with queen palms that swayed in the cool breeze. There was an unobstructed view of the ocean.

Their surroundings were serene, which made the recent tumult inside the mansion seem all the more out of place.

"Drink?" he asked Adam, who'd taken a seat on one of the bar stools.

"Booker's Bourbon, thanks."

From there, the conversation quickly moved to local business and politics. By an unspoken agreement, he and Adam put the ugly scene inside behind them as quickly as possible.

"The president of the Miami Business Council is

retiring next year," Stephen found himself observing after several minutes.

"Yeah, I know," Adam said. "I've been thinking of running to be his replacement."

Stephen shook his head. "The Business Council wants to uphold a certain image. Only married men have ever won election." He raised his glass and took a sip of his drink. "And you and I, little brother, are far from the image they want."

He and his brothers had well-earned reputations as players. Except now, Parker was married, and he'd probably be heading the same way soon, too, though he didn't feel the need to share that news with Adam just yet.

"So, what are you going to do about Jade? I'd like to meet her." Adam paused. "I'm an uncle, and I didn't even know it!"

"Try finding out that three years ago you became a father," Stephen replied ruefully. "And don't worry, you'll get to meet her."

All the Garrisons would, even if he had to move heaven and earth to make it happen.

His brows snapped together as he recalled Megan's accusation that he'd cheated. He could barely remember the night she'd referred to, or the woman who may or may not have tried to come on to him. But he knew he'd never two-timed anyone.

Still, he'd have to jog his memory somehow about

the night she was talking about. It infuriated him even now that she had continued to be skeptical even in the face of his denial.

"How *did* you feel when you found out you had a child?" Adam asked, curiosity lacing his words.

Stephen considered his brother's question. As he looked out at the water, Megan's words came back to him. *You wouldn't be thrilled to discover I was pregnant.*

Four years ago, he'd been happy to live in the moment. Yes, he'd given a passing thought to the fact that Megan was the one woman he could settle down with, but he hadn't taken any concrete steps in that direction. The truth was he'd have been blown away to discover he was a father.

Now, though, he thought about the little girl he'd seen yesterday. She looked like him, and he'd felt an instant connection.

He knew he wanted to be a father to Jade.

"It was unbelievable," he said, his gaze moving from the ocean to his brother. "She looks just like a Garrison, and the protectiveness automatically kicked in."

In fact, he was mad as hell at being shortchanged on the past three years.

"I've heard having a daughter changes everything for guys," Adam commented. "Suddenly you can't look at women the same way."

Tell me about it, Stephen thought, his mind traveling over all the women who'd blended into his past. Adam was right. He wouldn't want Jade to grow up and fall for the kind of smooth operator he'd been for most of his adult life.

"So, you're going to publicly acknowledge her?" Adam shook his head doubtfully. "I hope you know what you're getting into. As much as I hate echoing our mother, what do you know about Megan Simmons?"

"Enough," he said shortly.

"I remember meeting her when you dated four years ago," Adam went on. "Think she's one of those women who believes getting knocked up by a rich guy is like hitting the jackpot?"

"Shut up, Adam."

"No, really," his brother pressed.

"You don't know anything about it. She was hiding the kid's existence from me. I found out *accidentally* when I showed up at her house unannounced."

Adam whistled. "Well, that puts a different spin on things. I won't bother asking why you showed up at her house without an invitation." His brother gave him a sly look. "Still carrying a torch?"

"Shut up," he said, and downed some more of his drink.

It was late Sunday afternoon, and she and Anna Cross—no, Anna Garrison now, Megan corrected herself—sat at her dinette table enjoying some coffee and sinfully good Tres Leches cake.

Jade was playing in the living room, where they could hear and sometimes see her.

The house was big enough for Jade to play in, but small enough for just two people. Megan was glad now she'd taken up Anna's lease when she'd moved back to Miami. At the time, Anna had no longer needed the house in Coral Gables because she was marrying Parker Garrison.

Jade's uncle.

Of course, that meant Anna was Jade's aunt.

She really needed to 'fess up, Megan thought, looking at her friend.

She steeled herself and took a deep breath. "I have something to tell you."

"Mmm?" Anna responded, cutting off another piece of cake with her fork. "I shouldn't, but this is so—so yummy—"

"Jade is a Garrison."

Anna stilled for a moment, then her fork clattered against her plate. *"What?"*

Anna stared at her in disbelief, a dozen questions flitting across her face.

Megan rubbed clammy hands against her shorts. "Before you came to Miami four years ago, I dated Stephen Garrison."

"Stephen—?"

Megan nodded.

"I didn't even know the two of you had been involved!"

"It wasn't a long relationship." Though it had left its permanent mark. "It ended badly, and once it did, I was reluctant for a long time to share the details with anyone."

Now, though, she decided to fill in Anna on her past relationship and recent conversations with Stephen. Once she was done, she said, "He's threatened to go public. And he demanded I marry him."

"I can't believe you didn't tell him about Jade," Anna said. "Not that I'm passing judgment. It's just that I think I'd have found it hard to keep it secret."

And that was why, Megan thought, she hadn't confided in her closest friend about the details of Jade's paternity. She knew Anna would be working at Garrison, Inc. headquarters, and she didn't want to burden her friend with an explosive secret about the boss's brother.

Of course, she'd been tripped up by *not* having confided in Anna.

Anna looked thoughtful now that she seemed to have recovered from the initial shock. "I *knew* there was something between you and Stephen. I got some hints from Stephen's reaction when I mentioned you at dinner once. You also seemed to have a funny reaction at my wedding when he was heading our way."

"Actually, Stephen discovered I was back in Miami when you mentioned it to him," Megan said.

Anna's brow furrowed. "Oh, Megan, I'm *so* sorry! I didn't know how it would cause problems! All I wanted to do was send some business your way."

"Thanks." She reached out and patted Anna's hand soothingly. "I know you had the best intentions."

"And you know," Anna went on, "you *can* help Stephen. The Jefferieses are pressing *hard,* helped along by what Parker thinks is a corporate spy within the Garrison organization." Her lips twisted. "For a while, Parker—and, I guess, Stephen, as well— thought *I* was the spy."

"Yes, you explained it to me." She withdrew her hand and waved it around vaguely. "But now look at you. You're the glowing newlywed."

Anna laughed self-consciously, then murmured, "Parker…"

"*Believe me,* I'm very familiar with the charms of the Garrison men." Megan nodded her head toward the front room. "I have a daughter to prove it."

"But you don't regret Jade, do you?"

"No, of course not. She's wonderful. But now I have Stephen to deal with."

"All the Garrison men are alike," Anna observed obliquely. "What are you going to do?"

Megan sighed. "I'm not sure. Any suggestions?"

"Why don't you agree to marry him?"

"Are you serious? I can't!"

Obviously, Anna's eyes were clouded by love, Megan thought.

"Why not?"

Two simple words, and yet they dredged up a wealth of emotion, Megan thought. She was dangerously weak where Stephen was concerned, despite *everything*.

She'd seen that herself since he'd walked into her life again. It had been the same old feeling of excitement and overwhelming awareness—as if she couldn't stop arguing with him, and the only way to deal with it was to give in to the itch to jump his bones.

"He's a cheat," she contented herself with saying.

"Are you sure?" Anna pressed.

"You mean, am I sure I saw a woman with disheveled clothing emerging from Stephen's yacht, claiming to have seen more of him than his famous cleft chin?" Megan asked sarcastically. "Then, yes, I'm sure."

Anna cocked her head. "Well, even if he did cheat, that was four years ago. Now you have a child together. Think about Jade."

In fact, she had been thinking about Jade. Until now, Jade hadn't had a father in her life—though her own parents and family had been around in Indianapolis to shower her with love.

"You know," Anna went on, "being married to Stephen might not be so bad. It would take away some worries. Jade would grow up with everything money has to offer. You wouldn't have to worry about arriving at some complicated arrangement with Stephen for him to see her."

Yes, she thought, but she didn't know if *she* could take living under the same roof with Stephen. Sharing his bed...

Just being in the same room with him made her tense, jittery, and acutely aware of herself as a woman.

And she definitely couldn't risk her heart again. She'd cried for days, heartsick, when she'd discovered his betrayal four years ago.

At the time, she hadn't told him she was pregnant because she was sure a marriage between them would have been a disaster: he'd have cheated—he'd already proven himself capable of it—and she'd have wound up divorcing him to save herself.

There was *no way* she could marry him.

No way...no way...no way...

Unless...unless, of course, she could marry him without risking her heart again.

She paused.

Now, *there* might be a way out of her dilemma....

Six

Stephen stepped out of the elevators at Garrison, Inc., and the receptionist gave him a wide smile.

"Hi, Sheila."

"Hello, sugar." Sheila batted her eyelashes at him, and purred, "Come to make my day?"

He laughed. "I wish I could, honey, but duty calls."

Sheila pretended to pout.

The blue-eyed, blond, ex-Playboy bunny was his type, but this time, he knew his heart wasn't in their customary banter.

Damn Megan.

"Parker in his office?" he asked.

Sheila nodded.

"Thanks," he said, then walked down the hall.

He greeted Mario, who was pushing a mail cart and had been with the company since John Garrison's day, then a human resources person named Roberta, who was a recent hire.

All the while, he keenly observed every employee he passed. Someone in the firmament at Garrison, Inc. was passing along information to the Jefferies brothers, and until they discovered who it was, he and Parker and every other executive had to be careful about what they said and did within range of others.

Just last month, someone had accessed Parker's office computer and forwarded an e-mail they'd planted to Jordan Jefferies.

At his brother's partially closed office door, he rapped with his knuckles.

When he strode in, Parker said, "I hear congratulations are in order."

Closing the door, Stephen made for one of the leather chairs positioned before his brother's desk. "Thanks, but save it for after the wedding."

He was here because he and Parker had a Monday-morning appointment scheduled with Brandon Washington, the Garrison family lawyer. Brandon was always punctual, so Stephen knew he'd be here soon.

He caught his brother's raised eyebrows as he settled into his chair. "Somehow I knew the news would reach you one way or another."

Parker leaned back in his mesh swivel chair and tapped his fingertips together. "Maybe not the way you expected, Anna."

That caught his attention. "Anna?"

"I guess it's all right to disclose this now, since I also discovered you've been letting the news be known yourself." His brother paused. "Anna was over at Megan's place yesterday afternoon, and they had a little powwow."

Stephen felt his nostrils flare. "Tell me the wife encouraged Megan to do the sane thing."

Parker chuckled. "Define *sane*."

"Stuff it, Parker."

"Whoa, whoa, go easy here. I just discovered I'm an uncle."

Stephen let go with an expletive.

Parker eyed him. "You know, I should have known the minute I hired Megan four years ago that you'd find her irresistible. Of course, a redhead with flashing green eyes would send you down for the count."

"Yeah, well, I'm up again, and I intend to win this match. Why the hell didn't you tell me Anna and Megan were friends?"

His brother shrugged. "I had no idea myself until recently. It never came up. In fact, the first time I saw Megan again was at the wedding."

"You haven't reacted to my news with the same

suspicion it's been greeted with in other quarters," Stephen observed.

"Well, I *did* hire Megan, and I *am* married to Anna."

Just then a knock sounded, and both brothers turned to look at the door.

"Come in," Parker called.

Brandon walked in. "Good morning." He shut the door behind him. "I'm glad to see you're both here."

Stephen and Parker stood, and the men all shook hands.

Brandon took the other chair facing Parker.

"So what do we have, Brandon?" Stephen asked, as he and Parker sat back down.

"Cassie Garrison is still refusing to deal," Brandon stated matter-of-factly.

Stephen suppressed a snort of disgust.

At the reading of his father's will two months ago, he, along with the rest of the family, had discovered John Garrison had fathered a daughter during an extramarital affair with Ava Sinclair, a local he'd met in the Bahamas.

On top of it all, it turned out that the daughter was Cassie Sinclair, the manager of the Garrison Grand-Bahamas hotel, and that she, along with the five legitimate Garrison siblings, had inherited shares in the family business.

Stephen's lips twisted. Cassie Sinclair now chose to go by the name Cassie Sinclair Garrison.

Something had to be done.

So far, Cassie had resisted Parker's overtures and refused to turn over her shares in the Garrison empire.

"She apparently just wants to be left alone to run the Garrison Grand-Bahamas," Brandon said.

"No dice," Parker responded.

Brandon sighed. "I'm not getting anywhere by phone. Frankly, our best option is if I go down there and try to negotiate in person for a deal to buy her out."

Parker laced his fingers together. "I have no problem with that plan." Parker glanced over at Stephen for his assent before looking back at Brandon. "We're willing to pay—within reason."

Brandon named what he'd offered as a reasonable price for Cassie's shares, and Stephen's hand flexed on his armrest.

"You lowballed her first?" Stephen heard himself ask.

"Of course," Brandon said.

Stephen trusted Brandon like a brother. The Washingtons—Brandon and his father before him—had been the family legal advisors for years. Still, it was vitally important they get this problem with Cassie wrapped up soon and to their satisfaction. They couldn't let the future of the Garrison empire rest with an unknown quantity—a potential loose cannon.

"And if she still refuses to sell after I approach her in person?" Brandon asked, voicing the question on all their minds.

"Everyone has their price," Parker said grimly. "We'll have to think about how much more we're willing to offer."

Stephen arched a brow. "Or we can borrow a page from the world of celebrity." He looked over at Brandon. "When you get down there, why don't you first see if you can dig up some dirt on Cassie's past? It'll give us some leverage to force her hand."

Parker nodded thoughtfully. "With stakes like this, I'll take any ammunition I can get."

When Megan walked into Stephen's office at Garrison, Inc., she had some design plans in hand. But more importantly, she had a decision.

Stephen stepped around his desk and strode toward her.

"I've drawn up some preliminary plans," she said. "You can take a look at them at your leisure, and then we can discuss them. Anything can be changed, of course."

He took the plans from her and dropped them on a nearby table. Then he shut his office door and braced his arm there. "Well?"

They both knew the real topic of this meeting.

She told herself she wasn't afraid of him. She

wasn't afraid of the vast Garrison family wealth and influence. But she had to face reality.

She chewed her lip. "I've thought about your proposal."

His *proposal* had been a far cry from her girlhood dreams, but those she'd buried along with their relationship four years ago.

"Good. I expected you to."

She walked farther into the room, and he followed.

Stephen's immense office had a view of the beach and endless blue water. His desk stood in front of floor-to-ceiling windows, and off to one side were a sofa and chairs arranged around a low table.

Like the rest of the hotel, the office was light and airy. The only thing she'd change was the abstract artwork. Though she was sure it was all very valuable, she'd prefer to see something less geometrical and more soft, maybe impressionist.

But more importantly, the view from Stephen's windows said everything, and *that* she couldn't change. She watched as a toned blonde walked past to head into the hotel.

She turned toward Stephen.

His too-handsome face gave nothing away.

Nervous energy thrummed through her. She rubbed a palm against her taupe linen skirt. "I've decided to accept your proposal."

His eyes shot dark fire, and she could read the

triumph in them. "We'll have the wedding next weekend."

Her stomach flipped over. "*Next weekend?* That's not enough time!"

She'd thought she'd have more time to adjust to the idea of being Mrs. Stephen Garrison.

"You've already had four years," he said in a clipped voice, as if he'd read her mind.

"A week is not enough time to plan a wedding—"

A grim smile slashed his face. "It is if we have it here at the Garrison Grand, where *conveniently* I'm the boss. In fact, I just put together Parker and Anna's wedding in a short time."

"I have a job I just started," she began.

"You won't need to do anything but show up."

She stared at him doubtfully.

"Let's seal the deal." He looked at her innocently. "I hope that's okay?"

Then before she could react, he pulled her into his arms, and his lips came down on hers.

First there was the warm pressure of his mouth, then he slipped inside, his tongue touching and coaxing hers.

Hot, sweet sensation flooded her, and a rainbow of colors danced behind her eyelids.

When he eventually pulled back, he gave her a heavy-lidded look. "Just like I remembered," he murmured.

She touched her fingertips to her lips, feeling him there still.

Ordinarily, the stolen kiss might have sparked her ire, but under the circumstances, it reminded her of what she had to do.

She dropped her hand. "I forgot to mention something," she said hoarsely.

"What's that?"

She took a breath. "I have a couple of conditions of my own."

His look turned guarded. "Shoot."

"I want to wait until after the wedding to explain to Jade that you're her biological father."

He looked ready to argue, so she rushed on. "I want to give her time to adjust. It's enough for the moment that I'm springing this wedding on her."

"Aren't you just drawing this out when it would be better to explain the whole thing at once?"

She shook her head. "I want her to get used to you...get to know and—and like you, first, without putting any sense of obligation on her three-year-old shoulders."

"Fine," he said, though she knew he still wasn't thrilled with her idea.

And now for the hard part, she thought.

"I'm agreeing to this marriage for Jade's sake," she said. "I know there'll be lots of advantages to growing up a Garrison and with you there to help raise her."

He nodded, as if he was glad she saw reason.

"That's why," she went on, her chin coming up, "this will be a marriage in name only. I'm doing this for Jade. I won't sleep with you, Stephen."

Something in his eyes flared, and his lips curled. "Strong words from a woman who just melted into my kiss."

"Those are my conditions," she repeated.

Their eyes held for one drawn-out moment.

"You'll get your own bedroom," he said finally.

She relaxed. She was thankful for the walls of a bedroom. Now she just had to work on shoring up the ones around her heart.

When she pushed back the tissue paper, Megan felt the breath leave her.

A short while ago, a messenger had delivered several boxes. She'd taken the delivery, puzzled but knowing from the sender's information that it came from Stephen. She'd wondered why he hadn't bothered to bring the boxes himself, since he was due to arrive in a short time.

Now, Megan let her fingers stroke over the smooth white satin revealed when she'd opened the first box.

A multitude of conflicting emotions stormed her.

She understood now why Stephen may have chosen to send the boxes by messenger before he arrived. Once she'd seen what he'd bought for her, he'd known she'd find it hard to resist.

Carefully, she lifted the gown from the box and examined it.

It was a backless sheath dress with a small swallowtail train made of satin overlaid with lace. The bodice, which had a sweetheart neckline, was held up by two spaghetti straps.

Simple but sexy, it would be spectacular with her flaming red hair, as well as show off her generous chest to advantage.

Stephen knew her so well. And *that,* she realized, was part of the problem.

She'd told Stephen she'd be wearing something practical—something she already owned—for the wedding. Instead, he'd overridden her.

He'd sent her this dress, and its message was clear: she was being served up as a delicious dessert he intended to savor.

Still, the dress was so beautiful, it brought tears to her eyes.

She'd once wished for happily-ever-after. Instead, she was getting an illusion.

A sham wedding leading to a fake marriage.

Tamping down a sudden well of emotion, she forced herself to open the rest of the boxes.

One box contained a pair of stylish stiletto sandals. Another held an adorable sleeveless flower girl's dress with a high ribbon waist and matching white sandals.

Her heart squeezed as she thought of Jade and how delighted she'd be.

When she opened the last box, however, her reaction changed, and she felt heat course through her.

The box contained a white bustier, matching lacy underwear and thigh-high hosiery.

Unbidden, images of modeling the sexy concoction for Stephen went through her mind.

Then, annoyed with herself, she let her hand drop away from the box.

Of course, Stephen had no trouble picking out her size. He was a connoisseur of the female form, she reminded herself. A playboy extraordinaire.

She was torn from her thoughts by the sound of the doorbell.

Moments later, she heard the sound of running feet.

"Mommy, there's someone at the door!" Jade called out.

"I'll be right there."

She and Stephen had agreed he'd come over on Wednesday night in order to ease the transition for Jade to the upcoming marriage.

She'd already explained to Jade as well as she could that she'd be getting married to Stephen and they'd be known as Megan and Jade Garrison.

Now, she prayed Stephen's get-to-know-you session with his daughter went well.

When she opened the door, with Jade peering around her, she was presented with an incongruous sight. Stephen held a bouquet of flowers in one hand, and a large brown-haired, brown-eyed baby doll in the other.

As annoyed as she'd just been with him, she couldn't help reacting with a laughing gasp.

His eyes met hers, and she saw laughter lurking within them. "She rode in the front passenger seat."

Wide-eyed, Jade stared at Stephen.

Megan covered her mouth.

Not a word, Stephen's eyes mockingly warned her. Then he stepped forward. "Hello, honey."

Megan stared at him—dressed as the consummate corporate executive in a charcoal business suit—before he bent forward and kissed her on the lips.

"We need to make this good for Jade," he murmured as he straightened.

She gave him a startled look, then closed the door behind him. What was he up to?

But Stephen was already looking down at his daughter. He smiled. "Hello, Jade."

Jade edged closer to her, and Megan put a comforting arm behind her.

"Hi," Jade said hesitantly.

Megan realized with a start that Jade was uncharacteristically shy. Apparently, it was one thing to enthusiastically point out a stranger—as Jade had done when Stephen had appeared in their backyard on Saturday—and another to welcome someone more permanent.

Megan prayed again or all their sakes that tonight went well.

Stephen held out the baby doll, which was dressed in pink and purple and wore a headband. "I have a present for you. This is Abby, and she's looking for a home."

Jade eyed the doll, then looked back at Stephen.

Megan saw a flicker of uncertainty in Stephen's eyes, and her heart went out to him. He was clearly lost.

"Stephen bought a gift for you, isn't that nice?" she said to Jade.

They'd agreed Jade would call him Stephen until she got used to him in her life.

Jade stepped forward, then took the doll and hugged it to her. "Thank you."

Megan watched as Stephen's eyes went to her again. "And these are for you."

The bouquet that he held out to her contained lilies mixed with lavender. Her favorite. He'd sent the flowers to her when they'd dated, and he'd remembered still.

"Thank you."

Their hands brushed over the flowers, and a sizzle

went through her. And though her mind flashed danger, her heart beat rapidly.

She steadied herself. "Why don't we go into the living room? Dinner is almost ready. Would you like anything to drink, Stephen?"

"A beer would be great."

Jade was already playing with her doll, and Stephen planted himself halfway between the kitchen and where the little girl sat.

Megan felt a small smile rise to her lips. Big, bad Stephen Garrison was in unfamiliar territory, rendered helpless by a three-year-old.

She could see the headline: Playboy Beaten by Child's Play.

When she came out with Stephen's beer, she noticed Jade looking at him from the corner of her eyes.

The little girl stood, then blurted, "Would you like to see my toys?"

She watched the play of emotions on Stephen's face, before he responded casually, "Sure. Let's see what you got, kid."

Her heart constricted as she watched Stephen follow Jade, and a variety of emotions swept over her.

Finally, she headed back to the kitchen. She had chicken Kiev in the oven and potatoes and broccoli on the stove.

Dinner would be a far cry from what Stephen was used to at Miami's top-tier restaurants, including the

ones within the Garrison Grand itself. She had to give
a nod to kid fare, but she reminded herself that
Stephen was better off finding out sooner rather than
later what parenthood was about. He was determined
to come into her life and Jade's, and she wasn't going
to sugarcoat it for him.

When she'd gotten everything on the table, she
went to find them—the most important person in her
life, and the one around whom her world had
revolved four years ago.

She located them in Jade's room.

"...and this is Holly, and that's Caroline," her
daughter said.

Megan watched as Stephen nodded. "Quite a
crowd."

Jade had all her dolls and stuffed animals lined
up, and apparently had been introducing them all
to Stephen.

"Dinner's ready," Megan heard herself say.

Stephen and Jade both turned to her.

"But, Mommy, I still need to introduce my dolls!"

"Later, sweetie."

Stephen winked. "I promise I'll come back after
dinner, pumpkin."

Jade pulled a face but trudged in the direction of
the kitchen.

Pumpkin?

It was a big turnaround from where Stephen and

Jade had been a mere thirty minutes ago, and Megan was reminded again of the fact that a three-year-old's worldview could do a one-eighty in a minute.

She watched Jade leave, then looked back at Stephen. "Quick work there."

He gave her a lazy smile. "Charm upsets you?"

She forced herself to shrug indifferently. "Your *legendary* charm. Why should I be surprised?"

"Afraid you'll fall under it again?" he challenged.

"I've been inoculated for life."

He chuckled as he sauntered toward her. "Don't worry. I leave my best for someone…special."

She sucked in a breath, but he didn't try to steal a kiss or make a pass.

Instead, he walked out of the room and followed Jade's lead.

She expelled the breath she was holding, then followed him out.

In the house's little dining area, she saw Stephen eyeing the floral display in the center of the table.

She'd set his bouquet there in a clear glass vase.

"Very nice," he commented, "if I do say so myself."

"I put them there so we wouldn't have to stare at each other across the table through dinner," she muttered in a low voice as she went past.

He had the audacity to laugh, which just sent a shiver through her because she remembered how much she'd always liked his laugh.

She felt his arm snake around her, and he gave her a quick kiss on the neck. "Glad you like them so much."

"You know flowers that stand for *devotion* are my favorite," she retorted.

At dinner, Jade kept up a steady stream of conversation with Stephen. She seemed openly curious about him now.

He handled her questions well, simplifying but never talking down to her, and it was clear that though he was still feeling his way, he was gaining confidence with every passing second.

Megan watched the interaction and thought they could all be any family having dinner together. Except this was a pretend family with an upcoming sham marriage.

Seven

So far, Stephen thought, things were working out as he'd planned.

Jade was warming to him, and while he had further to go with Megan, he knew at least that she was far from being immune to him.

"Want to see the rest of my dolls?" Jade piped up as soon as dinner was over.

"Sure."

Jade's face lit up. She ran around the table to grab his hand and tug him forward as he stood.

"Jade, we don't drag guests around like toys," Megan warned. "Stephen isn't Barney."

"Yes, Mommy," Jade responded without looking at her mother.

Stephen felt a smile pull at his lips.

She reminded him of himself when he was a little kid—full of boundless energy and enthusiasm. He wondered which parts of herself Megan saw in Jade.

It was still hitting him that this little girl was *his*. He wouldn't—couldn't—let her down.

Twenty minutes later, Jade was instructing him on tea party etiquette using her table-and-chair set and toy kitchen when Megan appeared in the doorway.

His eyes ate her up. He'd discarded his jacket and tie before dinner, but she was dressed even more casually in a flower-print short-sleeved blouse, tailored beige cropped pants and espadrille sandals.

Memories tugged and he remembered the way they used to dance together at some of Miami's hottest nightspots.

Their bodies had brushed, swayed and come together again. They'd tantalized each other before heading home to make passionate love on silk sheets.

Realizing he'd been staring at Megan and she'd begun looking back at him questioningly, he suddenly felt ridiculous.

It was absurd to be having sexy thoughts about Megan while he was sitting in a girly pink bedroom, waiting to drink pretend tea from a toy cup.

Covering his lapse, he said, "Have you shown Jade her flower girl dress?"

Megan hesitated, but Jade perked up, "Dress? What color?"

"Pink, of course," he informed her.

Jade squealed and clapped her hands. "Can I see? Can I see?"

Megan sighed. "It's on my bed, Jade."

Stephen noted Megan didn't seem too happy with his gift. He was doubly glad now he'd let the cat out of the bag and gotten the jump on her.

They followed Jade to Megan's bedroom, which was decorated in tropical colors of lime-green, peach and pink. White wicker furniture blended with a couple of antique pieces.

His eyes fell to the bed, where some of his purchases from yesterday lay in and out of their boxes. The lingerie he'd sent was nowhere to be seen but a tulle-and-satin flower girl dress with a wide sash and little rosebud embroidery along the neckline lay spread out across the bed.

Jade oohed and aahed over the dress before announcing, "I love it!"

"I wasn't sure of the size, so I had to guess."

"It's her size," Megan said gloomily from next to him.

He tossed her an amused look, and she raised an

eyebrow at him. Clearly there'd be a battle later, but he was more than up for it.

After Megan gave in to Jade's pleas to try on the dress, and the little girl had twirled around for them, Megan announced it was time for dessert.

They all went back to the dining room to have what Stephen discovered was Jade's favorite: mint chocolate chip ice cream with chocolate syrup.

Afterward, the three of them cleared the table and Megan said it was Jade's bedtime.

Jade put up some resistance, but gave up the fight when Stephen agreed to read a bedtime story.

Only after he'd read three of Jade's favorite stories were he and Megan able to head back to the living room.

Once there, Megan folded her arms. "I can't accept the gifts you sent."

"Then I suppose you're really not going to like this." He reached into his pocket, then picked up her hand and slid a ring onto her finger.

He heard her breath catch, hitch.

Yesterday, he'd gone to one of Miami's most exclusive jewelers and bought an engagement ring with a large Canadian diamond in the center flanked by two emeralds.

"The stones signify our yesterday, today and tomorrow," he told her. "I chose emeralds for your eyes."

"We're not having much of an engagement," she said, staring at the ring.

"We're just condensing the steps."

She looked up at him, then started to pull the ring off, but he stopped her.

Her chin came up. "Do you want a symbolic reminder of our yesterdays, Stephen?"

His mouth tightened. "Do you regret having Jade?"

"You know that's not what I meant!"

"Then what did you mean?" he challenged her. "Do I want to remember nights of mind-blowing sex? Do I want to remember the way we were so hot for each other, we couldn't be in the same room without getting turned on?"

Their eyes locked.

He'd opened the door, and their past came flooding back. One touch, one kiss, right now, and Stephen knew they'd both be swept away.

"I was waiting to discuss the packages with you, but now that you made her aware of the dress, Jade is all excited."

"Yeah, well, consider yourself outmaneuvered."

The air between them shimmered with sexual energy.

"And what about that kiss when you first walked in?"

He gave her a rakish smile. "What about it?"

"What did you mean by 'we need to make this good for Jade'?"

He sobered. "I mean, if this marriage is about doing what's best for Jade, then we need to make her believe we're happily married."

She stalked away, then whirled back. "You're just using Jade as an excuse."

Busted. "For what?" he asked innocently.

"You know what. To put the moves on me, hoping to get me back in bed."

"When we wind up back in bed, it'll be because you'll want it as badly as I do."

"You're not even going to try to deny it, are you?"

"In fact—" he glanced back toward Jade's room "—since Jade's asleep now, I'm going to suggest we practice." He took a step toward her.

Her eyes widened. "Definitely not necessary," she said sharply.

"But oh so enjoyable. Did you like the lingerie I sent?"

She flushed. "Strumpet & Pink. You *do* know your lingerie, and why am I not surprised?"

He was close enough now to see the pulse jump at the side of her throat.

He smoothed a lock of her hair with the back of his hand, and her eyes sparked before his gaze dropped to her mouth.

He'd always liked her fire. As much as he liked

her mouth, in fact. It was full and made for kissing. He remembered all she'd done with that mouth, and nearly groaned aloud.

"You had an amazing collection," he muttered against her lips, "and a fabulous body to go with it."

Then he kissed her, sinking into her with a hunger that surprised even him. There was a moment when she didn't react, but then her mouth opened to him.

He deepened the kiss and brought his hand up to cup her breast, feeling the nipple harden through the thin fabric of her bra and top.

Lust slammed into him, and just like that he was aroused.

She'd always been able to turn him on faster than any woman ever had, and apparently nothing much had changed.

He had to have her. In bed and out. He *would* have her.

It gave him some satisfaction to be in control—to be calling the shots. It was what he was used to.

But if he didn't stop this make-out session soon, he was in danger of losing it. Tonight wasn't the night for seduction—just for giving her a taste.

Jade was sleeping nearby, and he didn't want to scare Megan off a wedding when he almost had her where he wanted her.

He eased back from their kiss. When he raised his head, he met her lambent gaze.

"Was that kiss supposed to prove something to me?" she asked.

"Yeah. We won't have any problems convincing Jade." Hell, his body still raged for her, and it was only with effort he got it under control.

Her brows drew together. "Of course not. You're a playboy of mythical proportions."

He refrained from gibing about what proportions she was talking about. Instead, he said, "I won't cheat because my father was a cheater."

That got her attention.

"What?" She stopped, and her brow puckered again. "What do you mean?"

"I mean, my father had an extramarital affair, and we only found out about his twenty-seven-year-old love child at the reading of his will recently. Suffice it to say, the news wreaked havoc on the family, particularly my mother."

He filled her in on his family's discovery of the existence of Cassie Sinclair Garrison and her claim on the Garrison fortune.

"You do have problems, don't you?" she said. "The Jefferieses on one hand, and now your father's illegitimate child."

"Don't forget *my* illegitimate child, but I'm about to fix that situation."

Megan folded her arms. "So I'm supposed to conclude from the Cassie story that you've reformed?"

Her coolness and continued skepticism ate at him. He picked up his jacket from where he'd thrown it on the back of a chair at the beginning of the evening. "You're supposed to conclude we'll have a *real* marriage."

He gave her a lingering look—sparks shooting back and forth between them—before he let himself out of the house.

The wedding ceremony was held on a private slice of beach behind the Garrison Grand, where Parker and Anna's wedding had taken place the month before.

A floor had been laid over the sand, and folding chairs had been set up on either side of a makeshift aisle. Off to the side, adjacent to the hotel, was a canopied area that would serve as the location for an indoor-outdoor reception.

Because of the short notice, and the small number of guests, the local media had not caught wind of the pending nuptials.

Now, as Megan stood behind Jade and next to her father in the shade of the hotel's lobby, waiting for the string quartet to strike up Pachelbel's *Canon,* she was profoundly grateful for the relative privacy.

She was nervous enough as it was.

This week, she'd had to break the news to both her family and her employer that she was about to have a hasty wedding to Stephen Garrison.

Her parents and younger sister had known at least that Stephen was the father of her child, though they'd kept a vow of secrecy for the past four years.

She'd simply told them that she and Stephen had reconnected when she'd moved back to Miami and that the two of them had realized they were destined to be together.

Her mother had nonetheless worried about whether Megan was making the right decision, but Megan had kept a determined, upbeat front. Her entire immediate family had decided to fly down to Miami for the weekend for the ceremony.

Breaking the news to her coworkers at Elkind, Ross had been a trickier matter. They'd been surprised and even astonished to discover she and Stephen were going to marry. None of them had even been aware that she and Stephen had been involved in the past, because she'd been discreet about her affair with the middle Garrison brother four years before.

She'd had to explain that she and Stephen had reconnected over her work on the Garrison Grand and known immediately they'd made a mistake by parting ways.

Once she'd assured everyone that Elkind, Ross would continue to have the Garrison account, and she'd continue to work on it with the utmost professionalism, everyone's initial curiosity at least had been satisfied. Conrad Elkind was even attending the ceremony today along with his wife.

By far the hardest disclosure for her to deal with had been the announcement to the media. She'd helped Stephen draft a public statement that would be released right after the wedding. She'd combed over every word of the announcement of her marriage and the disclosure that Jade was Stephen's child.

She was suddenly recalled from her reverie as the instrumentalists struck up Pachelbel's *Canon*.

The assembled guests turned to look at her, and she in return surveyed them. Even Bonita Garrison was in attendance, though Stephen had warned her that his mother had drawn unpleasant comparisons between their situation and the hurt caused by her late husband's philandering.

Her eyes drifted to Stephen, and she only had eyes for him as she started down the aisle created by the partitioned guests.

His expression was carved in granite—except for his eyes. As she drew closer, she saw that his eyes shone with sensuous promise.

She had to remind herself it was a well-practiced look for him and she shouldn't attach too much significance to it.

Still, when she reached his side, and they turned to face the officiant, tears pricked her eyes and she trembled.

There were times when she'd wished Jade had had a father around, and now Stephen had stepped up to the plate—whether she wanted him to or not.

She handed her round bouquet of tightly packed roses to Jade.

"We have been called here today to witness Megan and Stephen being joined together in holy matrimony…"

As the officiant went on, she was very aware of Stephen standing by her side and she stole a look at him. He was steady as a rock, facing forward, his expression serious.

Maybe because he felt her observation, however, he turned his head and glanced down at her.

She blinked rapidly to clear the mist from her eyes.

"Who gives this woman to be wedded to this man?"

"I do!" Jade piped up, and the guests laughed.

She and Stephen laughed, too, and then her breath caught. She hadn't seen Stephen laugh like that in four years.

And all at once, it was time to say her vows.

"I, Megan, take you, Stephen, to be my husband…" Her voice came out a little unsteady, but Stephen held her gaze, refusing to let her look away.

When it was his turn, he looked into her eyes and spoke in a sure and clear voice. "I, Stephen, take you, Megan, to be my wife…"

His words gave her goose bumps, and the goose

bumps turned to a fine tremor when it was time to exchange rings.

She wondered if Stephen could feel her unsteadiness as he took her hand and slipped a filigreed platinum band next to her engagement ring.

"Take this ring as an eternal symbol of my love…"

She couldn't look away from him as he said the words and then it was her turn to repeat them back to him.

"…I now pronounce you…"

Married. The word echoed in her head, and she felt the full effect of its heady power.

Stephen had changed the course of her life already, and now he was her husband.

Her husband, and he was bending forward, a dark glimmer in his eyes and lust in his soul.

"Let's make it good for Jade," he murmured.

His lips touched hers, and before she could react, he'd deepened the kiss to a long and lingering one she felt down to the toes. Her hands curled into his upper arms.

The guests hooted and clapped.

Stephen straightened, and she took a deep breath. Then she hooked her arm through his and they walked past their guests and toward the hotel to the tune of "Ode to Joy."

Fortunately, once the reception started under tents set up on the beach, she was able to mingle among the guests and push aside—at least for the moment—the disturbing feelings Stephen aroused in her.

As she watched Jade dance with Stephen, Anna come over to congratulate her.

Her friend gave her a quick hug. "I'm so glad you married into the family, even if I have selfish reasons. The Garrisons *can* be intimidating."

"Tell me about it," Megan muttered. She'd met all of the Garrison siblings when she and Stephen had dated, so she had an inkling. Then she thought about how hard a time she had handling just Stephen.

Anna searched her face. "So are you satisfied with your decision?"

"Thanks for dispensing with the word *happy*," she responded. They both knew this forced marriage was anything but a joyous occasion.

"You should give Stephen a chance. He might surprise you."

"It'll be difficult to surprise me. This time I won't be shocked if I find another woman in his bed."

Stephen was still dancing with Jade, who was twirling around. It wasn't hard to see how they were related—the dark-haired little girl who was smiling and laughing, and the darkly gorgeous father who somehow managed to look comfortable dancing with an unpredictable partner.

"You shouldn't be such a cynic," Anna admonished.

Megan looked back at her. "It's precisely because

I don't think he can be faithful that I made sure this would be a marriage in name only."

"What do you mean?"

"I mean—and this is confidential—we won't be sleeping together."

Anna's eyebrows shot up. "Stephen agreed?"

She recalled Stephen's challenges, then his gambit regarding making things look good for Jade. "He agreed to separate bedrooms."

Anna looked at her shrewdly. "Uh-huh."

Megan glanced over at the man who'd sent her life careening off course ever since he'd stepped into it four years ago. "I won't lose my heart to him again," she said adamantly.

Eight

He was, Stephen decided, a masochist.

Looking at Megan in the wedding gown *he'd* picked out, all he wanted to do was spirit her away to a place where they could get naked and find feverish deliverance.

His yacht would serve the purpose well. He kept it nearby, and it was somewhere he could relax and get away from it all. Its satin-covered bed was his favorite place to make love, rocked by the soothing waves lapping the sides of the boat.

His body had been at a steady hum ever since he'd seen Megan start down the aisle. He hadn't been able to peel his eyes off her. She'd looked incredible in the simple but sexy gown he'd picked up for her at a high-end Miami boutique.

He was getting what he wanted, but he wanted her *willing*. Despite her attempt to make this a marriage of convenience, he planned to seduce her back into his bed—as the first step toward making them the family unit they should be.

He'd seen tears in her eyes during the ceremony, and had wondered whether they signaled sadness or happiness. When she was in his arms, he'd make sure she was beyond sadness or happiness. They'd just *fit,* as they had from the very beginning.

He absently twisted the ring on his finger.

"Still getting used to the feel? Don't worry, you will, faster than you can believe."

He turned at the sound of his brother's voice. "Hey, Parker."

"What are you thinking?"

"Nothing."

"*Nothing* is a lot when you're the groom, and it's your day," his brother commented.

Stephen watched Megan float among the guests. She stopped to speak with Conrad and his wife and accept congratulations.

"Be careful," Parker murmured, following the direction of his gaze. "At this rate, you'll be falling for her all over again, and she'll have you eating out of the palm of her hand."

"Not gonna happen."

He wanted Megan, but he was done with surprises coming out of left field. This time he was in control.

He scanned the guests, then gave his brother a lopsided smile. "I pulled this thing together in a week. I'm getting good at it. Think any of our other siblings wants a spur-of-the-moment wedding?"

Parker groaned. "Don't even think it. It's bad enough Brittany thinks she's getting hitched to a Jefferies."

"Speaking of which," Stephen responded, spying Brittany and her fiancé, Emilio Jefferies, "looks like some guests are heading our way."

"Yeah, *Jefferies,*" Adam grated as he joined them from where he'd been standing a few feet away.

Parker turned in the direction of their gaze, and watched, too, as their younger sister approached with the darker of the Jefferies brothers.

Stephen had gotten a chance to size the man up when Emilio had crashed Parker and Anna's wedding. Unlike his brother, Emilio was dark haired and olive skinned, his green eyes a startling contrast to his complexion.

From an investigative report that Parker had ordered, Stephen knew Emilio had been adopted. His mother had been the Jefferies' nanny, and he'd been born in Cuba.

"Hola," Brittany said, smiling as she came toward them holding Emilio's hand.

Emilio, in contrast, looked as guarded as he and his brothers probably did, Stephen noted.

"We just wanted to say congratulations, Stephen." She stepped forward and brushed his cheek with a quick kiss.

"Thanks, kiddo." Then he looked up, and said in acknowledgment, "Jefferies."

Emilio held out his hand. "Congratulations."

It was a bold move, and after a split second, he reached out to grasp Emilio's hand. "Thanks."

He and his brothers had their suspicions, but while signs pointed to corporate espionage by the Jefferieses, they'd yet to uncover the trail and, more importantly, find the culprit.

In the meantime, it was clear Emilio was devoted to Brittany, and Stephen figured that had to count for something—at least for a cool but civilized exchange of pleasantries at a wedding. And, if there was one thing he'd learned in the corporate world, it was never to let the competition see you sweat.

Parker looked narrow-eyed. "Good to see you, Jefferies."

Adam nodded his head in acknowledgment.

Brittany beamed, and Parker caught the look.

"It's easy to be charitable when this is one wedding Emilio isn't crashing," Parker said to his sister wryly.

Adam coughed to hide a laugh, and, if he wasn't

mistaken, Stephen thought, a glint of humor appeared in Emilio Jefferies's eyes.

As he turned to say something more to Brittany, however, he spotted one of his hotel employees wheeling in the table with the wedding cake.

He grasped his brothers' arms, and nodded at his sister and Emilio. "You'll excuse me. Business—of the pleasant variety—calls."

She'd visited Stephen's private estate near South Beach four years ago, but this time around it was home—and Megan found herself adjusting to the idea.

She and Stephen had agreed she'd give up the lease on the cute little house in Coral Gables and move into his four-bedroom Spanish Mission-style home. She knew the grounds of the estate included a pool, while the house itself had a gym and a home theater.

Even a little girl as active and rambunctious as Jade would have a hard time making a dent in such a place.

Megan consoled herself with that thought now, as she prepared to get out of her wedding gown and get ready for bed in the bedroom next to Stephen's.

Her room and Stephen's were separated only by a connecting bathroom, and Stephen had explained that while his bedroom was the master suite, hers had been set up as a baby's room by the house's previous owners. Since Jade was occupying the third bedroom, which was ideally configured for use as a child's room, and the fourth was being used by Stephen as a guest bedroom/upstairs office, there was no place else for her to stay.

She sighed now as she looked around the room, toying with the bouquet she'd held earlier in the day as she'd walked down the aisle.

The room was outfitted with Spanish colonial-style furniture, in keeping with the house's architecture. Rich, sturdy wood furniture contrasted with white walls and wrought-iron accent pieces.

Four years ago, when she'd spent nights at Stephen's estate, she'd imagined this room one day being used as a nursery for their child. Now Jade was already past the need for a nursery, and she and Stephen wouldn't have any more children.

The thought inexplicably depressed her, just as the entire day had been an emotional maelstrom for her.

After the wedding reception, she and Stephen had headed back to his estate and put a very tired Jade to bed. Jade had promptly fallen asleep in her new bedroom, down the hall from hers and Stephen's.

There hadn't been time to move all their possessions from the Coral Gables house to Stephen's place before the wedding, but since she'd already paid the current month's rent, she knew she had some time to move out, though she'd given notice she'd be giving up the lease.

With any luck, Jade would settle right into their

new routine. She'd still drop Jade off at preschool, and Tiffany would pick her up and babysit until Megan or Stephen got home from work.

Her thoughts were interrupted by Stephen's appearance in the open doorway of the connecting bathroom.

His eyes were shadowed in the low lighting afforded by her bedside lamp, and though she couldn't read his expression, her breath caught.

His tie hung loose around his neck. "Need some help?" he asked.

She dropped the bouquet of roses onto the bed. "Even if I did, asking you would be like asking a wolf to shepherd a lamb."

He flashed a smile and sauntered into the room. "Are you a lamb?" he murmured. "You're dressed in white…but not devoid of sin, from what I recall."

She tossed her hair, and moved to the bureau to remove her watch and earrings. "Spoken like a true scholar of the subject."

He laughed. "That's my girl."

"What do you want, Stephen?"

"In a word, you."

A tremor went through her at his words, despite her best attempts to steel herself against him. "Do I already need to remind you this is a marriage in name only?"

"I'm a patient man. I'm willing to wait for the pleasure of seeing you in that lingerie I sent you earlier in the week."

He moved up behind her and his hands clasped her shoulders. She stared at their image in the mirror in front of her.

She could feel the imprint of his body behind her, the male heat emanating from him and branding her. She picked up his masculine scent, one she recognized from four years ago and one which predictably awakened her senses.

He bent his head to nuzzle her neck, and her body reacted to remembered passion, as well as the image of the two of them together in the mirror.

His dark good looks were a perfect foil for her red hair and pale creamy skin.

His hands stroked up and down her arms, his mouth caressing the curve of her neck, then the shell of her ear...and the wisps of hair at her temple. Always teasing her.

Her nipples hardened, thrusting against the fabric of her gown.

She felt herself succumbing to him with mind-numbing ease, pulled under by a seductive undertow.

She turned in his arms, breaking free and intent on telling him off, but his mouth claimed hers before she could speak.

His lips moved over hers, taking control of the kiss, slipping past her barriers to touch her tongue with his and invite her to duel with him. Mate with him.

Her defenses came crashing down as the past

stormed back to greet them in all its passion and un-fettered need.

His mouth moved over hers with greater urgency, and his hands roamed her back, bringing her closer to the flame of his desire.

She felt his erection press against her.

Sexual need ate at her. It was even hotter than before. Even hotter than she remembered.

She felt his hand at her back, tugging the zipper of her gown downward.

With a last desperate effort, she pulled her mouth from his and pushed away from him.

He took deep breaths, his eyes dilated from arousal.

Her breaths matched his, and she ached all over. Especially in her heart.

She hugged the sagging bodice of her dress to her.

He reached for her again, and she took a step back.

"You can't deny we both want it," he said in a quiet voice.

She raised her chin. "I'm wise enough to know now that *wanting* doesn't mean *having*."

They locked eyes, and she watched his expression shutter.

"One of these days, you're going to realize you're not the only one who's changed in the past four years," he said evenly.

They both stood there for a moment, not moving, before he strode out of the room.

She watched him leave, fighting to slow her pulse. Then she turned toward the vanity table to pick up her brush—and the broken pieces of her shattered four-year-old control.

Stephen arrived home on Monday to relieve the babysitter. He and Megan had decided to try out staggering their workdays as much as possible so that one of them would almost always be with Jade and they'd use their babysitter only to fill in small gaps.

"Hi, Stephen," Tiffany said, giving him a bright smile.

The sitter couldn't be more than twenty-two or twenty-three, he'd concluded when he'd first met her. Today, she wore hip-hugging denim shorts and a sleeveless tee with the words Baby Phat in rhinestones across the chest. Her straight blond hair was pulled back in a ponytail.

He was familiar with Tiffany's type. Women like her roamed at the periphery of his world—through the Garrison Grand's celebrity-hosted events, and at hot spots like his brother's nightclub, Estate.

"Hey," he said in acknowledgment. "Everything go okay today?"

Tiffany nodded, looking a little tongue-tied, and Stephen recognized the reaction. In some ways he was even used to it.

He wasn't a movie star or rock sensation, but with

his looks and wealth, he'd inspired reactions ranging from no-holds-barred come-ons to stolen glances and coy smiles. As the owner of the Garrison Grand, he was considered the epitome of cool—as much as it amused him sometimes.

Like everyone else, Tiffany had reacted with surprise when he and Megan had announced they were getting married. Still, she seemed to accept the explanation Megan had given—that the two of them had realized when they'd reencountered each other that they wanted to be together.

If Tiffany had caught on that he and Megan had begun their marriage sleeping in separate beds, she hadn't said anything. And frankly, Tiffany's presence was another reason he'd put Megan in the room next to his—aside from the obvious one of wanting Megan close by. He didn't want the babysitter to be the source of idle gossip. There'd been enough speculation out there among the public and the press about his lifestyle.

He loosened his tie just as Jade bounded into the room, holding what he'd come to know was her Baby Alive doll.

"Hello, gorgeous." He crouched and opened his arms, and Jade threw herself into them.

He'd recently been instructed by his daughter, in a very important voice, about all the cool characteristics of Baby Alive.

He seemed to recall Brittany and Brooke having a similar doll when they were little—one that, as a prank, he'd put in the pool to see if it could swim—so the toy apparently had staying power. Go figure.

He also decided it was best if he didn't mention that particular prank to Jade—though his sisters might rat him out at some point. Old stunts like that could tarnish his budding reputation as a great dad.

After a moment, Jade pulled back from his embrace. "Hi," she said, somewhat shyly.

He noticed that, despite her initial exuberance, Jade seemed to be hesitant.

One step forward, two steps back, he thought. But he was in this for the long haul.

After Tiffany left, he and Jade played with some puzzles and simple board games in the den until Megan arrived home.

They went out to greet her in the foyer.

One look at Megan, and his body tightened, the way it always did around her.

A short brown skirt showed off her spectacular legs, which were accentuated by stone-embellished spike-heeled sandals. She was wearing a short-sleeved blouse with a tropical print and gold chandelier earrings.

"Mommy!"

"Hi, sweetie." Megan's eyes traveled from Jade to him, a question in her eyes. "How are you doing?"

"We were just playing board games," he supplied.

Games a lot simpler than the one he and Megan were playing.

He reached out to take her upper arm and swept Megan's lips with a kiss. Jade, he noticed, absorbed it all with interest.

"Come on," he said to both of them. "I grill some mean steaks."

"Hamburger," Jade responded.

He feigned a long-suffering sigh. "All right, hamburger for you." He touched her nose. "But only because I feel like playing short-order cook tonight."

"What's a short-order cook?" Jade asked.

He slanted her a look. "Anyone cooking for someone who can barely reach the light switch."

Jade giggled.

He guided the little girl forward with his hand on her shoulder. "Come on, I'll explain."

"I'll join you as soon as I change," Megan said from behind them.

He turned back to her, quirking a brow. "Need some help?"

The air crackled with energy.

"No, thank you," she said, looking at him disapprovingly.

He flashed her a wicked smile. "Your choice."

"Yes."

"But I'm hoping to win the lottery one of these days."

She gave him a quelling look before heading for the stairs.

Later, they wound up having dinner on the patio, where they were able to watch the lowering sun. He grilled on his outdoor range, and Jade got her wish when he served up a Cuban-style burger seasoned with chorizo.

Jade's questions and requests peppered the dinner conversation, and Stephen realized this was what he should expect from now on.

They were a little family, the three of them, he thought, and it felt good. More than good.

It should have taken him longer to adjust from being a practiced playboy with honed predatory skills to protective father and husband. But instead it felt like coming home.

After dinner, he and Megan sat back and watched Jade explore and play on the patio.

"You're good with her," she remarked.

He leaned back farther in his chair. "She seemed a little hesitant when I came home today, though."

"That's natural."

He looked over at Jade. "Yeah, but I'm wondering whether something more is going on."

When Jade eventually came back over to join them, Megan leaned toward her. "Did you have a good day today, sweetie?"

Jade nodded, hopping back into her chair and taking a drink from her cup.

"Did you have fun at preschool?"

"Yes."

"Did something happen at school?" Megan prompted some more.

This time, Jade looked at him from the corner of her eyes.

"Jade?"

Jade looked down at her now-empty plate, and said in a rush, "I told Emily I had a daddy because you got married. She said no, I had a *stepfather.*"

Oh, damn, Stephen thought.

He looked at Megan. It seemed as though their conversation with Jade was upon them faster than they'd anticipated.

Megan opened her mouth, but Stephen silenced her with a look.

"Jade, I *am* your daddy," he explained gently. "I was away for a little while, but I'm here now and will love you forever."

Jade looked up at him, such hopefulness in her eyes, it almost killed him.

"Do you understand?" he asked.

The little girl nodded. "Uh-huh."

"And even if I was your stepfather, I wouldn't love you any less."

Jade blinked, then blurted, "Can I call you Daddy?"

His heart did a weird twist.

"Of course," he said, his voice coming out unexpectedly hoarse.

"You'll never know how much I regret not being around when you were a baby," he said.

Jade got down from her chair and threw her arms around him.

His eyes met Megan's over Jade's dark head, and he thought he saw a sheen of tears in them.

Nine

On Saturday, Stephen took them out on his yacht, a sixty-foot Sea Ray.

Jade had pleaded to see the boat, and though Megan had her suspicions about how her daughter had gotten the idea in her head, she gave in.

Stephen had been so good with Jade this past week. The three of them had even toured the Garrison Grand early one evening, seeing the suite that Stephen kept there for his—now their—personal use. She couldn't deny him or her daughter the fun of an outing on Biscayne Bay.

From what she remembered, the yacht, named *Fishful Thinking,* was Stephen's prized possession.

The two of them had spent many carefree hours on it, making love and just relaxing and enjoying each other…until she'd discovered she wasn't the only woman he'd been entertaining aboard.

Now, as she stood in the stateroom, running a brush through her hair near a small mirror, she pushed the uncomfortable thought aside.

Stephen had killed the engine and dropped anchor so that the boat bobbed in the water.

After she and Stephen had taken turns diving and swimming off the side of the boat, they'd had lunch. Then Jade—worn out by the excitement of being on a yacht for the first time—had lain down for a nap.

Her daughter was asleep now on the bunk in the guest stateroom, so there was no innocent little girl around to run interference between her and Stephen. Megan sought to quell the nervousness that seized her.

As if conjured by her thoughts, Stephen appeared. He looked relaxed, fit and tanned in swim trunks and a short-sleeved navy T-shirt he'd donned after his swim.

"Hey, there," he said, resting his hand on the top of the door frame.

"Hi." She hated that he looked so at ease when she was a bundle of nerves. She'd intentionally put on a short skirt over her halter-top emerald bathing suit, but she still felt exposed.

It didn't help she'd seen amusement in the depths of Stephen's eyes when she'd done so, as if he saw right through her maneuver.

Now, as he looked her up and down, her body hummed in reaction. She prayed her nipples wouldn't harden, betraying her even more.

Despite the ease with which he'd assumed a fatherly role in Jade's life, she had to remember he was a rat and their relationship was *all business,* including this marriage.

"What are you doing?" he asked.

"Trying to get some knots out of my hair." Her hair had dried from her dip in the water earlier, but despite having had it in a ponytail, it had gotten tangled by the wind and water.

He continued to watch her with the same searing gaze he'd had when she'd stripped down to her bathing suit earlier.

"Jade wants to learn how to swim," she blurted.

His lips curved in the lopsided smile that never failed to send heat shooting through her. "I want to teach her. If she'd grown up here, near the water, she might already know how."

Surprisingly, she couldn't detect a hint of reproach in his voice. "She'd love to learn."

He stepped forward. "Here, let me help you."

She lowered the hand with the brush to her side.

"What?" she asked, though she'd heard him perfectly well. Her mind had just stopped at the image of Stephen touching her hair.

He grasped her wrist and gently removed the brush from her nerveless fingers. Then he stepped behind her, and she felt the movement of thick bristles from her scalp to the curling edges of her wavy hair.

She also felt his presence as he shifted against her—saw it in the small mirror in front of her—and her pulse picked up.

His skin gave off the scent of fresh air, salty water and sunscreen—and healthy male sweat.

They stood in silence. He lifted first one lock of hair, then another, pulling the brush through from root to tip.

She felt the air around her grow hot and heavy, until she had to concentrate on keeping her breathing even.

"Just like a mermaid," he murmured, arranging one curling edge over her shoulder before lifting another section of hair.

"No fins," she said automatically, and couldn't believe how breathless she sounded.

He chuckled, then sobered.

"I've been thinking about your accusation, and I've done some research," he said. "I looked back over my business diary from four years ago to try to refresh my memory about the night you were talking about."

She stiffened. "I'm surprised you didn't attempt hypnosis."

He laughed shortly before going on. "We hosted a party that night for an up-and-coming British rock group, and there were plenty of celebrity hangers-on involved. The woman you saw that night was there on a lark. She must have followed me back from the Garrison Grand, or gotten a tip from someone there that I owned a yacht."

"I wonder how she could have gotten the impression you were open to a brief encounter," she remarked acerbically.

He didn't react, apparently refusing to be baited by her sarcasm. "I admit I had a reputation as a player, and since you weren't around that night, someone thought I was fair game."

"I bet," she said unbendingly.

"But I did not sleep with that bottle blonde," he continued inexorably. "She sneaked aboard, but I sent her packing the second it became clear why she was there."

"How do you explain the fact she was still straightening her clothing when I saw her?" Megan asked. She didn't want to give him a chance to clarify things, but curiosity got the better of her.

In the mirror, she saw Stephen's lips twist. "I'm betting she saw you coming—maybe even recognized you—and decided to put on a show out of spite."

She finally felt herself relax a little at his words, despite her best intentions.

"You already think I'm a cheater," he said, as if

reading her mind. "I'm not about to compound my problems by becoming a liar, too."

"How do I know you won't cheat now?" she asked, her eyes meeting his in the mirror. "You're still the head of the Garrison Grand and—" she gestured around her "—you've still got this yacht. Women will want to come on to you."

He showed her the hand with his wedding ring. "This is your insurance."

She looked at his plain platinum band. "A wedding ring isn't considered an obstacle by some women."

"I just admitted that *at the time* you met me I had a reputation—"

She raised her eyebrows. "Really? The fact that you had to jog your memory speaks volumes." Though her words were sharp, it was getting hard to maintain her edge when he was practically giving her a scalp massage. "You couldn't even remember the woman who showed up that night."

"But I could never forget you," he said against her temple. "That's why I turned her away."

She felt his words with shattering force. Her walls where he was concerned—never sturdy to begin with—crumbled some more.

"I want to make love," he stated, and her insides turned to mush.

"That's not a good idea," she managed to say through a constricted throat.

"On the contrary," he responded, tossing the brush aside. "I think it's the best idea I've had in a *long* time."

He spun her around to face him, and her hands fell against his chest.

He dipped his head, and his mouth plundered hers. Tongues touched and lips moved, shifted, caressed, and just like that, the dam burst.

She moaned low in her throat.

His fingers delved into her hair, undoing his handiwork as he pulled her head back. His mouth skimmed along the side of her neck.

"I want you so damn much," he muttered.

Her hands moved to grip his shoulders, anchoring herself in a world gone topsy-turvy.

When his mouth met the obstacle of her bathing suit, his fingers went to the clasp of the halter top and released the bonds that kept her from him. Her breasts spilled forward, and his hands came up to palm and stroke them, rubbing folds of nylon across sensitized nipples.

The force of their desire came roaring to life, the way it always had.

They couldn't get enough of each other. Mouth fused to mouth, and his hands shot down, skimming under her skirt to grasp her buttocks and bring her flush against him to feel the strength of his need.

The past had been a glorious ride before she'd been thrown, but it had brought her Jade, and now suddenly she wanted to reach out again with both hands to grasp the sunshine, feeling reckless—no, feeling like a gambler.

She felt the strong beat of his heart and felt the thrilling excitement of wanting to be joined with him.

Her skirt hit the floor, and their hands roamed with increasing urgency. Her fingers stroked and delved, retracing every luscious inch of him that had been imprinted on her memory.

During the years they'd been apart, she'd still dreamed about him—fantasized about him. It hadn't mattered that she'd thought he was a cheat. Her heart at night was free to roam where her mind would not allow itself to go when she was awake.

Now, he pulled away from her and yanked his shirt over his head, exposing a chest she'd itched to touch ever since he'd stripped down to his bathing trunks for their swim earlier.

Her fingers danced over defined muscle, until she gave in to the urge to place openmouthed kisses where her hands had just been. His skin tasted warm, salty and sun-kissed.

With an oath of frustration, he bent and pulled down his swim trunks.

His impressive erection sprang free, exciting her even more.

She quivered, her body tightening—a reaction that echoed those she'd felt whenever they were together.

"I've got to have you," he said, and her senses ran riot.

He hooked his thumbs under the fabric of her swimsuit and pulled it off her.

His mouth came down to ravage hers. After a moment, he hooked his foot behind her ankle, sliding her leg forward and throwing her off balance so they both tumbled onto the bed next to them.

He feasted on her breasts, then found all her pleasure points: the hollow behind her ear…the curve of her breast…her inner thigh…her instep. All the while she did a slow slide to mindless desire.

And still he played with her.

He was a master at bringing her vibrantly to life.

She raked her hands down his back as he kissed her hip bone, then the indentation it formed.

When he touched her welcoming wetness with his hand, she sucked in a breath, tensing.

"Relax," he murmured.

How could she relax when she could hear the dark intent in his voice? She could feel his breath against her, and her pulse accelerated.

The first touch of his mouth sent waves of sensation surging through her.

"Stephen."

He growled against her damp heat, then delved in to pleasure her with his mouth.

She turned her head toward the mattress, her hands grasping the sheets.

She moaned, sighed and careened toward release. Within moments, she trembled against him before sinking back against the mattress, weak and fulfilled.

Seconds later, she watched as he moved up next to her and looked over at a nearby drawer. "Damn it. I just realized I don't have any protection."

"I haven't been with anyone since our affair." She was desperate for him, otherwise she'd never have been so direct. Her body was still wet and wanting.

He looked at her questioningly, then his eyes kindled.

"With a small child, there hasn't been time for anything," she explained.

"I'm healthy," he said.

She nodded.

"But you could get pregnant," he went on, holding her gaze.

Her heart flipped. "Or not. It's the wrong time of the month."

The truth was there were times when she'd been sad that Jade might not have any siblings. She'd foreclosed other possibilities when she'd married Stephen. *Why not take this?* her heart whispered.

"We're married," he said, his erection resting against her. "This time it's you and me in it together, either way."

"We've already made that bargain," she responded in a low voice, though she knew another child hadn't factored into their arrangement.

Her green light was the last encouragement he needed.

His mouth claimed hers, and with his lead, their need for each other was stoked to a blistering height once more.

When he finally sank into her, she expelled a breath on a long sigh.

"I know, baby," he murmured, soothing her. "Let me give you what you want—what we both need."

She caught his rhythm as effortlessly as she always had. It was a dance they'd always performed well, moving with primal instinct.

He thrust, sending her higher and higher. She clung to him, moaning, reaching, and leaving herself open to feeling.

Then, just when she thought the tension couldn't build up anymore, the coil within her released, and she shattered.

She felt him strain back, thrust one final time, and with a guttural groan, climax after her.

"Everyone, this is Jade," Stephen said, his hand resting on his daughter's shoulder.

Stephen's siblings stepped forward in turn to greet Jade.

Megan wet her lips nervously.

All the Garrisons had gathered, including Parker and Anna. Anna had said she'd show up to give moral support, and now Megan was glad for it.

Though Stephen's family had seen Jade at the wedding, this Sunday-night dinner at the Garrison estate would be their first opportunity to really interact with her.

This was also her own very first visit to the Bal Harbour estate, Megan reflected. She'd never stepped inside Stephen's parents' mansion during their fling, but she was here now as his wife and the mother of their child.

She let her gaze travel over her surroundings with a designer's practiced eye. The foyer was designed to impress—intimidate even—as was the entire estate.

The double-height foyer was dominated by an immense stone fireplace, before which were arranged various armchairs and sofas. Thick stone Corinthian columns supported graceful archways. To one side, a wide stone staircase led to a second level, where a gallery, bracketed by more stone columns, ran around the perimeter of the room and gave a glimpse of the rooms on the upper level.

Four years ago, she'd met all the Garrison siblings at one event or another. Parker, of course, she'd worked for, and she and Stephen had partied at

Adam's nightclub, where she'd also met the twins, Brittany and Brooke.

She wished, however, that she'd also met Stephen's mother back then. The matriarch of the clan had greeted her stiffly at the wedding and now held back, surveying the scene.

When all of Stephen's siblings had stopped fussing over Jade, Stephen's mother looked down at her granddaughter.

"Come here, little girl," Bonita said, and after a slight hesitation, Jade stepped forward.

Megan could feel Stephen tense beside her.

She'd dressed Jade in a sleeveless emerald-green dress, tying her daughter's hair back with a ribbon. She'd wanted Jade to make the best impression possible. She could deal with rejection for herself, but she wanted Jade to be accepted—embraced even—by the Garrisons.

So far, to her relief, all of Stephen's siblings had reacted warmly, surpassing expectations that she'd tried to keep in check so as not to be disappointed.

Now, though, she held her breath as Bonita grasped Jade's chin and tilted her face up so she could examine the little girl's face.

Seconds ticked by, and Megan felt as if everyone else in the room was holding their breath right along with her.

"There's no mistaking the fact you're a Garrison," Bonita stated finally. "The image of your father, in fact."

Though there was no visible softening of Bonita's features, everyone seemed to relax slightly. The lack of censure in Bonita's voice made it likely this evening at least might pass without incident.

"I'm your grandmother," Bonita said. "You may call me Grandmother."

Bonita dropped her hand, and Jade nodded, wide-eyed.

Megan's shoulders lowered. Stephen had filled her in on the fact that Bonita had a drinking problem that had become exacerbated recently. She'd stated that his mother could prove difficult about accepting what were, in her view, a mistress and out-of-wedlock child into the family.

Yet, it seemed Bonita's affection for her son had won the day, and Megan felt her tension ebb some more.

As people began to mingle and talk, waiting for dinner to be served in the dining room, Stephen moved away to speak with Adam, and Brittany approached her.

Stephen's sister squeezed her arm. "I'm so happy for you and Stephen."

Megan put a smile on her face. "Thanks, and likewise for you and Emilio." She looked over Brittany's shoulder. "Where is he by the way?"

Brittany laughed. "Busy with El Diablo."

Megan nodded. "He must work hard. That restaurant has gotten great reviews for its food and ambience."

Brittany leaned in. "Between you and me, I think it's just as well he isn't here. We're still easing our way with the family."

"Tell me about it," she responded ruefully. "I was nervous about coming tonight. Everyone had to be on their best behavior for the wedding, but tonight is a different matter."

"You're doing great," Brittany said, then looked across the room at Stephen. "You know, I suspected Stephen was carrying a torch for you after your breakup."

Megan felt a flutter, but then reminded herself that Brittany was hardly an impartial party.

"Not our playboy action hero," she said glibly.

"He matured, too," Brittany insisted. "Since you left, he built up the Garrison Grand even more. I think he poured himself into it, and in the process, he took a good hotel and made it great."

"I can't disagree there," Megan murmured, looking across the room now, too. Stephen had studied her plans for the hotel's conference and business center and made some modifications to make the renovation even more state-of-the-art. She had to admit he knew his stuff.

"My only concern was that he was becoming just a little too focused and ruthless," Brittany went on, turning to look at her again. "Now that he's married, I can stop worrying."

If only Brittany knew the half of it, Megan thought.

Of course, Brittany wanted to believe she and Stephen had found a happily-ever-after—she was in love herself. From what Stephen had told her before the wedding, Megan knew Brittany was newly engaged to Emilio Jefferies and planning a splashy wedding.

But she also knew her own situation was far different. Stephen's ruthlessness hadn't ebbed a bit, and she and Stephen had married for convenience.

She almost blurted out the latter to Brittany, but she contented herself with saying, "Jade's certainly had an effect on him."

After Stephen's sister had moved off to speak with her twin, Megan found herself mulling over the weekend's events.

Yesterday, when they'd gotten home from their outing on the yacht and put Jade to bed, she'd fallen asleep herself atop her own bed. After changing into her sleep tee, she'd meant to lie down only for a few minutes before doing some work-related reading. Instead, in the morning, she'd woken up under some blankets. She'd realized Stephen must have come in at some point and covered her up, and a wave of awareness had washed over her, despite her best efforts.

Then today, she and Stephen had both been so

busy with Jade, there'd been no time to talk. In many ways, though, she'd been grateful for the distraction.

True, yesterday the sex between her and Stephen had been fantastic. Their unbridled need had proven to her once again that, where Stephen Garrison was concerned, she had no self-control.

Yet though she believed Stephen's explanation of what had happened—or, rather, what had *not* happened—that night four years ago on his boat, she wasn't sure what they had between them now was more than just good sex.

Yes, he wanted her back in his life, but it was because he thought the two of them should raise Jade together. He wanted to be fully involved in his daughter's life, and the only way to do that was to include Jade's mother in a package deal.

Undeniably, on the yacht yesterday, she'd had a moment of recklessness that might have made her pregnant again—though the possibility was unlikely. At least this time, though, she was married and had already committed to raising one child with Stephen.

But she knew better than to risk her heart again. Stephen had never said he loved her, and given the long line of women in his life—despite Brittany's claim about his newfound maturity—she doubted he ever would. She might be the most memorable in his long line of conquests, but he'd given her no reason to believe she'd ever been more.

Still, because she'd rejected him four years ago, he saw her as a sexual challenge now. She belatedly realized she'd all but waved the red flag in front of him when she'd announced she wouldn't sleep with him.

Stephen had a strong sex drive, and she was his wife. If no longer in name only, she reminded herself, still just out of convenience.

Ten

Stephen had the chance to speak to his mother alone after the family dinner. He stopped her at the base of the foyer staircase.

Good thing that today she seemed more sober than usual. Still, he had a good hunch she'd been heading upstairs to her stash of liquor.

"You're out of control," he said without preamble.

She raised an eyebrow haughtily. "Excuse me, but I have no idea what you mean."

He had to give his mother credit. Even struggling with an addiction to alcohol, she was still the grand dame. But he knew where the truth lay.

"Let's dispense with the subterfuge," he said.

If possible, Bonita seemed to freeze even more. "I'm your mother. I won't have you speaking to me this way."

With her hand on the railing, Bonita took a step up, but he placed his hand over hers, halting her progress.

"I'm talking about your drinking, Mother. It's started to affect the entire family, and it's consuming your life."

Bonita straightened, her spine stiffening with outrage. "How dare you? Wasn't I polite and cordial to your wife and daughter? Didn't I welcome them into my home?"

"Your drinking is upsetting the whole family," he continued implacably.

Bonita's eyes snapped with anger. "How dare you speak to me about *upsetting* this family? Your father cheated and imperiled the family fortune, and you've decided to follow in his footsteps."

He sighed. The family peace that had prevailed tonight appeared to be over. He'd figured Megan would come into this at one point or another.

"Your accusations are off the mark. I didn't cheat on my wife—" Though Megan had thought he'd cheated on her before they were married, he decided his mother didn't need to know about a false accusation "—and I sure didn't jeopardize the family fortune. Parker and I are working to get this situation with the woman in the Bahamas straightened out. The *only* parallel with Dad is that I had a child out of wedlock, but I don't regret Jade's existence for a second."

His mother's lips thinned. "And now your mistress has joined the family, too. You outdid your father in that department, Stephen."

He held on to Bonita's hand when she tried to ascend. "Make no mistake, Mother. Megan *is* part of this family, and she's here to stay. I won't tolerate your being rude to her."

Then because of his purpose in seeking out his mother tonight, and because he could read the turbulence and pain in her eyes unusually well at the moment, he softened his voice. "Get yourself some help, Mother. Otherwise, we'll have to do it for you."

After a tense moment during which neither of them spoke, Bonita extricated her hand from his and went up the stairs without a look back.

Watching his mother depart, Stephen reflected on her accusations, and his thoughts naturally turned to the status of his relationship with Megan.

Yesterday had been fantastic. He'd taken Megan and Jade for an outing aboard his prized yacht and had been able to share one of his favorite pastimes with his daughter for the first time. Life didn't get any better.

On top of it all, his and Megan's lovemaking had been as explosive as ever. He meant to repeat the experience as soon as possible. Tonight, if he could arrange it.

Yesterday, when Megan hadn't seemed to mind the possibility of getting pregnant again, he'd nearly blown his cool right then with his blinding need to have her.

Now, the thought of having more children with her made his pulse quicken all over again. This time he wanted to be around for all of it. He wanted to experience the wonder of pregnancy with her. He wanted to be there when their child was born.

He wanted Megan in his bed, in his life. Period.

If Megan didn't realize it already, he was going to set out to prove it to her.

Their marriage in name only was about to become a marriage in every possible way.

When they got home from Bonita's estate, Megan helped Jade get ready for bed, then tiptoed out of her daughter's room while Stephen read a bedtime story.

Returning to her own room, she thought about how wonderful it would be to luxuriate in a warm bath for half an hour. She'd survived the evening, and all she wanted to do now was relax.

Instead, however, she opted for a quick shower in the adjoining bathroom. A hot shower would do the trick almost as well to relieve her tight muscles. And it had the added benefit of being relatively fast—no need to worry too much about Stephen moving around in the next room.

She stripped, then walked into the bathroom and got the water running in the shower. Stepping into the stall, she sighed and closed her eyes as hot jets of water pounded her.

All in all, she had to admit the evening hadn't gone *badly*. Bonita—judging from what Stephen had told her beforehand by way of warning—seemed to have behaved fairly well.

And Stephen's siblings had been warm, welcoming and nonjudgmental. They appeared to accept that whatever her relationship with Stephen had been, and whatever reasons she'd had for not telling Stephen about Jade, it was all water under the bridge now that she and Stephen were married.

She sighed again.

"Need me to do your back?"

She gasped and jerked around.

Stephen stood outside the shower stall, and from his lazy, amused tone, he'd gotten quite an eyeful.

"What are you doing here?" Surprise made her tone sharp.

His lopsided grin emerged. "I knocked on your bedroom door, and when I got no response, I came in." His eyes crinkled. "I thought you might have fallen asleep on the bed—again."

"Well, as you can see, I'm taking a shower!"

His eyes traveled downward. "Yeah, I can see all right—"

"What do you want?"

His eyes came back to hers. "Take a guess."

She regretted her choice of words. "I'll be out soon."

She made her tone repressive. They needed to talk, that was for sure—but not here and now! She used her pointed tone to mask her susceptibility.

She felt vulnerable and exposed, not to mention that standing before him naked was doing strange things to her insides.

Stephen's grin only widened. "Sure about the back scrub?"

"No, thanks."

"I'll try to get over the devastating rejection."

"I know it doesn't happen much, but join the masses."

His eyes glinted at her humor. "Do you remember the showers we took together?" he murmured. "We'd wind up late for work."

She certainly *hadn't* forgotten. How could she? She'd replayed those scenes in her mind too many times over the years.

She moved to turn off the shower. "I've grown up," she responded.

"So have I," he drawled, turning toward the door, "but that doesn't exclude indulging in some fun."

Judging by their encounter yesterday, she'd have to agree with him. Mercifully, though, she was spared a response as he walked out of the room.

* * *

Twenty minutes later, she wandered downstairs in her bare feet, a satin robe over a matching knee-length gown. Damp tendrils of hair lay against her shoulders. She hadn't completely succeeded in keeping her hair dry despite tying it up for the shower.

She found Stephen in the spacious living room. The lights were turned down low, and the voice of Harry Connick, Jr. crooning "Only You" sounded softly in the background.

Stephen stood holding two wineglasses filled with red wine. He held one out to her.

A little flame she was all too familiar with ignited inside her.

She'd sought him out for a talk—the recent episode in the shower had convinced her they were past due for one—but this wasn't quite the ambience she was expecting.

"Relax," he said, as if reading her mind.

She realized her only hope rested with appearing cool and nonchalant. Stephen would exploit any hint of responsiveness to his advantage.

With that thought, she took the wineglass from him—ignoring how the brush of their hands sent a tingling through her—and sat with him on the couch.

"Thanks for coming to the family dinner tonight," he said. "I know it was stressful for you."

"It's important for Jade to meet your family," she

said, glad to be on a safe topic. "She is the first grand-child, after all."

She took a sip of her drink. She'd expected him to immediately begin putting the moves on her, so he'd thrown her off with his comment.

Still, it was hard not to be aware of him. He was impossibly masculine in black pants and an open-collar white shirt. His shirtsleeves had been rolled back to expose the dark hair of his arms.

Now, he nodded. "I know some of my siblings would have bet good money against my being the father of the first grandchild. We almost beat Parker and Anna to the altar, too."

She looked down into her glass. "Your mother behaved well."

She hadn't gotten a warm, fuzzy feeling from Bonita Garrison, but she was happy the woman had been polite and accepting of Jade.

"For a change," Stephen said.

She looked up at him again. "Do you ever worry about drinking yourself?"

He shook his head. "No, I set clear limits to when I'll drink, and I can stick to them. Besides—" he shot her a significant look "—I get into enough trouble without bringing alcohol into it."

She knew he was thinking about their relationship and, specifically, about the child they'd produced.

"You haven't told me about your years in Indianapolis," he said abruptly.

She shrugged. "There isn't much to tell. I was raising a child with help from my family."

She talked then about her life in Indiana. She told him about her family and friends, and the funny little things that had happened to her.

"How did you support yourself?" he asked.

"I did small contract jobs for family, friends and neighbors." She shrugged again. "You know, helping someone remodel a kitchen or add on to a house."

His lips tightened.

"I know what you're thinking," she said. "Don't say it."

"We're married now," he responded. "That's what counts."

"Yes, about that—"

She wet her lips, then stopped as she saw he'd focused on the action.

"Are you going to express regrets about accusing me of cheating?" His eyes held hers steadily. "You should have faced me four years ago with your suspicions."

"I was wrong not to face you," she admitted, knowing she owed him that, at least. "You'll never know how many times I've wondered over the years whether I made the right decision for Jade."

He looked mollified.

She took a deep breath. "But I've also come to

the realization that meeting that woman that night was just the catalyst for my leaving. I knew what your life was like—"

His brows snapped together.

"—and we were having a no-strings affair."

He leaned forward to place his wineglass on the end table. "Oh, there were strings, baby, make no mistake about it."

She put down her wineglass, too, and rose. "That's why yesterday shouldn't set a pattern."

He got to his feet, too. "I agree."

"You do?" She couldn't keep the surprise from her voice. Well, *that* was easy.

His arms snaked around her. "Next time, it's going to be dry land or nothing. A small cabin like that isn't big enough for our kind of—" his eyes gleamed "—physically demanding lovemaking."

She nearly choked.

"Hey, I'm a *big* guy."

This time, she did splutter, but she could see from the amusement on his face that he was enjoying toying with her—enjoying having her wonder exactly what he meant by *big*.

A smile teased his lips. "Four years ago, we were closer to being kids. We could have made do with a park bench. Now, as you've pointed out, we're seeing the wrong side of thirty."

"I said *I* was grown-up—"

His head came down, and he claimed her mouth.

Behind her eyelids, the world erupted in color. Her mind swam.

Pressing his advantage, he plundered her mouth, making her open to him. Making her feel.

She moaned low in her throat, even as a part of her mind fought for control.

After several moments, she tore her mouth from his. "Stephen—"

In response, he bent her backward, and her robe fell open. He trailed his lips down her throat, lingering over the pulse under her jaw.

Pulsating awareness sang through her veins and gathered at the juncture of her thighs.

Oh. "We have to talk—"

"Trust me on this one, Meggikins," he said thickly. "There are actions more valuable than words right now."

"I'm not sure that's the saying," she said somewhat breathlessly, raising her head. He used to call her Meggikins all the time before she left Miami. This was the first time he'd used her old nickname in his previous sweet, unsarcastic way.

"Whatever," he responded. "There are times when we guys call it right."

He was getting it more than right, she thought. He was playing her like a virtuoso handling a Stradivarius.

He stared at the silky nightgown revealed by her

open robe. She could tell he'd focused on her nipples, which had tightened and now jutted against the thin material of her gown.

His eyes darkened, his face growing taut with desire. "Do you know I fantasized about you?" He shook his head slowly. "It used to drive me crazy that I kept thinking about you when you'd been the one to walk away."

"That's why you want me now. I'm a novelty. The one who dumped you." She guessed this wasn't the time to tell him she'd dreamed about him, too. It would be like adding fuel to the fire. She could feel his erection pressed against her.

He shook his head again, his brows coming together. He gave her a little shake. "Don't give me that garbage. You're the mother of my child."

Her heart plummeted, even as she told herself she shouldn't care whether he saw her as just a mother or not at all.

"We can barely be in the same room without wanting to get it on," he said huskily.

Her heart skipped a beat. "Lust."

"Sexual attraction," he contradicted. "It's more than a lot of other people have."

But it wasn't enough for her. "What happens when it all fades?"

"It hasn't in four years."

She shook her head in denial.

His eyes gleamed. "Do you need me to show you again just how much it can be worth?"

His hand skimmed up her thigh, raising her gown and robe. His head lowered.

"We shouldn't," she whispered.

"What?" he muttered against her mouth. "We're married. We're legal. We're not inebriated."

"This isn't what I signed up for."

"Hell, me, too, but sometimes you just have to run with it."

He hoisted her up and fastened his mouth to hers.

Oh, damn. She'd underestimated just how hard it would be to live under the same roof and resist him. And he wasn't making it any easier on her.

In the background, Harry Jr. had faded into the slow, sultry tones of Norah Jones.

Without breaking contact, Stephen used one hand to pull her panties off, then sat back on the couch with her.

Her legs came down on either side of him, straddling him.

He rubbed her sensitized nipples and made a guttural sound of pleasure.

Yes, her mind whimpered.

She'd gone so long without. So long without him. Yesterday, the dam had burst, and now all her desires came pouring forth.

He kissed her jaw, then pushed the robe off her shoulders so that it dropped to the floor. He kissed her neck, her shoulder and her collarbone, then gave her a little love bite.

She fumbled with the buttons of his shirt, sliding against him, needing him to fill the dull ache inside her.

Eventually, with a groan, he stilled her hands against his shirt. He grasped the bottom of her gown and pulled her last article of clothing over her head before tossing it aside.

Turning back to her, he reached between them. He delved, testing her with his fingers and finding her wetness.

And she savored his touch. Her eyes closed, her back arched, and her breathing became shallow. She clenched around him.

"That's right," he muttered. "Come to me, my mermaid."

She opened her eyes and looked at him.

From the harsh, intent look on his face, she knew he was ready. *She* was ready.

He withdrew his hand, and with quivering fingers, she helped him undo his belt and free himself.

She held his gaze as she sank down on him, joining them and making them both sigh with pleasure.

She rode him then with sweet rhythm while he whispered encouragement in her ear.

Slowly, slowly, they climbed to the pinnacle together.

When she peeked at him and saw his jaw was

locked, she realized only iron control kept him from taking her wildly. She knew he was waiting for her—trying to make this good for her.

And with that awareness, all her nervous tension broke and she found a magnificent release.

He caught her when she came, taking over in the last few moments and thrusting up to meet her with a deep groan as he shook and strained one last time.

Eleven

On Friday, Megan met Anna for lunch at La Loggia, near Elkind, Ross's offices downtown.

After they'd ordered, Anna said, "Marriage seems to agree with you."

"Does it?" Megan remarked, lifting her water glass.

"Mmm-hmm," Anna persisted, a teasing light in her eyes. "You look as if you've been having lots of sex—and enjoying it."

She choked on a sip of water. *"What?"*

"Are you okay?" Anna responded, laughing.

"How would you know that?" She felt as if she were wearing an *H* for *horny* emblazoned on her knit top.

Anna gave another tinkling laugh. "Simple.

I'm married to a Garrison, too, and I'm also a newlywed."

Megan resisted the urge to cup her hot cheeks.

The past week had been crazy. She and Stephen were married parents of a young child, and they were conducting a passionate affair.

The couch…the desk…the breakfast table. They were sneaking around a three-year-old. They'd even put his gift of lingerie to good use.

Just last night, after they'd put Jade to bed, Stephen had bent her forward over the desk in his study and had intercourse with her.

Anna took a sip from her water glass, seemingly reading Megan's silence for the admission it was. "Mmm-hmm. Persuasive, was he?" she murmured.

Megan groaned and hid her face behind her hands.

"Oh, Anna," she said when she looked up, "we've been on a roller coaster this past week."

Her friend laughed again. "So you're having wild, uninhibited sex with your husband. What's wrong with that?"

Everything.

"He… We…"

Anna's lips twitched. "I understand. Stephen's an attractive guy with a healthy sex drive and he wanted to get it on with you."

Megan expelled a breath and nodded. "The rat. He's reneging on the terms of this marriage."

Her friend placed a hand over her heart melodramatically. "How? By wanting to have sex with you, his wife, rather than someone else?"

"When you put it that way, it sounds so reasonable."

"It *is* reasonable."

Rather than concede, however, she held on doggedly to her position, which she nevertheless knew was fast becoming unsustainable.

Still, she felt compelled to set the record straight on one score. "It turns out he wasn't having sex with anyone else four years ago, either."

Anna raised an eyebrow, and Megan recounted Stephen's story to her.

"And I believed him," she said when she finished.

"So," Anna said, "everything should be great now, right?"

She shook her head. "*No*. Don't you see?" she said, her voice almost a wail. "I was vulnerable to believing that woman four years ago because Stephen had such a reputation as a player, and nothing has changed, and—and, oh God, I may be falling for him again!"

Panic roiled her stomach.

She was in love with him. Maybe had always remained a little in love with him.

Anna patted her hand.

She looked at her sister-in-law, her eyes pleading. "Why, why, why did he have to insist on this marriage? We could have come to an arrangement that allowed him to see Jade!"

Anna shook her head. "Megan, Megan, look around!" Anna glanced to one side of them, then to the other. "Do you know how many men have looked over at us—at you—since we arrived? You're a tall, gorgeous redhead who attracts more attention than a neon sign in the desert. Of course Stephen wanted to slap a ring on your hand as soon as possible!"

Megan closed her eyes, sucked in some deep, controlling breaths, then looked at her friend again.

"You're fearful right now, that's all," Anna said. "Believe me, I understand. I was just there. Falling in love is scary. And then there are all those trust issues."

"I know," she said matter-of-factly.

Trust. Anna and Parker didn't have the lengthy tortured history she and Stephen did and yet Anna knew about the importance of that little word.

Just then, the waiter approached with their food.

All through lunch, however, Megan wondered about her new discovery and how she was going to handle it.

She was in love with Stephen Garrison. Again.

A storm was on the way. Stephen looked up at the sky from the deck of *Fishful Thinking*. Fortunately, the storm wasn't a hurricane—at least for now.

Still, it would hit over the weekend, and he wanted to make sure his yacht was prepared.

Though the staff at the marina could do the work for him, *Fishful Thinking* was his baby, and he liked to get personally involved when he could.

The yacht needed to be tied up with longer, sturdier lines, and as a precaution, he needed to clear out some of his personal possessions.

He headed below deck, then turned at the sound of someone clambering aboard.

Retracing his steps, he felt a smile rise to his lips. Megan was early.

They'd agreed last night to meet at the marina after work and have a Friday night out. He'd been looking forward to it all day.

But as he came up on deck again, he saw his visitor wasn't Megan, but their babysitter.

Tiffany was dressed as if she was heading out for a night on the town. She was wearing a sheer blouse, black miniskirt and heels, and her face was more made-up than usual.

He remembered now mentioning to the babysitter that he'd have to tie up his boat at the Miami Beach Marina after work today.

"What's up, Tiffany?" His thoughts automatically went to his daughter. "Is something wrong with Jade?" he asked, his voice coming out sharp.

"No, no, no," Tiffany said on a breathless laugh,

walking toward him. "I dropped her off at her friend Gillian's birthday party earlier."

He relaxed. "Well, if you're thinking you need to babysit, there are crossed wires. My sister-in-law, Anna, is supposed to pick her up from the party—" he consulted his watch "—in a little over an hour."

He and Megan had agreed Anna and Parker would take Jade for the evening while they went out for a quick dinner, just the two of them. Anna had been thrilled at the prospect of babysitting.

"No crossed wires," Tiffany said easily, her gaze focused on his face, "and there's plenty of time for what I came to discuss."

"Oh, yeah?"

She nodded to the stairs. "Can we talk somewhere more private?" She hugged herself and looked around. "It's windy out here."

"Yeah, with good reason. There's a storm coming ashore," he said, but nevertheless turned to lead the way.

"I've never been aboard before," Tiffany said from behind him once they were in the narrow corridor below deck. "Is this where you nap?"

He turned around to see Tiffany peering into the master cabin.

"Yup," he said, then braced his hands on his hips. He'd dressed in pants and an open-collar shirt for work today because he'd known he'd be heading over to the yacht to meet Megan for dinner. "Now why don't you tell me what this is about?"

Tiffany straightened and peeked up at him through her lashes. "Better yet, I'll show you."

She stepped forward and fastened her mouth to his.

It happened so fast, he didn't have a chance to react. In the tight confines of the yacht's passageway, there wasn't much room to move.

Still, it was the last thing he'd been expecting from Tiffany, so for a second he remained immobile.

She pressed closer, going up on tiptoe, her arms snaking around his neck.

"Mmm," she murmured.

As she moved her mouth over his, his brain snapped on. *What the hell.*

He reached for her arms and tugged them from his neck.

She touched his chest, looking up at him pleadingly. "Do me."

He opened his mouth, flabbergasted.

"Excuse me."

He and Tiffany both turned to look at the end of the passageway.

Megan stood rigidly, silhouetted by the light, then spun on her heel.

Stephen cursed. "Megan, wait!"

He started after her, but Tiffany fisted her hand into the back of his shirt, stopping him.

He turned back, his brows snapping together. "What the hell are you doing?"

"Let her go, Stephen."

"She's my wife!"

Tiffany smirked. "C'mon, I know you're not sleeping with her. She's been in the guest bedroom."

Oh, hell. Yes, Megan's stuff still remained in the guest bedroom, but he'd been having a damn good week, seducing Megan at every opportunity—making headway, or so he thought. And now this.

Tiffany trailed a hand down his chest. "I know a virile guy like you must have a difficult time doing without," she said, lowering her voice invitingly. "So, here I am."

He removed her hand from his chest. "You don't know a thing," he said coldly.

The first glimmer of uncertainty entered the babysitter's eyes. "C'mon, Stephen. Everyone knows you play the field—"

"Past tense there, honey." In fact, in the last couple of years, his reputation had been based more on past public perception than on reality.

He glowered at her. "What's your game?"

Tiffany affected a pout. "Nothing! You're one of the sexiest, hippest guys in Miami. Everyone knows about the Garrison brothers. I wanted to see what all the fuss was about."

Stephen sighed inwardly. He'd been reduced to a

notch on the bedpost, and the irony wasn't lost on him. Aloud, he said, "You're going to explain to Megan *exactly* what happened here."

"That we were kissing?" Tiffany smirked again. "I think she saw that for herself."

"No, that you came on to me unexpectedly."

Tiffany's jaw set mulishly. "I can't do that."

"You *can,* and you *will.*" He resisted the urge to shake some sense into her.

"If I say that, I'll never get another child-care job! I have to stick to the story it was mutual."

He was surprised and even a bit impressed at how much she'd thought this through. It made him wonder, though, just how many guys Tiffany had come on to in the past. He'd been at the receiving end of enough conniving women to be sort of jaded about the type.

"You won't get a job based on the recommendation I'd give you," he gritted.

She folded her arms. "At least my way I'll have a fighting chance. It'll be my word against yours."

Tiffany had cost him, and cost him big, with Megan, but Stephen suddenly felt an iota of sympathy for the babysitter. She was young and impressionable, and obviously looking for love in all the wrong places.

"Stop chasing a rainbow. Fame and being hip isn't all it's cracked up to be," he advised.

Then he turned away to try to find his wife.

* * *

Megan blindly found her way back to her car. She got behind the wheel and her brain went on automatic pilot as she steered out of the parking lot.

It was just like four years ago. A wild affair where she couldn't see straight, then blindsided by a betrayal.

She should have known. She should have known.

Once a cheater, always a cheater, the naysayer within her chanted.

She made herself relive the pain of catching Tiffany and Stephen in an intimate embrace.

At least four years ago she'd been spared the visual evidence. Then she'd gone only on the word of a woman she hadn't met before. *That,* and Stephen's playboy reputation.

This time, she'd witnessed the cheating herself.

As she made a left turn at a stoplight, she realized she couldn't go home—or rather, to Stephen's estate near South Beach. He'd be there, and she needed time to think.

Her cell phone rang, and she ignored it. She recognized the ring as Stephen's,

Her mind raced ahead. The Garrison Grand was also off-limits for obvious reasons. Under other circumstances, she might have turned to Anna for help, but Anna was now married to Stephen's brother.

With that thought, her mind went to Jade. At least

she wouldn't need to worry about her daughter tonight. She knew Anna would be happy to take care of Jade for as long as needed.

Her cell phone rang again, and she turned it off with one hand.

She realized after a moment that she could always go to the little house in Coral Gables. She had the lease until the end of the month, and some of her furniture and belongings were still in the house.

Her mind made up, she turned the car west.

A short time later, when she reached her former home, she let herself in, kicked off her sandals and turned her phone back on.

The screen on her cell flashed information on several missed calls from Stephen. Cynically, she wondered what explanation he'd come up with this time.

Then she searched for and found Anna's number. When her sister-in-law picked up, she said, "Anna, it's Megan."

"Hi! I was just about to go get Jade—"

"Listen, would you mind keeping her until tomorrow?"

"Of course I don't mind," Anna responded. "We'll just run by the Garrison Grand on the way home and pick up some stuff for her from your suite."

Like Stephen, Megan knew, Parker and Anna maintained a suite at the Garrison Grand for personal use.

"Thanks," Megan said, relief making her relax. "I

left some clothes over there when Jade got a tour of her father's hotel."

The father who had just proved once again he was a lying, cheating, untrustworthy rat.

"You and Stephen want the evening to yourselves, hmm?" Anna asked teasingly.

"Something like that." Megan heard her voice wobble. "Just tell Jade I love her and I'll see her tomorrow."

"Is something wrong?" Anna asked, her voice suddenly tinged with worry. "You sound a little strange."

Sudden, unexpected tears clogged her throat. Damn it. She'd thought she had this under control.

"Everything's fine," she managed. "See you tomorrow."

After disconnecting, she looked around.

She was beginning to rethink her idea of staying in Coral Gables tonight. It might not be the first place Stephen thought to look for her, but it might occur to him if he reflected on it a bit.

With that thought, she strode purposely into her former bedroom and gathered up some clothes. She packed an ancient overnight bag.

She needed to ponder what to do, she thought, feeling sick to her stomach. This time, it would be hard for her to cut and run. She and Stephen were married, and there was a three-year-old child involved.

She knew he'd come after her—because of Jade, of course.

She couldn't believe she'd opened her heart to him again. *The jerk.*

She swung her overnight bag off the bed with more violence than necessary. *The philandering snake.*

This time, though, she decided her reaction would be different—not only because it had to be, but because she wanted it to be.

She walked toward the front door.

She wasn't going to be a passive victim. She wasn't meekly going away.

Outside, she locked up the house, tossed her overnight bag into the car, and got behind the wheel.

Jaw set, she knew exactly where she was going. First steps first.

She was checking into one of the Garrison Grand's rival hotels. It was just too bad the Hotel Victoria wasn't open yet.

Twelve

By the time Stephen got to the marina's parking lot, Megan was gone. Annoyed with himself for letting Tiffany slow him down, he whipped out his cell to try to reach Megan by phone.

When she didn't pick up then or on subsequent calls, he held out slim hope the reason was because she was driving. More likely, she'd drawn her own conclusions about the scenario that had apparently played out before her eyes.

He swore under his breath. He had to find her and fix this situation. He knew appearances were damning, but he had to convince her of the truth.

Just the thought she might walk away from him again made him nearly break out in a sweat.

He strode to his car, which was parked nearby. He was willing to do this the hard way—by process of elimination.

First, he headed to the most likely place he'd find her—his estate near South Beach.

When he didn't find her there, he grimly headed back out to his car. He decided to check his suite at the Garrison Grand next.

Before pulling out of his drive, however, he called Anna. It occurred to him Megan wouldn't do anything without making sure Jade was taken care of. Parker's wife might therefore be able to give him some leads.

When his sister-in-law picked up, he said, "Hi, Anna. Is Jade with you?"

"Yes, she's right here. I just got back from picking her up."

At least he knew where Jade was, Stephen thought, some of his tension easing. "Is Megan there?"

There was a pause on the line, and he could practically see Anna frowning.

"I thought she was with you," his sister-in-law said.

"There's been a…misunderstanding. Has she tried to contact you?"

"As a matter of fact, she did—"

Stephen's hand tightened on the phone.

"—but she didn't say where she was. She asked if I could keep Jade until tomorrow. Of course I said it was okay. I just stopped by your suite at the Garrison Grand on the way home and picked up some clothes for Jade."

Damn. Still, now he knew Megan wasn't at the hotel.

"Thanks, Anna," he said. "I'll be in touch. Give Jade a kiss for me."

"You know," Anna put in, "Megan said nearly the same thing when I talked to her. She wanted me to tell Jade she loved her."

At least, Stephen thought, there was one thing he and his wife agreed on at the moment. They were united in their love and concern for Jade.

"Are you sure everything is all right?" Anna asked.

"It will be soon," Stephen assured her.

When he ended the call, he sat and gazed down his driveway for a moment.

Now he knew Megan wasn't at the Garrison Grand, he was at loose ends. He'd covered the most logical bases, and Megan wasn't answering her phone.

He squinted into the distance, then realized there was one place he hadn't tried yet.

After turning the key in the ignition, he pulled away from the house and headed to Coral Gables.

Megan woke up disoriented.

She was in a strange room. A *hotel* room.

Then the drama of the previous evening came rushing back, and along with it, the queasy feeling there was no way to fix what was wrong with her life.

It was a feeling she'd had once before, when she'd found herself pregnant and alone, having realized the father of her child thought of her as nothing more than a fling.

Luckily, she'd found a hotel room yesterday. With the impending storm, there had been a number of last-minute cancellations of weekend reservations.

While she'd been tossing and turning in bed last night, she'd also come to a resolution.

The last time she'd caught Stephen cheating, she'd turned and run. She hadn't even sought an explanation from him. This time, though the evidence against him was damning, she wouldn't make the same mistake.

Now, after she showered, dressed and ate a light breakfast delivered by room service, she put in a call to Tiffany.

When the babysitter picked up, she announced without preamble, "You're fired."

"Megan?"

"Yes, it's me," she said crisply. "As of today, your services are no longer required."

"I can explain—"

"I'm sure you can," she responded, "but I don't want to hear it."

Afterward, she checked herself out of the hotel and headed for Stephen's estate.

She'd bolted, just like four years ago. But now, she was turning around and fighting.

Last night had to rank as the most miserable night of his life, Stephen reflected. Megan hadn't come home, and he hadn't been able to find her.

He poured himself another morning cup of coffee and paced back and forth in his kitchen.

He'd been up since six—not that he'd gotten much sleep. Though it was only late morning, he'd showered, dressed in jeans and a casual shirt, and been prowling around restlessly for what seemed like eons.

Yesterday, when he'd arrived at the house in Coral Gables, he'd discovered Megan wasn't there. However, he'd run into a neighbor who said she'd thought she'd seen Megan's car parked in front of the house not too long before.

Cursing his bad timing, but realizing he'd run out of options, he'd returned to his estate near South Beach.

Now, he looked outside at gray storm clouds and a steady rain.

Damn it. The storm was closing in, and if he didn't find Megan soon, he'd have to ride out the storm here—alone and without resolution.

The only silver lining was that Megan had asked

Anna to hold on to Jade only until today. That meant—at least he hoped it did—that Megan was bound to show up sooner rather than later.

He'd already phoned Anna this morning and told her to give him a call if Megan stopped by to pick up Jade. He'd sensed that his sister-in-law had questions but was refraining from asking them.

He knew Megan couldn't just take off this time. She had a partnership in her firm and a three-year-old who couldn't be uprooted easily. There was also a storm coming ashore. And most importantly, he'd find her—no matter how long it took—and make her see the truth.

Itching to do something *now,* however, he dialed the sitter. Perhaps Megan had contacted Tiffany. She'd seemed angry enough last night to let loose with some choice words aimed at the both of them.

When Tiffany picked up, he said, "It's Stephen. Have you heard from Megan?"

There was a pause. "You know, for no longer being in your employ," Tiffany drawled, "I sure do get a lot of calls from Garrisons."

Suddenly alert, he asked, "What do you mean you're no longer employed?"

"By you and your wife. She fired me."

Stephen felt his spirits lift, but he nevertheless asked sarcastically, "Even after your explanation that it was supposedly mutual?"

"It didn't get that far. She didn't even give me time to explain!"

At a sound behind him, he swung around and his eyes locked with Megan's.

"Talking to the other woman?" she asked, arching a brow.

"Gotta go, Tiffany," he said absently, then disconnected. He stared at Megan, willing her to be more than a figment of his imagination.

She looked like a mermaid that had been washed ashore and up to his doorstep. She was wearing a rain-splattered flower-print sundress, the shoulder straps of which cleverly continued beneath her breasts, outlining them. Her long red hair hung down her back, drops of rain reflecting the light cast by the overhead in the kitchen.

The way she looked right now, she took him back four years. Back to when she was still willing to play the seductress and he was her eager victim. Back to when things had been right between them.

He fought the urge to grab her and pull her into his arms. He settled for setting down the phone and walking toward her. "I didn't know where you were."

"Then let me put your mind at ease," she said, planting her handbag on a nearby chair. "The Tides Hotel."

Ouch. "You know how to hit a guy when he's down, don't you?"

"Funny, I thought I was the one who was down, and you—" her eyes went to his crotch "—were the one who was up."

She was taking no prisoners, he thought with an inner grimace. Still, ridiculously, he felt turned on.

"I thought you were going to bolt like before," he said.

"Can't." She shrugged and held up her hand. "I'm married to you this time."

He was close enough to glimpse uncertainty beneath her cool reserve, and he pressed forward. "I'm not letting you go."

Her eyes flashed. "You strong-armed me into this marriage—"

"Damn right, I did."

"I fired Tiffany."

"But you can't fire me."

"But I can divorce you," she said, her chin coming up.

His jaw set. *Like hell.*

"Were you carrying on with her?" she asked.

The question hung in the air between them. "Would you believe me if I said no?"

"Would any reasonable person?" she tossed back.

"I'm not giving you a divorce," he said implacably, "so forget it."

Megan watched the man she loved walk toward her, and held her breath.

His eyes were like hot coals, belying an expression carved in granite.

Yet beneath his hard, uncompromising attitude, she sensed a hint of vulnerability, and her heart somersaulted.

"I fired Tiffany before she gave me an explanation," she said.

He nodded. "I know. She told me. Why?"

"Maybe I learned from my mistakes," she said in a low voice. "Maybe I decided this time that if I was going to exact payment, it should fall on both guilty parties."

He nodded. "*Maybe,* but is that the real reason?"

He stopped in front of her, and she shook her head slowly, holding his gaze.

Her lips parted. "I didn't want an explanation. I was talking to Anna recently, and she mentioned the issue of *trust.* It's what was lacking the last time in our relationship. I like to think I learn from my mistakes."

"It looks bad—"

"Incriminating. So incriminating, in fact," she said, "that after the initial shock, I realized no one could be that stupid."

His face relaxed, his shoulders lowering.

"Who'd try to have a romantic encounter on his yacht when he knew his wife was due to meet him there soon?"

"When he'd gone to all the trouble of strong-arming the same wife into marrying him," he supplied.

"Exactly." She'd thought this through the night before—when she'd had a chance to calmly assess what had happened.

"I'm getting rid of *Fishful Thinking*," he said hoarsely.

Her eyes widened. "But you love that boat."

He stepped forward. "I love you more."

A crazy joy swept through her.

He raised his hand and pushed hair away from her face. "The yacht doesn't suit my lifestyle now, but there's an acquaintance who's expressed interest in buying it on more than one occasion."

His lips quirked in the lopsided smile that she'd always loved. "He used to be a rival of mine in Miami's playboy sweepstakes."

"You don't say," she said, a teasing tone creeping into her voice.

"I'm also stepping away from being the public face of the Garrison Grand."

She went still. "*What?* You can't do that."

"I can and I will," he responded, looking at her tenderly. "I don't need to be partying when what I really want is to be home."

It was a grand gesture, and sudden tears choked her.

"Are you going to say it?" he asked. "Because I'm prepared to wage a campaign if I have to."

"I love you!" She flung the words at him, even her vision blurred. "There, I said it. Are you happy now? You arrogant, ruthless—"

He yanked her into his arms. "I'm all those things and worse," he muttered, "but I love you."

Then he silenced her with a kiss. He didn't ask, he took, and they both gave themselves up to the kiss with wild abandon.

She'd taken the long way, she thought, but she finally had what she'd been looking for.

When his lips eventually moved away from hers, he trailed kisses along her cheek and to the hollow of her throat.

"You know," she joked breathlessly, her heart feeling lighter than it had in years, "if this keeps happening, I'm going to have to lock you up to keep women away from you."

"Don't worry, Meggikins," he said, his fingers searching for the zipper to her dress, "I intend to become the most family-oriented guy around. I want more kids, and I'm definitely going to enjoy making them."

She pretended to look shocked. "We can't spend all our time in bed!"

As if in response, he nuzzled her neck.

"Is this how men communicate their feelings?" she teased, her breath catching.

"What can I say? I'm a man of action."

His response elicited an involuntary laugh, even as he nibbled along her shoulder, sending waves of lush desire through her.

"We need to pick up Jade from Anna's before this storm really hits," he said reluctantly, kissing the tops of her breasts.

"Mmm," she responded. "I called Anna and Parker right before I got here. They're bringing over Jade shortly."

"In that case, we'll have to hurry."

Another laugh escaped her. "At this rate, I'll be pregnant in a month."

He raised his head to look at her seriously. "We talked about it in an 'if it happens' sort of way, but we can wait if you want to."

She shook her head. "I don't want to. Jade is going to be four, and I'd like her to have a sibling or two before she gets too much older. Now I'm a partner at Elkind, Ross, I've got some leverage as far as organizing my work schedule and taking a leave. I'll just have to space my projects further apart."

He smiled. "You'll have no problem getting clearance from your current client."

Then he lifted her onto the nearby kitchen table, bunching her dress around her hips in the process.

"The kitchen table—?"

"We haven't used it yet. Let's tick it off our list."

She slid back on her elbows to keep her balance. He was aroused, and she was weak-kneed.

"It's been one of my fantasies for a long time," he admitted, grasping her hips to pull the panties off her.

"How long?" she asked throatily.

"Too damn long," he responded. "Since you left."

She watched as he divested himself of some clothing. "Ah, those fantasies of yours…"

He looked at her, passion dilating his eyes. "We're about to make one of them come true."

"I'd dream about you, too, you know. I couldn't stop myself."

He stilled, looking at her. "Oh, yeah?"

His pose was all male swagger, tinged with hunger. She nodded.

He smiled. "Care to share?"

She shook her head. Just the thought made her—

"You're blushing." He leaned forward with wicked intent, bracing his arms on either side of her. "I'll just have to make you—"

"Nothing will make me spill my secrets," she said on a breathless laugh.

But he was already tracing a hot path to her cleavage, making her gasp.

"Whisper them to me…"

And she did, as they had grinding, pulse-throbbing sex on the kitchen table.

Later, as they were straightening their clothes, Stephen said, "After you saw Tiffany kissing me on the yacht, I thought I'd lost you for good."

"Was *she* kissing *you?*"

He nodded.

Megan was glad for the confirmation that her faith hadn't been misplaced. "I overheard you on the phone asking Tiffany about her explanation that it was supposedly mutual."

His lips twisted. "Yeah, that's her story, and she's sticking to it."

"It wouldn't have mattered," she responded. "I'd already made up my mind, but accidentally hearing your part of the phone conversation earlier was nice validation."

Stephen shook his head. "She's fairly savvy for a mixed-up kid."

Megan wondered whether she'd missed some signs where the babysitter was concerned. "I hired her through a child-care agency. She was available to babysit during the hours I needed because she's an aspiring dancer and attends classes in the evenings."

"Well, I'll be around to help now," Stephen said. "We'll continue adjusting our schedules to accommodate Jade, and I'll hire a live-in housekeeper. When I was a single guy, I didn't feel the need for permanent staff, but that's changed now."

She thought about Stephen's statement earlier. "I don't want you to give up the yacht for me."

"Not for you. For us."

"But we'll need *Fishful Thinking* to entertain all those kids you're planning to have," she teased.

He looked at her for a moment, then slipped his hands around her waist. "Do you know how much I love you?"

"Tell me again," she said, smiling as she placed her hands on his chest.

He gave her a quick kiss. "I don't think I ever got over you."

"Definitely likewise," she responded.

"You were right, you know," he added. "Until you walked away, I'd never had the experience of being dumped. It was a bitter pill, especially since I'd been crazy about you."

Her heart swelled. "Walking away from you was one of the hardest things I've ever done, even though I believed at the time that you'd cheated."

"I got a necessary dose of humility," he admitted. "After that, I toned down the playboy lifestyle and focused on building up the Garrison Grand."

"And got wonderful results for it," she said. "The Garrison Grand is considered the premier hotel in South Beach."

"Thanks, but I consider my greatest accomplishment to be Jade."

Her heart spilled over. "I feel the same way," she said softly.

He gave her a lingering kiss. "You hold my heart in your hands. You always have."

She raised her hand and stroked his face. "I never would have guessed. You looked so forbidding the day you walked into my office at Elkind, Ross."

"I was angry," he said, giving her a lopsided smile, "but I was determined to get you back in my bed."

"Oh?" She arched a brow.

"No woman has turned me on as much as you do," he said. "I was determined to reignite our affair and break it off only when I wanted to this time. Of course, I wasn't yet admitting to myself that time might be *never*."

"Silly man," she said, her eyes misting. "So desperate, you had to blackmail me into marrying you."

"Not one of my finer moments," he admitted. "I wanted to believe I was in control, but the reality was the opposite."

He was laying himself bare for her, and joy bubbled up inside her again. Before either of them could say anything else, however, the doorbell rang.

"Jade," she said.

Stephen nodded. "I'll get it."

Moments later, he walked back into the kitchen, trailing an exuberant Jade. Parker and Anna followed behind.

"Mommy!" Jade rushed forward, and Megan bent and wrapped her daughter in her arms.

"I played board games with Aunt Anna and Uncle Parker! And I got ice cream! And Gillian's party was great, and—"

Everyone laughed.

"Slow down there," Stephen said, ruffling Jade's hair.

Megan watched as Anna looked at her, a question in her eyes.

"Is everything okay?" Anna asked, her gaze going from her to Stephen.

"Perfect now," Megan said.

Stephen slipped his arm around her and pulled Jade close to him with his other.

Megan smiled at Anna, trying to communicate that everything truly was fine now. The message seemed to come across because, after a moment, her sister-in-law smiled back and squeezed Parker's hand.

"Now that I've been to Gillian's house, I know what I want!" Jade piped up.

"What?" she and Stephen asked in unison.

"A little brother or sister," Jade announced, then ducked under Stephen's arm and skipped away. "*I* get to tell them what to do!"

Megan felt herself heat, and Stephen laughed.

Anna and Parker looked amused but knowing.

"Uh-oh," Stephen said. "I think we're in trouble."

"She's definitely *your* daughter," Megan teased, looking up at him with her heart in her eyes, "and we've definitely come home to stay."

* * * * *

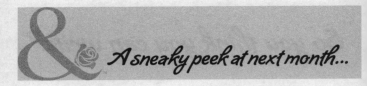

By Request

RELIVE THE ROMANCE WITH THE BEST OF THE BEST

My wish list for next month's titles...

In stores from 19th October 2012:

☐ Sultry Nights – Abby Green, Annie West & Cathy Williams

☐ Miracle Christmas – Amy Andrews, Shirley Jump & Cara Colter

3 stories in each book - only £5.99!

In stores from 2nd November 2012:

☐ The Garrisons: Cassie, Adam & Brooke – Brenda Jackson, Emilie Rose & Catherine Mann

...ble at WHSmith, Tesco, Asda, Eason, Amazon and Apple

Just can't wait?

...an buy our books online a month before ...hit the shops! **www.millsandboon.co.uk**

1012/05

Special Offers

Every month we put together collections and longer reads written by your favourite authors.

Here are some of next month's highlights— and don't miss our fabulous discount online!

On sale 19th October   **On sale 2nd November**   **On sale 2nd November**

The World of Mills & Boon®

There's a Mills & Boon® series that's perfect for you. We publish ten series and, with new titles every month, you never have to wait long for your favourite to come along.

Blaze.
Scorching hot, sexy reads
4 new stories every month

By Request
Relive the romance with the best of the best
9 new stories every month

Cherish
Romance to melt the heart every time
12 new stories every month

Desire
Passionate and dramatic love stories
8 new stories every month